Alexander Murdoch

The Scottish poets recent and living

Alexander Murdoch

The Scottish poets recent and living

ISBN/EAN: 9783337234041

Printed in Europe, USA, Canada, Australia, Japan

Cover: Foto ©Andreas Hilbeck / pixelio.de

More available books at **www.hansebooks.com**

THE
SCOTTISH POETS

RECENT AND LIVING

BY

ALEXANDER G. MURDOCH

WITH PORTRAITS

GLASGOW: THOMAS D. MORISON
LONDON: HAMILTON, ADAMS & CO.
1883.

GLASGOW
PRINTED BY HAY NISBET AND CO.,
STOCKWELL STREET.

PREFACE.

In submitting a new edition of *Recent and Living Scottish Poets* to the favour of the public, the author desires to recapitulate what he said in the preface to the former edition,—namely, that the greater portion of the work appeared first as a series of brief Biographical Sketches in the newspaper press during the year 1880. These Sketches, with emendations and additions, were issued in book form early in the following year.

The work having gone out of print almost immediately on publication, he now has the pleasure of issuing an augmented and thoroughly revised edition, which, he hopes, may meet with similar success. Many new names have been added, and the whole work has been thoroughly sifted and re-arranged with a view to completeness without indiscriminate superfluity. Obviously, in a work of this kind, the chief merit must consist in *selection*, rather than in amplification; and while the compiler does not arrogate entire success in this respect, he can honestly aver that he has discharged conscientiously, and to the best of his ability, a somewhat delicate task, and he flatters himself that the most censorious reader will scarcely find a single poem or lyric included in the volume which does not show appreciable poetic fancy, united to an intelligent and painstaking exercise of the mechanical function of verse-making.

The author further desires to state, that the biographical sketches here presented are original and authentic, and can in each case be regarded as thoroughly trustworthy. In no case, where direct fact was to be obtained by personal communication, has the writer culled his information from irresponsible sources.

ALEXANDER G. MURDOCH.

GLASGOW, *December*, 1882.

ERRATUM.

Page 69, *for* Mediterranean *read* Mediterraneum.

CONTENTS.

LIST OF PORTRAITS.

THE

SCOTTISH POETS:

Recent and Living.

SANDY RODGER.

A MAN of genuine humour, and the author of several well and widely-known songs, ALEXANDER RODGER was born at East Calder, Midlothian, 16th July, 1784. His father (originally a farmer on the ground of Haggs, adjacent to the small hamlet of Dalmahoy) became latterly landlord of the village inn at Mid-Calder. He appears to have been unfortunate in his business ventures, and finally went abroad, leaving the future poet to the care of his maternal relatives at Glasgow. Young RODGER had been apprenticed to the trade of a silversmith in Edinburgh, but had only completed one year of his apprenticeship when the interruption of his removal to Glasgow occurred. He was, thereafter, persuaded to engage himself in the service of a respectable hand-loom weaver, who resided at the old Drygate Toll, adjacent to the venerable city cathedral.

In 1806 he entered the connubial state, removing shortly afterwards to Bridgeton, then an eastern suburb of Glasgow, where he continued to reside till his death. In conjunction

2

with his poetical gift, he had early shown a taste for music, and finding his limited income as a working weaver inadequate for the support of a growing family, he supplemented his weekly wage by teaching music to such pupils as friendship put in his way.

Thus circumstanced, the poet's life flowed placidly on, until the time of the Radical troubles, about 1819 or 1820. RODGER was a working weaver, and a weaver in those days was nothing if not political. But our poet was more than merely a noisy Radical. He was by nature a man of broad and warm sympathies, whose soul resented every species of tyranny, whether of political or class bondship. He could not, therefore, long remain a passive spectator of the exciting mob-meetings which were being daily convened everywhere around him. Impelled by his strong instincts, he left the loom and identified himself with a then newly started and violently Radical newspaper, called *The Spirit of the Union,* the proprietor of which was shortly afterwards apprehended on a charge of sedition, tried, found guilty, and sentenced to penal servitude for life.

RODGER thereupon returned to the shuttle, but being marked as a disaffected person, he was shortly afterwards apprehended and thrown into prison, along with many others, on the scare occasioned by the publication of the famous "Treasonable Address," issued by a bogus "Provisional Government." A rather good story is related of the poet at this trying period of his history. When his house was searched for seditious publications, previous to his apprehension, RODGER handed the Sheriff's officer the Family Bible as the only treasonable book in his possession, for proof of which, he referred the aghast official to the Chapter on Kings, in the first Book of Samuel.

On his liberation from confinement, he obtained a situation in the Barrowfield Print Works as inspector of cloths, in which situation he remained for nearly eleven years, and it was during this tranquil period of his life that he found leisure to indite some of his happiest effusions. He edited with much acceptance several of the series of *Whistle Binkie,* and was latterly employed on the staff of the *Reformer's Gazette* newspaper, continuing there until his death, which event occurred on the 26th September, 1846.

In estimating RODGER's genius, the stirring and troubled times in which he lived and took active part must not be overlooked. Much of what he indited was of a necessarily ephemeral character. He wrote immediately for the hour, had the applause of his fellows, and was satisfied with the effort if the end aimed at was thereby advanced or secured. His political and satirical effusions are thus now almost forgotten, and on the few popularly-worded lyrics, which in his happier and less stormy hours he incidentally chanced to write, his future fame as a Scottish minstrel must rest. His mind was of an essentially popular cast. Devoid of imagination his verses are pervaded by a lively fancy and a humorous satire which never fail to interest and amuse. In domestic poetry he is noticeably happy, and has succeeded in writing many genuine and successful lyrics.

Although not a born native of Glasgow, he was, nevertheless, so long and so actively associated with its affairs as a life-residenter, and in a certain sense as a public man, that he may be fairly called a Glasgow poet. His worth, both as a man and a poet, was not entirely overlooked by his fellow-citizens during his lifetime. In 1836 about two hundred of his admirers entertained him to a public festival, and presented him with a purse of sovereigns by way of adding comfort to his closing years.

His remains were interred in the Glasgow Necropolis,

where a handsome monument, showing a profile of the poet's homely face, attests in sculptured letters that he who sleeps below was in life a poet, a humorist, and a true man, whom adversity could not depress nor popularity enfeeble.

—::—

ROBIN TAMSON'S SMIDDY.

My mither men't my auld breeks,
  An' wow! but they were duddy,
And sent me to get Mally shod
  At Robin Tamson's smiddy;
The smiddy stands beside the burn
  That wimples through the clachan,
I never yet gae by the door,
  But aye I fa' a-lauchin'.

For Robin was a walthy carle,
  An' had ae bonnie dochter,
Yet ne'er wad let her tak' a man,
  Tho' mony lads had socht her;
But what think ye o' my exploit?
  The time our mare was shoeing,
I slippit up beside the lass,
  And briskly fell a-wooing.

An' aye she e'ed my auld breeks,
  The time that we sat crackin',
Quo' I, my lass, ne'er mind the *clouts*,
  I've new anes for the makin';
But gin ye'll just come hame wi' me,
  An' lea' the carle, your father,
Ye'se get my breeks to keep in trim,
  Mysel' an' a' thegither.

'Deed lad, quo' she, your offer's fair,
  I really think I'll tak' it,
Sae, gang awa', get out the mare,
  We'll baith slip on the back o't;

For gin I wait my faither's time,
  I'll wait till I be fifty ;
But na ! I'll marry in my prime,
  An' mak' a wife most thrifty.

Wow ! Robin was an angry man,
  At tynin' o' his dochter ;
Thro' a' the kintra side he ran,
  An' far an' near he socht her ;
But when he cam' to our fire-end,
  An' fand us baith thegither,
Quo' I, gudeman, I've ta'en your bairn,
  An' ye may tak' my mither.

Auld Robin girn'd an' shook his pow,
  Guid sooth ! quo' he, you're merry,
But I'll just tak' ye at your word,
  An' end this hurry-burry ;
So Robin an' our auld wife
  Agreed to creep thegither ;
Now, I hae Robin Tamson's pet,
  An' Robin has my mither.

——::——

MARRY FOR LOVE.

When I and my Jenny thegither were tied,
  We had but sma' share o' the world between us ;
Yet lo'ed ither weel, and had youth on our side,
  And strength and guid health were abundantly gi'en us ;
I warsled and toil'd through the *fair* and the *foul*,
  And she was right carefu' o' what I brought till her,
For aye we had mind o' the canny auld rule,
  "Marry for love, and work for siller."

Our bairns they cam' thick—we were thankfu' for that,
  For the *bit* and the *brattie* cam' aye alang wi' them ;
Our *pan* we exchanged for a guid *muckle pat*,
  And somehow or ither, we aye had to gi'e them.

Our laddies grew up, and they wrought wi' mysel',
  Ilk ane gat as buirdly and stout as a miller,
Our lasses they keepit us trig aye, and hale,
  And now we can count a bit trifle o' siller.

But I and my Jenny are baith wearin' down,
  And our lads and our lasses hae a' gotten married ;
Yet see, we can rank wi' the best i' the town,
  Though our noddles we never too haughtily carried.
And mark me—I've now got a braw *cockit hat*,
  And in our *civic building* am reckon'd a pillar ;
Isna THAT a bit honour for ane to get at,
  Wha married for love, and wha wrought for siller ?

——::——

BLYTHE JAMIE M'NAB.*

GAE find me a match for blythe Jamie M'Nab ;
Ay, find me a match for blythe Jamie M'Nab ;
The best piece o' *stuff* cut frae Nature's ain wab,
Is that prince o' guid fellows—blythe Jamie M'Nab.

In her kindliest mood Madame Nature had been,
When first in this warld Jamie open'd his e'en,
For he ne'er gied a whimper, nor utter'd a sab,
But hame he cam' lauchin—blythe Jamie M'Nab.

In process o' time Jamie grew up apace,
And still play'd the smile on his roon' sonsie face ;
Except when a tear, like a pure hinny-blab,
Was shed o'er the wretched by Jamie M'Nab.

And Jamie is still just the best o' guid chiels,
Wi' the cheerfu' he lauchs, wi' the waefu' he feels ;
And the very last shillin' that's left in his fab,
He'll share wi' the needfu'—blythe Jamie M'Nab.

* Long connected with the *Glasgow Herald* newspaper, and said to be well entitled to the high praise accorded him by the poet.

Blythe Jamie M'Nab is sae furthy and free,
While he's crackin' wi' you, while he's jokin' wi' me,
That I wad wish nae better than twa hours' confab
Owre a horn o' guid yill wi' blythe Jamie M'Nab.

And Jamie M'Nab is nae thin airy ghaist,
For he measures an ell and twa-thirds roon' the waist;
Yet a wittier wag never trod on a slab,
Than that kind-hearted billie—blythe Jamie M'Nab.

Yes, Jamie has *bulk*, yet it damps na his glee,
For his flashes o' fancy come fervid and free;
As bright frae his brain as if lively Queen Mab
Held nightly communings wi' Jamie M'Nab.

He tells sic queer stories, and rum funny jokes,
And mak's sic remarks upon a' public folks,
That time rattles by like a beau in a cab,
While sittin' and list'ning to Jamie M'Nab.

I carena for Tory—I carena for Whig—
I mindna your Radical raver a fig;
But gie me the man that is staunch as a stab
For the richts o' his *caste*, like blythe Jamie M'Nab.

Amang the soft sex, too, he shows a fine taste,
Admiring what's lovely, and handsome, and chaste;
But the lewd tawdry trollop, the tawpie, and drab,
Can never find favour wi' Jamie M'Nab.

Some folks, when they meet you, are wonderfu' fair,
And wad hug ye as keen as a Noraway bear;
The next time they see you, they're soor as a crab,
That's never the gate wi' blythe M'Nab.

No! Jamie is ever the same open wight,
Aye easy and pleasant frae morning till night;
While ilk man, frae my Lord down to plain, simple Hab,
Gets the same salutation frae Jamie M'Nab.

Had mankind at large but the tithe o' his worth,
We then might expect a pure heaven on earth;
Nae rogues then wad fash us, wi' *grip* and wi' *grab*,
But a' wad be neebors—like Jamie M'Nab.

Lang, lang may the sonsy GUIDMAN o' the *Herald*
Wi' Jamie M'Nab wauchle on thro' this warld ;
And when, on Life's evening, cauld Death steeks his gab,
May he mount up on high wi' blythe Jamie M'Nab.

—::—

COLIN DUNLAP.*

WE'RE muckle obligéd to ye, Colin Dunlap,
We're muckle obliged to ye, Colin Dunlap,
Ye're truly a worthy auld patriot chap,
To enlighten you're country sae, Colin Dunlap.

Ye patronise lear, and ye propagate light,
To guide erring man in the way that is right ;
Ne'er under a bushel your candle you clap,
But let it lowe openly, Colin Dunlap.

A burning and shining light close by the Clyde,
Illuming the country around, far an' wide ;
Ye bleeze like a beacon upon a hill-tap—
A general benefit, Colin Dunlap.

Frank Jeffrey, and Chambers, and Brougham, and so forth,
Diffuse their cheap tracts to enlighten the earth ;
Mony thanks to the chiels for this praiseworthy stap ;
But mony mae thanks to *you*—Colin Dunlap.

Your light unto *me* has been better than theirs ;
For aye when in Glasgow at markets or fairs,
And daundering hame rather light in the tap,
Ye're a lamp to my feet, worthy Colin Dunlap.

The burns and the bog-holes, the dubs and the dykes,
The howes and the humplocks, the sheuchs and the sykes,
And ilk thing 'gainst whilk my heid I might rap,
Ye help me to shun them a', Colin Dunlap.

* For the better understanding of the above poem, it may be stated, that Colin Dunlop, Esq., was in his day the principal proprietor of Clyde Iron Works, whose large smelting furnaces still send out, in particular states of the night atmosphere, an immense volume of light.

Even spunkie himsel' is nae bogle to me,
When owre moor and moss I march hameward wi' glee;
Wi' my stick in my neive, in my noddle a drap,
Cheer'd onward by thee, my guide, Colin Dunlap.

The sun I'd like weel, gin the sun wad bide still,
But then ilka nicht he slides doon yont the hill,
Like a plump ruddy carle gaun to tak' his bit nap,
But you ne'er forsake us sae, Colin Dunlap.

Na, waur! ilka winter he's aff and awa',
Like our fine bloods to Italy shunning the snaw,
Scarce deigning a blink owre a hoary hill-tap,
But you're ever wi' us, kind Colin Dunlap.

The moon does fu' weel when the moon's in the lift,
But, oh, the loose limmer tak's mony a shift,
Whyles here, and whyles there, and whyles under a hap;
But your's is the steady light, Colin Dunlap.

Na, mair!—like true friendship, the mirker the night,
The mair you send out your vast volume o' light;—
When sackcloth and ashes the heavens enwrap,
'Tis then you're maist kind to us, Colin Dunlap.

The day and the night unto you are the same,
For still ye spread oot you're braid sheet o' red flame;
When this weary warld soundly tak's its bit nap,
You sleep not, you slumber not, Colin Dunlap.

The folks about Glasgow may brag o' their gas,
Whilk, just like a' glaring things pleases the mass;
Gin they're pleased wi't themsel's I'll ne'er snarl nor snap,
Quite contented wi' you, friendly Colin Dunlap.

Ay, aften I'm muckle behanden to you,
While wauchlin' alang between sober an' fu';
Wi' a stoiter to this side, to that side a stap,
Ye show me the gate aye, kind Colin Dunlap.

Gin neighbouring farmers felt gratefu' like me,
They'd club a' thegither, a present to gie—
A massy punch-bowl, wi' a braw mounted cap,
To the man that befriends them aye, Colin Dunlap.

I ken for mysel' that a gift I intend—
To ane that sae aften has proved my guid friend—
O' a braw braid blue bonnet, wi' strawberry tap,
To be worn aye on New'r-days by Colin Dunlap.

I canna weel reckon how lang ye hae shined,
But I'm sure its as lang as my mither has mind;
And in a' that lang while there has ne'er been a gap
In your body o' light, canty Colin Dunlap.

O lang may ye shine to enlighten us here,
And when ye depart to some new unknown sphere,
That to shine on mair glorious may still be your hap,
Is the prayer o' your weel-wisher, Colin Dunlap.

——::——

SANCT MUNGO.

(THE PATRON SAINT OF GLASGOW.)

SANCT MUNGO wals ane famous sanct,
  And ane cantye carle wals hee,
He drank o' ye Molendinar Burne,
  Quhan bettere hee culdna prie;
Zit quhan he culd gette strongere cheere,
  He neuer wals wattere drye,
Butte dranke o' ye streame o' ye wimpland worme,
  And loote ye burne rynne bye.

Sanct Mungo wals ane merrye sanct,
  And merrylye hee sang;
Quhaneuer he liltit uppe hys spryngе,
  Ye very Firre Parke rang;
Butte thoch hee weele culd lilt and synge,
  And mak sweet melodye,
He chauntit aye ye bauldest straynes,
  Quhan prymed wi' barlye-bree.

Sanct Mungo wals ane halie sanct,
  Farre famed for godlye deedis,
And grete delyte hee daylye took,
  Inn countynge owre hys beadis;

Zit I, Sanct Mungo's youngeste sonne,
Can count als welle als hee ;
Butte ye beadis quilk I like best to count
Are ye beadis o' barlye-bree.

Sanct Mungo wals ane jolly sanct :—
Sa weele hee lykit gude zil,
Thatte quhyles hee staynede hys quhyte vesture,
Wi' dribblands o' ye still ;
Butte I, hys maist unwordye sonne,
Haue gane als farre als hee,
For ance I tynde my garmente skirtis,
Throuch lufe o' barlye-bree.

WILLIAM FINLAYSON.

The field of Scottish poetry is so richly dowered with the song-jewels of native genius that unassuming merit is apt to be taken at its own disparaging value and conveniently overlooked. William Finlayson, a poet of real, though homely merit, was born at Coustonholm, Pollokshaws, on 12th January, 1787, and died at his son's residence, Leith, as lately as 1872, the precise date of his demise being the 1st of the October of that year. He was one of a family of ten children, his father being Alex. Finlayson, of Custer-holm, and his mother Janet Glen, of the Cowglen there. He wrote the majority of his published poems while still resident in Pollokshaws as a working weaver. Through the influence of Mrs. Smith, of Jordanhill, to whom he was distantly related, he got an appointment in the Excise, in which service he remained for nearly forty years. In 1815 his poems and songs were issued in a collected form under the title of *Simple Scottish Rhymes.* The little volume, unpretentious in tone and appearance, possesses, as we have said, real though homely merit, and evinces on the part of the author the possession of native poetic genius. Finlayson in his day corresponded with and enjoyed the friendship of Tannahill. He was a man of quiet habits, and was locally much and deservedly respected.

—::—

GEORDIE'S MARRIAGE.

O, KEN ye that Geordie and Jean
  Are cried in the chapel on ither?
And that we are a' to convene
  On Friday to loop them thegither?
The lassie is handsome and fair,
  Has plenty of beauty and braw things;
And the clatterin' gossips declare,
  To furnish a house she has a' things.

Though Geordie has little laid by
  To serve the important occasion,
Nane need to gang hungry, or dry,
  Gin they ha'e a stout inclination;
His mither, a pensie auld wife,
  Has vow'd to preside at the table,
And she can plan things to the life,
  An's willing, and hearty, and able.

O' haggises, lang-kail, and pies,
  And birsled sheep's-heids there are plenty;
Wi' a patfu' o' guid monie-plies*
  To taste ony mouth that is dainty.
Then, fiddler, your fiddle-string stent,
  And play us up *Scamber-cum-scratch-me;*
This e'ening on dancing I'm bent,
  Gin the bridegroom's guidmother 'ill match me.

---

* A decoction of tripe.

Sae, the fiddler he lilted and play'd,
  And the young yins I wat werna idle,
While the auld bodies tippled, and pray'd
  For a blessing to follow the bridal;
But the main twa deserted the fiel',
  And skulkit unseen frae the weddin';
And some think they'll never dae weel,
  As naebody witness'd their beddin'!

—::—

POESY.

O Poesy! how often hast thou sooth'd
  The latent throbbings of a broken heart!
  How often hath thy heaven-bequeathèd art
The rugged pathway of my wanderings smooth'd!
  If, unawares, the bashful crimson steal,
In public, o'er my colour-changing cheek,
  In solitude I consolation feel,
And find, with thee, joys many dare not seek!
  Still may the numbers, rolling on supine,
Dispel my mental, melancholy gloom!
  Thine is the art—the powerful charm is thine,
On desert hills to make an Eden bloom;—
  To raise the soul o'er every human woe,
  And all the vain contempt a scoffing world can show.

ARCHIBALD MACKAY.

A genuine, though homely poet, Archibald Mackay, author of *Ingleside Lilts,* was born at Kilmarnock in 1801. Receiving an ordinary school education, he was thereafter sent to work at the loom. Not relishing the occupation of weaving, however, he after a time finally abandoned the loom, and acquiring a knowledge of the handicraft trade of bookbinding, continued, until recently, to prosecute that business. Like all other true poets, he was early devoted to the cultivation of the muse; and in 1828 he acquired local fame by the publication in that year of a metrical tale entitled *Drouthy Tam*, which ran through several editions. Encouraged to renewed efforts by the success of his first poetic venture, he issued, in 1830, a modest little book of poems, which was well received, and which was subsequently re-issued in an augmented form in 1855, under the distinctive title of *Ingleside Lilts*. A fresh edition was published in 1863. Mr. MACKAY, in addition to his poetic labours, is also the author of a well-known *History of Kilmarnock*, besides having been, in the course of a long life, an extensive contributor to the various local journals. As a poet, his verses are characterised by simplicity of thought and fancy, with pleasing natural expression. In subject, as in treatment, he is invariably sensible and homely, and never appears puffed up with a big and pretentious ambition. His best-known effusion, *My First Bawbee*, is replete with happy conceptions, and native, knackie clink, and has that easy and catching natural flow which invariably gains an immediate entrance to the popular mind. There are many other capital poems in the book, and the beautiful song, *Be Kind to Auld Grannie*, is full of the tenderest feeling poetically expressed. His efforts in English verse are almost uniformly good, particularly so the well-sustained poem on *The Bard*, which originally appeared in *Chambers's Journal*. Born in 1801, as we have already said, Mr. MACKAY is now (1882) in his 82nd year. A poetic octogenarian is truly a rare sight. Poets, as a rule, usually die of disappointment before attaining the end of the tether scripturally allotted to man. Mr. Mackay's career has therefore been presumably encouraging, and many admirers of Scottish poetry (not local friends only, but the reading public generally,) will rejoice to hear that the aged author of *My First Bawbee* is still with us, wearing his weight of years well, and happy in his local surroundings. He still resides in his native town of Kilmarnock, keeping a small book shop in Titchfield Street, wherein he is daily at the service of the public for a sale across the counter, or for a share in a furthy twa-handed Scotch crack.

——::——

MY FIRST BAWBEE.

O nane, I trew, in a' the earth, was happier than me,
When in my wee breeks pouch I gat my first bawbee;
I turn'd it roun' an' roun' wi' pride, syne toddled aff wi' glee,
To spend on something that was guid, my first bawbee.

I met auld Granny at the door; quo' she—"Noo, Rab, tak' care,
Nae feckless whigmaleeries buy when ye gang to the fair;
A gaucy row, or sonsie scone, is best for ane that's wee;
Mind, muckle lies in how ye spend yer first bawbee."

But Granny's words were sune forgot when to the fair I gaed,
An' saw sae mony ferlies there on ilka stan' array'd;
I glow'rt at this, I glow'rt at that, wi' roving greedy e'e,
An' felt dumfounder't how to spend my first bawbee.

Here apples lay in mony a creel, a' temptin' to the view,
Wi' plums an' pears, whase very look brocht water to the mou';
An' there were tosh wee picture books, spread oot sae fair to see,
They seem'd to say—"Come here an' spend your first bawbee."

I kent the ane wad gust the gab, the ither tell me how
Cock Robin fell that waefu' day the Sparrow drew his bow,
But baith, waesucks, I couldna get, and sae, wi' tearfu' e'e,
I swither't lang on whilk to spend my first bawbee.

At length, a wheedlin' Irish loon began to bawl an' brag—
"Come here," said he, "my little lad, and thry my lucky bag!
If you have but one copper got, for it you may get three;
Sure, never venture, never win! come sport your bawbee."

Thocht I, this is the verra thing; I'll mak' my bawbee twa,
An' syne I'll get the plums an' pears, the picture books an' a';
Sae, at the "bag" I tried my luck, but hope was dung ajee;
A *blank* was mine, an' sae I lost my first bawbee.

A tear cam' happin' owre my cheek, as sad I danner't hame,
The hunger rumblin' up an' doon, like win' within my wame,
I telt auld Granny a' my tale—"Ye've gane faur wrang," quo' she,
"But muckle guid may yet come oot yer first bawbee."

An' true she spak'; my loss was gain; it taught me usefu' lair;
It made me aft since syne tak' tent o' mony a gilded snare;
An' still, when rogues, to catch the plack, their fleechan phrases gi'e,
A something whispers—"*Robin, mind your first bawbee.*"

——::——

BE KIND TO AULD GRANNIE.

Be kind to auld Grannie, for noo she is frail,
As a time-shatter'd tree bending low in the gale.
When ye were wee bairnies, tot, totting about,
She watch'd ye when in, an' she watch'd ye when out;
An' aye when ye chanc'd in your daffin an' fun,
To dunt your wee heids on the cauld stancy grun',
She lifted ye up, an' she kiss'd ye fu' fain,
Till a' your bit cares were forgotten again.
    Then, be kind to auld Grannie, for noo she is frail,
    As a time-shatter'd tree bending low in the gale.

When first in your breast rose that feeling divine,
That's waked by the tales an' the sangs o' langsyne,
Wi' her auld-warl crack she wad pleasure inspire,
In the lang winter nichts as she sat by the fire;
Or melt your young hearts wi' some sweet Scottish lay,
Like "The Floo'rs o' the Forest," or "Auld Robin Gray."

Though eerie the win' blew around ha' an' cot,
Grim winter an' a' its wild blasts were forgot.
Then, be kind to auld Grannie, for noo she is frail,
Like a time-shatter'd tree bending low in the gale.

An' mind, though the blythe day o' youth noo is yours,
Time will wither its joys, as wild winter the floo'rs;
An' your step that's noo licht as the bound o' the roe,
Wi' cheerless auld age may be feeble and slow;
An' the friends o' your youth to the grave may be gane,
An' ye on its brink be left tott'rin alane;
O, think how consoling some friend would be then,
When the gloaming o' life comes like mist owre the glen.
Then, be kind to auld Grannie, for noo she is frail,
Like a time-shatter'd tree bending low in the gale.

WILLIAM MILLER.

NURSERY poetry, existing for long in a fugitive form, got a distinct embodiment in Scottish literature by the poets of the *Whistle-Binkie* school. One of the best known of these successful, though humble, contributors to Doric minstrelsy, was WILLIAM MILLER, who was a native of Glasgow, having been born in the "Briggate," August, 1810.

"A merry spot it was in days of yore,"

he was wont to say of it, and his early remembrances of the now tatterdemalion locality were bright and happy. He was afterwards removed to Parkhead, a village a short way east of Glasgow, where he spent his boyhood; and showing mental precocity was intended for the profession of medicine. He attended college in pursuance of that object, but a sudden and debilitating illness, with which he was seized while still a mere youth, altered that intention, and he was subsequently apprenticed to the trade of a wood-turner, which handicraft business he continued to follow till death. He was accounted a good workman, and is said to have had no superior for speed and excellency at the bench.

He early exhibited a talent for neat verse-writing, and before he had reached his 20th year was in the habit of contributing to the poetical columns of the local prints. In 1832 the remarkable series of original, pathetic, and humorous poems and lyrics—afterwards collected under the title of *Whistle-Binkie*—first began to be issued. The publication attracted favourable public attention, and the Scottish poets of the day clustered round it like bees round the summer flowers. MILLER was an early and valued contributor to its choice pages, and the publication therein of *Wee Willie Winkie*, with other kindred gems, first gave him fame as a true, though homely, poet.

It was not until 1863 that MILLER ventured on independent publication in a volume. His muse had never been prolific, but his liltings were choice if few. In that year appeared his thin quarto volume entitled *Nursery Songs and other Poems.* The book was well received by the Scottish press, but did not sell fast. Estimating his genius, one is struck by the *singleness*—if we may be allowed the expression—of the string on which he thrums. He has but little imagination and no humour. His poetic range is indeed limited, but within that narrow range his note of song is unquestionably exquisite. His fine poem on *Hairst* is an exceedingly chaste and beautiful production, and his *Lady Summer* is justly accounted one of the daintiest morsels of the Scottish muse.

In the latter part of 1871 he fell ill, and his health continuing to rapidly fail, he was removed to Blantyre at the generous wish of the late James Ballantyne, Esq., wholesale jeweller, Glasgow. Mr. Ballantyne's family took a deep and loving interest in their aged ward. He never rallied, however, and coming back to Glasgow, died there, August 20th, 1872. He was interred in Tollcross burying-ground, and a small but compact granite monument was subsequently erected to his memory within the Necropolis of Glasgow.

In person, WILLIAM MILLER was tall, with sharp, well-cut features, his countenance being ennobled by a fine lofty forehead, which at once bespoke his poetic gifts. He had a kindly way, and a quick manner of speaking, with a hurried nervous gait, and was, perhaps, not unconscious of his supremacy as the poet of child-life. Robert Buchanan, a competent critic, felicitously styled him the "Laureate of the Nursery," and that happily-distinctive appellation he is likely to permanently retain.

——::——

WILLIE WINKIE.

WEE Willie Winkie rins through the toun,
Up stairs and doun stairs in his nicht-gown,
Tirling at the window, crying at the lock,
"Are the weans in their bed? for it's noo ten o'clock."

"Hey, Willie Winkie, are ye coming ben?
The cat's singing gray thrums to the sleeping hen;
The dog's spelder'd on the floor, and disna gie a cheep;
But here's a waukrife laddie that winna fa' asleep."

Onything but sleep, you rogue! glow'rin like the moon;
Rattling in an air jug wi' an airn spoon.
Rumblin', tumblin', round about, crawing like a cock,
Skirlin' like a kenna-what, wauk'nin' sleeping folk.

"Hey, Willie Winkie—the wean's in a creel!
Wamblin' aff a body's knee like a very eel.
Ruggin' at the cat's lug, rav'llin' a' her thrums—
Hey, Willie Winkie—see, there he comes!"

Wearied is the mither that has a stoorie wean ;
A wee stumpie stousie that canna rin his lane ;
That has a battle aye wi' sleep, before he'll close an e'e—
But a kiss frae aff his rosy lips gies strength anew to me.

—::—

LADY SUMMER.

Birdie, birdie, weet your whistle !
Sing a sang to please the wean ;
Let it be o' Lady Summer
Walking wi' her gallant train !
Sing him how her gaucy mantle
Forest-green trails owre the lea,
Broider'd frae the dewy hem o't
Wi' the field-flowers to the knee !

How her foot's wi' daisies buskit,
Kirtle o' the primrose hue ;
An' her e'e sae like my laddie's,
Glancing, laughing, loving blue !
How we meet on hill and valley,
Children sweet as fairest flowers,
Buds and blossoms o' affection,
Rosy wi' the sunny hours.

Sing him sic a sang, sweet birdie !
Sing it owre and owre again ;
Gar the notes fa' pitter patter,
Like a shower o' summer rain.
"Hoot, toot, toot !" the birdie's saying,
"Wha can shear the rigg that's shorn ?
Ye've sung brawlie simmer's ferlies,
I'll toot on anither horn."

—::—

THE WONDERFU' WEAN.

Our wean's the most wonderfu' wean e'er I saw,
It would tak' me a lang summer day to tell a'

His pranks, frae the morning till nicht shuts his e'e,
When he sleeps like a peerie, 'tween faither and me.
For in his quate turns, siccan questions he'll speir :
How the moon can stick up in the sky that's sae clear?
What gars the wind blaw? and wharfrae comes the rain?
He's a perfect divert: he's a wonderfu' wean.

Or wha was the first body's faither? and wha
Made the very first snaw-shower that ever did fa?
And wha made the first bird that sang on a tree?
And the water that sooms a' the ships on the sea?—
But after I've tell't him as weel as I ken,
Again he begins wi' his "Wha?" and his "When?"
And he looks aye sae watchfu' the while I explain,—
He's as auld as the hills—he's an auld-farrant wean.

And folk wha ha'e skill o' the bumps o' the head
Hint there's mae ways than toiling o' winning ane's bread;
How he'll be a rich man, and ha'e men to work for him,
Wi' a kyte like a bailie's, shug-shugging afore him,
With a face like the moon, sober, sonsy, and douce,
And a back, for its breadth, like the side o' a house.
'Tweel, I'm unco ta'en up wi't, they mak' a' sae plain—
He's just a town's talk—he's a by-ord'nar wean!

I ne'er can forget sic a laugh as I gat,
When I saw him put on faither's waistcoat and hat;
Then the lang-leggit boots gaed sae far owre his knees,
The tap loops wi' his fingers he grippit wi' ease.
Then he march'd through the house—he march'd but, he march'd ben,
Sae like mony mae o' our great little men,
That I laugh'd clean outright, for I couldna contain,
He was sic a conceit—sic an ancient-like wean.

But 'mid a' his daffin' sic kindness he shows,
That he's dear to my heart as the dew to the rose;
And the unclouded hinnie-beam aye in his e'e
Mak's him every day dearer and dearer to me.
Though fortune be saucy, and dorty, and dour,
And glooms through her fingers, like hills through a shower,
When bodies hae got a bit bairn o' their ain,
How he cheers up their hearts—he's the wonderfu' wean.

HAIRST.

THO' weel I lo'e the budding spring, I'll no misca' John Frost;
Nor will I roose the simmer days at gowden autumn's cost:
For a' the seasons in their turn, some wish'd-for pleasures bring,
As hand in hand they jink aboot like weans at jingo ring.

Fu' weel I mind how aft ye said, when winter nichts were lang,
"I weary for the simmer woods, the lintie's tittering sang;"
But when the woods grew gay and green, and birds sang sweet and clear,
It then was, "When will hairst-time come, the gloaming o' the year?"

Oh, hairst-time's like a lipping cup that's gi'en wi' furthy glee!
The fields are fu' o' yellow corn, red apples bend the tree;
The genty air, sae ladylike, has on a scented gown,
And wi' an airy string she leads the thistle-seed balloon.

The yellow corn will porridge mak', the apples taste your mou',
And owre the stibble riggs I'll chase the thistle-down wi' you;
I'll put the haw frae aff the thorn, the red hip frae the brier—
For wealth hangs in each tangled nook in the gloaming o' the year.

Sweet hope! ye biggit ha'e a nest within my bairnie's breast—
Oh! may his trusting heart ne'er trow that whiles ye sing in jest;
Some coming joys are dancing aye before his langing een—
He sees the flower that isna blawn, and birds that ne'er were seen;—

The stibble rigg is aye ahin'; the gowden grain afore;
And apples drop into his lap, or row in at the door!
Come, hairst-time, then, unto my bairn, drest in your gayest gear,
Wi' saft and winnowing win's to cool the gloaming o' the year.

GEORGE PAULIN.

A POET of a high order of merit, GEORGE PAULIN was born at Horndean, a village in the parish of Ladykirk, Berwickshire, August 15th, 1812. He was educated at the Grammar School of Selkirk, went to Edinburgh University in 1832; took various prizes in the Humanity, Greek, Logic, and Moral Philosophy Classes between 1832 and 1838; was successively Parochial Schoolmaster in Newlands, Peebleshire, and in Kirknewton, Edinburghshire, till 1844, when he was appointed Rector of the Irvine Academy, which appointment he held till the autumn of 1877, when he finally resigned it. On his retirement from the rectorship of Irvine Academy, his old pupils presented him with £1000 as a token of their admiration of his abilities, and their esteem for his private character.

In 1876, he issued at the suggestion of very many friends, a selection of his poems under the title of *Hallowed Ground and Other Poems.* The piece which gives the book its name was a Prize Poem, written for Prof. Wilson's class in September, 1838. The learned professor declared the poem to be the finest he had ever received, a tribute of which the author might justly feel proud. The poem is a noble conception, most effectively wrought out, equal to Campbell's *Pleasures of Hope* in fire and nervous energy, and more than equal to that brilliant performance, in nobility of sentiment, and true reach of thought.

Mr. PAULIN is the Whittier of Scotland. He resembles the grand old American Quaker poet in head and face, as well as in the Christian sentiment and purity of his alternately splendid and charming verse. Viewed as a whole, his volume may be fairly judged as the noblest contribution made to the shrine of Scottish Poesy for the last quarter of a century.

We extract a portion of the principal poem under the title of

HALLOWED SCENES.

They rise before me, robed in many hues,—
Distant and dim with years, or brightly near—
The mouldering records of a bygone year,
When Greece own'd heroes, Helicon a muse—
The high blue hills that cleft the Grecian heaven,
When sunn'd with glory's beam, and cleave it still,—
The eternal City, with its splendours riven
By conquering Time from its own palace-hill—
And later hallow'd (not less true to fame),
Helvetia's mountain-land of liberty.
The island heights that despots quake to name,
Guarded by valour and the rolling sea;
And, holier far, the plains by angels trod,
What time a lowly wanderer, faint and poor,
Walk'd o'er the Syrian sands—the incarnate God
Who paved with burning suns heaven's palace floor,
And toil'd with humble men by Galilee's lone shore!—

They rise before me, bursting through the veil
Of bygone years; and many a scene beside,
Of its own land the glory and the pride,
Hallow'd for ages by the poet's tale.
I see a million swords flash back the sun
From high Octa's base, and Malia's shore;
I hear the Persian shout, "The pass is won!"
I see their glittering myriads downward pour:
Thermopylæ! thy own Three Hundred stand
Before me as they stood when round their lord
They vowed to die, or save their fatherland
With Freedom's keen and consecrated sword.
There stood—there fell Leonidas, and round
(With twice ten thousand foes) his little band;—
Their fall hath sanctified that gory ground,
Their fall hath hallow'd all that wondrous land,
And still the Egean hymns their dirge by Malia's strand.

Gray Marathon! the pilgrim turns to thee,
Flashes Athena's banner on his sight,
And all the glittering splendour of the fight—

The plume, the shield, the sword, the prostrate tree,
Rolls on the Mede's interminable host,
Stand firm and stern and mute the patriot few:
See yonder hero, Athens' proudest boast,
With joyous look the moving myriads view:
The war-peal bursts—the dawning light of heaven
Blends the wild strife of freeman and of slave;
And see, before the avenging banner driven,
To shun the sword the Persian seeks the wave
To fetter freedom in her loved retreat;
In pride of power the despot left his throne,
He chain'd the floods that lash'd his worshipp'd feet,
But found Miltiades and Marathon,—
And bent his haughty crest a present God to own.

Clime of the ancient but undying glory!
Birth-place of freedom, valour, love, and song!
Fain would the pilgrim, lingering, dwell among
Your haunted heights and vision'd vales of story;
Fain would he linger by Cithæron's steep,
And kneel upon the shores of Salamis;
Wander a while where Leuctra's heroes sleep,
And muse o'er Sparta's tomb where adders hiss;
Stand mournfully where old Athenæ stood,
And fair Ilyssus roll'd its flower kiss'd-stream,
And Plato walked in triumph's noblest mood,
Amid the youthful blooms of Academe:
For time that steals from beauty, power, and fame,
Adds to the charm that wins the poet's eye—
To each loved scene whose old familiar name
Link'd with the soul's bright youth, can only die
With poesy divine and high philosophy.

On fancy's bark the pilgrim quits the land
Of freedom's birth, and skims the Ionian tide.—
Before him, in its old heroic pride,
He sees the city of the Cæsars stand;
And there the stern dictator,—on his brow
The majesty of empire and its care;—
Content and poor, he guides his humble plough,
And toils for bread his little ones may share.

There sits the stern tyrannicide, whose doom
(His country's laws from tyrant scorn to save)
Consign'd his valorous offspring to the tomb,
Himself with blighted heart to wish the grave.
There Cato stands, and flings his honest frown
On Rome's degenerate wealth, and shakes the soul
That quails before the splendours of a crown ;
While Tully points to Greece and glory's goal,
And o'er the tyrant's head bids Roman thunders roll.

Another clime !—the pilgrim knows it well—
Oft has his soul with Alpine thunders been,
And oft the bursting avalanches seen
Roll stormy music o'er the land of Tell.
See where the keen-eyed archer stands amid
His bold compatriots on the mountain's brow ;
His eye pursues the eagle's flight, till hid
Beyond the clouded peaks of Alpine snow ;
Then with his little band he bends his knee,
And vows to heaven, upon that hoary height,
That the wild hills that nursed its plume, should be
Unchain'd and tameless as the eagle's flight.
And how he kept his vow, the Switzer boy
Sings to his comrade's pipe upon the fell,
Tending their flock in freedom and in joy ;
And to the stranger points with bosom's swell,
Where stood the humble cot of glorious William Tell.

The rush of waves—the voice of many floods—
Old ocean's music, meets the pilgrim's ear ;
Grim frowning rocks their giant heights uprear
Around Britannia's hills, and streams, and woods :
Bewilder'd is his eye ; for who can count
Those fanes in sunshine and in shade that lie,
Studding each down, and dell, and hoary mount,
Beneath the blue of Albion's cloudy sky !—
The dim cathedral's high and solemn pile,
Whence float to heaven old England's songs of praise,
Whence peal'd the ancestral worship of our isle,
Tuned to the organ's swell of other days ;

The ivied church, where England's noble poor
Mingle their prayers on day of holy rest,
That he who bade their mountains stand secure,
And fix'd their isle a gem on ocean's breast,
Should bid their fathers' fanes and fatherland be blest.

And Scotia ! gleaming o'er thy lowland sod,
And up thy highland heights amid the heather,
Fanes where thy Sabbath-honouring children gather
To pay their vows to Scotia's covenant God.
They pour the reverence of the simple heart
In solemn melody and humble prayer ;
And with their dearest blood would sooner part,
Than see the altar-spoiler enter there !
And Scotia's emigrant when far away
Amid the forest stillness of the West,
Oft from the banks of Tweed or Highland Tay,
Lists the loved tones steal o'er the ocean's breast !
They lead him back to childhood's happy home,—
The village church beside the old yew-tree,
The silent Sabbath, when he loved to roam
In fields, to hear the hum of heather bee
Float in the hallow'd air from brake and flowery lea.

They lead him back to where, in days of yore,
The austere sires of Scotland's freedom stood
Banded to save the Bibles which they bore,—
Their heritage of hope, from men of blood.
The trembling boy—the parent, grey with years
And bent with toil—the widow poor and old,
Driven houseless forth by persecuting spears,
To shiver on the bleak and wintry wold.
Their blood hath nursed a tree that will not die,—
That braved the blast, and still the blast shall brave ;—
And Scotland will not own the ungenerous eye,
That beams not proudly o'er her martyr's grave.
And haply, too, they lead him back to where
The Southern plume lay low on Bannockburn ;
He sees the Bruce his Carrick falchion bare ;
And patriot chiefs, where'er his eye may turn,
Start from their hollow'd bed—the thistle-tufted urn.

JAMES SMITH.

A MAN of true poetic genius and versatile mind, JAMES SMITH is a native of Edinburgh, having been born in St. Mary's Wynd, March 2nd, 1824. His father, a coach-lace weaver, apprenticed him to the business of a printer in his eleventh year, at which calling Mr. SMITH continued to work up till 1869. In that year he was appointed librarian to the Edinburgh Mechanics' Library, a post which he still continues to fill with acceptancy and trust. On the completion of his apprenticeship he afterwards "tramped"—travelled is the polite term—through a great part of England and Ireland, acquiring thereby such a practical trade experience as only travel can competently give. Returning to Edinburgh, he again wrought there as a journeyman printer for a number of years, and was afterwards "reader," and, later on, manager of Aikman's Law Printing House in Hanover Street, where he superintended the printing of the "Daily Rolls of Court of Session" for a period of thirteen years. This situation he left in consequence of the business having been transferred to another party, our author coming down to the rank and file of the working operative class once more. His career at this period was much and deeply chequered. Domestic affliction of the most trying kind succeeded on trade misfortune; but the resolute and admirable spirit of the man rose superior to his crushing environments, and he found consolation and hope in the consciousness of daily duties faithfully and unfailingly done, and in the sweet, pensive, and ever-present solace of his ingenious muse.

His first volume of verses—which was "set up" and

printed in leisure hours by his own hands—was early in 1869 re-published by the Messrs. Blackwood of Edinburgh, under the title of *Poems, Songs, and Ballads*. The volume, which was received with universal favour, at once established his reputation as a Scottish poet. The book has since reached a fourth edition. SMITH's poetry is full of animation and graphic realism, and the author shows throughout his book the power to draw the tear as well as the ability to raise the laugh. In this way he has embalmed some of his heart experiences in the saddest and sweetest settings of verse. This very fine quality of pathos in Mr. SMITH's poetry is all the more noticeable, as the slap-dash, rumble-tumble, laugh-at-care nature of the majority of his humorous Scotch sketches and stories is quite proverbial. He has all the versatility of the true poet, and can alter his note of song at will. In the vein of children's poetry he has never been surpassed. His *Wee Joukydaidles*, as a graphic and life-like photograph of a steerin', dish-breakin', sugar-lickin' Scotch wean, is perfection of its kind, and in the pathetic vein, his *Wee Pair o' Shoon*, as a tenderly suggestive poem, is treasured up in many a bereaved mother's heart, and is unquestionably one of the truest notes of pathos in the language. In a lighter vein, his *Merry Bridal o' Frithmains* is one of the happiest and most graphic contributions to modern Scottish poetical literature.

Personally, Mr. SMITH is a most loveable man. He is full of candour, and his manners partake of the abrupt and unstudied simplicity of a thoroughly honest and conscientious mind. On the shortest acquaintance you instinctively feel that you could as implicitly rely upon his spoken word as on his written signature. He has written very profusely, and a large proportion of his work is imperishable, being already bound up with the best of the current literature of the country. The subjoined small tribute to Mr. SMITH's delightful genius—which has the merit of sincerity—seems not out of place here :—

TO JAMES SMITH.

"O rare Ben Jonson!" cried an early wit,
In eulogy of him who sat and heard
The voice of Shakspeare, and with him confer'd,
Permitted in his presence oft to sit;
And if, dear friend, at loss fit words to snatch,
I cry, glad-voiced—"O rarest Jamie Smith!"
That of itself would be meet praise wherewith
Thy worth and happy genius both to match.
The favourite thou of all the fabled Nine,
Striking at will sweet-toned or saddening chords,
Or calling up in rumble-tumble line
Fun's farcic group upon the roaring boards;
Whilst unto thee the higher praise is due—
Thou brave-soul'd bard, to life and duty true!

—Alex. G. Murdoch.

A very pleasant fact remains to be added. In May, 1875, a number of the poet's friends and admirers, including the gifted and highly popular Earl of Rosebery, presented Mr. SMITH with a purse containing two hundred guineas as a token of their admiration of his genius and character. Despite the harassing worry of his busy and chequered life, he still enjoys excellent health and perfect mental vigour. His writings, in great part, are likely to secure permanent popular appreciation.

——::——

WEE JOUKYDAIDLES.

WEE Joukydaidles, toddlin' oot and in :
Oh, but she's a cuttie, makin' sic a din !
Aye sae fou' o' mischief, an' minds na what I say :
My very heart gangs loup, loup, fifty times a day !

Wee Joukydaidles—Where's the stumpy noo ?
She's tumblin' i' the cruivie, an' lauchin' to the soo !
Noo she sees my angry e'e, an' aff she's like a hare !
Lassie, when I get ye, I'll scud ye till I'm sair !

Wee Joukydaidles—Noo she's breakin' dishes ;
Noo she's soakit i' the burn, catchin' little fishes ;
Noo she's i' the barn-yard, playin' wi' the fouls—
Feeding them wi' butter-cakes, snaps, an' sugar-bools.

Wee Joukydaidles—Oh my heart it's broke !
She's torn my braw new wincey, to mak' a dolly's frock.
There's the goblet owre the fire ! the jaud ! she weel may rin !
No a tattie ready yet, an' faither comin' in !

Wee Joukydaidles—Wha's sae tired as me !
See ! the kettle's doun at last ! waes me for my tea !
Oh, it's angersome, atweel, an' sune'll mak' me grey :
My very heart gangs loup, loup, fifty times a day !

Wee Joukydaidles—Where's the smoukie noo ?
She's hidin' i' the coal-hole, cryin' "Keekybo !"
Noo she's at the fireside, pu'in' pussy's tail—
Noo she's at the broun bowl, suppin' a' the kail !

Wee Joukydaidles—Paidlin' i' the shower—
There she's at the wundy ! haud her, or she's owre !
Noo she's slippit frae my sicht : where's the wean at last ?
In the byre amang the kye, sleepin' soun' and fast !

Wee Joukydaidles—for a' ye gi'e me pain,
Ye're aye my darlin' tottie yet—my ain wee wean !
An' gin I'm spared to ither days—Oh may they come to pass !—
I'll see my bonnie bairnie a braw, braw lass !

——::——

BURD AILIE.

Burd Ailie sat doon by the wimplin' burn,
  Wi' the red, red rose in her hair ;
And bricht was the glance o' her' bonnie black e'e,
  As her heart throbb'd fast and sair ;

And aye as she look'd on ilk clear wee wave,
  She murmur'd her true love's name,
An' sigh'd when she thocht on the distant sea,
  And the ship sae far frae hame!

The robin flew hie owre the gowden bloom,
  And he warbled fu' cheerilie;
"Oh, tell me—oh, tell me, my bonnie wee bird,
  Will I ever my true love see?"
Then saftly and sweetly the robin sang—
  "Puir Ailie! I'm laith to tell;
For the ship's i' the howe o' a roarin' wave,
  And thy love's i' the merlin's cell!"

"Oh, tell me—oh, tell me, thou bonnie wee bird,
  Did he mind on the nicht langsyne,
When we plighted our troth by the trystin' tree?
  Was his heart aye true to mine?"
"Oh, fond and true," the sweet robin said,
  "But the merlin he noo maun wed;
For the sea-weed's twin'd in his yellow hair,
  And the coral's his bridal bed!"

Burd Ailie lay low by the wimplin' burn,
  Wi' the red, red rose in her hair;
But gane was the glance o' her bonnie black e'e,
  And the robin sang nae mair;
For an angel cam' doon at the fa' o' the nicht,
  As she murmur'd her true love's name,
And took her awa' frae a broken heart,
  And the ship that wad ne'er come hame!

——::——

THE WEE PAIR O' SHOON.

Oh, lay them canny doon, Jamie,
  An' tak' them frae my sicht!
They mind me o' her sweet wee face,
  An' sparklin' e'e sae bricht.

Oh, lay them saftly doon beside
  The lock o' silken hair;
For the darlin' o' thy heart and mine
  Will never wear them mair!

But oh! the silvery voice, Jamie,
  That fondly lisp'd yer name,
An' the wee bit hands sae aft held oot
  Wi' joy when ye cam hame!
An' oh, the smile—the angel smile,
  That shone like simmer morn;
An' the rosy mou' that socht a kiss
  When ye were weary worn!

The eastlin' wind blaws cauld, Jamie—
  The snaw's on hill and plain—
The flow'rs that deck'd my lammie's grave
  Are faded noo, an' gane!
O, dinna speak! I ken she dwells
  In yon fair land aboon;
But sair's the sicht that blin's my e'e—
  That wee, wee pair o' shoon.

——::——

THE LINTWHITE.

A LINTWHITE sat in her mossy nest,
  Ae eerie morn in spring,
An' lang she look'd at the cauld grey lift,
  Wi' the wee birds under her wing.
An' aye as she lookit, wi' shiverin' breist
  Sae waesomely she sang:
"O tell me true, ye winds that blaw,
  Why tarries my love sae lang?

"I've socht him down i' the fairy glen,
  An' far owre the lanely lea;—
I've socht him down i' yon saft green yird,
  An' high on the birken tree;—

I've socht till the wee things cried me hame,
   Wi' mony a heavy pang;
O tell me true, ye winds that blaw,
   Why tarries my love sae lang?"

"O waly!" the norland breezes moan'd,
   "Sae weel may thy heart be sair;
For the hawk's awa' with thy ain true love,
   An' he'll sing thee a sang nae mair!
Fu' wae was his fate on yon auld aik tree,
   That aft wi' his warblin' rang!
Noo speir nae mair, wee shiverin' bird,
   Why tarries thy love sae lang!"

The lintwhite flew frae her mossy nest,
   For she couldna thole the sting;
An' she flichter'd east, and she flichter'd west,
   Till she droukit her downy wing;
An' aye as she flutter'd the lee-lang day,
   Sae wild an' sae shrill she sang:
"O tell me—tell me true, ye winds,
   Why tarries my love sae lang?"

——::——

THE WALY QUEEN.

The waly queen gaed by ae nicht
   As eerie fell the gloamin',
An' far owre mony a dowie dell,
   The waly queen gaed roamin';
When owre a lanely birken shaw,
   Where cushets aft were crying,
She glinted through a silvery cloud,
   And heard a maiden sighing.

"O thou that dwells aboon," she cried,
   "Where angel shadows hover,
Thy pity show, sweet Lady Moon,
   An' tell me o' my lover.

A blude-red rose he gied to me,
In a' its simmer blossom;
But dowie is the bonnie flower
That noo lies in my bosom."

Fu' saftly sigh'd the waly queen,
"Sae weel may be thy sorrow,
For owre thy fondest love on earth,
Nae mair shall dawn the morrow.
Wi' broken sword, an' shatter'd helm,
He sleeps in yon green loanin';
An' owre his lanely bed o' rest,
The dreary winds are moanin'."

Bricht radiance fill'd the birken shaw,
The streamlet sparkled clearly,
As dounward fell the crystal tears
For him she lo'ed sae dearly.
Then sabbin' sair, she breath'd his name,
Her weary heart resigning,
An' owre her locks o' yellow gowd,
The waly queen was shining.

——::——

I'LL SING MY SANG WHATE'ER BETIDE.

Oh, what reck I tho' Poortith's blast
Blaws owre my biggin', cauld and keen?
An' what tho' kind and generous hearts
Are no sae rife as they hae been?
Tho' selfish Greed an' crabbit Spleen
Stand gloomy glowerin' side by side;
Yet cantily I'll play a spring,
An' sing my sang whate'er betide!

This warl's nae weary bed o' thorns,
For a' the dolefu' moan that's made;
Yon sun that shines on silken braws,
Blinks cheery on my auld grey plaid!

Sour Discontent shrinks back dismay'd,
  When heart loups high wi' sturdy pride;
Sae cantily I'll play a spring,
  An' sing my sang whate'er betide.

  My housie's nae great boast I trow—
A wee wee but—a wee wee ben;
  Yet lauchin' face maks denty ha',
An' that's what lordies seldom ken.
Wi' wife an' weans I blithely fen',
  As doun Life's stream we saftly glide;
Sae cantily I'll play a spring,
  An' sing my sang whate'er betide!

  Despondency's a beggar born—
Lang may his back be at the wa'!—
  Yet gin he daur to show his pow,
My chanter I'll the louder blaw!—
The darkest nicht brings aye the daw:
  The thistle has its downy side;
Sae cantily I'll play a spring,
  An' sing my sang whate'er betide!

  Puir dowie chield, that's skin an' bane
Wi' nocht but borrow'd misery—
  Wha canna pree the gowden joys
That bloom 'neath Freedom's rosy sky;
Greet out your fill; I carena by,
  Tho' fools may sneer, an' gowks deride;
I'll play wi' pith a canty spring,
  An' sing my sang whate'er betide.

NORMAN MACLEOD, D.D.

THE late Dr. NORMAN MACLEOD was one of the many clergymen who have not deemed it a reflection to indulge an odd leisure hour in the genial cultivation of the muse. One of the "crackiest" and most valued correspondents of Robert

Burns was the Rev. John Skinner, the author of that blythest and best of old Scottish songs, *Tullochgorum.* Fifty years ago Robert Montgomery attained a brief popularity in his Glasgow pulpit through his published poetry, and was in a fair way of obtaining immortality as well, if the omniscient Macaulay had not in an excess of critical severity suddenly *sat on him.* In our own day we had lately in Glasgow, and have now in Edinburgh, the well-known and gifted Dr. W. C. Smith, of *Olrig Grange* celebrity. And although the few poems accredited to the late Dr. NORMAN MACLEOD are mere side-lights of an otherwise great and popular mind, they are not the less welcome as genuine additions to the Doric minstrelsy of our time.

NORMAN MACLEOD was born at Campbeltown, June 3rd, 1812. He was descended from an ancestry of regularly qualified and ordained ministers. His first charge was that of the Parish of Loudon, Ayrshire. In 1843, during the troubles consequent on the "Disruption," he was translated to the pastorate of Dalkeith. His growing reputation as a worker and preacher soon marked him out for still more conspicuous church services, and early in 1851 he was transferred to one of the most important charges in Scotland —that of the Barony Parish of Glasgow. His fame had preceded him, and thousands flocked to his ministrations. His style to the last was masculine, sensible, and convincing, rather than florid or rhetorical, and the popularity with which he was surrounded cheered and supported him to the end. He was a large-minded man, of broad and warm sympathies, and had the elevation of the working-classes much at heart. A popular feature of his ministry for years was his Sunday evening services for people in working clothes, which were very largely attended, and were productive of lasting good.

On the publication of *Good Words*, in 1860, he was entrusted with the control of that magazine, and continued to successfully edit it till his death. The connection between the editor and the publisher—Mr. Alexander Strahan—was of the most cordial nature, reflecting honour on both gentlemen. In 1869 he was elected with acclamation to the Moderator's Chair in the General Assembly. In the previous year he had been commissioned by the Assembly to visit and report on the Mission-field of the Church in India, and his health, sensibly declining under the fatigue of foreign travel, never thoroughly regained its tone. On June 16th, 1872, he died resignedly and full of honours, having just completed his sixtieth year.

His death, as will be vividly remembered, produced a wide-spread feeling of regret, and he was mourned by all sects and classes as a lost leader in Israel. He sleeps in Campsie churchyard, in the quiet shadow of the hills near which his boyhood was passed, leaving his Church and his country the legacy of a great and enduring name. He was succeeded in the editorship of *Good Words* by his brother, the Rev. Donald Macleod, D.D., of Park Church, Glasgow, himself a preacher of distinguished ability and grace.

One of the most genial characteristics of his versatile mind was a keen sense of the ludicrous—a passion which seized him at the unlikeliest moments. His broadly-humorous verses on *Captain Frazer's Nose*, were mostly written, his appreciative biographer—Rev. Donald Macleod, D.D.—tells us, when he was "enduring such pain, that the night was spent in his study, and he had occasionally to bend over the back of his chair for relief."

In the autumn of 1881, it may be mentioned, a handsome statue of Dr. Macleod was erected at Infirmary Square, directly facing the church within whose walls he had ministered so lovingly and so long. The statue is in bronze, and is elevated on a massive granite pedestal. It represents MACLEOD at his prime, and is accounted one of Mossman's most successful works.

TRUST IN GOD.

COURAGE, brother! do not stumble,
  Though thy path is dark as night;
There's a star to guide the humble;—
  Trust in God, and do the right!

Let the road be long and dreary,
  And its ending out of sight;
Foot it bravely, strong or weary;—
  Trust in God, and do the right!

Perish "policy" and cunning—
  Perish all that fears the light!
Whether losing, whether winning;—
  Trust in God, and do the right!

Trust no forms of guilty passion,
  Friends can look like angels bright;
Trust no custom, school, or fashion—
  Trust in God, and do the right!

Trust no party, church, or faction;
  Trust no leaders in the fight;
But, in every word and action,
  Trust in God, and do the right!

Some will hate thee, some will love thee,
  Some will flatter, some will slight;
Cease from man, and look above thee—
  Trust in God, and do the right!

Simple rule, and safest guiding;
  Inward peace, and inward light;
Star upon our path abiding—
  Trust in God, and do the right!

A MOTHER'S FUNERAL.

Ah ! sune ye'll lay yer mither doon in her lanely bed and narrow ;
But, till ye're sleeping by her side, ye'll never meet her marrow !
A faither's love is strong and deep, and ready is a brither's,—
A sister's love is pure and sweet—but what love's like a mither's?

Ye maunna greet owre muckle, bairns, as round the fire ye gaither,
And see the twa chairs empty then, o' mither and o' faither ;
Nor dinna let yer hearts be dreich, when wintry winds are blawin',
And on their graves, wi' angry sugh, the snelly drift is snawin' ;

But think of blyther times gane by—the mony years of blessing,
When sorrow pass'd the door, and nane frae 'mang ye a' were missing.
And mind the peacefu' gloamin' hours when the out-door wark was endin',
And after time, when auld grey heads wi' yours in prayer were bendin'.

And think hoo happy baith are noo, abune a' thocht or tellin' ;
For they're at hame, and young again, within their Faither's dwellin'.
Sae gin ye wish to meet up there yer faither and yer mither,
O love their God, and be gude bairns, and O love ane anither !

——::——

CURLER'S SONG.

A' nicht it was freezin', a' nicht I was sneezin' ;
  "Tak' care," quo' the wifie, "gudeman, o' yer cough ;"
A fig for the sneezin', hurrah for the freezin' !
  This day we're to play the bonspiel on the loch !
Then get up, my auld leddy, the breakfast get ready,
  For the sun on the snawdrift's beginning to blink,
Gie me bannocks or brochan, I am aff for the lochan,
  To mak' the stanes flee to the tee o' the rink !

Chorus—Then hurrah for the curlin' frae Girvan to Stirlin' !
  Hurrah for the lads o' the besom and stane !
  "Soop it up !" "ready noo !" "clap a guard !" "steady noo !"
  Oh ! curlin' abune every game stan's alane !

The ice it is splendid, it canna be mended—
  Like a glass ye may glow'r on't and shave aff your beard;
And see hoo they gether, comin' owre the brown heather,
  The servant and master, the tenant and laird!
There's brave Jamie Fairlie, he's there late and early,
  Better curlers than him or Tam Conn canna be.
Wi' the lads frae Kilwinnin', they'll send the stanes spinnin'
  Wi' *whirr* an' a *curr* till they sit roun' the tee.
    Then hurrah, etc.

It's an unco-like story that baith Whig and Tory
  Maun aye collyshangie like dogs owre a bane;
And a' denominations are wanting in patience,
  For nae kirk will thole to let ithers alane;
But in the frosty weather let a' meet thegither,
  Wi' a broom in their haun' and a stane by the tee,
And then, by my certes, ye'll see hoo a' parties
  Like brithers will love and like brithers agree!
    Then hurrah, etc.

——::——

CAPTAIN FRAZER'S NOSE.

O! if ye're at Dumbarton Fair,
Gang to the Castle when ye're there,
And see a sicht baith rich and rare—
    The nose o' Captain Frazer!

Unless ye're blin' or unco glee't,
A mile awa' ye're sure to see't,
And nearer han' a man gangs wi't,
    That owns the nose o' Frazer.

It's great in length, it's great in girth,
It's great in grief, it's great in mirth,
Tho' grown wi' years, 'twas great at birth—
    The nose o' Captain Frazer!

I've heard volcanoes loudly roarin',
And Niagara's waters pourin',
But oh! gin ye had heard the snorin'
    Frae the nose o' Captain Frazer!

To wauken sleepin' congregations,
Or rouse to battle sleepin' nations,
Gae wa' wi' preachin's and orations,
And try the nose o' Frazer !

Gif French invaders try to lan'
Upon our glorious British stran',
Fear nocht if ships are no at han',
But trust the nose o' Frazer !

Just crack that cannon owre the shore,
Weel ramm'd wi' snuff: then let it roar
Ae heilan' sneeze ; and never more
They'll daur the nose o' Frazer !

If that great nose is ever deid,
To bury it ye dinna need ;
Nae coffin made o' wood or lead
Could haud the nose o' Frazer !

But let it stan' itsel', alane,
Erect, like some big druid stane,
That a' the warld may see it's bane,
In memory o' Frazer !

PROFESSOR J. S. BLACKIE.

No name is better known in Scotland at the present day than that of John Stuart Blackie, Professor of Greek, in the University of Edinburgh. The son of a banker, he was born at Glasgow, July 28, 1809. His father, who had originally migrated to Glasgow from Kelso, removed to Aberdeen while his son was yet a boy, becoming agent for the Commercial Bank there. The future professor, who was of precocious smartness, began his education at a private school, and at the age of twelve years became a student at Marischal College. After four years' attendance there, he removed to Edinburgh, pursuing for three years theological studies in the University of that city. He afterwards proceeded to the Continent, assiduously prosecuting his studies at Gottingen and Berlin, completely mastering the language, and enriching at the same time his quick and marvellously receptive mind with the immortal treasures of German Literature. Proceeding next to Italy, he resided for fifteen months at Rome, devoting himself to the study of the language and literature of that country, and to the recondite study of Archæology. Returning to Scotland, he completed and published his celebrated translation of Goethe's *Faust*, which immediately established his claim as an accomplished German scholar.

Having finally given up the idea of entering the Church, and becoming thus, to use his own facetious phraseology, a "stickit minister," he studied law, and was called to the Scottish bar in 1834. He did not, however, prosecute the legal profession to practical ends, but continued a devoted and successful student of the much more congenial pursuits of literature.

In 1841 his devotion to literary concerns was rewarded by an appointment to the Professorship of Humanity (Latin Literature) in his native Marischal College, Aberdeen; a post which he honourably filled for nearly eleven years.

While a Professor in Aberdeen, he boldly initiated, against much obfuscated opposition, certain valuable university reforms which have since then been generally adopted.

In 1852 he was honoured with the appointment he still holds—Professor of Greek, in the Edinburgh University. Shortly after his election he travelled in Greece, residing at Athens for three months, initiating himself while there into a fluent use of the living Greek language, as well as familiarising his mind with the everyday manners and customs of the people.

At this period began the publication of those translations of Homer, in four volumes, along with repeated volumes of original descriptive and narrative verse, which so amply reflect the impulsive and reflective side of his vivacious and wonderfully versatile mind. In 1857 appeared *Lays and Legends of Ancient Rome.* In 1860, *Lyrical Poems.* In 1870, he issued a volume of *War Songs for the Germans;* and in 1872 appeared his best known poetical work, *Lays of the Highlands and Islands.* As recently as 1876 he published a fresh volume of poetry, entitled, *Songs of Religion and Life.*

Besides the list of works adverted to, the energetic Professor is also the author of a good half-dozen prose works on various recondite subjects, a convincing proof, if proof were needed, of Professor Blackie's amazing industry, and apparently inexhaustible fertility. His recent successful exertions on behalf of a Gaelic Chair in Scotland will be fresh in every reader's mind.

In addition to his labours as an original author, Professor Blackie has lectured with great acceptance on various topics, and on innumerable platforms. His mind is of a quick, bold cast, and he has, at all times, the fearless courage of his convictions, in consequence of which virtue, he has become the most widely quoted of platform speakers. He can never possibly be dull or uninteresting in a book, or in debate, as he unites, in high perfection, the two popular qualities of humour and animation. As a poet, he is distinguished for sense, enthusiasm, and melody.

In private company, the worthy Professor—still hale and hearty—is understood to be the soul of innocent geniality.

He has a strong array of attached personal friends, stands well with the public, and, as he still enjoys perfect mental health and vigour, he may be expected to still further enrich the imperishable song-treasures of his beloved Scotland.

——::——

BEAUTIFUL WORLD!

Beautiful world! though bigots condemn thee,
My tongue finds no words for the graces that gem thee!
Beaming with sunny light, bountiful ever,
Streaming with gay delight, full as a river!
    Bright world! brave world!
      Let cavillers blame thee!
    I bless thee, and bend
      To the God who did frame thee!

Beautiful world! bursting around me,
Manifold million-hued wonders confound me!
From earth, sea, and starry sky, meadow and mountain,
Eagerly gushes Life's magical fountain.
    Bright world! brave world!
      Though witlings may blame thee,
    Wonderful excellence
      Only could frame thee!

The bird in the greenwood his sweet hymn is trolling,
The fish in blue ocean is spouting and rolling!
Light things on airy wing wild dances weaving,
Clods with new life in Spring swelling and heaving!
    Thou quick-teeming world,
      Though scoffers may blame thee,
    I wonder, and worship
      The God who could frame thee!

Beautiful world! what poesy measures
Thy strong-flooding passions, thy light-trooping pleasures!
Mustering, marshalling, striving, and straining,
Conquering, triumphing, ruling, and reigning!

Thou bright-armied world!
So strong!—who can tame thee?
Wonderful power of God
Only could frame thee!

Beautiful world! while godlike I deem thee,
No cold wit shall move me with bile to blaspheme thee!
I have lived in thy light, and when Fate ends my story,
May I leave on Death's cloud the bright trail of Life's glory!
Wondrous old world!
No ages shall shame thee!
Ever bright with new light
From the God who did frame thee!

—::—

JOHN THE BAPTIST.

Who is he in hairy raiment
Clad, i' the wilderness
Preaching freely without payment
Truth and righteousness?
Whoso hears, and not despises,
Him with water he baptises,
In the contrite hour;
Whoso hears with haughty scorning,
Him he smites with holy warning,
And with prophet's power.

Swarms the city from its corners,
Motley bad and good;
Thoughtless hearts and hoary mourners
Haste to Jordan's flood;
Some for sin their souls abasing;
Some to feed their eyes with gazing;
Some to search and try
With captious craft the shaggy Preacher,
And themselves to teach the Teacher;
Some they know not why.

Comes the Rabbi, with a stately
  Measured gravity;
With a solemn air, sedately
  Comes the Pharisee;
Wide his robe, and on the border
Sacred texts, in well-match'd order,
  Show his purpose plain.
With a nice and fenced existence
Far to keep, at holy distance,
  Every look profane.

Comes fat Priest, and Pontiff portly,
  Each with bloated face;
Comes Herodian, smooth and courtly,
  With a gay grimace.
Comes the Essene from his station
Of secluded contemplation
  With mild gravity;
With an eye of twinkling keenness,
And a smile of cold sereneness,
  Comes the Sadducee.

Comes the Soldier, firm and steady,
  Frolicsome and gay,
With a quick hand ever ready
  For the rising fray.
Comes the Usurer, dry and meagre,
Comes the Publican, sharp and eager
  For great Cæsar's penny.
With a train of silken pages
Comes the rich man; with scant wages
  Come the burden'd many.

What saith he, the wayside Preacher,
  To this motley crew?
Doth he come a cunning teacher
  Of lore strange and new?
Hath he drawn without omission,
Point for point, a long confession,

To inform the brain?
Piled a proud word-architecture,
Fenced it round with nice conjecture,
And distinctions vain?

Hath he won a girth to measure
God, a chain to bind
The Infinite, and mapp'd at leisure
The omniscient Mind?
Hath he trimm'd an old Theogony,
Cumbrous rear'd a new cosmogony,
To employ the schools?
Not with speculation vainest
Preacheth he;—with wisdom plainest,
And with simplest rules.

Thus he speaks—"Repent! repentance
Smooths Messiah's way;
'Tis an old and weighty sentence,
Weigh it well to-day.
Hast thou nursed a sin?—confess it;
Hast thou done a wrong?—redress it;
And, with just desire,
Ask no more than what is due thee;
Be content, when offered to thee,
Is thy lawful hire.

"Say not, with vain pride elated,
'God's own people we,'
Tracing high a hoary-dated
Patriarch pedigree.
Peopled earth is thickly studded
With the children, common-blooded,
Of the Great I AM.
From the hard flint, at his pleasure,
God can raise up without measure
Sons to Abraham.

"Hear, whose barren trunk hath cumber'd
Now too long the ground.
Saith the Lord, your days are number'd;
Hark! with crushing sound,

Falls the axe that fells the fruitless !
Toils he not with labour bootless
  Who now smites the tree.
He his winnow'd wheat shall garner,
But like empty chaff the scorner
  Burn like chaff shall he."

Thus he preach'd to great and small men,
  Of the human right ;
Like the blessed sun, on all men
  Shedding simple light.
O ! wise are they who list such preaching,
Not too high for common teaching
  In life's common ways ;
Not with proud pretence ballooing,
Nor with gay parade festooing,
  To catch the public gaze.

Flap who will the air-borne pinion,
  Sweeping far and free ;
Solid earth be my dominion,
  Baptist John, with thee !
In the plainest path of duty,
Stamping daily things with beauty,
  I with thee will tread ;
Where thy warning fingers pointed
I would follow, where th' anointed
  Saviour lowly led !

——::——

POUR FORTH THE WINE !

Pour forth the wine ! the ruby wine !
And with thine eyes look into mine,
  Thou friend of olden days !
Heap up the blazing logs. Not here
On this grey ridge of granite drear,
Boon April spends her flow'ry cheer,
  To wake the poet's lays.

The east wind, through th' ungenial day,
  Blows meagre, thin, and chill,
And laggard winter's freezing ray
  Gleams from the snow-patch'd hill.

Pour forth the wine! the ruby wine!
And with thine eyes look into mine,
  Thou friend of olden days!
Cheer me with love and truth; for I
Oft seek in vain, beneath the sky,
The true heart, from the open eye
  That looks with guileless gaze.
A cold and caution-crusted race
  Here fans few joys in me;
But when I see a clear, bright face,
  I flourish, and am free!

Pour forth the wine! the ruby wine!
And with thine eyes look into mine,
  Thou friend of olden days!
Speak of devotion's fiery breath,
Friendship and love more strong than death,
And high resolve, and manly faith,
  That walks in open ways.
Look as thou didst long years ago,
  And read my heart with thine,
That Love and Truth may freely flow,
  To bless the ruby wine!

PROFESSOR NICHOL.

A POET of imaginative power, and fine taste, JOHN NICHOL Regius Professor of English Language and Literature in the University of Glasgow, was born at Montrose, 1833. His late gifted father—who was Professor of Astronomy at

Glasgow—is remembered as a man of a lofty and speculative genius, as well as a lecturer of brilliant and popular power.

The present Professor was appointed to the high office he now holds, in 1861. He is a man of more than mere academic culture, and has successfully attested his claim to a foremost place in the ranks of present-day English-writing poets, by the publication, in 1873, of his lofty historical drama of *Hannibal*. In 1881, his well-won fame was assured and widened on the appearance of his latest poetical work—*The Death of Themistocles and other Poems*. In other congenial walks, the able and learned Professor is also very favourably known. Two volumes of *Tables of Ancient Literature and History*, and of *European Literature and History*, respectively attest his painstaking industry and learned research, and are valued as admirable aids to the student of history, as well as to all such as desire to carefully revise their recollection of literary and historical facts. A volume of *Critical Estimates* has also proceeded from his cultured pen, with other recondite efforts in philosophy and criticism.

——::——

THE CORNISH COAST.

Far in the west a windy music rings
 The names of citadels of dim renown—
Of Lyonnesse, the sunken beach of Kings,
 Tintagel's height, and mystic Uther's crown.

It tells of fights a thousand years ago,
 Of banners waving round the rocky wall;
The strifes of heroes, and their overthrow,
 When the same surges wail'd for Arthur's fall!

Old monks are chaunting, in forgotten towers,
 To kneeling knights; and, under shade, is seen
Launcelot, stealing from the royal bowers,
 With guilty Guinevere, the glorious queen.

High on the guarded mount the archangel's sword
  Wrathfully gleams on Marazion's spoil;
And ruin'd chieftains cross the craggy ford,
  While grim Tregeagle plies his endless toil.

The wraiths of ages pass, of leagued crusades,
  Plantagenet, and stately Tudor days;
With fleeing foemen, and with mourning maids,
  And rival Roses sung in vanish'd lays.

Fair, 'mid the changeful lights of stranded Time,
  Are April spring-tides, mingling smiles and tears,
Serener loves that sue for softer rhyme,
  Beauties that blush, like morning, through the years.

But the winds whistle to a sterner time,
  The breakers boom along the barren shore,
Recalling in the notes of some wild rune,
  Th' invader's pride, th' avenging battle's roar.

I see the galleons of insulting Spain,
  The sport of northern gales and English skiffs;
I hear the loud laugh of the Cornish main,
  And Freedom shouting from her iron cliffs.

Another valour reigns, th' adventurous heart
  Rifles from regions far the teeming shires,
The fastness falls, appears the thronging mart,
  And, o'er the labouring mine, the furnace fires.

Still in dark nights the wrecking tempest raves,
  That toss'd the Norland pirates of fierce fame;
While captains, loyal to their heaving graves,
  Bear through the storm an undiminish'd name.

Fresh fancies stir us, as the ages roll;
  Still, underneath the varying effort, lies,
Ebbing and flowing, the same human soul,
  And the old Priest returns in altered guise.

These rocks re-echo the resounding voice
  Of the great Preacher with the narrow creed,
Pressing our rich life to a single choice,
  Yet serving hungry soil with fruitful seed.

A new day dawns, and grants a grander grace
  Than thine, good shepherd of the Cornish fold;
We read the mighty records of our race,
  And trust the eternal forces as of old.

We have the faith that's in the stars above—
  The sky, the hills, the message of the sea,
Are signs of wonder, majesty, and love,
  The beacons of a nobler earth to be.

—::—

MARE MEDITERRANEAN.

A LINE of light! it is the inland Sea,
  The least in compass and the first in fame;
The gleaming of its waves recalls to me
    Full many an ancient name.

As through my dreamland float the days of old,
  The forms and features of their heroes shine:
I see Phœnician sailors bearing gold
    From the Tartessian mine.

Seeking new worlds, storm-toss'd Ulysses ploughs
  Remoter surges of the winding main;
And Grecian captains come to pay their vows,
    Or gather up the slain.

I see the temples of the "Violet Crown"
  Burn upward in the hour of glorious flight:
And mariners of uneclips'd renown,
    Who won the great sea-fight.

I hear the dashing of a thousand oars,
  The angry waters take a deeper dye;
A thousand echoes vibrate from the shores
    With Athens' battle-cry.

Again the Carthaginian rovers sweep,
  With sword and commerce, on from shore to shore;
In visionary storms the breakers leap
    Round Syrtes, as of yore.

Victory, sitting on the Seven Hills,
Had gain'd the world when she had master'd thee:
Thy bosom with the Roman war-note thrills,
Wave of the inland sea.

Then, singing as they sail in shining ships,
I see the monarch minstrels of Romance,
And hear their praises murmur'd through the lips
Of the fair dames of France.

Across the deep another music swells,
On Adrian bays a later splendour smiles;
Power hails the marble city where she dwells
Queen of a hundred isles.

Westward the galleys of the Crescent roam,
And meet the Pisan challenge in the breeze,
Till the long Dorian palace lords the foam
With stalwart Genovese.

But the light fades, the vision wears away;
I see the mist above the dreary wave.
Blow winds of Freedom, give another day
Of glory to the brave!

PRINCIPAL SHAIRP.

A POET of fine feeling, and of deep and true sympathies, John Campbell Shairp, LL.D., Principal of the University of St. Andrews, was born at Houston House, Linlithgowshire, July 13th, 1819. He was educated at Glasgow University, and at Balliol College, Oxford. Shortly after his graduation at the latter University he was appointed assistant-master of Rugby School, where he remained till 1857. Following that, he held the Professorship of the Humanity Chair in the St. Andrews University, and was subsequently appointed Principal of that College.

A poet at heart, the learned Principal issued in 1864, a volume of exquisite verse, entitled, *Kilmahoe, A Highland Pastoral, with other Poems.* The volume is admittedly one of the very finest of recent contributions to modern poetical literature, combining scholarship with distinct originality, and evincing on every page, the finest lights and shades of poetic feeling, with the most engaging grace and modulation of verse.

Principal Shairp is also the author of *Studies in Poetry and Philosophy*, of a volume of *Lectures on Culture and Religion*, of an able and valuable critical estimate of Burns, contributed to the *English Men of Letters* series, and of numerous effective contributions to current magazine literature.

——::——

THE CLEARANCE SONG.

FROM Lochourn to Glenfinnan the grey mountains ranging,
Nought falls on the eye but the changed and the changing,
From the hut by the lochside, the farm by the river,
Macdonalds and Camerons pass—and for ever.

The flocks of one stranger the long grass are roaming,
Where a hundred bien homesteads smok'd bonnie at gloamin,'
Our wee crofts run wild wi' the bracken and heather,
And our gables stand ruinous, bare to the weather.

To the green mountain sheilings went up in old summers
From farm-town and clachan how many blithe cummers !
Though green the hill-pastures lie, cloudless the heaven,
No milker is singing there, morning or even.

The Chiefs, whom for ages our claymores defended,
Whom landless and exiled our fathers befriended,
From their homes drive their clansmen, when famine is sorest,
Cast out to make room for the deer of the forest.

Yet on far fields of fame, when the red ranks were reeling,
Who press'd to the van like the men of the sheiling?
Ye were fain in your need Highland broadswords to borrow:
Where, where are they now, should the foe come to-morrow?

Alas for the day of the mournful Culloden!
The Clans from that hour down to this have been trodden;
They were leal to their Prince, when red wrath was pursuing,
And have reap'd in return but oppression and ruin.

It's plaintive in harvest, when lambs are a-spaining,
To hear the hills loud with ewe-mothers complaining—
Ah! sadder that cry comes from mainland and islands,
The sons of the Gael have no home in the Highlands!

——::——

THE BUSH ABOON TRAQUAIR.

Will ye gang wi' me and fare
To the bush aboon Traquair?
Owre the high Minchmuir we'll up and awa',
This bonnie summer noon,
While the sun shines fair aboon,
And the licht sklents saftly doon on holm and ha'.

And what wad ye do there,
At the bush aboon Traquair?
A lang dreich road, ye'd better let it be,
Save some auld skrunts o' birk
Which i' the hillside lirk,
There's nocht i' the warld for man to see.

But the blithe lilt o' that air—
"The Bush aboon Traquair"—
I need nae mair, it's eneuch for me;
Owre my cradle its sweet chime
Cam' soughin' frae auld Time,
Sae tide what may, I'll awa' and see.

And what saw ye there,
At the bush aboon Traquair,
Or what did you hear was worth your heed?

I heard the cushies croon,
Through the gowden afternoon,
And Quair burn singin' doon to the vale o' Tweed.

And birks saw I three or four,
Wi' grey moss bearded owre,
The last that are left o' the birken shaw,
Whaur mony a summer e'en,
Fond lovers did convene,
Thae bonnie, bonnie gloamings that are lang awa'.

Frae mony a but and ben,
By muirlan', holm, and glen,
They cam' ane hour to spen' on the greenwood sward;
But lang hae lad and lass
Been lying 'neath the grass,
The green, green grass o' Traquair kirkyard.

They were blest beyond compare,
When they held their trystin' there,
Amang the greenest hills shone on by the sun;
And syne they want a rest—
The lownest and the best—
I' Traquair kirkyard when a' was done.

Now the birks to dust may rot,
Names of lovers be forgot,
Nae lads and lasses there ony mair convene;
But the blythe lilt o' yon air
Keeps the bush aboon Traquair,
And the love that ance was there, aye fresh and green.

——::——

CHANGE.

O mighty mountain pass! from eldest time
Organ of tempest-breath and roar of river!
And can it be thy heritage sublime
Is forfeit now for ever?

Shall all that man hath done not once have drown'd
The mountain music that abides in thee?
Save for a moment, when thou heardest sound
The onset of Dundee.

One single hour, and all again was dumb!
But overcrowing Tummel's loudest fall,
And Garry's thunder, hark the railway come
Harsh shrieking over all!

Ah, what down-crashing! fall thy kingly ones,
Rock-moor'd old oaks, and tempest-soughin' pine,
And birches that have gleam'd in summer suns,
Shimmer'd in white moonshine.

Along these mountains must we never more
See silver mists unmixed with railway steam?
Nor hear, without the train's intruding roar,
Pure voice of wind and stream?

GEORGE MACDONALD, LL.D.

There is a certain type of poetic genius which owes almost all its witchery—thought, colour, and fancy—to the hectic flush of youth, and once dis-illusioned it is ever afterwards nerveless for higher and better work. True genius, however, finds a new vantage ground for thought in the added experience of years, and changes only to assume higher and wider form and power. To this latter type of mind, the subject of this sketch essentially belongs. Born at Huntly, Aberdeenshire, in 1824, George Macdonald is now in his fifty-eighth year, and his later contributions to fiction and poetry only reveal in clearer light the wonderful resources and native richness of his fine genius. His father bore the same Christian name, and the poet claims maternal descent from a very old Highland family. He early gave tokens of future literary distinction, and when a mere boy is said to have shown a great aptitude for improvising tales. Statements of this kind irresponsibly made, however, must be received with caution, as rumour has proverbially a rather fertile imagination. Leaving school he entered and studied at King's College, Aberdeen, securing in time the degree of M.A. His father was a staunch Congregationalist—a strict sect, much akin to the Baptists in church government and practice—and he was careful to have his promising son educated in the views of that church sect. But the young student, earnest and thoughtful, and aided by the light of an informing genius, carried on and completed in the depths of his own mind and heart, a higher and wider education than the formal teachings of creeds or schools could bestow. From an early period he had assiduously devoted himself to the concerns of literature, and first sought recognition as a poet, by the publication, in 1855, of a semi-dramatic poem, entitled *Within and Without.* The book was received with much favour by the critics, and secured a wide acceptance at the hands of the reading public. This has been followed up from time to time, and in rapid succession, by numerous other works in prose and verse, which have made the name of GEORGE MACDONALD familiar wherever the English language is spoken or read. Possessed of undeniable poetic genius, he super-adds to that many splendid and special gifts. The spiritual element in his poems and stories is ever present, and very remarkable. He is eminently introspective, and his sentences, suggestive always of profound thought, glow often-times with a strange far-off luminosity, like the traditional nimbus round the brow of the pictured Christ. He has of late years come to be better known as a novelist than as a poet, and the secret of his undeniable success in the important department of story-writing is to be found in the breadth and universality of his human sympathy. He is the novelist of Christian morality, in the highest and best sense of the term, and invariably succeeds in lifting his readers to the healthful table-land of an elevated spiritual plane, ennobling thereby the very name of the art. It is of GEORGE MACDONALD as a poet, however, that we have in this notice more immediately to speak, and detailed criticism may be fitly summarised by briefly remarking that in the poetic department, as in fiction, his powers are consecrated with a rare and faithful devotion to his sense of duty as a Christian writer. He is also the author of a volume of *Unspoken Sermons*, and preaches from dissenting pulpits occasionally. His pulpit ministrations are characterised by simplicity and depth—his style being impressive rather than eloquent. Relative to his poetry, the compactness, and designedly unadorned simplicity of his style are both fairly evidenced in the following little piece, in which a whole love-drama is suggestively outlined in two short verses :—

PARTED!

"ANNIE, she's dowie, an' Willie, he's wae,
What can be the maitter wi' siccan a twae?
For Annie she's fair as the first o' the day,
An' Willie he's honest, an' stalwart, an' gay.

"Oh, the tane has a daddy, is poor an' prood;
The tither a minnie, wha cleiks at the gowd;
They lo'd ane anither, an' said their say,
But the daddie and minnie they pairtit the twae!"

Perhaps the best evidence of the value of his verses is to be found in the fact, that despite the exceeding plainness of their verbal dress, they are warmly cherished in the reader's heart. Divested of the ordinary embellishments of poetry, they are still felt to be poetry, and the genius of verses which can survive a crucial test of that kind is beyond rational question. His mind is still fertile and strong, and his love of and capacity for work undiminished, and favoured with continued health, English literature is likely to be still further enriched by his gifted pen.

The subjoined unique and impressive little poems—*This Side an' That*—*Wha's my Neibor*—and *The Twa Bawbees*—were originally contributed to the Glasgow *Weekly Mail*, to which journal Dr. Macdonald has contributed some of his finest prose stories. The perusal of them, we doubt not, will induce many to earnestly wish that Dr. MACDONALD may yet find opportunity to paraphrase, in like manner, the whole of the parables of Christ; a work which, once accomplished, Scotland would not willingly let die.

——::——

THIS SIDE AN' THAT.

A GODLY BALLANT.

THE rich man sat in his father's seat—
  Purple an' linen, and a' thing fine!
The puir man lay at his gate i' the street—
  Sairs an' tatters, an' weary pine!

To the rich man's table ilk dainty comes;
  Mony a morsel gaed frae't, or fell;
The puir man fain wad hae dined on the crumbs,
  But whether he got them I canna tell.

Servants quate, saft-fittit, an' stoot,
  Stan' by the rich man's curtain'd doors;
Maisterless dogs that rin about,
  Cam to the puir man an' lickit his sores.

The rich man dee'd, an' they buried him gran';
  In linen fine his body they wrap;
But the angels tuik up the beggar man,
  An' laid him doon in Abraham's lap.

The guid upo' this side, the ill upo' that—
  Sic was the rich man's waesome fa';
But his brithers they eat, an' they drink, an' they chat,
  An' carena a straw for their father's ha'.

The trowth's the trowth, think what ye will;
  An' some they kenna what they wad be at;
But the beggar man thocht he did no that ill,
  Wi' the dogs i' this side, the angels o' that.

—::—

WHA'S MY NEIBOR?

Doon frae Jerus'lem a traveller took
  The laigh road to Jericho;
It had an ill name an' mony a crook,
  It was lang an unco howe.

Oot cam the robbers, an' fell on the man,
  An' knockit him on the heid,
Took a' whauron they could lay their han',
  An' left him nakit for deid.

By cam a minister o' the kirk:
  "A sair mishanter," he cried;
"Wha kens whaur the villains may lirk?
  I'se haud to the ither side."

By cam an elder o' the kirk,
  Like a young horse he shied;
"Fie! there's a bonnie morning's wark!"
  An' he sprang to the ither side.

By came ane gaed to the wrang kirk;
  Douce he trotted alang;
"Puir body!" he cried, an' wi' a yerk,
  Aff o' his cuddy he sprang.

He ran to the body, an' turn'd it owre:
  "There's life i' the man," he cried;
He wasna ane to stan' an' glow'r,
  Nor haud to the ither side.

He doctor'd his wounds an' heised him on
  To the back o' the beastie douce ;
An' held him on, till a weary man,
  He langt at the half-way hoose.

He ten'd him a' nicht, an' at dawn o' day :
  "Laudlord, latna him lack ;
Here's auchteen pence, an' ony mair outlay,
  I'll settle as I come back."

Sae nae mair, neibors, say na the word,
  Wi' hert aye arguin' an' chill ;
Wha is the neibor to me, O Lord ?
  But wha am I neibor till ?

——::——

THE TWA BAWBEES.

STATELY, lang-robit, an' steppin' at ease,
  The rich man gaed up the temple ha' ;
Hasty, an' grippin' her twa bawbees,
  The widow cam after, boo'd an' sma'.

Their gowd rang lood as it fell, an' lay
  Yellow an' glintin', bonnie an' braw :
But the folk roun' the Maister heard him say,
  The puir body's bawbees war mair than it a'.

——::——

ANE BY ANE.

(From STRAHAN & Co.'s *Cabinet Edition of Geo. Macdonald's Poems.)*

ANE by ane they gang awa',
The Gaitherer gaithers great an' sma',
Ane by ane mak's ane an' a'.

Aye when ane sits doon the cup,
Ane ahint maun tak' it up,
Yet thegither they will sup.

Golden-heided, ripe an' strang,
Shorn will be the hairst ere lang,
Syne begins a better sang!

—::—

BABY.

Where did you come from, baby dear?
Out of the everywhere into here.

Where did you get those eyes so blue?
Out of the sky as I came through.

What makes the light in them sparkle and spin?
Some of the starry spikes left in.

What makes your forehead so smooth and high?
A soft hand stroked it as I went by.

What makes your cheek like a warm white rose?
I saw something better than any one knows.

Whence that three-corner'd smile of bliss?
Three angels gave me at once a kiss.

Where did you get this pearly ear?
God spake, and it came out to hear.

Where did you get those arms and hands?
Love made itself into bonds and bands.

Feet, whence did you come? you darling things!
From the same box as the cherub's wings.

How did they all just come to be you?
God thought about me, and so I grew.

But how did you come to us? you dear!
God thought about you, and so I am here.

PROF VEITCH
Wm McDOWALL
REVd Dr HATELY WADDELL
NEMO ME IMPUNE LACESSET
JAMES NICHOLSON
WILLIAM WATT
JAMES NORVAL

WILLIAM THOM.

A poet of true genius, William Thom, known to fame as "The Inverurie Poet," was born at Aberdeen, in 1789. In his tenth year the boy-poet was put to a cotton factory; became a handloom weaver to trade; married early, and suffered many privations through protracted family sickness and want of work. In the year 1844 he ventured on the publication of a little volume, entitled *Rhymes and Recollections of a Handloom Weaver*, which was prefaced by a brief autobiographical sketch, and was well received by the Scottish press. The true note of pathos undertoning the affecting story of his life touched all hearts, and the destitute poet was tendered pecuniary aid, as well as public poetical recognition. After a second visit to London, in which he was unsuccessful in attempting to establish himself in connection with the press, he returned to Scotland, taking up his abode in Dundee, where, losing heart, his irregular habits became confirmed, and after a brief period of penury and distress, he died in the spring of 1848. For purity of sentiment and dialect, and unaffected simplicity of pathos, very many of Thom's lyrics will compare favourably with the choicest effusions of the modern Scottish muse.

—::—

THE MITHERLESS BAIRN.

When a' ither bairnies are hush'd to their hame
By aunty, or mither, or frecky grand-dame;
Wha stands last an' lanely, an' naebody carin'?
It's the puir doited loonie—the mitherless bairn!

The mitherless bairn creeps to his lane bed,
Nane covers his cauld back, or haps his bare head:
His wee hackit heelies are hard as the airn,
An' lithless the look o' the mitherless bairn.

Aneath his cauld broo siccan dreams hover there,
Of hands that used kindly to kame his dark hair;
But morning brings clutches, a' reckless an' stern,
That lo'e na' the locks o' the mitherless bairn.

Yon sister that sang owre his saftly-rock'd bed,
Noo rests in the mools whaur her mither is laid:
The faïther toils sair the bit bannock to earn,
An' kens na' the wrangs o' his mitherless bairn.

Her spirit that fled in the hour o' his birth,
Still watches his wearisome wand'rings on earth;
Recording in heaven the blessings they earn,
Wha couthilie deal wi' the mitherless bairn.

Oh, speak him na' harshly—he trembles the while,
But bends to your bidding, an' blesses your smile;
In their dark hour o' anguish the heartless shall learn
That God deals the blow for the mitherless bairn!

HEW AINSLIE.

HEW AINSLIE, one of the best and most characteristic of modern Doric song writers, was born on the 5th of April, 1792. He was a native of Ayrshire, having been born at Bargeny Mains in the parish of Dailly, where his father followed the occupation of a baker, and was for years employed in the service of Sir Hew Dalrymple. AINSLIE was sent in early boyhood to the Parish School of Ballantrae, but completed his education at the Ayr Academy. At the age of sixteen, while still a tall, raw, unformed lad, he entered, through the influence of a relative, the writing chambers of a legal gentleman in Glasgow; but the protracted confinement of the desk proving injurious to his health, he hastily threw up his situation, and lived for a time with some relatives at Roslin. The poet's father, along with his family, removed thither shortly afterwards; Hew in the interval having been successful in his application for a clerkship in the General Register House, Edinburgh.

While still a clerk in the Register House, he had entered into the state of matrimony, and finding his means unequal to the comfortable up-bringing of a fast-increasing family, he resolved on emigration to America as a chance for possible fortune, or at least as a timely escape from impending penury. Accordingly, he set sail for New York in the midsummer of 1822, and having contracted for the purchase of a small farm, he lived for three years at Rensselaer, in the State of New York. The venture was only moderately successful, and giving up possession of his farm, he next tried for a short time the new social system of Robert Owen, philosopher and philanthropist, at his working settlement, New Harmony, Indiana. Note the title, *New Harmony*, and reflect how much it promises and implies. New Harmony Settlement was the pet conception of a large-hearted man of genius, who wished to make everybody happy, and life worth the living for. But, alas for the sin-blots and petty jealousies of the common heart! The idea, beautiful in theory, was in practice a sad failure. Ainslie, watchful of its spirit, early observed this, and speedily abandoned his connection therewith. Nothing daunted, however, Ainslie, who was a man of more than ordinary energy and resource, immediately ventured upon fresh speculations, erecting for a joint-stock company several brewery establishments in various districts in the State. Removing to New Albany

Indiana, he latterly erected a brewery establishment on his own account, which was burned shortly after completion. Subsequently, until he finally retired from the concerns of active life, he devoted himself to the occupation of superintending the erection of mills, factories, and breweries in different parts of the Western States.

AINSLIE was early devoted to the composition of verses, having drawn, probably, like many others, his first inspiration from Burns. He had published in early manhood, on the occasion of a return visit to Scotland, a volume of prose and poetry entitled *A Pilgrimage to the Land of Burns*, in which the entire section of Ayrshire and Dumfriesshire is descriptively and poetically gone over. The Doric is mostly used throughout; and the book is interesting, being replete with characteristic observation and reflection. A second volume from his pen, entitled *Poems, Songs, and Ballads*, was published at New York in 1855. As late as 1864, being then in his seventy-sixth year, AINSLIE made a second return visit to his native Scotland, and was well received by friends and admirers of his genius everywhere. He latterly fixed his abode at New Jersey, in the immediate neighbourhood of New York, where he died, in 1877, a ripe octogenarian.

The poems and lyrics of AINSLIE are full of character, and are remarkable for strength rather than for refinement of thought or diction. It was fortunate for his reputation that he wrote almost exclusively in the expressive dialect of Scotland, as the cast of his mind and sympathies were so characteristically Scottish, and even local, that he could not, presumably, have succeeded well in pretentious English verse.

HEW AINSLIE is not, perhaps, one of the few poets whom publishers find it profitable to reprint entire, but many of his spirited and characteristic lyrical pieces have found a wide popular acceptance; and when Scotland comes to finally make up her list of imperishable song-jewels, AINSLIE's claim to permanent recognition cannot consistently be overlooked.

——::——

THE ROVER O' LOCHRYAN.

THE Rover o' Lochryan he's gane
  Wi' his merry men sae brave;
Their hearts are o' the steel, and a better keel
  Ne'er bowl'd owre the back o' a wave.
It's no' when the loch lies dead in his trough,
  When naething disturbs it ava;
But the rack and the ride o' the restless tide,
  Or the splash o' the grey sea-maw.

It's no when the yawl an' the light skiffs crawl
  Owre the breast o' the siller sea,
That I look to the west for the bark I lo'e best,
  An' the rover that's dear to me;
But when that the clud lays its cheek to the flood,
  An' the sea lays its shouther to the shore;
When the win' sings high, and the sea-whaups cry,
  As they rise frae the whitening roar.

It's then that I look to the thickening rook,
  An' watch by the midnight tide;
I ken the win' brings my rover hame,
  An' the sea that he glories to ride.
Oh, merry he sits 'mang his jovial crew,
  Wi' the helm heft in his hand,
An' he sings aloud to his boys in blue,
  As his ee's upon Galloway's land:

"Unstent and slack each reef an' tack,
  Gie her sail, boys, while it may sit;
She has roar'd through a heavier sea afore,
  An' she'll roar through a heavier yet.

When landsmen sleep, or wake an' creep,
In the tempest's angry moan,
We dash through the drift, and sing to the lift
O' the waves that heaves us on."

DOWIE IN THE HINT O' HAIRST.

It's dowie in the hint o' hairst,
At the wa-gang o' the swallow,
When the win' grows cauld, and the burns grow bauld,
And the wuds are hingin' yellow;
But oh, it's dowier far to see
The wa-gang o' her the heart gangs wi',
The dead-set o' a shinin' ee—
That darkens the weary world on thee.

There was mickle love atween us twa—
Oh, twa could ne'er be fonder;
And the thing on yird was never made,
That could ha'e gart us sunder.
But the way of Heaven's abune a' ken,
And we maun bear what it likes to sen'—
It's comfort, though, to weary men,
That the warst o' this warld's waes maun en'.

There's mony things that come and gae,
Just kent, and just forgotten;
And the flow'rs that busk a bonnie brae,
Gin anither year lie rotten.
But the last look o' that lovely e'e,
And the dying grip she gave to me,
They're settled like eternity—
Oh, Mary! that I were wi' thee.

THE LAST LOOK O' HAME.

Bare was our burn brae, December's blast had blawn,
The last flow'r was dead, an' the brown leaf had fa'n:

It was dark in the deep glen, hoary was our hill ;
An' the win' frae the cauld north cam heavy and chill :
When I said fare-ye-weel, to my kith and my kin ;
My barque it lay a-head, an' my cot-house ahin';
I had nought left to tine, I'd a wide world to try ;
But my heart it widna lift, an' my e'e it widna dry.

I look'd lang at the ha', through the mist o' my tears,
Where the kind lassie lived I had ran wi' for years ;
E'en the glens where we sat, wi' their broom-cover'd knowes,
Took a hand on this heart that I ne'er can unlowse.
I ha'e wander'd sin' syne, by gay temples and towers,
Where the ungather'd spice scents the breeze in their bowers ;
Oh ! sic scenes I could leave without pain or regret ;
But the last look o' hame I can never forget.

HENRY GLASSFORD BELL.

A MAN of distinguished forensic abilities, as well as a poet of fine voice, HENRY GLASSFORD BELL was born at Glasgow in 1805. His father was an advocate, and removing with his family to Edinburgh in 1811, the future poet spent his early years in that city, and was educated at the Edinburgh University. He evinced an early and decided predilection for literary pursuits, and succeeded in establishing the *Edinburgh Literary Journal* in 1829. That journal he successfully conducted for a period of three years, at the expiry of which time he passed advocate, and devoted himself afterwards more exclusively to the dry studies of law. In 1839 he was appointed Sheriff-Substitute for Lanarkshire, and in 1869 was promoted to the high office of Sheriff-Principal, on the death of his distinguished colleague, Sir Archibald Alison, the responsible duties of which important office he fulfilled with distinction till death, which event occurred, January 7th, 1874.

Although a bred lawyer, and the son of a lawyer, HENRY GLASSFORD BELL never forgot his early love for literature and the muses. Nature had made him a poet before the accident of education and position had constituted him a formal lawyer. And a poet he remained till the end, by instinct and by preference. During his long and busy life he issued in all some twelve volumes of original matter, comprising poems, literary, moral, and critical essays, tales, and recondite papers on law. His last published volume, *Romances and Minor Poems*, exhibits the poet grave with years, and full of sage sad wisdom, but playful and kindly-humorous in spirit, reviewing the past with manly satisfaction rather than with weak regret. Many of these beautiful poems are eminently quotable, and will be perused by all readers of taste with pleasure; but on his earlier and finer poem of *Mary, Queen of Scots*, his fame as a poet will ultimately rest. It is a richly-phrased, finely-melodious, and singularly impressive poem.

Regarding his qualities as a man, a city newspaper remarked at his death, that "though his works were good, and his work was excellent, the man was more excellent still. As with Irving and Chalmers, and his old friend John Wilson of *Blackwood's Magazine*, what he has left behind can give no adequate impression of the space he filled in the minds and hearts of those who were privileged to enjoy his companionship. He was in some respects the last of a race—*ultimus Romanorum*—of the men who could think, and talk, and revolve great problems in their minds, and yet keep a cheerful face before all the world. With that world he was always on good terms, but without surrendering an inch of his independence."

SHERIFF BELL, in addition to his other accomplishments' was an eloquent platform speaker, and very many will vividly remember the portly form and sonorous voice of the man as he descanted on congenial and inspiring themes. He was a warm and chivalrous admirer of the beautiful but unfortunate Queen Mary, and it may be said of him, that he could not see her frailties for tears.

——::——

MARY, QUEEN OF SCOTS.

I LOOK'D far back to other years, and lo! in bright array,
I saw, as in a dream, the forms of ages pass'd away.

It was a stately convent, with its old and lofty walls; [falls;—
And gardens, with their broad green walks, where soft the footstep
And o'er the antique dial-stones the creeping shadow pass'd,
And, all around, the noon-day sun a drowsy radiance cast.
No sound of busy life was heard, save, from the cloister dim,
The tinkling of the silver bell, or the sisters' holy hymn.
And there five noble maidens sat, beneath the orchard trees,
In that first budding spring of youth, when all its prospects please;
And little reck'd they, when they sang, or knelt at vesper prayers,
That Scotland knew no prouder names—held none more dear than theirs;—
And little e'en the loveliest thought, before the Virgin's shrine,
Of royal blood, and high descent from the ancient Stuart line;
Calmly her happy days flew on, uncounted in their flight,
And, as they flew, they left behind a long-continuing light.

The scene was changed. It was the court—the gay court of Bourbon—
And 'neath a thousand silver lamps, a thousand courtiers throng;
And proudly kindles Henry's eye—well pleased, I ween, to see
The land assemble all its wealth of grace and chivalry;—
Grey Montmorency, o'er whose head has passed a storm of years,
Strong in himself and children, stands the first among his peers;
And next the Guises, who so well Fame's steepest heights assail'd,
And walk'd Ambition's diamond ridge, where bravest hearts have fail'd—

And higher yet their path shall be, stronger shall wax their might,
For before them Montmorency's star shall pale its waning light.
Here Louis Prince of Condé wears his all unconquer'd sword,
With great Caligni, by his side—each name a household word!
And there walks she of Medicis—that proud Italian line,
The mother of a race of kings—the haughty Catharine!
The forms that follow in her train, a glorious sunshine make—
A milky way of stars that grace a comet's glittering wake;
But fairer far than all the rest,—who bask'd on fortune's tide,—
Effulgent in the light of youth,—is she, the new-made bride!
The homage of a thousand hearts—the fond, deep love of one—
The hopes that dance around a life whose charms are but begun—
They lighten up her chesnut eye, they mantle o'er her cheek,
They sparkle on her open brow, and high-soul'd joy bespeak.
Ah! who shall blame, if scarce that day, through all its brilliant hours,
She thought of that quiet convent's calm, its sunshine and its flowers!—

The scene was changed. It was a bark that slowly held its way,
And o'er its lee the coast of France in the light of evening lay;
And on its deck a lady sat, who gazed with tearful eyes
Upon the fast-receding hills, that dim and distant rise.
No marvel that the lady wept—there was no land on earth
She loved like that dear land; although she owed it not her birth;
It was her mother's land, the land of childhood and of friends—
It was the land where she had found for all her griefs amends—
The land where her dear husband slept—the land where she had known
The tranquil convent's hush'd repose, and the splendours of a throne;—
No marvel that the lady wept—it was the land of France—
The chosen home of chivalry—the garden of romance!
The past was bright like those dear hills so far behind the bark;
The future, like the gathering night, was ominous and dark!
One gaze again—one long last gaze—"Adieu, fair France to thee!"
The breeze comes forth—she is alone on the unconscious sea.

The scene was changed. It was an eve of raw and surly mood,
And in a turret-chamber high of ancient Holyrood
Sat Mary, listening to the rain, and sighing with the winds
That seemed to suit the stormy state of men's uncertain minds.

The touch of care had blanch'd her cheek—her smile was sadder now,
The weight of royalty had press'd too heavy on her brow;
And traitors to her councils came, and rebels to the field;—
The Stuart sceptre well she sway'd, but the sword she could not wield.
She thought of all her blighted hopes—the dreams of youth's brief day,—
And summon'd Rizzio with his lute, and bade the minstrel play,
The songs she loved in early years—the song of gay Navarre;—
The songs perchance that erst were sung by gallant Chatelar;
They half beguiled her of her cares, they sooth'd her into smiles,
They won her thoughts from bigot zeal, and fierce domestic broils;—
But hark! the tramp of armèd men! the Douglas' battle-cry!—
They come—they come—and lo! the scowl of Ruthven's hollow eye!
And swords are drawn, and daggers gleam, and tears and words are vain,
The ruffian steel is in his heart—the faithful Rizzio's slain!
Then Mary Stuart brush'd aside the tears that trickling fell:
"Now for my father's arms!" she said; "my woman's heart, farewell!"

The scene was changed. It was a lake with one small lonely isle,
And there, within the prison-walls of its baronial pile,
Stern men stood menacing their queen, till she should stoop to sign
The traitorous scroll that snatch'd the crown from her ancestral line:—
"My lords, my lords!" the captive said, "were I but once more free,
With ten good knights on yonder shore, to aid my cause and me,
That parchment would I scatter wide to every breeze that blows,
And once more reign a Stuart queen o'er my remorseless foes!"
A red spot burn'd upon her cheek—stream'd her rich tresses down,—
She wrote the words—she stood erect—a queen without a crown!

The scene was changed. A royal host a royal banner bore,
And the faithful of the land stood round their smiling queen once more;—
She staid her steed upon a hill—she saw them marching by—
She heard their shouts—she read success in every flashing eye;
The tumult of the strife begins—it roars—it dies away;
And Mary's troops and banners now, and courtiers—where are they?
Scatter'd and strewn, and flying far, defenceless and undone—
O God! to see what she has lost, and think what Guilt has won!

Away! away! thy gallant steed must act no laggard's part:
Yet vain his speed, for thou dost bear the arrow in thy heart.

The scene was changed. Beside the block a sullen headsman stood,
And gleam'd the broad axe in his hand, that soon must drip with
blood.
With slow and steady step there came a lady through the hall,
And breathless silence chain'd the lips, and touch'd the hearts of all.
Rich were the sable robes she wore—her white veil round her fell—
And from her neck there hung the cross—the cross she loved so well!
I knew that queenly form again, though blighted was its bloom—
I saw that grief had deck'd it out—an offering for the tomb!
I knew the eye, though faint its light, that once so brightly shone—
I knew the voice, though feeble now, that thrill'd with every tone—
I knew the ringlets, almost grey, once threads of living gold—
I knew that bounding grace of step—that symmetry of mould!
Even now I see her far away, in that calm convent aisle,
I hear her chant her vesper-hymn; I mark her holy smile;—
Even now I see her bursting forth upon her bridal morn,
A new star in the firmament, to light and glory born!
Alas! the change! she placed her foot upon a triple throne,
And on the scaffold now she stands—beside the block, alone!
The little dog that licks her hand, the last of all the crowd [bow'd.
Who sunn'd themselves beneath her glance, and round her footsteps
Her neck is bared—the blow is struck—the soul is pass'd away;
The bright—the beautiful—is now a bleeding piece of clay!
The dog is moaning piteously; and, as it gurgles o'er,
Laps the warm blood that trickling runs unheeded to the floor!
The blood of beauty, wealth, and power—the heart blood of a queen—
The noblest of the Stuart race—the fairest earth hath seen—
Lapp'd by a dog!—Go, think of it, in silence and alone;
Then weigh against a grain of sand, the glories of a throne!

PROFESSOR VEITCH.

JOHN VEITCH, LL.D., Professor of Logic and Rhetoric in the University of Glasgow, author of *Hillside Rhymes,* issued from the Glasgow press in 1872, and a later volume of verse, *The Tweed, and Other Poems*, which appeared in 1875, was born at Peebles, October 24th, 1829. Receiving the elementary part of his education at the Grammar School of his native town, he afterwards entered the Edinburgh University, where he achieved distinction as a student in Logic and Moral Philosophy, receiving shortly after the completion of his course the honorary degree of M.A., and subsequently that of LL.D. In 1860 Dr. Veitch was appointed to the Chair of Logic and Rhetoric in St. Andrew's University, and four years afterwards was appointed to the same high office in the University of Glasgow, which position he still holds.

Metaphysics, one would think, is about as far removed from poetic contemplation as mathematics. Nevertheless, Dr. Veitch, in the publication of the volumes of graceful verse already named, has evinced the possession of a fine poetic vein of thought and feeling—quiet, meditative, and unimpulsive, like the Tweed of which he so pleasingly sings, flowing sweetly on, in sunshine and shadow, through the richest pasture land of Border chivalry and song. Fine, delicately-drawn description, intermingling with Wordsworthian feeling and reflection, encased in an appropriately graceful setting of verse, are the Professor's most obvious poetical characteristics. In a review of *Hillside Rhymes*, a competent writer in the *Scotsman* newspaper said—"Next to an autumn day among the hills, commend us to poems like these, in which so much of the finer breath and spirit of those pathetic hills is distilled into melody."

Dr. Veitch, it should be stated, is also the author of a translation of the *Works of Descartes*, and of *Lucretius, and the Atomic Theory*, with several minor exercises in biography and metaphysics.

EXTRACTS FROM "THE TWEED."

Tweed, most thy gentle spirit loves the smile
Of Heaven's own face,—amid the dappled light
Of spring, when soft white showers, from passing clouds
That mottle light the blue of space o'erhead,
First glisten on the green of birken leaves,
And sprinkle all the haughs with twinkling rain;
While, in the sunny blinks between the show'rs,
The primrose blessing sends from woody braes.
The linnet strains its note to voice the joy
That pulses in the air; the sounding stream
For very gladness gleams; the speckled trout,
Drawn from dark depths of winter pools, disport
In overflow of life and innocence;
And 'neath the airy insects' sun-bright dance,
Make quiet circlings o'er the spreading face,
Complacent, of the pool with pleasure moved.

How deep the soul is moved on autumn e'vе,
When spreading haughs are ripe with golden grain,
And God's rich bounty blesses all the strath,
To eye the moon, new risen, stay high-poised,
Full-globed, on upmost rim of eastern hill,
Whence, for brief space, she loving looks aslant
The westward glen, till its low shadows break
In brightness, through the joy to meet her gaze;
And then, well-pleas'd with greeting of the earth,
Floats calm away to her own silent heaven,
And reigns in full possession of the sky.

THE HERD'S WIFE.

In a lone herd's house, far up i' the Hope,
By the hill wi' the winter cairn,
She paced the floor i' the peat-fire glow,
In her airms she clasp'd her bairn!

Out in the night the snow storm's might
  Tore wild around the door;
"Oh! waes me for my ain guidman
  Up on that weary moor!

"I canna hide that gruesome sough,
  That swirl o' blindin' drift;
There's no a star in a' the sky,
  Nor a glint o' moon i' the lift!

"Has the crook o' my lot then cam' sae soon
  On oor gleesome wedding day?
Wi' the ae bloom o' the heather braes
  Is my blessing sped away?

"Oh, bonnie a' through was oor year,
  Frae Spring to Lammas-tide;
There was joy in the ee'-blinks o' morn,
  Was I wrang in wishin' 'twad bide?

"But little thocht I that the hay
  Deep owre the haugh and the lea—
(Our first crop he sae blythely maw'd)
  Was the last we thegither wad see!

"Have I lov'd him owre muckle, O, Lord,
  Thinkin' mair o' his smile than thine?
Oh, on earth I had nane but himsel—
  To be my sweet bairnies and mine!"

She paced up and down, the bairn in her grip,
  That knew not her sad unrest;
And about it her airms she clasp'd,
  Press'd it, how close, to her breast!

High on the blast rose a piteous whine,
  She thrill'd as 'tween hope and fear,
'Twas the pleading wail of faithful "Help,"
  But alone,—no master there!

No warm hearth seeks the dog to-night,—
  His face is set to the storm,—
He's come from where his master lies,—
  He'll guide to the snow-numb'd form!

One tender look has the wife for "Help,"
A tear-eyed glance for her child,
Out will she 'mid the fearsome night,
For him wha lies on the wild.

With milk in vial, her sole resource,—
Laid in the warmth of her breast,—
She and "Help" 'gainst the 'wildering snow,
To her God she leaves the rest!

Fearless she faced the gruesome sough,
And swirl of blindin' drift,
There wasna a star in a' the sky,
Nor a glint o' moon in the lift!

Bare-headed slept he 'neath the mound,
Where the wreath was owre him laid,
There in the folds of the winding snow,
"Help" found him wrapt in his plaid!

Oh! how she clasp'd him there, and pour'd
Life warmth through his chilled frame!
Heaven tenderly look'd on her wifely love—
He breath'd, and bless'd her name!

JOHN BRECKENRIDGE.

In Blackie's *Book of Scottish Song*, edited by Alexander Whitelaw, and published in 1843, the following note is prefixed to the celebrated poem, *The Humours o' Gleska Fair*:—"We can learn nothing of the author beyond that his name was Breckenridge, and that he was a compositor to trade." The editors of several subsequent similar publications have gone on repeating the error embodied in this note, for Breckenridge was a weaver, and never had aught to do with type-setting. In several collections of humorous

Scottish poetry, the poem named is held to be anonymous, which, during the lifetime of the author it practically was. Having learned that BRECKENRIDGE was a handloom weaver in his day, resident in Parkhead, an eastern suburb of Glasgow, we lately made a visit of note-taking inquiry to to that ilk, and getting a cue, we were directed to auld Watty Trum'ull (Walter Turnbull), still resident in the village, and now well-nigh an octogenarian, who knew BRECKENRIDGE intimately—was, in fact, one of his "jamb freen's"—and who at once proceeded to put us into possession of many facts and anecdotes relative to the life-history of the hitherto unknown poet. These facts we summarise in the following brief sketch.

JOHN BRECKENRIDGE, author of *The Humours o' Gleska Fair*, was born in Parkhead, about the year 1790. He was bred to the trade of a handloom weaver, at which occupation he wrought until reaching the years of early manhood. Being of a vivacious spirit, and fond of active life, he joined the Lanarkshire Militia, serving a term of five years, a considerable portion of which period was passed in Ireland. Returning to his native village, he got married, and succeeded his mother in a small, but thriving grocery business, in the Main Street. The shop is now occupied as a district Post Office. Here he wrote humorous rhymes, and made capital fiddles, the fame of which travelled to London in some unexplained way, as he had several English purchasers who paid him high prices for his instruments. He seems to have been a sort of universal genius, and that, too, without the shadow of pretence. He was a *crack* hand at the loom. He made famous rhymes, and equally famous fiddles. He "wrote like copperplate," we have been assured, and was one of the blythest and best of men. He had no love of money, but simply wished to achieve an honest "thro'-

gaun" in life. Neither had he any ambition for poetic fame. He wrote rhymes to please himself and his special fireside friends, and never would allow one of them to pass into print. The publication and popularity of *The Humours o' Gleska Fair* was achieved against his will. An MS. copy of the poem had come into the possession of Livingstone, the famous Scottish vocalist, who sung it into extensive repute. BRECKENRIDGE never completely forgave him. About 1840 he fell ill, and died of a lingering internal disease. When he felt his end approaching, he caused his wife to bring out a drawer where his papers were kept, and petitioned her to subject them, one and all, to a fiery baptism. Poems, songs, and epigrams, replete with native genius and humour, were, one by one, remorselessly consigned to the flames. Beyond what may have existed in the menory of contemporaries, not a scrap was saved. He is known to have written many poems and lyrics, of superior native genius, which have all been lost. Our informant, old Walter Turnbull, still retains on his memory imperfect scraps of several of his homely effusions. There was a song, he remembers, named *Mirren Shaw*, the opening verse of which ran thus—

> Ae mornin' clear, as Mirren Shaw
>   Gaed out to flit her wee bit yowe,
> She met a youth, fu' trig an' braw,
>   Come whistlin' owre the whinny knowe.

On a certain "Ne'e'r-day nicht," BRECKENRIDGE and a few friends were gathered together in the "Bull Tavern," which still stands. They were met to pledge success to Gilbert Watson, a local baker, who was just starting business on his own account. Gibbie stood the pies, and the company the porter. BRECKENRIDGE was requisitioned to poetically open the ball, which he did in the following verses :—

It's auld Ne'e'r-day nicht an' we're met in the "Bull,"
Wi' oor hearts dancin' licht, an' a bowl flowin' full,
Let envy and spite throw aff a' disguise,
And drink to young Gibbie that's gien us the pies.

Noo, here's to us a', man, wife, lad, and lass,
In peace and good humour this nicht let us pass;
An' when on the morrow we think on the fray,
May conscience against us hae naething to say.

To John Williamson, a particular friend of the poet, BRECKENRIDGE addressed a rhymed "Epistle" in happy terms, a portion of which is still remembered—

My worthy freen', an' social sowl,
As ever sat before a bowl,
Wi' you I'd sit an' never growl,
  Till the sun blinks through in the mornin'!

Your blythesome face I like to see,
Ye're aye sae fu' o' social glee,
It's I could sit an' crack wi' thee
  Till the wee sma' hours o' the mornin'!

Nae cankert wife oor peace annoys,
Nae argument oor mirth destroys,
True freen'ship sweetens a' oor joys,
  An' mak's us blythe till the mornin'!

BRECKENRIDGE, we should state, was a very temperate man, and sinned in poetic fancy, rather than in act.

He owned during the latter period of his life a small grocery business, and one of his last injunctions to his wife was that she "wisna to be sair on the folks that were awn (owing) them, as she would maybe manage to fen in a decent way without it." The anecdote is characteristic of BRECKENRIDGE, and was in keeping with the actions of his whole life. He was "deil-fond o' fun, an' whyles sae fu' o' mischief that there was nae fennin' wi' him," but he never betrayed a friendship, never harassed a debtor, and was never known to do a mean or an ungenerous act.

Personally, BRECKENRIDGE was a man of modest presence, small in stature, and rotund in form, with a blythe expression of countenance, dark bright eyes, and a brow so ample that he was nick-named "brooie" when a boy.

We have thus, in brief terms, floated a new life into Scottish poetical literature, and as the particulars have been corroborated in great part by a distant relative of the deceased poet, whom we also interviewed, the interesting narrative may be accepted as trustworthy.

THE HUMOURS O' GLESKA FAIR.

THE sun frae the eastward was peeping,
And braid through the winnocks did stare,
When Willie cried—"Tam, are ye sleeping?
Mak' haste, man, and rise to the Fair;
For the lads and the lassies are thranging,
And a' body's now in a steer;
Fye, haste ye, and let us be ganging,
Or, faith, we'll be langsome I fear."

Then Tam he got up in a hurry,
And wow but he made himsel' snod,
And a pint o' milk brose he did worry.
To mak' him mair teugh for the road.
On his head his blue bannet he slippet,
His whip o'er his shouther he flang,
And a clumsy oak cudgel he grippet,
On purpose the loons for to bang.

Now Willock had trysted wi' Jenny,
For she was a braw canty quean,
Word gaed that she had a gey penny,
For whilk Willie fondly did grean.

Now Tam he was blaming the liquor ;
  Yae night he had got himsel' fou,
And trysted gleed Maggie MacVicar,
  And faith he thocht shame for to rue.

The carles, fu' cadgie, sat cocking
  Upon their white nags and their brown,
Wi' snuffing, and laughing, and joking,
  They soon canter'd into the town ;
'Twas there was the funning and sporting,
  Eh, lord ! what a swarm o' braw folk,
Rowly-powly, wild beasts, wheels o' fortune,
  Sweety stan's, Maister Punch, and Black Jock.

Now Willock and Tam geyan bouzie,
  By this time had met wi' their joes ;
Consented wi' Gibbie and Susy
  To gang awa' down to the shows ;
'Twas there was the fiddling and drumming,
  Sic a crowd they could scarcely get through,
Fiddles, trumpets, and organs a-bumming ;
  O, sirs ! what a hully-baloo.

Then hie to the tents at the paling,
  Weel theekit wi' blankets and mats,
And deals seated round like a tap-room,
  Supported on stanes and on pats ;
The whisky like water they're selling,—
  And porter as sma' as their yill,—
And aye as you're pouring they're telling,
  "Troth dear, it's just sixpence the gill !"

Says Meg—"See yon beast wi' the claes on't,
  Wi' the face o't as black as the soot,
Preserve's ! it has fingers and taes on't—
  Eh, sirs, it's an unco like brute !"
"O, woman, but ye are a gomeral,
  To mak' sic a won'er at that,
D'ye na ken, you daft gowk, that's a mongrel,
  That's bred 'twixt a dog and a cat."

"See you souple jaud how she's dancing,
Wi' the white ruffled breeks and red shoon,
Frae the tap to the tae she's a' glancing,
Wi' gowd and a feather aboon.
My troth, she's a braw decent kimmer,
As I have yet seen in the Fair."
"*Her* decent!" quo' Meg, "she's a limmer,
Or, faith, she would never be there."

Now Gibbie was wanting a toothfu',
Says he "I'm right tired o' the fun,
D'ye think we'd be the waur o' a mouthfu'
O gude nappy yill and a bun?"
"Wi' a' my heart," Tam says, "I'm willing—
'Tis best for to water the corn;
By jing, I've a bonnie white shilling,
And a saxpence that ne'er saw the morn."

Before they got out o' the bustle,
Poor Tam got his fairing I trow,
For a stick at the Ginge'bread play'd whistle,
And knockit him down like a cow.
Says Tam, "Wha did that? deil confound him—
Fair play, let me win at the loon!"
And he whirl'd his stick round and round him,
And swore like a very dragoon.

Then next for a house they gaed glow'ring,
Whar they might get wetting their mou',
Says Meg, "Here's a house keeps a pouring,
Wi' the sign o' the muckle black cow."
"A cow!" quo' Jenny, "ye gawky!
Preserve us! but ye've little skill,
Ca' ye that in rale earnest a hawky?—
Look again and ye'll see it's a *bull*."

But just as they darken'd the entry,
Says Willie, "We're now far enoo,
I see it's a house for the gentry—
Let's gang to the Sign o' the Ploo."

"Na faith," then says Gibbie, "we'se raither
  Gae danner to auld Luckie Gunn's,
For there I'm to meet wi' my faither,
  And auld uncle John o' the Whins."

Now they a' snug in Luckie's had landed,
  Twa rounds at the bicker to try;
The whisky and yill round was handed,
  And baps in great bourocks did lie.
"Blind Aleck" the fiddler was trysted,
  And he was to handle the bow;
On a big barrel-head he was hoisted,
  To keep himsel' out o' the row.

Ne'er saw ye sic din and guffawing,
  Sic hooching and dancing was there,—
Sic rugging, and riving, and drawing,
  Was ne'er seen before in a Fair.
For Tam, he wi' Maggie was wheeling,
  And he gied sic a terrible jump,
That his head cam' a rap on the ceiling,
  An' clyte he fell doon on his rump.

Now they ate and they drank till their bellies
  Were bent like the head o' a drum,
Syne they raise, and they caper'd like fillies,
  Whene'er that the fiddle play'd—bum.
Wi' dancing they now were grown weary,
  And scarcely were able to stan',
So they took to the road a' fu' cheery,
  As day was beginning to dawn.

WILLIAM M'DOWALL.

POETRY, like an ever-flowing fount, breaks through all repressing influences, and finds expression everywhere—at the plough-tail, in the noisy workshop, in the lowly cot and in the lordly palace, in the sculptor's studio, and in the editor's room.

WILLIAM M'DOWALL, poet, local historian, and journalist, was born at Maxwelltown, Kirkcudbrightshire, on the 21st July, 1815. He was educated at Dumfries Academy, and evincing strong literary instincts, he became editor of the *Dumfries and Galloway Standard*, in 1846. In 1867 he issued the *History of the Burgh of Dumfries*, a work of much local value. In 1870 appeared his deeply interesting little work—*Burns in Dumfriesshire.* In 1876 he issued *Memorials of St. Michael's*—the old Parish Churchyard of Dumfries. In addition, Mr. M'DOWALL is the author of several valuable contributions to the *Encyclopedia Britannica.*

Regarding the poetical side of his mind, it may be mentioned, that although his fancy has been very much subordinated to the exacting duties of his editorial position, he has never quite forgotten his early affection for the muse. By a necessity of his mental nature he was a poet before he became a journalist, and as early as 1844 he issued a small volume of verses under the title of the *Man of the Woods and other Poems*, which was very favourably received, and is long since out of print. The poem which gives the book its title, is a series of lofty contemplations on nature, life, death, and immortality, expressed in felicitous, and oftentimes eloquent verse. It makes, all through, very impressive reading, and the hand of the true poet is frequently discovered in those deft touches of fancy and phraseology which only genius can frame. His *Martyr of Erromanga*, which is rather lengthy for quotation, is a poem of much power and beauty, and the touching verses—*Burns on his Death-bed*, were much and deservedly admired on their first production, and will be read with appreciative interest as long as the affecting incident which they illustrate is remembered in connection with Burns's name.

Personally, Mr. M'DOWALL is much and widely respected as a man of genius and fine moral worth. In politics he is a Liberal, and still conducts with great success the influential newspaper so long associated with his name. A revised and enlarged new edition of his poems is now in course of preparation, we understand, and in June of the present year (1882) he issued a small handbook of interesting reading on physiognomy, under the title of *The Mind in the Face.*

—:—

BURNS ON HIS DEATH-BED.*

Soon will life's weary whirl be done,
  And I shall reach the peaceful grave;
Soon shall my latest sands be run,
  And passion's tempest cease to rave.
The goal of death and darkness won—
  This chequer'd scene no more to see;
Yet, let me view again the sun—
  It winna shine sae lang for me.

Unbind the veil that hides his face,
  And draw yon envious screen aside,
Then shall his gladsome radiance chase
  The mists which o'er my couch preside.

---

* "A night or two before Burns left Brow, he drank tea with Mrs. Craig, widow of the minister of Ruthwell. His altered appearance excited much silent sympathy; and the evening being beautiful, and the sun shining brightly through the casement, Miss Craig (afterwards Mrs. Henry Duncan) was afraid that the light might be too much for him, and rose with the view of letting down the window blinds. Burns immediately guessed what she meant; and, regarding the young lady with a look of great benignity, said—'Thank you, my dear, for your kind attention; but, oh! let him shine! he will not shine long for me!' The poet died a few days afterwards at Dumfries."—*Land of Burns.*

Ere yet the ebon gates are barr'd
  Upon my hours of grief and glee,
Sweet sun, my earnest cry regard ;
  Ye winna shine sae lang for me.

Break forth as thou wert wont to shine,
  When in thy glorious light I trod,
To trace the links of love divine,
  From nature up to nature's God.
Meet emblem of that mighty One,
  Thy face reveal, and seem to be
A token of His mercy shown ;
  For nane can need it mair than me.

No more I see thee paint the plain,
  Or pierce the leaf-embattl'd shade,
Or mirror'd in the trembling main,
  Or glist'ning in each dewy blade.
But thou canst make the clay-built cot
  Seem blythesome as yon lily lea ;
Not all forlorn the poet's lot,
  Since thou dost shine aince mair on me.

Thou stay of life, and source of light !
  How doubly dear thy presence now,
When shadows, as of endless night,
  Are gathering o'er my throbbing brow !
Prized wer't thou in my songful prime—
  And precious must thou ever be ;
Though swiftly comes a mirk, mirk time,
  When thou shalt shine nae mair for me.

The sunless grave ! no straggling ray
  Of thine can reach its dread recess ;
Nor would the soul-deserted clay
  Be conscious of its warm caress.
Yet grieve I not, by care opprest,
  To meet the doom I soon maun dree ;
Since, though it shade thy beams sae blest,
  'Twill scatter far the clouds frae me.

IN TROQUEER CHURCHYARD.

HAIL, hoary Ash ! whose hallow'd shade
O'er-canopies the slumbering dead,
And casts congenial gloom around
The precincts of this holy ground !
Now age amongst thy leaves has crept,
And from thy form its freshness stript ;
Time on thy trunk his hand has laid,
And, pointing to the tombs, has said—
"Ere long to death thy head must bow,
And thou shalt be as these below ;
Thy youth—thy prime—thy autumn past—
Be levell'd with the earth at last."
But though life's close be thus reveal'd,
Strength still remains its germ to shield—
Strength to sustain the tempest's shock,
And long its fiercest fury mock,
To keep thee pillar'd on the plain,
Life's emblem in the grave's domain,
Whilst marking, 'neath thy foliage shrin'd,
The sons of men to dust consign'd.

There, where thy farthest boughs extend,
His relics rest, who call'd me friend.
Shed o'er him, Tree, one wither'd leaf,
And share and mitigate my grief.
Here Beauty's final couch is made,
Her flowery diadem decay'd ;
Oh, cruel death ! that needs must fare
Upon such dainties choice and rare.
Here, in his tent, the soldier tried,
Who ne'er from foeman turn'd aside ;
If courage with the grave could vie,
Thou wouldst not thus inglorious lie.
This tablet speaks a son of fame,
That consecrates a lowlier name ;
For here, around, the rich and great
With humble beggars congregate,

Bed-fellows all—a motley throng,
Yet sound their dreamless sleep, and long;
They slumber peaceful, side by side,
'Neath stoneless turf, or pile of pride;
And pomp would scarce her children know
In the vast commonwealth below!
Whilst thou, old tree, o'er all look'st down,
As if thou wor'st a kingly crown,
And these, so lowly at thy feet,
Were prostrate slaves thy rank to greet:
Creation's lords they claim'd to be;
Vain title! since the grey ash tree,
Once scorn'd, perchance, in triumph waves
His budding sceptre o'er their graves.

Rejoice, old Monarch, whilst thou may!
Thy term of triumph speeds away;
These sever'd leaves, with dirge-like call,
But ante-date their parent's fall;
And tell, what thou wouldst fain mistrust,
That trees, as well as men, are dust.
Alas, for thee! once downward cast,
Thy proud pre-eminence is past.
Alas for thee! once swept from view,
No summer shall thy strength renew—
A prisoner in oblivion's womb,
Heir of no second birth or bloom,
How are thy sylvan honours shed,
Thy garniture and glory fled!
The tones which earth's foundation shake,
And bid the sentient clay awake,
Which break corruption's bands of might,
Shall never on thy chains alight,
Nor vivifying force impart,
For *unredeemed dust thou art.*
But those who sleep beneath thy shade,
Shall hear and heed the summons made;
And on thy conqueror, Death, look down,
And claim the imperishable crown.

GLORIOUS BRUCE OF ANNANDALE!

Suggested by the Movement for a Memorial to the Hero-King at Lochmaben.

HEY! the Lord of Annandale!
Howe! the Lord of Annandale!
Auld Scotia hero-king we hail—
The Glorious Bruce of Annandale!

A blessin' on Lochmaben towers!
A blessin' on Lochmaben bowers!
Which sent us him' of bairns the wale,
A richt gude son of Annandale!
Hey! the Lord of Annandale! &c.

When crafty Comyn sought the croun,
And tried to keep puir Scotland doun;
Wha smote him through his plated mail?
'Twas Bruce the Lord of Annandale!
Hey! the Lord of Annandale! &c.

He raised the flag of freedom true,
And follow'd wheresoe'er it flew;
But lang did England's micht prevail
Out owre the Bruce of Annandale.
Hey! the Lord of Annandale, &c.

They hunted him through moor and glen,
And thought his hiding place to ken;
But syne they learn'd anither tale,
Frae Bruce, the Lord of Annandale!
Hey! the Lord of Annandale, &c.

A tale of wonder and deray,
The desperate deer has turn'd to bay!
The Southern dogs look dowf and quail
Before the Bruce of Annandale.
Hey! the Lord of Annandale!

Around him frien's are gathering fast—
Anither blow!—the best—the last—
Now, Isleman, Lowlander, and Gael,
Lay on for Bruce of Annandale!
Hey! the Lord of Annandale! &c.

By Bannock's stream the blow is struck—
Through patriot pith and valour's luck
The land is freed, baith hill and vale,
Thanks to the Lord of Annandale!
Hey! the Lord of Annandale! &c.

Lang years since then hae passed away,
But Bruce's name defies decay:
This statue, which fair hands unveil,
Tells how he's loved in Annandale.
Hey! the Lord of Annandale! &c.

——::——

AULD DUMFRIES, FAIR DUMFRIES.

AULD Dumfries, fair Dumfries, for ever dear to me,
Seated where in cosy bield the Britons planted thee;
Water'd by the wimpling Nith, girt by guardian hills,
Looking in thy winsome face, pride my bosom fills;
Ilka feature glads the e'e, to the memory brings
Mony thochts o' tenderness, and blinks o' by-gane things,
What time the buirdly Romans ruled the country wide,
Lang before the Lion-King claim'd thee for his bride.
Fair Dumfries, rare Dumfries, for ever dear to me:
Dower'd by nature's dainty hand, the bonniest place I see.

In mony a border battle ye bore a double share;
In mony a feudal foray ye suffer'd sad and sair.
Wasted by the Southron loons, laid in ashes black,
Swith ye aye got up again, and paid the reivers back;
Dool to the faithless dyke that ever loot them in!
But blessings on the strong arms that made them hameward rin!
Ance Charlie wi' his Hielanders your aumrie emptied clean,
But the puir lad had scarce a plack, or he wadna been sae keen.
Fair Dumfries, rare Dumfries, for ever dear to me:
In spite o' by-gane broileries the bonniest place I see.

Owre the caul the waters dance, wi' a pleasant croon,
Welcome to your charm'd ear as laverock's voice in June;
And minglin' wi' the canticles which through your bowers rang
For precious simmers five arose an everlasting sang:

'Twas loud and lown, 'twas blythe and sweet, 'twas Sorrow's sel'
by turns,
Its singer was your ain great son, and Coila's minstrel Burns ;
And since they laid him in the mools, the sacred solemn trust
Is yours, to tent wi' miser care the poet's sleepin' dust.
Fair Dumfries, rare Dumfries, for ever dear to me :
Burgh of the poet's shrine, the bonniest place I see.

Auld Dumfries, fair Dumfries, sae auld and yet sae new,
Growin' bigger every year, and bonnier to the view :
Wi' ha's and kirks fu' splendid, and birring busy mills,
Where Industry sae eident, the horn o' plenty fills ;
Wi' braw villas buskit, and crown'd wi' steeples five,
My blessin' be on you and yours ; lang may ye thrive !
Wi' rowth o' bairns about ye, better ne'er hae been,
A' loyal to their mither dear, the dainty Southern Queen.
Fair Dumfries, rare Dumfries, for ever dear to me :
Of burgh-toons the pick and wale, the bonniest place I see.

JAMES HEDDERWICK, LL.D.

A DISTINGUISHED journalist and poet, JAMES HEDDERWICK was born at Glasgow, 18th January, 1814. He was early put to work at the types in his father's printing establishment, but showing decided literary tastes and capacity, he removed to London in his sixteenth year, attending the University there, and carrying off a first prize for rhetoric. In his twenty-third year he became sub-editor of the *Scotsman* newspaper, doing conspicuously good service for that journal, and enjoying the personal friendship and society of the most eminent of the Edinburgh *literati*. In 1842 he returned to Glasgow, to start, in connection with a city merchant, the *Citizen* newspaper, which secured immediate public attention and favour. The *Citizen*, in its old broad-sheet form, held for many years a most influential position amongst the leading Scottish newspapers, and to the end was one of the choicest mediums of communication between the public and struggling genius that Scotland possessed. It is still represented, in a modified form, in the *Weekly Citizen*, a journal of literary selections. Himself a poet of finished taste, the editor, JAMES HEDDERWICK, quickly recognised and fostered into public favour the fine voice of poetical genius wherever heard. Therein Alexander Smith, the author of the celebrated *Life Drama*, flung with lavish hands the first-fruits of his opulent genius. Hugh Macdonald first found effective voice there, and therein David Wingate dropped star-songs, transplanted from the midnight of the mine. On that altar poor James Macfarlan, a crushed flower of song, poured out his earliest breathings in verse; and a little later the clear and perilously high-pitched voice of David Gray, author of *The Luggie, and other Poems*, first arrested the public ear, his efforts ending in a book, a biography, and an early death. The story of the young poet's struggles, as narrated by his biographer, touched all hearts, and has embalmed his name amongst the inheritors of unfulfilled renown. For years also, and while still a very young man, and unknown to fame, William Black, the popular novelist, contributed poems and sketches regularly, and with acceptance, to the literary columns of the *Citizen*.

In 1844 HEDDERWICK issued his first volume of poems, which were received with much favour, establishing the author's claim as a poet of delicate taste, and the rarest beauty. In 1859 appeared his second volume, *Lays of Middle Age*, which assured and heightened his fame. For a brief period he conducted a weekly periodical, entitled, *Hedderwick's Miscellany*; and in 1864 he established his most successful venture, the *Evening Citizen*, which occupies at the present day a leading position amongst Scottish daily newspapers. A few years ago he had the degree of LL.D. conferred on him by the Senatus of the Glasgow University, and the honour gave general public satisfaction.

As a poet, HEDDERWICK is remarkable for grace, refinement, and beauty of diction, rather than for *sans culottes* strength. His fancy is airy and bright, his observation of nature keen and truthful, and his rhythm mellifluously sweet and graceful. He is a man of great and varied literary experience, and his judgment and taste in matters appertaining thereto are unquestionable. Dr. HEDDERWICK's latest volume, *The Villa by the Sea, and other Poems*, recently issued from the Glasgow Press, has been very favourably received.

——::——

WAITING FOR THE SHIP.

Now he stroll'd along the pebbles, now he saunter'd on the pier,
  Now the summit of the nearest hill he clomb;
His looks were full of straining, through all weathers foul and clear,
  For the ship that he was weary wishing home.

On the white wings of the dawn, far as human eye could reach,
  Went his vision like a sea-gull's o'er the deep;
While the fisher's boats lay silent in the bay and on the beach,
  And the houses and the mountains were asleep.

'Mid the chat of boys and men, and the laugh from women's lips,
  When the labours of the morning were begun,
On the far horizon's dreary edge his soul was with the ships,
  As they caught a gleam of welcome from the sun.

Through the grey of eve he peer'd when the stars were in the sky—
  They were watchers which the angels seem'd to send;
And he bless'd the faithful lighthouse, with its large and ruddy eye,
  For it cheer'd him like the bright eye of a friend.

The gentle waves came lisping things of promise at his feet,
Then they ebb'd as if to vex him with delay;
The soothing wind against his face came blowing strong and sweet,
Then it blew as blowing all his hope away.

One day a wiseling argued how the ship might be delay'd—
"'Twas odd," quoth he, "I thought so from the first;"
But a man of many voyages was standing by and said—
"It is best to be prepared against the worst."

A keen-eyed old coast-guardsman, with his telescope in hand,
And his cheeks in countless puckers 'gainst the rain,
Here shook his large and grizzled head, that all might understand
How he knew that hoping longer was in vain.

Then silent thought the stranger of his wife and children five,
As he slowly turn'd with trembling lip aside;
Yet with his heart to feed upon his hopes were kept alive,
So for months he watch'd and wander'd by the tide.

"Lo! what wretched man is that," asked an idler at the coast,
"Who looks as if he something seem'd to lack?"
Then answer made a villager—"His wife and babes are lost,
Yet he thinks that ere to-morrow they'll be back."

Oh! a fresh hale man he flourish'd in the spring-time of the year,
But before the wintry rains began to drip—
No more he climb'd the headland, but sat sickly on the pier,
Saying sadly—"I am waiting for the ship."

On a morn, of all the blackest, only whiten'd by the spray
Of the billows wild for shelter of the shore,
He came not in the dawning forth, he came not all the day;
And the morrow came—but never came he more.

——::——

THE LINNET.

Tuck, tuck, feer—from the green and growing leaves;
Ie, ie, ie—from the little song-bird's throat;
How the silver chorus weaves in the sun and 'neath the eaves,
While from dewy clover fields comes the lowing of the beeves,
And the summer in the heavens is afloat!

Wye, wye, chir—'tis the little linnet sings;
  Weet, weet, weet—how his pipy treble trills!
In his bill and on his wings what a joy the linnet brings,
As over all the sunny earth his merry lay he flings,
  Giving gladness to the music of the rills!

Ic, ic, ir—from a happy heart unbound;
  Lug, lug, jee—from the dawn till close of day!
There is rapture in the sound as it fills the sunshine round,
Till the ploughman's careless whistle, and the shepherd's pipe are
  And the mower sings unheeded 'mong the hay! [drown'd

Jug, jug, joey—oh, how sweet the linnet's theme!
  Peu, peu, poy—is he wooing all the while?
Does he dream he is in heaven, and is telling now his dream,
To soothe the heart of pretty girl basking by the stream,
  Or waiting for her lover at the stile?

Pipe, pipe, chow—will the linnet never weary?
  Bel, bel, tyr—is he pouring forth his vows?
The maiden lone and dreary may feel her heart grow cheery,
Yet none may know the linnet's bliss except his own sweet dearie,
  With her little household nestled 'mong the boughs!

——::——

SORROW AND SONG.

Weep not over poet's wrong,
  Mourn not his mischances;
Sorrow is the source of song,
  And of gentle fancies.

Rills o'er rocky beds are borne
  Ere they gush in whiteness;
Pebbles are wave-chafed and worn
  Ere they show their brightness.

Sweetest gleam the morning flowers
  When in tears they waken;
Earth enjoys refreshing showers
  When the boughs are shaken.

Ceylon's glistening pearls are sought
In its deepest waters;
From the darkest mines are brought
Gems for beauty's daughters.

Through the rent and shiver'd rock
Limpid water breaketh;
'Tis but when the chords are struck
That their music waketh.

Flower's, by heedless footstep press'd,
All their sweets surrender;
Gold must brook the fiery test
Ere it shows its splendour.

When the twilight cold and damp,
Gloom and silence bringeth,
Then the glow-worm lights its lamp,
And the night-bird singeth.

Stars come forth when night her shroud
Draws as daylight fainteth;
Only on the tearful cloud
God his rainbow painteth.

Weep not, then, o'er poet's wrong,
Mourn not his mischances;
Sorrow is the source of song,
And of gentle fancies.

———::———

THE SKYLARK.

Whither away, proud bird? is not thy home
On earth's low breast?
And when thou'rt wearied, whither shalt thou come
To be at rest?
Whither away? the earth with summer bloom
Is newly dress'd!

From the soft herbage thou has brush'd in showers,
The glistening dew,
And upwards sprung to meet the blue-eyed hours
Seen peeping through!
Has earth no spell to bind? have wilding flowers
No power to woo?

Rapt flutterer! I partake thy high delight—
Thy holy thrill;—
Upward and upward in thy tuneful flight
Thou soar'st at will!
Perch'd on the highest point of heavenward sight,
I see thee still!

Oh, marvellous! that thou, a thing so small,
The air should'st flood
With song so affluent and musical!
Most tiny cloud
In the blue sky, raining o'er earth's green ball
Music aloud!

What ear such sweet enchanting melody
Could every cloy?
The pulsing air high-heav'd with ecstasy,
Thy wings up-buoy!
Methinks bright morning hath commission'd thee
To speak its joy!

Night, rich in jewels as an Ethiop queen,
On spray and stem—
On every little flower and leaflet green
Has left a gem,
And gentlest airs tell sweetly they have been
A-wooing them!

Glad nature seems the freshness to partake
Of Eden's birth,
And every sound that hails the morning's break
Has tones of mirth;
Whilst thou, to sing the glorious day awake,
Soar'st high o'er earth!

God of the morning! with adoring eyes
To Thee we bow!
Thou mad'st the lark a preacher in the skies,—
I hear it now!
The air is fill'd with blended harmonies--
Their author—Thou!

ROBERT CHAMBERS, LL.D.

THE names of William and Robert Chambers are known and respected wherever intelligence exists. Their adventurous enterprise in the book publishing world, their unwearied personal industry, and the great credit attached to the firm represented by their names, are matters within the knowledge of all. It is of ROBERT CHAMBERS we have in this brief notice to do, and only with one side of his variously-gifted mind. Endowed with an intellect of extraordinary capacity and power, and full-handed with self-chosen literary toil, ROBERT CHAMBERS had hidden away in his versatile mind a somewhat neglected poetical gift, which, under cultivation, might have yielded the amplest reward. Born 10th July, 1802, in Peebles,—lying in the pastoral valley of the Tweed,—he was educated at the village schools, but was removed to Edinburgh while still a boy. He was intended for the ministry, but family misfortune interfering with that project, he had to forego the advantage of a University education, and pushing ahead for himself, he opened a small second-hand bookshop in Leith Walk, Edinburgh, in his fifteenth year, his stock being mostly made up of the wreck of the family library. He was a devoted lover of Auld Scotland, and produced, by his own unaided labours, over seventy goodly volumes, illustrative of her literature, social life, antiquities, and general history. In 1832, William, the elder brother, projected *Chambers's Edinburgh Journal*, and from the first ROBERT was an efficient and unwearied contributor. His delightful papers—humorous, pathetic, and descriptive—assisted materially in its early and certain success. As an instance of private generosity, the profits of the first edition of his *Life and Letters of Robert Burns*, amounting to over £200, were handed over to the daughters of Burns's surviving sister. In 1863, the Senatus of the University of St. Andrews conferred on him the honorary degree of LL.D. With the opening of 1871 he fell seriously ill, a victim in a great measure to his own unremitting industry, dying 17th March, 1871.

One of the happiest humorous efforts of ROBERT CHAMBERS is his reply to Outram's *Annuitant*, which, in itself, is a poem of most capital Scottish humour. Outram, who was editor of the *Glasgow Herald* for nearly thirty years, is the author of a posthumous volume, of *Legal Lyrics*, issued in 1874, by the eminent publishers, Wm. Blackwood & Sons. Outram was born in the vicinity of Glasgow in 1805, and died at Rosemore, Holy Loch, 16th September, 1856. We quote a portion of his famous poem, *The Annuity*, to enable the reader to fully appreciate ROBERT CHAMBERS's graphic and happy reply.

——::——

THE ANNUITY.

BY GEORGE OUTRAM.

I GAED to spend a week in Fife—
  An unco week it proved to be,
For there I met a waesome wife,
  Lamenting her viduity.

Her grief brak' out sae fierce and fell,
I thocht her heart wad burst the shell;
And I was sae left to mysel'—
  I sell't her an annuity.

The bargain lookit fair eneugh—
  She just was turn'd o' saxty-three;
I couldna guess'd she'd proved sae teugh
  By human ingenuity.
But years have come, and years have gane,
And there she's yet as stieve's a stane;
The limmer's growing young again
  Since she got her annuity.

She's crined awa' to bane an' skin,
  But that it seems is nocht to me;
She's like to live, although she's in
  The last stage o' tenuity.
She munches wi' her wizen'd gums,
An' stumps about on legs o' thrums,
But comes—as sure as Christmas comes—
  To ca' for her annuity.

I read the tables drawn wi' care
  For an Insurance Company;
Her chance o' life was stated there
  Wi' perfect perspicuity.
But tables here or tables there,
She's lived ten years beyond her share;
An's like to live a dozen mair
  To ca' for her annuity.

Last Yule she had a fearfu' hoast—
  I thought a kink might set me free—
I led her out, 'mang snaw and frost,
  Wi' constant assiduity.
But deil may care! the blast gaed by,
And miss'd the auld anatomy;
It just cost me a tooth, forbye
  Discharging her annuity.

If there's a sough o' cholera,
  Or typhus, wha sae gleg as she!
She buys up baths, an' drugs, an' a',
  In siccan superfluity!
She doesna need—she's fever proof—
The pest walk'd o'er her very roof;
She tauld me sae, and then her loof
  Held out for her annuity.

Ae day she fell, her arm she brak',
  A compound fracture as could be;
Nae leech the cure wad undertak',
  Whate'er was the gratuity.
It's cured! she handles't like a flail,
It does as weel in bits as hale;
But I'm a broken man mysel'
  Wi' her, and her annuity.

Her broozled flesh and broken banes
  Are weel as flesh and banes can be;
She beats the taeds that live in stanes
  An' fatten in vacuity!
They die when they're exposed to air,
They canna thole the atmosphere;
But her! expose her onywhere,
  She lives for her annuity.

. . . .

I'd try a shot; but whar's the mark?
  Her vital parts are hid frae me;
Her backbane wanders through her sark,
  In an unkenn'd cork-screwity.
She's palsified, and shakes her head
Sae fast about, ye scarce can see't;
It's past the power o' steel or lead
  To settle her annuity.

She might be drown'd; but go she'll not
  Within a mile o' loch or sea;
Or hang'd—if cord could grip a throat
  O' siccan exiguity.

It's fitter far to hang the rope—
It draws out like a telescope :
'Twad tak' a dreadfu' length o' drop
To settle her annuity.

. . . .

The Bible says the age o' man
Threescore and ten perchance may be ;
She's ninety-four.—Let them wha can
Explain the incongruity.
She should hae lived afore the flood ;
She's come o' patriarchal blood ;
She's some old Pagan mummified,
Alive for her annuity.

. . . .

The water-drap wears out the rock,
As this eternal jaud wears me.
I could withstand the single shock,
But no the continuity.
It's pay me here, and pay me there,
And pay me, pay me, evermair ;
I'll gang demented wi' despair—
I'm *charged* for her annuity.

—::—

THE ANNUITANT'S ANSWER.

My certy ! but it sets him weel
Sae vile a tale to tell o' me ;
I never could suspect the chiel'
O' sic disingenuity.
I'll no be ninety-four for lang,
My health is far frae being strang,
And he'll mak' profit, richt or wrang,
Ye'll see, by this annuity.

My friends, ye weel can understand
This world is fu' o' roguery ;
And ane meets folk on ilka hand
To rug, and rive, and pu' at ye.

I thocht that this same man o' law
Wad save my siller frae them a',
And sae I gave the whilliewha
  The note for the annuity.

He says the bargain lookit fair,
  And sae to him, I'm sure 'twad be ;
I got my hundred pounds a year,
  An' he could well allow it tae.
And does he think—the deevil's limb—
Although I lookit auld and grim,
I was to die to pleasure him,
  And squash my braw annuity ?

The year had scarcely turn'd its back
  When he was irking to be free—
A fule the thing to undertak',
  And then sae sune to rue it ye.
I've never been at peace sin' syne—
Nae wonder that sae sair I coyne—
It's jist through terror that I tyne
  My life for my annuity.

He's twice had pushion in my kail,
  And sax times in my cup o' tea ,
I could unfauld a shocking tale
  O' something in a cruet, tae.
His arms he ance flang round my neck—
I thought it was to show respeck ;
He only meant to gie a *check*,
  Not for, but to, the annuity.

Said ance to me, an honest man,
  "Try an insurance company ;
Ye'll find it an effective plan
  Protection to secure to ye.
Ten pounds a year !—ye weel can spare't !—
Be that wi' Peter Fraser wared ;
His office syne will be a guard
  For you and your annuity."

I gaed at ance an' spak' to Pate
  O' a five hundred policy,
And "Faith!" says he, "ye are nae blate;
  I maist could clamahewit ye.
Wi' that chiel's fingers at the knife,
What chance hae ye o' length o' life?
Sae to the door, ye silly wife,
  Wi' you and your annuity."

The procurator-fiscal's now
  The only friend that I can see;
And it's sma' thing that he can do
  To end this sair ankskewity.
But honest Maurice has agreed
That if the villain does the deed,
He'll swing at Libberton Wyndhead
  For me and my annuity.

——::——

SCOTLAND.

SCOTLAND! the land of all I love, the land of all that love me;
Land, whose green sod my youth has trod, whose sod shall lie above me.
Hail, country of the brave and good; hail, land of song and story;
Land of the uncorrupted heart, of ancient faith and glory!

Like mother's bosom o'er her child, thy sky is glowing o'er me;
Like mother's ever-smiling face, thy land lies bright before me.
Land of my home, my father's land, land where my soul was nourish'd;
Land of anticipated joy, and all my memory cherish'd!

Oh Scotland, through thy wide domain, what hill, or vale, or river,
But in this fond enthusiast heart, has found a place for ever?
Nay, hast thou but a glen or shaw, to shelter farm or shieling,
That is not garner'd fondly up within its depths of feeling?

Adown thy hills run countless rills, with noisy, ceaseless motion;
Their waters join the rivers broad, those rivers join the ocean:
And many a sunny, flowery brae, where childhood plays and ponders,
Is freshen'd by the lightsome flood, as wimpling on it wanders.

Within thy long-descending vales, and on the lonely mountain,
How many wild spontaneous flowers hang o'er each flood and fountain!
The glowing furze, the "bonny broom," the thistle, and the heather;
The blue-bell, and the gowan fair, which Childhood loves to gather.

Oh, for that pipe of silver sound, on which the shepherd lover,
In ancient days, breath'd out his soul, beneath the mountain's cover!
Oh, for that great lost power of Song, so soft and melancholy,
To make thy every hill and dale poetically holy!

And not alone each hill and dale, fair as they are by nature,
But every town and tower of thine, and every lesser feature;
For where is there the spot of earth within my contemplation,
But from some noble deed or thing has taken consecration?

Scotland! the land of all I love, the land of all that love me;
Land, whose green sod my youth has trod, whose sod shall lie above me.
Hail, country of the brave and good; hail, land of song and story;
Land of the uncorrupted heart, of ancient faith and glory!

JAMES NICHOLSON.

A PROLIFIC and successful contributor to the Doric minstrelsy of the present day, JAMES NICHOLSON was born at Edinburgh, October 21, 1822. His parents belong to the humbler classes. In his seventh year the family removed to Paisley, but the blight of severe domestic trial occurring in his father's household, put its mark on the succeeding years of our poet's early life. Removing in course of time to the village of Strathaven, young Nicholson became a "herd-boy" for some time. Afterwards he engaged himself to a sheep-farmer in the immediate neighbourhood, but the monotony of his occupation proving distasteful, he broke his engagement by stealing out from the farm-house one fine midsummer night, and setting off on foot to Edinburgh.

Here he put up with his grandfather for a length of time, applying himself to the trade of tailoring until something better might fortunately turn up. Returning to Strathaven at his father's request, he engaged himself to a tailoring firm there, in whose service his father acted as foreman; and getting on rapidly in the practice of his trade, he was soon able to do the work of an ordinary hand, though receiving for his week's produce a greatly inferior wage. At the age of twenty-one he got married, and set up in business for himself, but the venture was not so successful as to encourage him to retain it. He had early shown a predilection for poetry, joined to a deep love for botany, and all his leisure hours--which were scant enough—were now lovingly divided between the two sister studies. Unsuccessful in business, Nicholson fell back to his handicraft work again. In 1853 he obtained a situation as foreman tailor in a public institution in Glasgow, which situation he still worthily retains.

Regarding the literary side of his life, Mr. NICHOLSON, it should be mentioned, has for the greater part of his life warmly identified himself with the temperance movement, and has frequently and effectively employed his pen in the service of that excellent cause. He has written much and well, and his spare hours are still ungrudgingly given to the informing study of books, to occasional solicitations of the Doric muse, and to the ardent pursuit and study of his beloved wild-flowers. While his muse but seldom attempts the higher flights of poetry, there is a pervading humanity and reality in his verses which cannot fail to arrest and please. It is in the simplest and the homeliest subjects that his genius shows to the most advantage. Therein he is always relishable, and his humour—which is of itself invariably good—receives an added piquancy in the use of an apt and graphic Doric which few could successfully imitate, and none may surpass. In the course of his long and active life, Mr. NICHOLSON has issued several volumes of verse and prose, some of which have reached second and third editions.

Many of NICHOLSON's humorous poems have taken a sure hold on public favour. His *Oor Wee Kate* and his highly-humorous *Im-phm!* are known everywhere, and very warmly prized, and his *Jenny wi' the Lang Pock* is a distinct addition to the nursery minstrelsy of Scotland.

Mr. NICHOLSON, it need scarcely be mentioned, is a man of excellent character, and is much respected by a wide circle of admiring friends.

——::——

OOR WEE KATE.

WAS there ever sic a lassie kent, as oor Wee Kate?
There's no a wean in a' the toun like oor Wee Kate;
Baith in an' oot, at kirk an' schule, she rins at sic a rate,
A pair o' shoon jist last a month wi' oor Wee Kate.

I wish she'd been a callan, she's sic a steerin' quean—
For ribbons, dolls, an' a' sic gear, she doesna' care a preen,
But taps an' bools, girs, ba's, an' bats, she plays wi' ear' an' late;
I'll hae to get a pair o' breeks for oor Wee Kate.

Na, what d'ye think? the ither day, as sure as ony thing—
I saw her fleein' dragons, wi' maist a mile o' string;
Yer jumpin' rapes, and peveralls, she flings oot o' her gate,
But nane can fire a towgun like oor Wee Kate.

They tell me on the meetin' nicht she's waur than ony fule,
She dings her bloomer oot o' shape an' mak'st jist like a shule;
The chairman glooms an' shakes his heid, an' scarce can keep his seat;
I won'er he can thole sic deils as oor Wee Kate.

But see her on a gala-nicht, she's aye sas neat an' clean—
Wi' cheeks like ony roses, an' bonnie glancin' een—
An' then to hear her sing a sang, it's jist a perfect treat,
For ne'er a lintie sings sae sweet as oor Wee Kate.

An' yet there's no' a kinder wean in a' the toun, I'm sure;
That day wee brither Johnny dee'd, she grat her wee heart sair:
In beggar weans an' helpless folk she taks a queer conceit—
They're sure to get the bits o' piece frae oor Wee Kate.

Gaun to the kirk the ither day she sees a duddie wean
Wi' cauld bare feet an' bruckit face sit sabbin' on a stane;
She slipt the penny in his haun' I gaed her for the "plate:"
The kirks wad fa' if folk were a' like oor Wee Kate.

For a' she's sic a steer-about, sae fu' o' mirth an' fun,
She taks the lead in ilka class, an' mony a prize she's won—
This gars me think there's maybe mair than mischief in her pate,
I wish I saw the wisdom teeth o' oor Wee Kate.

——::——

WHO ARE THE HEROES?

Who are the heroes?—the men who labour.
  Who are the kings?—the brave who toil.
Not by the rifle, not by the sabre,
  Claim we a right to the fruits of the soil.

What though we own no fertile acres,
  What though no lands in tenure we hold,
Ours is the might, for we are the makers—
  Ours are the hands that gather the gold.

We are the sinew and bone of the nation,
  We are the walls our isle to defend;
Firm is the throne that has for foundation,
  The hearts of a people on which to depend.

Down with all tyrants! away with oppression!
  What though we own but an isle of the sea,
Earth is our work field, labour our mission,
  Let who will worship wealth, we are the free!

Treasures of home, so dear to our bosoms,
  Be our endeavour still to improve,
Dear to the workman his fair buds and blossoms,
  Faithful his friendship, deathless his love.

May the Almighty still guard and defend us
  From every vice that would us ensnare;
Shades of our fathers! to bless, still attend us;
  God save the labourer! still be our prayer.

A GLEN AMONG THE HILLS.

The sun had roll'd behind the western wave,
  Leaving behind a track of golden spray;
Soft evening crept around us silent, save
  The tide that lapsing left the sandy bay.

'Twas God's sweet sabbath: we had spent it well,
  Not worshipping, as wont, in cushion'd pew,
But far away within a Highland dell,
  Where purple heath and azure hare-bells grew.

'Mid rocks fantastic, where white cascades dash'd,
  Leaping from caves their winter floods had made,
To foamy ire their tortur'd waters lash'd,
  Till lost in depths where agile minnows play'd.

Like a great chalice in the hand of God,
  That grand old glen brimm'd o'er with joyous light;
On high the clouds like glowing chariots rode,
  Flecking with shade each hill and mountain height.

Who would not worship God in such a place?
  To us it seem'd a glimpse of paradise,
Where silent joy lit up each flow'ret's face,
  While love shone through the dew-gems in their eyes.

Such was the day; more beauteous still the night
  Crept dreamily o'er moorland, field, and fell,
While softly dawn'd from heaven a holier light
  Above the hills that hid our Highland dell.

'Twas not the shifting pale Aurora light,
  Nor the red radiance of the planet Mars—
The soft effulgence of the Queen of Night,
  Nor yet the dewy lustre of the stars.

Ah no ! it made the star-lamps twinkle dim,
Deep'ning the shades that lay on tower and tree,
While rose the mountain ridge clear-cut and grim
Like some huge monster stranded 'mid the sea.

We sat and gaz'd with longing earnest eyes
Along the line of soft celestial light,
As if awaiting, from the silent skies
Reveal'd, some wondrous vision of the night.

We seem'd to feel on the surrounding air
The tread of angels—felt their presence near ;
The heavens seem'd wrapt in ecstasy of prayer,
The glittering star-worlds blending sphere with sphere.

Such blissful sights and scenes to mortal eyes
May well compensate for life's countless ills ;
God grant to each the power to realise
His presence shed at midnight on the hills.

—::—

JENNY WI' THE LANG POCK.

Jenny wi' the lang pock,
Haste ye owre the main,
Lampin' wi' yer lang legs,
Plashin' through the rain ;
Here's a waukrife laddie
Winna steek his e'e,
Pit him in yer lang pock
An' dook him in the sea.
Oh, dear me ! whan 'ill Jenny come?
Wheesht ! I think I hear her cryin' doun the lum ;
Fie, awa', Jenny ! we dinna want ye here—
A' the bairns are in their beds—a' but Jamie dear.

Gudesake ! noo I hear her !
There's she's on the stair,
Sapples o' the sea-bree
Stickin' in her hair,

Hushions on her bare legs,
  Bauchles on her feet,
Seeking waukrife bairnies
  Up an' doun the street!
Oh, losh me! There's she's at the sneck,
Stoitin' owre the stair-heid—may she break her neck!
Cuddle down fu' cosy—that's my ain wee lamb;
Dinna spurtle wi' yer feet, or ye'll wauken Tam.

Jenny's nae awa' yet,
  Sae ye manna greet;
There she's on the door-mat
  Scufflin' wi' her feet,
Wabblin' wi' her lang legs,
  Sneevlin' through her nose,
Hirslin wi' her lang pock,
  Aff Jenny goes!
Oh, losh me! there's she's back again,
Listenin' wi her lang lugs for a greetin' wean!
Fie, gae bar the door, Jean, thraw aboot the key—
Na, she winna get ye, ye're owre dear to me!

Whaur's the body gaun noo?
  Up the ither stair,
At oor neebor's door she's
  Tirlin' I declare!
Cryin' through the key-hole
  Like a roopit sheep,
"Hae ye ony weans here
  Winna fa' asleep?"
Oh, losh me! hae they let her in!
Wha's that sprechin, makin' sic a din?
No oor Jamie, for he is sleepin' soun',
Like a bonnie rose-bud in the month o' June.

Jenny wi' the lang pock,
  Ye may tak' the road,
A' the bairns are safe noo
  In the lan' o' nod;

Losh! can that be John's fit
Comin' up the stair?
No ae bit o' supper yet
Ready, I declare.
Oh, dear me! rest for me there's nane,
Pity on the mither that's plagued wi' sic a wean!
Yet at him the very cat daurna wink an e'e,
For he's the darlin' o' my heart, an' a' the warl' to me.

HUGH MACDONALD.

HUGH MACDONALD, best known to fame as the author of a very successful book of *Rambles Round Glasgow*, was a native of the East-end of Glasgow, having been born in Rumford Street, Bridgeton, on the 4th of April, 1817. His parents were in humble circumstances, and their family being numerous, the subject of this sketch had necessarily to forego, at a very early age, the benefits of the school. While still a very little boy he entered the Barrowfield Block-Printing Works, and very soon became regularly apprenticed to that trade. Having completed his term of servitude and saved a little money, he unsuccessfully tried shop-keeping in his native district of Bridgeton, and thereafter, having lost his little all, he returned to the block-printing business, finding employment at Colinslie, near Paisley. While working here he continued to reside in Bridgeton, walking the distance there and home again, morning and evening, a walk in all of sixteen miles; rather a heavy stretch, when we take into consideration that he wrought ten or twelve hours per day as well. MACDONALD, however, had a genius for walking (if the phrase is allowable), and the time spent on the journey to and from his place of toil was economised to good ends by useful observation, and the perusal of congenial books. The pleasant result began to be seen about this period, in the frequency with which his name was to be met with appended to poems and sketches contributed to the local journals.

When about thirty-two years of age he was promoted to the sub-editorship of the *Citizen* newspaper, which post he filled with credit for years. While acting in this capacity he wrote and contributed to that journal the series of sketches now forming his popular book of *Rambles Round Glasgow*. He afterwards edited for a short time a paper called the *Glasgow Times*, and subsequently accepted a position on the staff of the Glasgow *Morning Journal*, which connection he sustained until his death, an event which happened March, 1860, in his forty-third year. His directly literary life, extending as it did over a period of eleven years, was not quite exclusively devoted to mere prose writing. He indited much, and excellent, lyrical and descriptive verse. Looking through his poems one is struck with the frequent allusions to flowers, and the warm and repeated eulogies on the genius and character of his beloved Burns with which the volume abounds. Those who knew MACDONALD best while living, will, we daresay, be best able to poetically appreciate him in his book. His love for the flowers, they must well know, was no mere fancy, but a genuine passion. And if we are at all to stop to estimate him as a doric poet, it cannot—even in view of his *Burnsiana* verses—be as a mere imitator of the embayed ploughman bard. The influence of Burns is indeed sensibly felt in HUGH MACDONALD's poetical writings, but not more so than the influence of Ramsay and Ferguson is known to exist in Burns. The semi-imitation of Burns in HUGH

MACDONALD'S case, and in the case of some few others, perhaps, proceeded from a poetic mental affinity rather than otherwise.

Apart from his reputation as a local man of letters, HUGH MACDONALD was widely respected and warmly loved as a genial companion and friend. He was, constitutionally, incapable of literary jealousies, and was the first to call attention to the genius of Alexander Smith, poor unfortunate James Macfarlan, and others. His death, which was sudden, came upon his immediate friends and the public as a startling surprise. He had proceeded on a Saturday forenoon to gather some of his loved Spring flowers at Castlemilk, a few miles south of Glasgow, and returning the same afternoon took to his bed and expired the next day. A sum of money approaching to £900 was publicly collected for the benefit of his widow and young family shortly after the poet's death. He was interred in the Southern Necropolis, Caledonia Road, Glasgow. A small headstone, erected to the memory of his first wife, marks the spot. In 1878 a few surviving admirers of the poet erected a handsome Memorial Fountain on the Gleniffer Braes, overlooking the site of one of his happiest lyrical effusions—*The Bonnie Wee Well on the Breist o' the Brae.* In 1881 the said Memorial Fountain was removed to Glasgow, and now occupies a prominent site on the "Green" of that city.

——::——

THE WEE PRIMROSE.

ON a green mossy bank, 'neath a bonnie birk tree,
By a burnie that danced to its ain voice o' glee,
A sweet yellow primrose, on March ope'd her e'en,
Like wee starnies o' gowd in a bricht clud o' green.

O sweet sang the merle in the hour o' her birth,
An' the lark tauld his joy frae the lift to the earth ;
While the wud-mouse peep'd out frae a grey lichen'd stone,
To welcome the floo'r that bids winter begone.

Though March whussilt keen through the cauld drapeless wud,
The bonnie birk tree 'gan to smile an' to bud ;
Sayin' Summer is near, since the primrose is come,
I'll don my green kirtle, an' welcome her home.

The wee robin cam' there wi' his sere-breasted bride,
An' they biggit their nest at the primrose's side ;
An' sweet frae the birk tree he sang air an' late,
To soothe the bit heart o' his bonnie wee mate.

——::——

THE WEE WEE MAN.

A WEE wee man, wi' an unco din,
  Cam' to our bield yestreen,
And siccan a rippit the body rais'd
  As seldom was heard or seen ;—
He wanted claes, he wanted shoon,
  And something to weet his mou',
And aye he spurr'd wi' his tiny feet,
  And blink'd wi' his e'en o' blue.

His face, which nane had seen before,
  Thrill'd strangely through ilk min',
Wi' gowden dreams frae mem'ry's store,
  Of loved anes lost langsyne.
A faither's brow, a mither's e'en,
  A brither's dimpled chin,
Were mingled a' on that sweet face,
  Fresh sent frae a hand abune.

Oh ! soon ilka heart grew great wi' love,
  And draps o' joy were seen
To trinkle fast o'er channell'd cheeks,
  Where streams o' wae had been.

A welcome blithe we gie'd the chiel,
  To share our lowly ha';
And we rowed him warm in fleecy duds,
  And linen like Januar snaw.

Our guidman has a way o' his ain,
  His word maun aye be law—
Frae Candlemas to blithe Yule e'en
  He rules baith great and sma';
But the howdie reign'd yestreen, I trow,
  And swagger'd baith butt and ben—
Even the big arm-chair was push'd agee
  Frae the cosie chimley en'.

The guidman snoov'd about the house,
  Aye rinnin' in some ane's way,
And aft he glanc'd at the wee thing's face,
  On the auld wife's lap that lay;
His breast grew great wi' love and pride,
  While the bairn was hush'd asleep,
And a gush o' blessings frae his heart
  Came welling, warm and deep.

"I canna boast o' gowd," quoth he,
  "My wealth's a willing arm;
Yet health and strength and wark be mine,
  And wha shall bode thee harm?
To fill thy wee bit caup and cog,
  And gie thee claes and lair,
Wi' joy and sweet content I'll strive
  Through poortith, toil, and care."

There's joy within the simmer woods,
  When wee birds chip the shell,
When firstling roses tint wi' bloom
  The lip of sunlight dell;
But sweeter than the nestling bird,
  Or rose-bud on the lea,
Is yon wee smiling gift of love
  To a fond parent's e'e.

MY AIN HEARTHSTANE.

'Tis sweet, when smiling Simmer flings her mantle o'er the lea,
When scented flow'rs unfold their bloom and birds are a' in glee,
To wander wi' the wimplim burn, or 'mang the woods alane;
But sweeter, dearer to the heart, our ain hearthstane.

When gloamin' spreads out-owre the scene her dewy wings o' grey,
And brings the ploughman frae the furr', the shepherd frae the brae,
How sweet the winsome wifie's smile the prattlin o' the wean,
That welcome weary labour to his ain hearthstane.

My hame is but a lowly beild, a wee bit but and ben,
A kame into a croodet byke that grandeur disna ken;
Yet pride within her lofty wa's amid her menial train,
Micht envy me the treasures of my ain hearthstane.

Of gowd or gear I mauna speak; fause fortune's still my fae;
She's grudg'd me e'en the timmer spoon—the breeks o' hodden grey;
Our kail she aye sends through the reek, and clean we pike the bane;
Yet love makes licht o' poortith at my ain hearthstane.

Owre weel I love, wi' genial friends, a social nicht o' glee,
When sang and crack around the bowl gar a' life's shadows flee;
But bicker-joys are fleeting a', and sune the heart is fain
To toddle hame repentant to its ain hearthstane.

There's jags on ilka path o' life, in ilka cup there's ga';
But poortith 'bides the sairest dunts on mortal pows that fa';
For lowly toil meets cankert words and looks o' sour disdain,
And Worth maun snool to screen frae Want her ain hearthstane.

We've a' our ain bit weird to dree, our ain bit wark to dae,
And some maun hurkle doon the howe, while ithers speel the brae;
But in the dub or on the dyke, ye'll find its a' in vain
To look for lasting pleasure aff your ain hearthstane.

——::——

THE BONNIE WEE WELL.

The bonnie wee well on the breist o' the brae,
That skinkles sae cauld in the sweet smile o' day,
And croons a laich sang a' to pleasure itsel'
As it jinks 'neath the brecken and genty blue-bell.

The bonnie wee well on the breist o' the brae,
Where the hare steals to drink in the gloamin' sae grey;
Where the wild moorlan' birds dip their nebs and tak' wing,
And the lark weets his whistle ere mounting to sing.

Thou bonnie wee well on the breist o' the brae,
My mem'ry aft haunts thee by nicht and by day;
For the friends I ha'e lov'd in the years that are gane
Ha'e knelt by thy brim, and thy gush ha'e parta'en.

Thou bonnie wee well on the breist o' the brae,
While I stoop to thy bosom, my thirst to allay,
I will drink to the lov'd ones who come back nae mair,
And my tears will but hallow thy bosom sae fair.

Thou bonnie wee well on the breist o' the brae,
My blessing rests with thee, wherever I stray;
In joy and in sorrow, in sunshine and gloom,
I will dream of thy beauty, thy freshness, and bloom.

In the depths of the city, 'midst turmoil and noise,
I'll oft hear with rapture thy lone trickling voice,
While fancy takes wing to thy rich fringe o' green,
And quaffs thy cool waters in noon's gowden sheen.

JAMES NORVAL.

A STUDY of poetry, along with an ordinarily close attention to the habits and actions of the poetic *genus* generally, reveals the anomaly of youthy rhymsters indulging in the special luxury of premature publication while their muse is still imitative, and before their thoughts can be justly called their own, with the opposite spectacle of men of experienced and matured minds hesitating distrustfully over such an action. To the latter, and perhaps wiser, class of poets must be relegated the name of JAMES NORVAL, a Calton bard, who has been associated with the east-end of Glasgow, as a resident working weaver, for the space of a life-time. Born April 29th, 1814, he is now in his 68th year. He is a native of Parkhead—an eastern suburb of Glasgow, but was removed while still a child to the quadrangular row of tenements known as the old *White Hooses*—referred to in *My Ain Gate En'*—at the foot of Bellgrove, Gallowgate, long since taken down.

His mother—who was full of old ballads and witch stories—early imbued his mind with the love of Doric poesy, and while still a young man he had so far overcome the obstruction of a defective education as to be able to contribute with frequency snatches of graphic minstrelsy to the Poets' Corners of some of the better known of the local Scottish newspapers.

Mr. NORVAL'S life has all along been chequered to a degree with the harassments which commonly hedge about the lives of the lowly born—want of work, pinched circumstances, and consequent domestic troubles—but has otherwise been uneventful and ordinary. Though possessed of strong native poetic feeling and instinct, he has never allowed the study of verse-making to dominate his life, but has wisely made it only a subsidiary consideration—a mere solace for leisure hours. The cast of his mind is essentially realistic, and he has no patience with the elaborate creations of the Tennysonian school of poets, but finds a wholesome "grup" in the writings of Burns, Tom Campbell, Hew Ainslie, and Henry Scott Riddell, with others of that direct-speaking and masculine-minded class of poets. His verses are, all through, the immediate reflection of his mind and heart at the moment of composition. Thus, in his *Auld*

Man's Sang the exclamation is genuine and the regret real—

> Oh, gin I was young again !
>   Hech-howe, gin I was young again !
> Chasing bumbees owre the plain
>   Is jist an auld sang sung again !

To the nursery literature of Scotland, he has also contributed several very relishable pieces.

His muse is mostly retrospective in the selection and treatment of subjects. He has a warm nook in his heart for the pure, though fleeting, joys of childhood, with its merry laughter and prattle, its sunshine and its truth, and its happy memories of blue skies and green fields, with brattling burns, and wee birds, and bright flowers; and when his muse depicts these memorial recollections of child-life and its happy associations, he is invariably pleasing and interesting to a marked degree. In satire, he wields a scathing pen. But perhaps the very best effort of his genius is to be found in his fine verses on *The March Win'*. Brief in detail, but essentially dramatic in conception and execution, we take that poem to be one of the best idiomatic pieces in the Scottish dialect. His range is limited, but within that certain radius he is happily successful. He has not yet ventured on the publication of a volume. There is no reason why it should be longer withheld. NORVAL's poems, if issued in a small collected form, would indubitably receive a warm welcome at many a Scottish fireside. Home-loving Scotchmen would everywhere thank him for them; and when that event is accomplished, his future reputation as a characteristic Scottish poet will be secure.

THE MARCH WIN'.

THE March win' sat gurlin' on he room winnock sill,
At the deid hour o' nicht; an' his gurl boded ill.
He gar'd the doors an' winnocks shake, syne roar'd doun the lum—
"Are ye there, frail man! Hoo! I'll kill ye gin I come!"

"Kill me gin ye come, will ye, catwuttet auld fule?
Hoots! ye couldna sned the shank o' a wee puddock stule!
Cam ye here to bullirag? Your threats I lichtly dree,
For my life's in the haun's o' my Maker, wha's on hie,
An' quakesna at the snash o' a braggart like thee."

"Ha! ha! ha!" lauch'd the win'; "e'en sneer gin ye will;
But I hae the power to threaten—certes, I can kill!
I could mak' yer heart cauld, an' your een stane blin';
My sooth! he maun be bauld that wad daur the March win'."

"My sooth! he maun be bauld? Feich! the auld boul's rinnin' wud;
Gae 'wa' an' fley the bairns wi' your white stoorie clud.
Turr the thack aff the roof, whup its strae owre the linn,
I carena a boddle for your heel-hackin' win',
Ye lee like a banker when he spoolies wi' a *grin*."

"I've smote the bonny bride, 'mid her bridesmaids young and fair:
I've fell'd the beggar loon ;. I've chok'd the baron's heir;
I've slain the radiant saint, an' the bloated in his sin,
An' the bauldest doff their caps to the keen March win'."

"Weel, I wadna doff my cowl, nor wad I jee my wig
To sic a sprowsin' fule—to sic a leein' prig—
That comes like a thief i' the middle o' the nicht;
Gin ye'd come like a man, 'mid the noon's rosy licht,
I wad ding ye wi' a sun-glaff, ye frozen-saul'd wicht."

"Frozen-saul'd wicht!" said ye; "then ye'll dree the wicht's power.'
Syne he gied me sic a worryin', fegs I mind it to this hour;
He fill'd me fu' o' gellin' pains frae ankle-bane to chin;
He brang the measles 'mang the weans, an' spreckled a' their skin;
It's easy work to count their gains that daur the March win'!

MY AIN GATE EN'.

I've climb'd the lofty mountain, I've cross'd the gowling sea;
I've rested by the fountain that gushes 'neath the lea;
I've been amang the truly great, alack, but even then,
My heart grew grit wi' yearning for my ain gate en'.

Oh, dear to me the scenes at my ain gate en'—
The wifies and the weans at my ain gate en';
There's no a spot on a' the earth that I sae brawly ken,
As the hamely auld white hoosies at my ain gate en'.

It isna for their grandeur—they hae nae gaudy show;
It lack's a' dignity o' art, that lowly cottar's row,
Wi' its quaint auld teekit roofs, and ilk cosie butt and ben,
Whaur dwelt the douce and decent at my ain gate en'.

I've had muckle fun and daffin roun' my ain gate en';
Joy and comfort aye gaed lauchin' roun' my ain gate en';
Yet there's a'e bit mournfu' nook, a bonny fairy den,
Whaur I buried a pet Robin, at my ain gate en'.

Oh, I grat owre that wee birdie till I sca'ded baith my een,
And I buskit a' the yirdie wi' the wild flowers frae the green,
And I thocht there was nae loss like mine within a' human ken,
Sae sicker is first sorrow at our ain gate en'.

Hae ye seen a wardless outcast cut aff frae freens and hame,
A-pining for that ingle, wi' its soul-stirring flame;
What can thro' a' his bleeding heart sic thrills o' pleasure sen'
As a weel-kent bairn-time story o' his ain gate en'?

A blink o' sweet remembrance glints owre his scowling broo,
A bygane blue-ee'd lassie is beside him sittin' noo;
Again he wreathes her sunny hair wi' fox-bells doun the glen,
And he hears the waters rushing by his ain gate en'.

O'! an unca witching charm has our ain gate en';
And we shrink frae change as harm to our ain gate en';
Frae the peasant on the lea to the wealthy and the hie,
We've a' a warm heart-liken to our ain gate en'.

THE AULD STAIRHEID.

At hin hairst—when leaves are cast in humplocks on the blast,
Which rushes doun the bleak glen wi' a mad bull's speed—
The bairns hurry in, seekin' shelter frae the win',
In a helter-skelter rin, to the auld stairheid;

Whaur grannie's sitting rocking, knitting gutcher's stocking,
The kittlin's gowfin' here and there, the clew and the threed;
The bairnies gie a skirl, as kitt gar's the ba' play birl—
Sends it spinning wi' a swirl owre the auld stairheid.

Auld grannie lift's her han's, and stamps her fit, and bans;
Paiks them ane and a' for a mischief-brewing breed;
Tells them a fleesum tale, that gars their wee hearties quail,
As the dead leaves breenge like hail 'gainst the auld stairheid.

May a' that's gude protect her; she's gied them a' a lecture,
Hoo wilfu' bairns were serv'd that ca'd guid men chuckle-heid,
Twa red wud beasties cam', and fell on them ram-stam;
Rave them spawl frae spawl; och, and left them bluidy deid.

Whae'er glories in mischief, or guffaws at grannie's grief,
Are aye seen by an e'e that has never steek'd nor jee'd;
And in his ain guid time, when you've tint your youthfu' prime,
He'll bring my words to min', when I'm moolin' 'mang the deid.

She gies them crumpy farls, to mend their fykes and quarrels,
And they nip and brak' to mirls a' their twal-hours breid;
And, aiblins, ere they stop they'll play at a wee shop—
Trowth, there's mony a huxter schul'd on an auld stairheid.

The purse-proud hae their braws, and the lordly hae their ha's;
While the miser, skinny loon, starves 'tween his gowd and
greed;
But the memories o' oor youth wi' its sunwinks and its truth,
Shimmers like the flowery south, round the auld stairheid.

Awa' wi' your gewgaws, and your thieveless hums and haws—
On warm hearts they fa' like a blad o' frozen leed;
The auld leeve wi' the past, whaur Hope's pennant crown'd the
mast,
And their beacon through life's blast was that auld stairheid.

WILLIAM WATT.

A CHARACTERISTIC Scottish poet of capital ability and of more than merely local fame, WILLIAM WATT, was born at West Linton, Peeblesshire, in 1792; but was early placed under the care of his paternal grandmother at the village of East Kilbride, owing to his father, who was a native of that village, having enlisted into the army while the future poet was still a child. After a brief and broken attendance at school, he was ultimately apprenticed to the weaving trade; and being a close reader of books when opportunity allowed, with a certain restless instinctive longing for poetic voice and fame, he forthwith began the cultivation of the three sister arts of poesy, painting, and music, but, to the last, was principally engrossed with poesy. In 1831 he entered the married state, and two years afterwards secured an appointment as parish precentor, at a modest salary. In 1835 he published his collected poems and songs in a volume. The book sold well, but the publisher being unsuccessful in business, WATT received no pecuniary benefit from the venture. A second augmented edition of his songs was issued in 1844, and it also proved a profitless venture, through an almost similar unfortunate circumstance. WATT sang well, and had a distinct talent for original musical composition. In addition, he had a fine taste for decorative painting, and was locally celebrated as a *crack* hand at painting coats of arms, "Lodge" flags, and the like artistic work.

WILLIAM WATT, it may be mentioned, inherited poetic genius from his father, who wrote several humorous and patriotic songs, and it will be our pleasant duty, to call attention to his son, Alexander Watt, who inherits, at the present day, a fair share of his late father's musical and poetical abilities. The closing period of WILLIAM WATT's life was chequered by misfortune and domestic bereavement, and his Caledonian lyre was for years almost silent for sorrow. In the April of 1859 he died, regretted by a wide circle of admiring friends. His widow still survives.

WILLIAM WATT's claim to the recognition as a characteristic Scottish song-writer, is now pretty generally conceded, but his writings are not so well known as their merits would seem to warrant. He was a man of kindly and simple habits, and of wide and generous sympathies. His muse was buoyant, fertile, and spontaneous in its flow. His ever fresh and popular *Kate Dalrymple* will alone insure him a lasting niche in the temple of fame. It is unquestionably one of the happiest effusions of the modern Scottish muse.

——::——

KATE DALRYMPLE.

IN a wee cot-house far across the muir,
  Where the peesweeps, plovers, and whaups cry dreary,
There lived an auld maid for mony lang years,
  Wham ne'er a wooer did e'er ca' his dearie.
A lanely lass was Kate Dalrymple,
A thrifty quean was Kate Dalrymple;
Nae music, exceptin' the clear burnie's wimple,
Was heard round the dwellin' o' Kate Dalrymple.

Her face had a smack o' the gruesome and grim,
  Whilk did frae the fash o' a' wooers defend her;
Her lang Roman nose nearly met wi' her chin,
  That brang folk in min' o' the auld witch o' Endor.
A weagle in her walk had Kate Dalrymple,
A sneevil in her talk had Kate Dalrymple;
And mony cornelian and cairngorm pimple
Did bleeze on the dun face o' Kate Dalrymple.

She span tarry woo' the hale winter through,
For Kate ne'er was lazy, but eident and thrifty ;
She wrocht 'mang the peats, coil'd the hay, shore the corn,
And supported hersel' by her ain shift aye.
But ne'er a lover cam' to Kate Dalrymple,
For beauty and tocher wanted Kate Dalrymple ;
Unheeded was she by baith gentle and simple,
A blank in the warld seemed puir Kate Dalrymple.

But mony are the ups and downs in life,—
Aft the dice-box o' fate's jumbled a' tapsalteerie ;
Sae Kate fell heiress to a friend's hale estate,
And nae langer for lovers had she cause to weary.
The Squire cam' a-wooing o' Kate Dalrymple,
The priest scrapin', booin', fan' out Kate Dalrymple ;
And on ilk wooer's face was seen love's smiling dimple,
And noo she's nae mair Kate—but *Miss Dalrymple.*

Her auld cuttystool, that she used at her wheel,
Is flung-by for the saft gilded sofa sae gaudy ;
And noo she's array'd in her silks and brocade,
And can rank noo for ruffs and muffs wi' ony lady.
Still an unco fash to Kate Dalrymple,
Was dressing and party clash to Kate Dalrymple ;
She thocht a half-marrow, bred in line mair simple,
Wad be a far fitter match for Kate Dalrymple.

She aftentimes thocht, when she dwelt by hersel',
She could wed Willie Speedystool the sarkin weaver ;
And now to the wabster she the secret did tell,
And for love or for int'rest, Will did kindly receive her.
He flang by his heddles for Kate Dalrymple,
He burnt a' his treddles doun for Kate Dalrymple ;
Though his right e'e doth skellie, and his lang leg doth limp ill,
He's wedded to and bedded noo wi' Kate Dalrymple.

ALEXANDER MACLAGGAN.

A POET of vigour and fertility, ALEXANDER MACLAGGAN was born at Brigend, Perth, 3rd April, 1811. His father, originally a farmer, settled in Perth as a manufacturer. Unfortunate in business he eventually removed with his family to Edinburgh, where the future poet was in time apprenticed to the trade of a plumber. He began to write poetry when a mere boy, and evinced in addition a very fine talent for pencil-sketching, which acquirement, however, the arduous duties of his calling very much repressed. In connection with his trade he spent a brief period in London, and, returning to Scotland, wrought two years in Dunfermline as a foreman plumber, and finally removed to Edinburgh, devoting himself almost exclusively to literary pursuits.

MACLAGGAN published in the course of his life-time several volumes of poems and songs, which were well received publicly, attracting the favourable attention of Lord Jeffrey, the Duke of Argyll, Dr. Guthrie, Professor Wilson, and other distinguished men of letters. In 1856 he received a modest Civil List pension. He died in Edinburgh so recently as 1879.

His poetry, although not of the highest order, is distinguished by vigour, sense, manly sentiment, and melodious flow. He is never mawkish in tone, but energetically strikes a true and hearty note, which invariably succeeds in awakening a responsive echo in the reader's breast. For pawkie, and quietly-effective characteristic Scotch humour, not a few of his Doric effusions stand unrivalled.

AULD ROBIN THE LAIRD.

AULD Robin, the laird, thocht o' changin' his life,
But he didna weel ken whaur to wale a guid wife.
A plump quean had he who had serv'd him for years ;
"Ho, Tibby, come here," an' lo, Tibby appears.
"Sit doun," said the laird, "ye are wanted awee."
"Very weel, sir," quo' Tibby, "sae let it be."

"Noo, Tibby," quo' he, "there's a queer rumour rins,
Thro' the haill countryside, that there's naebody spins,
Bakes, washes, or brews, wi' sic talents as you—
An' what a' body says, ye ken, maun be true ;
Sae ye ought to be gratefu' for their courtesie."
"Very weel, sir," quo' Tibby, "sae let it be."

"Noo, it seemeth but just an' richt proper to me,
You should milk your ain cow 'neath your ain fig-tree ;
That a servant sae thrifty a guid wife will mak',
It's as clear as daylicht, sae a man ye maun tak',
Wha will haud ye as dear as the licht o' his e'e."
"Very weel, sir," quo' Tibby, "sae let it be."

"The pearl may be pure, Tib, though rough be the shell—
So I am determin'd tae wed ye mysel'—
An' a' that a lovin' an' leal heart can grant
O' this world's wealth, lass, troth, ye shall nae want ;
Sae a kiss to the bargain ye maun gi'e to me."
"Very weel, sir," quo' Tibby, "sae let it be."

The weddin'-day cam', wi' bridecake an' buns,
Finding Tib i' the kitchen 'mang tubs, pats, and pans.
"Bless me," quo' the laird, "what on earth hauds ye here ?
Our friends are a' met in their braw bridal gear ;
Ye maun busk in your best, and that richt speedily."
"Very weel, sir," quo' Tibby, "sae let it be."

When the blessing was said, an' the feastin' was dune,
Tib crapt to her bed i' the garret abune ;
When she heard the laird's fit an' "rap" at her door,
She wonder'd—he ne'er took sic freedom before.

"Come Tibby, my lass, ye maun listen to me."
"Very weel, sir," quo' Tibby, "sae let it be."

"Noo, Tibby, ye ken, we were wedded this nicht,
An' that *ye* should be here, haith, I think is no richt:
It canna be richt; for when women an' men
Are wedded, they ought to be bedded, ye ken.
Sae come doon the stair, Tib, an' e'en sleep wi' me."
"Very weel, sir," quo' Tibby, "sae let it be!"

——::——

THE THISTLE.

Hurrah for the thistle! the brave Scottish thistle,
The evergreen thistle of Scotland for me!
A fig for the flow'rs, in your lady-built bowers—
The strong-bearded, weel-guarded thistle for me!

'Tis the flow'r the proud eagle greets in its flight,
When he shadows the sun with the wings of his might;
'Tis the flow'r that laughs at the storm as it blows,
For the stronger the tempest, the greener it grows!
Hurrah for the thistle, etc.

Round the love-lighted hames o' our ain native land—
On the bonneted brow, on the hilt of the brand—
On the face o' the shield, 'mid the shouts o' the free,
May the thistle be seen where the thistle should be!
Hurrah for the thistle, etc.

Hale hearts we ha'e yet to bleed in its cause;
Bold harps we ha'e yet to sound its applause;
How, then, can it fade, when sic chiels an' sic cheer,
And sae mony braw sprouts o' the thistle are here?
Then hurrah for the thistle! the brave Scottish thistle,
The evergreen thistle of Scotland for me!
A fig for the flow'rs in your lady-built bow'rs—
The strong-bearded, weel-guarded thistle for me!

"DINNA YE HEAR IT?"

'Mid the thunder of battle, the groans of the dying,
The wail of weak women, the shouts of brave men,
A poor Highland maiden sat sobbing and sighing,
As she long'd for the peace of her dear native glen.
But there came a glad voice to the ear of her heart,
The foes of Auld Scotland for ever will fear it ;
"We are saved !—we are saved !" cried the brave Highland maid,
"'Tis the Highlanders' slogan ! O dinna ye hear it ?"
Dinna ye hear it ? dinna ye hear it ?
High o'er the battle's din, dinna ye hear it ?
High o'er the battle's din, hail it and cheer it !
"'Tis the Highlanders' slogan ! O dinna ye hear it ?"

A moment the tempest of battle was hush'd,
But no tidings of help did that moment reveal ;
Again to their shot-shatter'd ramparts they rush'd—
Again roar'd the cannon, again flash'd the steel !
Still the Highland maid cried, "Let us welcome the brave !
The death-mists are thick, but their claymores will clear it !
The war-pipes are pealing 'The Campbells are coming !'
They are charging and cheering ! O dinna ye hear it ?"
Dinna ye hear it ? dinna ye hear it ? etc.

Ye heroes of Lucknow, fame crowns you with glory ;
Love welcomes you home with glad songs in you praise ;
And brave Jessie Brown, with her soul-stirring story,
Forever will live in the Highlanders' lays.
Long life to our Queen, and the hearts who defend her !
Success to our flag ! and when danger is near it,
May our pipes be heard playing "The Campbells are coming !"
And an angel voice crying, "O dinna ye hear it ?"
Dinna ye hear it ? dinna ye hear it ?
High o'er the battle's din, dinna ye hear it ?
High o'er the battle's din, hail it and cheer it !
"'Tis the Highlanders' slogan ! O dinna ye hear it ?"

P. HATELY WADDELL, LL.D.

ADMIRED by many as one of the finest literary geniuses of the present century, the Rev. P. HATELY WADDELL, was born May 19th, 1816, at Balquhaston, parish of Slamannan, Stirlingshire—where his father, James Waddell, was the last of the original proprietors.

He was educated for the ministry, and manifesting superior genius, was early called to a Free Church pastorate; but repudiating the narrowing formalities of sectarianism as opposed to the broad charity of Christ, he resigned that charge while still a young man, and has since occupied, with conspicuous ability, independent pulpits, first in Girvan, and afterwards in Glasgow.

In 1859, he presided in the "Cottage" at the Centenary of Burns, and has since given to the world one of the best editions of Burns, with a spiritual biography of the poet. Among other works of a kindred nature, he has devoted a large and handsome volume to demonstrate the authenticity of Ossian by identifying the scenes of Ossianic poetry with localities still recognisable both in Scotland and Ireland. This most able and erudite work has lately attracted the notice of most distinguished critics on the Continent, and has been epitomised in an elaborate review by Professor Ebrard, of Erlangen, in the *Conservative Monatsschrift* for March and April of 1881.

In 1871 the learned Doctor issued his celebrated translation of THE PSALMS FRAE HEBREW INTIL SCOTTIS, a work of remarkable interest; which was followed, in 1879, by the publication of a like translation of ISAIAH. The latter translation is said to correspond very closely with the original

Hebrew, both in style and rhythm, and is uniform in size and appearance with the former publication. As regards the translation of the entire Bible into Scottish—the original intention of the author—the prosecution of that design will depend, we understand, very much on circumstances; but at present (1881) the work is progressing with the book of Genesis.

Apart from the practical value of these translations, there can be but one opinion as to the care, scholarship, and research bestowed on the task. They are works of undeniable ability, evincing on the part of the translator, the possession of fine genius, correct taste, and supreme literary knowledge and skill. The chapters are replete with passages of surpassing beauty and purity of diction and rhythm. Many of the verses fall into the most natural poetic form. Thus in the last two verses of the fifty-second chapter of *Isaiah*—quoted on a succeeding page—the lines make quite delicious rhyme and rhythm—

Awa, awa, clean but frae the town;
Mak' nor meddle wi' nought that's roun':
Awa frae her bosom; haud ye soun',
  Wi' the gear o' the LORD forenent ye!
For it's no wi' sic pingle, ye'se gang the gate;
Nor it's no wi' sic speed, ye maun spang the spate:
For the LORD he's afore ye, *ere an' late;*
  An' Israel's God he's ahint ye!

Whatever comparative neglect they may be fated to presently suffer, Dr. WADDELL's translations are undoubtedly works of distinct genius, the value of which the passage of centuries will ineffably enhance. It needs no stretch of fancy to conceive of a time when a copy of the original edition of *The Psalms Frae Hebrew intil Scottis*, will draw a price equivalent to that now obtained for a copy of the Kilmarnock edition of Burns.

THE FIFTY-SECOND CHAPTER OF ISAIAH.

WAUKEN, O wauken; on wi' yer might, O Zioun! Cleed yo wi' yer braws, Jerusalem, Halie town! for nae mair sal win hame till thee, the ill-snedden tyke an' the loon.

2 Shake yersel weel frae the asse; up till yer dais sae heigh, Jerusalem! aff wi' the branks frae yer hals, Dochtir o' Zioun in thirldom!
(3) For JEHOVAH himsel, quo' he: Ye war trokit awa' without fee; an' it's no wi' a siller.plea, ye'se come hame again.

4 For it's sae quo' JEHOVAH himsel: My folk intil Ægyp lan', langsyne they gaed down till bide, [an' war keepit thar:] an' sin-syne, the Assyrian *han'* on their *head's* been an unco guide, till thring them sair:

5 What mair can I thole syne, 's JEHOVAH'S word; that my folk suld be stown for nought? Wha ring owre hem, they mak them till dree, quo' the LORD; an' my name, ilka day gangs for ought! (6)
Syne sae sal my folk weel ken my name; *they sal ken* i' that day, 'am the same *God* ay: I speak for mysel, an' come hame.

7 How braw on the hills sae heigh himlane, 's the feet o' the rinner wi' news till tell! wi' news it's a' lown, wi' word it's weel; wi' a sugh o' salvation for *ilka chiel;* that cries till Zioun, That God o' yer ain, he's King himsel!

8 Yer out-leukers syne, they sal lowse their tongue; they sal lowse their tongue, an' sal lilt fu' fain: they sal glow'r thegither, een till een; whan the LORD sal fesh hame again Zioun!

9 Blythe and break-out, lilt a' like ane, ye bourocks sae swak o' Jerusalem: for the LORD he has hearten'd his folk fu' kin'; he has e'en bought back Jerusalem.

10 The LORD he rax'd yont his halie arm, in sight o' the natiouns mony, O; an' ilk neuk o' the yirth sal tak tent an' learn, the health o' our God sae bonie, O!

11 Awa, awa, clean but frae the town; mak nor meddle wi' nought that's roun': awa frae her bosom; haud ye soun', wi' the gear o' the LORD forenent yo!

12 For it's no wi' sic pingle, ye'se gang the gate; nor it's no wi' sic speed, ye maun spang the spate: for the LORD, he's afore yo, *ere an' late;* an' Israel's God, he's ahint yo!

THE TWENTY-THIRD PSALM.

The Lord *is* my herd, nae want sal fa' me :

2 He louts me to lie amang green howes ; he airts me atowre by the lown watirs :

3 He waukens my wa'-gaen saul ; he weises me roun, for his ain name's sake, intil right roddins.

4 Na ! tho' I gang thro' the dead-mirk-dail ; *e'en thar*, sal I dread nae skaithin : for yersel *are* nar-by me ; yer stok an' yer stay haud me baith fu' cheerie.

5 My buird ye hae hansell'd in face o' my faes ; ye hae drookit my heid wi' oyle ; my bicker is *fu' an'* skailin.

6 E'en sae sal gude guidin an' gude-gree gang wi' me, ilk day o' my livin ; an' ever syne i' the Lord's ain howff, *at lang last*, sal I mak bydan.

JAMES BALLANTINE.

One of the best known of modern Scottish minstrels, James Ballantine was born in the West Port of Edinburgh, 11th June, 1808. The death of the poet's father—who was a well-to-do brewer—caused an alteration of his prospects in life, and James was in consequence early apprenticed to the trade of a house painter. He afterwards turned his attention to the art of glass painting with the most gratifying success, becoming in time the head of the eminent firm to which was entrusted the execution of the stained glass windows for the Houses of Parliament.

Mr. Ballantine wrote early and well. His muse is remarkable for its humour, spontaniety, and graphic force. He was, in his day, the principal contributor to *Whistle Binkie.* He died in Edinburgh so recently as December 18, 1877. Many of his lyrics will live as long as the Doric is known and read.

CASTLES IN THE AIR.

THE bonnie, bonnie bairn, wha sits poking in the ase,
Glow'ring in the fire wi' his wee round face;
Laughing at the fuffin' lowe, what sees he there?
Ha, the young dreamer's bigging castles in the air.

His wee chubby face, and his touzie curly pow,
Are laughing and nodding to the dancing lowe;
He'll brown his rosy cheeks, and singe his sunny hair,
Glow'ring at the imps wi' their castles in the air.

He sees muckle castles tow'ring to the moon,
He sees wee sogers pu'ing them a' doon;
Worlds whomling up and doon, bleezing wi' a flare—
See how he loups, as they glimmer in the air.

For a' sae sage he looks, what can the laddie ken?
He's thinking upon naething, like mony mighty men;
A wee thing maks us think, a sma' thing maks us stare—
There are mair folk than him bigging castles in the air.

Sic a night in winter may weel mak him cauld,
His chin upon his buffy hand will soon mak him auld;
His brow is brent sae braid, O pray that daddy Care
Would let the bairn alane wi' his castles in the air.

He'll glow'r at the fire, and he'll keek at the licht,
But mony sparkling stars are swallowed up by nicht;
Aulder een than his are glamour'd by a glare,
Hearts are broken, heads are turn'd, wi' castles in the air.

—::—

CONFIDE YE AYE IN PROVIDENCE.

CONFIDE ye aye in Providence, for Providence is kind,
And bear ye a' life's changes wi' a calm and tranquil mind;
Tho' press'd and hemm'd on every side, hae faith, and ye'll win thro',
For ilka blade o' grass keps its ain drap o' dew.

Gin reft frae friends, or cross'd in love, as whyles nae doot ye've been,
Grief lies deep hidden in your heart, or tears flow frae your e'en,

Believe it for the best, and trow there's good in store for you,
For ilka blade o' grass keps its ain drap o' dew.

In lang lang days o' simmer, when the clear and cloudless sky
Refuses ae wee drap o' rain to nature—parch'd and dry,—
The genial nicht, wi' balmy breath, gars verdure spring anew,
And ilka blade o' grass keps its ain drap o' dew.

Sae, lest 'mid fortune's sunshine, we should feel owre proud and hie,
And in oor pride forget to wipe the tear frae poortith's e'e,
Some wee dark clouds o' sorrow come, we kenna whence or hoo,
But ilka blade o' grass keps its ain drap o' dew.

P. M'ARTHUR.

A MAN of excellent character and sense, as well as a genuine, though homely, Scottish poet, Mr. P. M'ARTHUR was born on the busy banks of the Levern in the year 1805; died October, 1881. The Levern is a small stream which flows past the Abbey Parish of Paisley, near to Barrhead. As early as his eighth year he was withdrawn from the village school, and sent into the printfield as a "tear-boy," or assistant to a calico printer, and after a few years spent in this species of drudgery, he was regularly apprenticed to the trade of calico printing. He had very nearly completed his term of servitude to this branch of the trade when his masters, interesting themselves in his welfare, and noticing his talents for sketching, warmly proposed that he should at once enter upon a new apprenticeship to the higher and more remunerative profession of pattern designing. As his inclinations from his earliest years had leaned in that direction, he very gladly accepted the proposal, and the business of a pattern designer continued his regular occupation through life. It is pleasant to be able to state that our author's character and proficiency in business were such as to speedily gain for him a leading place in his profession, and his services were latterly transferred to a firm in Glasgow, where he secured the management of an important department, which responsible post he continued to retain with acceptancy until the infirmities of approaching age induced him to relinquish it. To a distinct talent for poetry he superadded a very superior ability for painting, and, during life, his leisure hours had all along been with equal love fairly divided between the two beautiful sister arts. It is, however, only with the poetical side of his mind that we have in this notice immediately to do, and although we judge his poetical talents as having been only partially developed, his muse, especially in its Doric liltings, is fairly entitled to appreciative recognition. The characteristics of his verses may be briefly stated as geniality, quiet humour, and good sense. Melodious in numbers, he is never vapid nor commonplace in sentiment, but writes with invariable piquancy and force. His Pegasus is a steady-going animal, which trots out merrily, never floundering in low puddles, nor kicking at the traces in a hectic over-heat, but moving along the road of the homely journey at an easy, even pace. A number of his more ambitious pieces have been incorporated into Messrs. Blackie's editions of *Scottish Songs and Ballads*, and have also obtained place in the *Harp of Renfrewshire*. In 1880 he issued a selection of his practical pieces in a volume, under the modest title of *Amusements in Minstrelsy*. The volume is a most relishable addition to Doric minstrelsy. The local poem entitled the *Burgh Toon o' Rutherglen* is a most graphic, felicitous, and richly enjoyable sketch. And amongst many other fine Doric pieces, there is a poem descriptive of the courtship and domestic experience of a pair of douce Robins of the wood, which is touched off with the quietest, but the rarest humour.

——::——

THE BURGH TOON O' RUTHERGLEN.

HA'E ye been owre on Cathkin side,
  An' seen between you an' the Clyde,
Some auld thack houses scatter'd wide,
  Kenn'd by the name o' Rutherglen?
A big jail near the market-place,
A kirk to keep the folk in grace,
A steeple wi' an auld clock face
  To tell the hours in Rutherglen.
    The ancient toon o' Rutherglen,
    The burgh toon o' Rutherglen;
There's few that leeve and dinna ken
    Aboot the folks in Rutherglen.

I ha'e been there when simmer days
Look'd doon the loan wi' scorchin' gaze,
Broon tannin' wi' their burnin' rays
  The folks who leev'd in Rutherglen.
Scarce ocht was heard, scarce ocht was seen,
An' shuttle strokes were far between;
But come wi' me to yonder green—
  The bleaching-green o' Rutherglen;
    Folks min' their health in Rutherglen,
    Far mair that wealth in Rutherglen;
To fecht the cock, or draw the brock's
    The hardest wark in Rutherglen.

Look doon by softly-murmurin' Clyde—
Wha are they stretch'd alang it's side,
Or squatterin' in the cooling tide?—
  The sportive youths o' Rutherglen.
At ease alang the grassy banks
The collier chiels are laid in ranks,
While lassies braw, wi' shapely shanks,
  Spread oot the claes frae Rutherglen.

There's maidens braw in Rutherglen,
A' roon Stonelaw an' Rutherglen;
An' what's far mair, guid as they're fair,
Sae ken the lads o' Rutherglen.

I widna like to speak owre lood,
Nor ca' them over ill or good,
I'd like to say just what I should
About the folks in Rutherglen.
Variety's the charm o' life—
A time o' fun, a time o' strife;
Whiles ane wad think war to the knife
Wad be the end o' Rutherglen.
There's monthly fairs in Rutherglen,
To droon their cares in Rutherglen;
The guidwives bake the teugh soor-cake
At Draigle Dubbs* in Rutherglen.

They've had, nae doot, great men o' sense,
Baith Provost Steel and General Spence,
Wha neither spared their time nor pence
To benefit auld Rutherglen.
Let deeds the Provost's virtues tell,
Like patriarch guid, he dug a well;
But had it been a whisky stell
'Twad pleas'd them mair in Rutherglen.
'Twasna the stuff for Rutherglen,
Some thocht it "buff" in Rutherglen;
Cauld water swipes ne'er cur'd the gripes,
Nor cheer'd the folk in Rutherglen.

* On the evening of the last market-day of the year in Rutherglen—called Draigle Dubbs Fair—the old women, dressed for the occasion, used to assemble in a house appointed for the meeting, and arranged themselves in a wide circle round the hearth. They then proceeded to knead what was called "sour cakes," handing the dough from one to another, till it was made as thin as a wafer, when it was baked on a "girdle." The custom seems to have been handed down to the folks of Rutherglen by the Druids, but is of still greater antiquity, as in Old Testament times it was connected with the worship of Baal.

When dargs are dune an' dressin's wrocht,
There's some amusement maun be socht,
For youth's no gi'en to dolorous thocht,
Nor sentiment, in Rutherglen.
The quoits, the bullets, or the ba'
Gowf'd up against the gavel wa',
Or kick'd alang, wi' cloit an' fa',
An' rough-spun words in Rutherglen.
A "roset" cloot in Rutherglen,
Bound ticht aboot in Rutherglen
Their broken banes an' achin' sprains,
Hales a' their sairs in Rutherglen.

When winter bares the Hangingshaw,
An' smoors the burgh toon in snaw,
Gang to yon loch up by Stonelaw,
Ye'll fin' the men o' Rutherglen,
A' roarin' owre the rendin' ice,
Or dealin' oot the dram an' slice;
They tak' their fun—are they no wise?
The blythesome men o' Rutherglen.
Wi' meat and drink frae Rutherglen,
They cheer each rink frae Rutherglen,
Till the stanes roar owre the hog score—
An' croon the tee for Rutherglen.

Are ye a man for Parliament,
On civic honours firmly bent?
Then, if ye want your siller spent,
Gang owre to ancient Rutherglen.
Ye'll fin' your frien's in grave debate,
Discussin' plans for Kirk an' State,
Owre foamin' jug an' reekin' plate—
The patriots true o' Rutherglen.
They sell nae votes in Rutherglen,
They're true-blue Scots in Rutherglen,
Rare honest-hearted burgh men
Wha rule the roast in Rutherglen.

In better days langsince gane by,
On commons free they fed their kye ;
A' yon green bank whaur colliers lie
  Belang'd to ancient Rutherglen.
But Council dinners were sae dear—
For Bailies aye like savoury cheer—
This gather'd debt frae year to year,
  An' maistly ruin'd Rutherglen,
    But brak nae hearts in Rutherglen,
    Guid cream an' tarts in Rutherglen ;
For Sunday rig, cross owre the Brig,
    Ye Glasgow folk, to Rutherglen.

Before St. Mungo raised yon pile,
Wi' Gothic arch and dreary aisle,
An' ghaist-like pillars, file on file,
  The warl a' kenn'd o' Rutherglen.
Ere the grey smith o' Molindaur
Had blawn his fire, or forg'd a bar,
Owre Scotland's region broad an' far
  The fame was heard o' Rutherglen.
    There's room for pride in Rutherglen,
    'Mang a' that bide in Rutherglen ;
Your purse-proud bodies—Glasgow men—
    Maun doff their cowls in Rutherglen.

If daurin' deeds demand oor praise,
Back to the Covenantin' days,
They set the hale Clyde in a blaze
  By what was done in Rutherglen.
Before the jail, e'en at the Cross,
They burn'd the king's commands to dross,
Scatterin' the ashes like dry moss
  Alang the streets in Rutherglen.
    They laugh'd, ha, ha ! in Rutherglen,
    At king an' law in Rutherglen,
At vile Dalziel, at Lauderdale,
    An' Clavers too, in Rutherglen !

In Rutherglen King Ruther sway'd ;
There some say, Wallace was betray'd ;
Frae Langside battle Mary fled
  Up the Mill Wynd o' Rutherglen.
Guid nicht, auld freens, I'll quit my quill ;
If I've said wrang, I meant nae ill—
I ne'er let wit aboot the bill*
  That brak your jail in Rutherglen !
    Noo, whaur's the toon like Rutherglen ?
    Richts frae the Croon has Rutherglen,
In charters granted, nane kens when,
    By oor auld kings to Rutherglen.

——::——

THE TWA ROBINS.

Red Robin leev'd doon in yon green bosky glen,
Awa' frae the wand'rin's o' cruel-e'ed men ;
Though Robin to strangers seem'd distant an' douce;
He aft used to ca' for a pick at my hoose.
I fed him wi' crum's o' the finest o' breid—
In truth he got a' that a mortal could need—
An' yet he turn'd tir'd o' his bachelor life,
An' resolv'd frae the green woods to wale a young wife.

The spring time cam' roon' an' he cock'd up his crest,
He trimm'd his broon wing, an' he smooth'd his red breast,
Then socht the high bough o' the fresh buddin' thorn,
Beginnin' his sang wi' the dawnin' o' morn.

---

* The "bill," or bull, referred to in a poem, not being much of a Sabbatarian, after having forded the Clyde somewhere from the Glasgow Green to the banks on the Rutherglen side, was seized upon by the Rutherglen authorities, and lodged in jail for misdemeanour. The prison door being out of repair, the way was barricaded by an old harrow. The prisoner, not relishing his confinement, lifted the harrow on his horns, and proceeded with it down the street, to the amazement of the burghers, as a trophy of victory over Rutherglen Municipal law. We have been told that the mere mention of this ludicrous affair to any of the Ru'glen youths of former days was the cause of many a hard-fought "stane" battle.

I watch'd my freen Robin, I heard his love lay;
Then I saw hoppin' near by his side on the spray
A bird o' his kind, though mair russet in hue,
Wha seem'd to say—"Robin, I'm deein' for you."

Rob boo'd like a gallant; they flutter'd, caress'd;
Nae doot they got wed, for they built a fine nest
Underneath the burn brae, whaur brackens grow green,
An' fresh hazle boughs mak' a sweet summer screen.
They busk'd it wi' fog roots, they twin'd it wi' hair,
They lin'd it wi' down, an' wi' feathers sae rare—
'Twas a bonnie-built bower, just meet for a bride,
An' young Mrs. Robin she e'ed it wi' pride.

Noo, mornin' an' e'enin', Rob trill'd his love note,
His fond heart seem'd swellin' high up to his throat;
'Twas the mornin' o' love—his heart was in tune;
But pleasure aft flits wi' the sweet honeymoon.
Oh, fast flew the sweet days, the time ne'er seem'd lang,
Aye chirpin' their love tales the green boughs amang;
Belyve, as was needed, by turns they wad rest
On the wee freckl'd pearlens she brocht to the nest.

An' sune yae fine morn, as if dune by a spell,
Sax wee downie craturs crapt each frae their shell;
They streetch'd out their bare necks an' heids a' thegither—
'Twas noo Robin kenn'd the real joys o' a faither.
In chorus they cried—"Gie us meat, gie us meat;"
Frae mornin' till e'enin' 'twas naethin' but eat;
Then prood Mrs. Robin, their fond broodin' mither,
Seem'd losin' her notion for Rob a'thegither.

Rob saw there was naethin' for him noo but toil,
He rang'd the green glen, an' he brocht them the spoil;
They ne'er seem'd contented, but wrangl'd for mair;
Puir Robin aft starv'd that his family micht fare.
Still Robin was faithfu', and Robin was true,
He caught the fresh worms 'mid the morn's siller dew;
O' things that were dainty he brocht them a share.
Quoth he—"For your comfort what can I dae mair?"

Still thrivin' they feather'd, till hame grew owre wee ;
At length twa rash youths, while attemptin' to flee,
Fell owre the grey crag, and were droon'd in the burn—
Sad, sorrowfu' news for auld Robin's return.
In twa-three days langer the rest took the wing ;
But the gorbie fared warst—'twas a puir silly thing—
Caught up by a weasel, an' ruthlessly strangl'd,
His frien's scarcely kenn'd him, sae sair he was mangl'd.

Poor Robin droop'd doon on his breast his wee head,
While aff through the woodlands his fine family sped ;
Follow'd closely behin' by their fond fleechin' mither ;
Cried Rob—"She's awa', an' I'll ne'er woo anither ;
Hoo cauldrife she looks noo on me since the morn
When she proffer'd her love while I sang on the thorn ;
I ha'e toil'd for her welfare till careworn an' bald,
But comfortless noo I'm left oot in the cauld."

He e'ed the bit hame that in hope he had made,
Sae lane an' forsaken, sae towzl'd and braid,—
Like the hoose o' the thriftless wha leeve withoot care—
Quoth Robin—"I'll build for sic vagrants nae mair.
But, oh ! it is awfu' what faithers maun bear—
What changes I've kenn'd since the Spring o' the year !
They've a' come in turn—love, sorrow, an' strife,"
And his sad bosom heav'd, as he sigh'd,—"Such is life !"

Wi' sorrowfu' e'e he look'd in at my door,
But he wasna sae spree as I'd seen him before ;
His wings were sair draigl'd, and bald was his crest ;
The feathers were torn frae his ance rosy breast.
He seem'd like a mortal whose schemes had been wreck'd ;
Sair bow'd doon wi' labour and sadly hen-peck'd.
Oh, nae mair in autumn I'll hear his refrain ;
He flutter'd awa'—I ne'er saw him again.

WILLIAM CAMERON
KENNETH McLACHLAN
JOHN YOUNG
COLIN RAE BROWN
ROBERT GEMMELL
J P CRAWFORD

DR. ANDREW CRAWFURD.

Andrew Crawfurd (as he chose to spell his surname) was the second son of Andrew Crawford, portioner, and Jean Adam, a country heiress, and was born at Johnshill, Lochwinnoch, on 5th November, 1786. In early life he was employed as a mercantile clerk in Paisley, in compliance with his father's inclination to make him a manufacturer. But he was bookishly inclined, took lessons in Latin, and attended classes in the Glasgow College for eight years.

His university career was of more than ordinary promise, and he obtained many prizes and honours. Obtaining a diploma from the Faculty of Physicians and Surgeons of Glasgow in 1818, he practised medicine in Rothesay during the years 1818-19, but he was seized with typhus fever in December of the latter year, and lingered long between life and death. He recovered unexpectedly from this serious illness, but with the loss of speech, the amputation of one leg above the knee, and palsy of the right side of his body. He was brought home to his own house at Johnshill, and recovered his health to a wonderful and unexpected degree. His future life was that of an invalid, however, and all the years of it were spent at his writing-table and amongst his books. But he was by no means a dull or sullen recluse. He was fond of company, and was much sought after by friends and visitors. He never recovered his power of speech further than a few brief interjections. His handwriting in early life had been bold and beautiful, but his right arm was now palsified and powerless. With persevering resolution of heart, however, he taught himself to write with his left hand, and took pleasantly to literary, genealogical, and antiquarian pursuits. He encouraged his friends to visit and talk to him, and it was wonderful how easily and gracefully he managed to keep them going with an occasional laugh, shake of the head, "aye, no, ou-aye," etc. His part of the conversation was supplied by writing, when needful, and as he had always a gauger's ink-bottle and quill hung upon a coat-button, with writing-paper beside him, he was never at any loss for remark or answer.

He possessed great knowledge of the "auld Scottis tung," and used it freely in his writings, and made up an *Eik* to Jamieson's Scottish Dictionary, which is yet, unfortunately, only in manuscript. Two copies of it are in existence, the original in three large quarto volumes and a transcript in five thinner ones. He also made up what he loved to call a "Cairn of Lochwinyoch, Renfrewshire, and West of Scotland Matters," which extends to forty-six substantial quarto volumes—a monument of painstaking industry—and, in addition to the rare and curious matter contained therein, much of it being illustrative of the words in the *Eik*, the volumes themselves are interesting to look at, as being mainly or altogether stitched and bound by his own industrious left hand, aided by the very slight help which his right arm and hand were latterly trained to afford. These interesting remains are now in the possession of his appreciative nephew, A. C. Young, Esq., Dowanhill, Partick. He was also a preserver of newspaper-cuttings, and these amount to nearly thirty quarto volumes, and serve to some extent to illustrate words in the *Eik* and matters in the *Cairn*. His peaceful and pleasant life wore itself out in these useful occupations and in kindred recreations, and he died at Johnshill on 27th December, 1854, shortly after entering upon his sixty-ninth year.

During his collegiate course he contributed largely to

sundry publications. In 1813 he assisted his early schoolmaster, Mr. John Mackinlay (a Lochwinnoch man) in *The Scotchman*, published in Paisley. He was the chief writer in the *Attic Stories*, a fortnightly periodical published in Glasgow in the year 1817; and the *Greenock Visitor*, during the year 1818, was liberally aided by his pen. He gathered into a couple of volumes many floating ballads in aid of his friend Motherwell's *Minstrelsy* about 1827, and contributed to the same friend's *Paisley Magazine* in 1828. Mr. David Robertson, the Queen's bookseller in Glasgow, began his *Laird of Logan* about 1835, and had DR. CRAWFURD'S assistance in all the issues of it up till about 1841. *Whistle Binkie* and the *Nursery Songs*, particularly the Scotch words in the latter, were helped by the willing and ever-ready Johnshill pen. To numerous other local publications DR. CRAWFURD was an unwearied and successful contributor, and it would be difficult to find a parallel to such varied and seemingly exhaustless literary fertility.

We append a few specimens of his poetical productions with the orthography slightly modernised. His translation of the *27th Ode of Horace* is a most graphic piece of Doric verse, and the morsel entitled—*A Glance Ayont the Grave*, makes both beautiful and impressive reading.

——::——

HORACE, BEUK 1, ODE 27.

TO HIS CRONIES.

[A translation of one of the Odes of Horace into our ancient vernacular tongue. The national allusions are accommodated to our own age and country, and the author styles his version an imitation.]

WHAT gars ye yoke in drucken tuilzies ?
And ape camstairy Irish bruilzies ?
Scotch drink was made to mak' ye happy ;
But ye sook skaith e'en frae the nappie !

Fy, quat your splores! hoo daur ye thump
Young Bacchus, couthie, quate an' plump?
The rude sheleilah's no a sicht
For peacefu' punch and cawnle-licht!
Whist, billies; cease your angry yabble,
And doucely lean you o'er the table.

Noo wad ye gar me drink my skair?
For ae propyne I'se birl richt fair—
Come, tell me, lad, an' dinna swither,
An' prove yoursel' a true-blue brither,
Tell me the lass has stown your heart;
And show the mark o' Cupid's dart.
What, winna ye the lassie name?
Then, here's guid e'en, I'se haud me hame.
But yet ye needna be sae sweir;
You twa, I'm sure, are feir for feir.
For ne'er your joe, nor ae-fauld flame,
Brocht you yet either skaith or shame.
Come tell her name, and be na sweir,
You'll lippen to a faithfu' ear.

What, sae ye sae! can that be true?
Wanweirdy wicht, sair, sair, ye'll rue;
The brawest leddie in the land
Wad at your biddin' gie her hand.
But what a vile wanwordy wooin'!
Ye're lairin' in the blackest ruin.
Nae witch that wakes at deid o' nicht,
Nae warlock in his cantrip-slicht,
Nae Gude that leeves aboon the lift,
Can raise you frae this eerie tift!

Tho' ye should mount the muse's naig,
You, elf-shot to the benmost core!
Fame couldna harl you up the craig:
Nae pow'r frae folly can restore.

THE POWER O' CONSCIENCE.

AYE! we may busk wi' rosie wreath
 The bitter cup o' care;
An' we may gar the drink aneath
 To skinkle bricht an' fair.

An' we may busk the face wi' smiles
 To hide the woundit heart;
An' fleech on mirth wi' flatterin' wiles
 To pu' awa' the dart.

An' we may jilt the suithfast frien'
 That snibs us when we sin,
And ilka hour in daffin' spen'
 To droon the voice within.

But yet the flow'rs—wi a' their pride
 The drink they canna sweeten;
An' yet the smirks—they canna hide
 The heart wi' canker eaten.

And conscience, tho' we've held her lang
 Hush't in a doverin' sleep,
Will rise belyve, refresh'd an' strang,
 An' gar us ruefu' weep.

——::——

A GLANCE AYONT THE GRAVE.

MY boyhood was a pleasant dreim,
 And noo I wake to prove it sae;
My youdith bleez't wi' hope's fair gleim,
 My manheid keps the thud o' wae.

The sunnie knowes that ainco were dear,
 I taigle on, aye fain to view;
The spunk o' life that lowe't sae clear,
 Is crynit to an aizle noo.

Is life a dulesum glamour a'?
  The wearie wraith o' daffin' past?
And are we bound by feydoom's law
  To lair in mirk wanhope at last?

Na! oor fate speils the hin'most breth,
  And skinkles like the star o' even',
And lichts the eerie glen o' deth,
  An' airts us to our beild in Hevin'.

WILLIAM CAMERON.

A SUCCESSFUL song-writer, WILLIAM CAMERON, was born in the parish of Dunipace, Stirlingshire, December 3rd, 1801. His father was a mill-owner, and the future poet was educated with a view to the ministry. The death of his father in 1819, however, altered his prospects in life, and he accepted an appointment as schoolmaster at the village of Armadale, near Bathgate. In 1836 he removed to Glasgow, where he successfully conducted business for over a quarter of a century. In 1877 he contracted a cold, which eventuated in an acute inflammation of the lungs, of which he died after a few days' illness.

Mr. CAMERON was a man of superior presence, and his songs represent only one side of a highly-gifted mind. As the author of several still popular songs his name is likely to be remembered.

MEET ME ON THE GOWAN LEA.

MEET me on the gowan lea,
  Bonnie Mary, sweetest Mary:
Meet me on the gowan lea,
  My ain, my artless Mary.

Before the sun sinks in the west,
And nature a' has gane to rest,
Then to my fond, my faithfu' breast,
Oh let me clasp my Mary.

The gladsome lark o'er moor and fell,
The lintie in the bosky dell,
Nae blyther than your bonnie sel',
My ain, my artless Mary.

We'll join our love-notes to the breeze,
That sighs in whispers through the trees,
And a' that twa fond hearts can please,
Will be our sang, dear Mary.

There ye shall sing the sun to rest,
While to my faithfu' bosom prest;
Then wha sae happy, wha sae blest,
As me and my dear Mary!

——::——

MORAG'S FAIRY GLEN.

Ye ken whaur yon wee burnie, love,
Rins roarin' to the sea,
And tumbles o'er its rocky bed,
Like spirit wild and free.
The mellow mavis tunes his lay,
The blackbird swells his note,
And little robin sweetly sings
Within the woody grot.
Then meet me love, by a' unseen,
Beside you mossy den;
Oh, meet me love, at dewy eve,
In Morag's Fairy Glen.

Come when the sun, in robes of gold,
Sinks o'er yon hills to rest,
And fragrance floating in the breeze
Comes frae the dewy west;

And I will pu' a garland gay,
  To deck thy brow sae fair;
For many a woodbine cover'd glade,
  And sweet wild flow'r is there.

There's music in the wild cascade,
  There's love among the trees;
There's beauty in ilk bank and brae,
  An' balm upon the breeze.
There's a' of nature and of art,
  That maistly weel could be;
An' O, my love, when thou art there,
  There's bliss in store for me.

——::——

BOTHWELL CASTLE.

By Bothwell Castle's ruin'd towers,
And lonely 'mang yon woody bow'rs,
There Clutha fondly winds around,
As loath to leave the hallow'd ground.

But where are now the martial throng?
The festive board, the midnight song?
The ivy binds the mould'ring walls,
And ruin reigns in Bothwell halls.

O deep and long have slumber'd now,
The cares that knit the soldier's brow;
The lover's grace, the manly pow'r,
In gilded hall, and lady's bow'r;

The smiles that fell from Beauty's eye,
The broken heart, the bitter sigh;
And deadly feuds have pass'd away:
Still, thou art noble in decay.

KENNETH M'LACHLAN.

A POET of acknowledged ability, KENNETH M'LACHLAN was born 5th May, 1815, and is descended from an ancient family, who were landed proprietors in Argyllshire, and were related to the M'Lachlans of Strathlachlan and Kilbride, the last possessor of the family estate having been ruined by his active participation in the romantic and tragic rebellion of '45. The poet's father, who was a shoemaker to trade, joined the 79th Highlanders, on the invitation of Sir Allan Cameron, who knew the history of the family, and was soon promoted to the rank of Colour-Sergeant and Master Shoemaker to the regiment.

Although born in the regiment, Mr. M'LACHLAN considers St. Mungo as his native city, his mother—who was a native of Glasgow—having returned home from abroad and settled in that city when he was only five months old. Completing an ordinary school education, he was afterwards bound apprentice to the block-printing trade with John M'Donald & Sons, Wellpark Print Works, Duke Street. The commercial crisis of 1842 occurring, he left Glasgow, and sought employment in London. Returning to Scotland, he settled for some time in Cathcart, where he got married, and where he continued to follow his trade until a second serious depression—occurring in 1854—compelled him to accept a situation in the Greenock Harbour Police Force, kindly offered him by the late Superintendent Mann.

For the past twenty years, Mr. M'LACHLAN has been a contributor to the poetical columns of the local press, and the encouragement he has all along received has been such, that he issued in rapid succession—*Progress of the Sciences; Hope's Happy Home; Scenes of the City by Night;* and his latest, and perhaps best work, the *Beauties of Scotland*, a lengthy poem of eloquent description, and flowing verse, replete with passages of heart-stirring patriotism, verbal splendour, and scenic beauty.

At the present time, Mr. M'LACHLAN is retired from active life, and owns a drapery establishment in the busy town of Greenock. Possessed of a fertile and flowing pen, Mr. M'LACHLAN has, in his time, contributed with acceptance to numerous journals and periodicals. He still occasionally engages in a "tussle" with the Muse, and has quite recently contributed several most interesting and able poems to the *People's Friend*, and to the local journals.

——::——

ON THE DEATH OF LONGFELLOW

THE AMERICAN POET.

THY end hath come! An end will come to all;
As dies each day, declining from the noon;
Here still a breathing world will wait the call
That each in turn must answer, late or soon.
Yet Earth will be re-peopled o'er and o'er
Ere one enrich in wealth of song that store
Bequeath'd by thee, sweet singer of the dulcet tune!

Hid not in clouds of dark bewildering haze—
Which oft conceal the poverty of thought,
While pomp of diction dazzles with the blaze,
And fire of wordy passion, roused and wrought
By furious affectation to appear
All glowing love, enduring and sincere—
Thine is affection deep and pure, without a blot.

Pure as the crystal bells upon the stream,
That sings for ever pure, hath been thy lays;

Gentle and sweet and loving is thy theme,
  And strains of music swelling to thy praise.
    Onward and upward, as the years grow old
    And change, yet still thy melodies will hold
The soul of fancy captive to thy winning ways.

The gems of wisdom fill thy *Psalm of Life*,
  Footsteps of angels *Voices of the Night;*
With toil the *Blacksmith* holds a willing strife;
  Evangeline hath charms of dear delight;
    The love of *Standish* given to his friend;
    And *Hiawatha's* legends wild, that end
When soars his warrior spirit to the Land of Light.

Sublimity and beauty fill the strains
  That best adorn the born-poet's muse;
The treasures of his wisdom are the gains
  We cherish by his teaching, that imbues
    The soul with moral virtue, or the mirth
    That ne'er contaminates, and brings to birth
The laughter of the gay—yet can the grave amuse.

Too full of true sincerity of soul,
  The world's frivolities were not for thee;
A flow of feeling, swelling to a whole,
  Tuned all thy numbers like a rippling sea
    That sings to heaven, as the boundless main
    Reverberates and re-echoes back again
The song that's never mute, and evermore shall be.

——::——

RAB M'LINTOCK'S PENNY WEDDIN'.

Ance on a time twa handsome youths,
  As simple as their hearts were lovin',
Wha thought the world a' guileless truths—
  A notion that would need some provin',—
Had made a vow to live as ane,
  But had nae plenishin' nor beddin',
And thought through Providence to gain
  Some down-sit by a Penny Weddin'.

At Martinmas it was to be,
  When country folk were routh o' siller,
And ploughmen chiel's had got their fee,
  Sae settled Rab, and named it till her.
Soon wi' the news the parish rang,
  Soon frien's and freme-folk got a bidden,
An' boon a' that was said or sang,
  Cam' Rab M'Lintock's Penny Weddin'.

The help o' fiddler Joe was got,
  Wi' poacher Pate, and Will the cadger,
And piper-major Johnie Groat,
  A pension'd Peninsula sodger;
And bellman Sandy, wi' the wife,
  And jolly Jim the auld gravedigger,
A' wags and wits o' country life,
  To mak' the fun and party bigger.

The great important day cam' roun',
  An' a' was bustle in the clachan:
Douce wives, wi' ilka haveral loon,
  Had their comments and roars o' lauchin.
The gallant piper led the van,
  On to the manse they cheer'd and tarried,
Till he wha could at length began,
  And join'd the couple—duly married.

Some had gi'en presents to the bride,
  And a' had paid their score o' siller,
Wi' ilka eatable beside,
  For weeks they had been bringin' till her.
At last the barn was seated fine,
  A' tables cled wi' every denty,
Then herds and cotters sat to dine
  On sonsie pies and haggis plenty.

The supper past, the floor was clear'd,
  And yill gaed roun' in jugs and bickers;
The bottl'd spirits cam' and cheer'd
  Their hearts wi' ilka kind o' liquors.

And o'er the snuff-mull cam' the crack
  On heavy craps and gaucy cattle ;
Auld folk, reflectin', lookit back
  On marriage joys and life's lang battle.

Pate roar'd the "Lass o' Ballochmyle,"
  Kate skirl'd the "Lads o' Gala Water,"
'Tween tragic scowl and idiot smile,
  The Bellman raved wi' stamp and clatter.
Syne Jim wi' "Wat and Meg" was thrang,
  But finished aff wi' "Nocht like Leather ;"
The "Cock's Craw" mixed wi' Geordie's sang
  O' "O'er the Moor amang the Heather."

The elder folk had toddled hame,
  The youngsters waited for the dancin' ;
A' join'd the reel wha werena lame,
  And hooch'd ! wi' antic steps, and prancin'.
Thus fled the nicht wi' toasts and sangs,
  And a' held on while they were able,
Till stools and seats together bangs
  As Pate falls flounderin' o'er the table.

Wi' "Babbity Bowster" cam' the end,
  Jean kiss'd her Jo, and Jock his Jenny,
Wi' after splores that werena kenn'd,
  That left them maist withoot a penny.
Syne beddin' time cam' on, and then
  The bride and bridegroom threw their stockin',
And they were caught by squintin' Jen
  And stutterin' Tam, 'mang gibes and jokin'.

Far on the road puir Jamie Bain,
  Wi' kindly heart as saft as butter,
Lay wi' his head upon a stane,
  His sturdy legs alang the gutter.
A' raise frae rest wi' rentin' heids,
  When conscience gie'd ilk ane their sentence ;
Pain is the price o' naughty deeds,
  And after folly comes repentance.

Meg wasna feckless, Rab was douce,
  Debauch had set their minds a-thinkin' ;
They mourn'd the wreck about their house,
  And vowed ne'er to indulge in drinkin'.
They lectures got frae feetless chairs,
  And sermons had frae broken dishes ;
For witless joys bring after cares,
  Sic pranks will ne'er content our wishes.

They plann'd together, toil'd and spared,
  And baith grew thrifty, leal, and willin' ;
But how he raise to be a laird
  Would take me here o'er lang the tellin'.
She's settled noo as grand-mamma,
  'Mang weel-clad bairns, brisk and healthy,
The blithe, respected pride o' a',
  And ranks hersel' amang the wealthy.

—::—

EXTRACT FROM "BEAUTIES OF SCOTLAND."

(Martyrdom of Sir William Wallace.)

Great-hearted Wallace, still unmov'd, unbent,
  Thy Country's love ! the passion of thy heart
  Stood firm, devoted, never to depart.
Thou wert a gift from the Eternal sent ;
  And as thy strength of arm, thy strength of will,
Unselfish, firm, in loyalty the same ;
  Thy life wed to thy cause, unshaken still ;
And thy great mind soar'd to a lofty aim,
Inspired to deeds eternal as thy fame !

Thou midst the faithless faithful stood alone,
  Whose spirit power could neither crush nor bind,
  No royal Prince by birth, but Prince in mind—
True when the noble, but the false, had gone

To sell the nation's birthright for a mess !
Like the apostates, Angus and Dunbar,
Whose high birth-boast but made their minds the less,
Whilst thine, still fixed as yonder polar star,
Shone through the storm, and dared the rage of war.

Thy country fell ; thou, her defender, came
And to oppression proud defiance hurl'd ;
Where Honour lauds thy daring through the world
It blasts aloud a tyrant's deed of shame !
That deed a thousand tongues could ne'er efface
With all that subtile sophistry could dole—
Still stands the inky, bloated, base disgrace ;
Black in that page of crime reveals the whole,
They mangled thee, but could not smite thy soul !

And treachery gain'd what power had ne'er subdued,
But meanly purchased by the price of blood ;—
The Judas-crime of old Robroyston Wood,
Sacred to shame, is with thy blood imbrued.
They sneer'd, and crown'd thee with a laurel crown,
But in their mocking blindness could not see
That they had crown'd with laurels thy renown.
Honour'd art thou, and all that fell with thee,
Thou patriot martyr ! monarch of the free !

——::——

OUR AIN BONNIE ISLE!

Gae, gather your laurels, your sons o' my hame,
And rise like our eagles on pinions o' fame ;
Your sinews are braced by the gales that blaw forth
Frae the rich caves o' Boreas 'neath snaws o' the north ;
Where Scotia fosters, o'er mountain and glen,
Her fresh rosy lasses and braw sturdy men ;
Surely Venus arose frae our waves, for her smile
Is bequeath'd to the maids o' our ain bonnie isle !

With a spirit in battle you stand till you "dee,"
And the same spirit bids you be noble and free ;

For your ain Scotland's credit, integrity brings
The honesty deep frae your heart's purer springs.
When you meet frae your hames in ocht climes 'tween the poles,
Nae cauld selfish swither the passions controls;
Wi' the wring o' the hand come the tear-showers the while
Frae the leal warm hearts o' our ain bonnie isle!

Though the climes o' the sun ha'e their flow'rets o' bloom,
The warm balmy breezes are sick wi' perfume;
The snake's in the grove, and the birds canna sing
Like the warblers that waken our valleys o' spring;
And the fame o' their plumage, that echoes sae loud,
But charms like the gay fading scene in the cloud;
And the voice o' the patriot stands up for the soil
O' grandeur and glory, our ain bonnie isle!

——::——

ROBERT LEIGHTON.

A POET of wide and excellent reputation, ROBERT LEIGHTON, was born in the "Narrow o' the Murraygate," Dundee, 20th February, 1822. He lost his parents while a boy, and found a home with an elder brother in Dundee. He received a fair amount of elementary instruction at school, but the best part of his education was self-acquired.

While still a youth he had discovered a facility for rhyming, which he sedulously cultivated in leisure hours. The study of poetry was a perennial delight to him, as the songs of his native land had been familiarised to his ears from infancy by the well-remembered accents of his mother's voice, whose kind, cheerful temperament, furnished him with an education of love.

The story of ROBERT LEIGHTON's life, if closely followed from this point, would not conduct us along flowery paths of poetic and contemplative indulgence. He early followed mercantile pursuits, and business was the exclusive occupation of his days,—excursions into the fields of nature and poesy their enjoyment and recreation.

In the autumn of 1850 he found a new meaning in life through his marriage with Elizabeth Jane Campbell, of Liverpool. Many years afterwards he thus reveals the trust and happiness of his wedded life—

> "I love our chapel for its beauty's sake,
> And for a promise on its altar laid;
> A promise that I did not need to make,
> And would not wish unmade."

In 1854 he accepted a responsible position in Ayr, as manager of the branch of a Liverpool firm, and while there, attended the Burns Centenary meeting, held within the "Cottage," and presided over by the Rev. Dr. P. Hately Waddell. This eloquent divine delivered on that occasion a glowing eulogy on Burns, and the next best event of the evening was the reading of an original poem by LEIGHTON on the inspired ploughman, under whose touch the trodden "daisy"

> "Blossom'd an immortal flow'r."

About 1860 his employers desired that his services should be transferred to the Liverpool house, and after a brief pleasure trip to America, he resumed his connection with the said employers, travelling during a large portion of each year in England, Scotland, and Ireland.

It was in the course of one of these journeys in 1867, that during a rough drive, he ruptured a blood-vessel, which brought on almost the only illness he had ever experienced, and which, after prolonged suffering, terminated fatally on the 10th May, 1869.

That LEIGHTON was a true poet, of high and pure aim,

none who have carefully read his *Records*, or his equally fine and thoughtful *Musings*, will for a moment dispute. Yet he is least known by his highest poetic works. He united to high thought and flowing English diction, a graphic realism of Scottish humour and dialect, the happy use of which brought him such an immediate popularity in life as his more elaborate efforts could scarcely be expected to command.

Personally, LEIGHTON was a man of cheerful temperament and genial parts, widely respected for his probity and honour, and beloved by all who were privileged to know him and to enjoy his friendship. He is survived by his widow—an excellent lady, who was devoted to him—and by a family of sons and daughters, all of whom are showing talent and character, worthy of the fame and good name of their late lamented father, and one of whom—Miss Alexis Leighton—recently made her debüt as a leading actress on the Liverpool stage.

JOHN AND TIBBIE'S DISPUTE.

JOHN DAVIDSON and Tibbie, his wife,
Sat toastin' their taes ae nicht,
When something startit on the fluir,
And blinkit by their sicht.

"Guidwife," quoth John, "did ye see that moose?
Whar sorra was the cat?"
"A moose?"—"Ay, a moose."—"Na, na, Guidman—
It wasna a moose, 'twas a rat."

"Ow, ow, Guidwife, to think ye've been
Sae lang aboot the hoose,
An' no to ken a moose frae a rat!
Yon wasna a rat! 'twas a moose."

"I've seen mair mice than you, Guidman—
  An' what think ye o' that!
Sae haud yer tongue an' sae nae mair—
  I tell ye, it was a rat."

"*Me* haud my tongue for *you*, Guidwife!
  I'll be maister o' this hoose—
I saw't as plain as een could see't,
  An' I tell ye, it was a moose!"

"If you're the maister o' the hoose,
  It's I'm the mistress o't;
An' *I* ken best what's in the hoose—
  "Sae I tell ye, it was a rat."

"Weel, weel, Guidwife, gae mak' the brose,
  An' ca' it what you please."
So up she rose, and made the brose,
  While John sat toastin' his taes.

They supit, and supit, and supit the brose,
  And aye their lips play'd smack;
They supit, and supit, and supit the brose,
  Till their lugs began to crack.

"Sic fules we were to fa' oot, Guidwife,
  Aboot a moose."—"A what!
It's a lee ye tell, an' I say again
  It wasna a moose, 'twas a rat!"

"Wad ye ca' me a leear to my very face?
  My faith, but ye craw croose!
I tell ye, Tib, I ne'er will bear't—
  'Twas a moose!"—"'Twas a rat!"—"'Twas a moose!"

Wi' her spoon she strack him owre the pow—
  "Ye dour auld doit, tak' that—
Gae to your bed ye canker'd sumph—
  'Twas a rat!"—"'Twas a moose!"—"'Twas a rat!"

She sent the brose caup at his heels,
  As he hirpled ben the hoose;
Yet he shoved oot his head as he steekit the door,
  And cried, "'Twas a moose! 'twas a moose!"

But, when the carle was fast asleep,
She paid him back for that,
And roar'd into his sleepin' lug,
"'Twas a rat! 'twas a rat! 'twas a rat!"

The de'il be wi' me if I think
It was a beast ava!—
Neist mornin', as she sweepit the fluir,
She faund wee Johnny's ba'!

JOHN YOUNG.

An energetic and successful cultivator of the Scottish muse, John Young, was born in "The Blue Raw," Milton of Campsie, Stirlingshire, on 17th November, 1825. His parents belonged to the agricultural class. In the hope of improving their position the family removed into the north-west quarter of Glasgow, the father beginning there the business of a cowfeeder in a small way, to which he subsequently added that of a contractor, or carter. Until overtaken by an accidental burning which disabled him ever afterwards from active work, our poet's chief occupation in life was that of a working carter. In his twenty-third year he got married, an event which he still regards as one of the wisest acts of his life. The domestic pleasure of "wife an' weans," however, he was fated only too shortly to enjoy. Domestic bereavements occurred in the death of a child and in the loss of a deeply-beloved mother, and hard upon these afflictions succeeded the accidental burning to which allusion has already been made. With a permanently maimed hand, and the almost total obliteration of his eyesight, the Poor's-house was the only alternative, and to that shelter of friendless want JOHN YOUNG had eventually to go, exchanging for its charitable cover his own little home, with all its fond and endearing, though humble, connections and heart-inspiring cheer. His life subsequently shows a power of will rightly directed, and a devotion to such opportunities of self-improvement as lay in his way, which his earlier life seems in no way to have forecasted.

A Poor-house poet was certainly something of a novelty. It was Orpheus conjuring the lyre with a Parochial suit on. JOHN's excellent book of verse—*Lays from the Poorhouse*—was accordingly largely and liberally subscribed for. On its publication, in 1859, the author was enabled to bid a final farewell to the walls which for six dreary years had afforded him a lonely shelter. The little book was very favourably received, and was so well bought up that the author was enabled to see, through the warm patronage bestowed on him, a solace and support for the remainder of his life in the honest prosecution of his art. He has since then issued several interesting volumes of verse.

Mr. YOUNG has an intelligent and well-informed mind, and writes with invariable accuracy and force. To say that his books are merely interesting would be to understate their poetical value. His verses are as full of merit, of a kind, and as worthy of recognition as those of any of our local singers. There is about his poems a geniality of phraseology and sentiment, a flavoursome mither wit and humour, and an inspiriting, masculine ring, which the dullest reader can scarcely miss, and the tone throughout is morally excellent. A fresh edition of his first book of verse—*Lays from the Poorhouse*—was issued in 1881, and may be had of the author, 3 Swan Street, Port-Dundas, Glasgow.

TOOTHACHE.

"Gie a' the faes o' Scotland's weal
A towmond's toothache."—*Burns.*

My sympathy wi' Robin gangs,
In yon well-worded spring,
'Bout cruel toothache's maddenin' stangs,
That gar'd him loup and fling.
An' wad ane ask me, how it comes
That I wi' Rab condole?
I hae twa auld stumps i' my gums,
Hard, hard eneuch to thole.

I've tried cre'sote, an' oil o' cloves,
I've stuff'd them fu' o' pepper,
Till they are burnt as broun's pan loaves,
But ne'er a hue they're better,
Till e'en the scruif-skin o' my moo
Hangs like an empty blether,
An' my puir lips are hard, I troo,
As ony weel-tann'd leather.

I've smok'd tobacco till I'm sick,
But a' to nae avail,
Close to the ribs I've held my cheek,
But that an' a' does fail.
I've tried the pow'r that's opium's,
I've cramm'd them wi' dry catten,
But o' the dardum i' my gums
It seems there's nae extrackin.

I've bor'd them wi' a wire red het,
Till I the thing hae thraw'd,
In short, a' plans I've tried, and yet
The vile stumps keep their haud.
An' waur than a', they're sae worn doun,
Till maistly oot o' sicht,
That no a dentist i' the toun
Could bring them to the licht.

They min' ane o' some cherish'd sins
  Caught in youth's giddy whirl,
He thinks them dead until he fin's
  Them gie anither dirl.
An' 'tweel I wat, few are exempt
  At times frae stings o' conscience,
That some part o' their life's been spent
  At best in hunting nonsense.

But here we ae advantage draw
  In getting a' things richted,
An' surely when the fee's sae sma',
  We wad do wrang to slicht it.
Ay, tho' the means whiles fail to cure
  Infected teeth o' smart aches,
We hae a panacea sure
  For curing sairest heartaches.

——::——

MY BIG JOCK.

I WONDER whaur the poets get sic wheens o' clever weans,
Whom they parraud and sprowse aboot in mony rousin' strains,
For waes my heart, I've yin at hame, the auldest o' my flock,
An' sic a sumph there never leev't as my big Jock!

He'd hardly skirl't into life—an' heth, he rowted weel—
Till Grannie Gossip pledg'd her aith he'd be a clever chiel;
A gown an' ban's, or lawyer's wig, fresh frae the barber's block,
He'd surely wear; but wae-sucks me, for my big Jock!

He's been at twenty schules, I'm sure, an' cost nae little cash,
For aye I hoped he yet micht win some laurels for the fash;
But a' his teachers are agree't they'll never maun to knock
Book-lear into the timmer heid o' my big Jock!

Some mithers brag o' cleanly bairns, but this is no my case,
Frae schule Jock's aft been lickit hame to wash his dirty face;

A feckless, lazy loon he is, wi' heid o' whinstane rock—
O' for some poother in the pow o' my big Jock !

An' yet, the laddie's ne'er been kenn'd for ony wicked ways ;
I never heard him tellin' whids, or swearin', a' his days ;
An easy-osy thieveless cuif, as soul-less as a rock—
O' for a twalmonth's sodgerin' for my big Jock !

Some think him silly, yet he kens hoo mony beaus mak' five,
An' freenly folks a few will hae't that he'll improve belyve,
An' aiblins tempt some thro-gaun lass to share the marriage yoke—
Ma wordie ! but she'll hae a prize in my big Jock.

Meanwhile, frae Linkumdoddie toon, on Tweeda's norlan' side,
To whaur the groozie Kelvin crawls into the savonry Clyde,
There's no a mither in the lan', I carena what's her flock,
Can turn me oot a bigger sumph than my big Jock !

JAMES P. CRAWFORD.

As the author of *The Drunkard's Raggit Wean*, JAMES P. CRAWFORD achieved a certain popularity a quarter of a century ago. That touching little lyric, simple in its pathos, and unassuming in its style, at once caught the popular heart, and was sung everywhere with acceptancy and universal favour. Mr. CRAWFORD was born in the beautiful village of Catrine, at the foot of the song-celebrated "Braes o' Ballochmyle," on the 14th of June, 1825. In 1840, and while still a mere boy, he removed to Glasgow, for the purpose of acquiring a better knowledge of the trade of a tailor, as followed by his father, and to which he was thus early apprenticed. Actively following up the trade of tailoring, he early established himself in business in Glasgow, and retained his connection therewith for over a quarter of a century. He has recently been appointed to a Registrarship in connection with the Govan Parochial Board, of which Board he was elected a member as early as 1856, and continues till now to take a deep interest in the administration of the Local Poor Law.

As a temperance song-writer of more than average merit and success, he has, in a certain measure, identified himself with the Teetotal Party. His first temperance effusion—*Bright Water for Me!* was a very promising forecast of his ability to shine in that special sphere. His second effort—*The Drunkard's Raggit Wean*, was a most successful song, as the reader must know, and immediately gained for the author popularity and name. The song is not a great poetical effort by any means, but it secured a favour with the public, which more elaborate works of art seldom achieve. It is curious to know that the song was composed inside a city U.P. Church one Sunday afternoon, in the September of 1855. It was certainly a daring act of the poet—this sacrifice of a Sunday sermon at the shrine of Poesy; but the words of the sermon very probably fell still-born from the pulpit, while the song, winged with music, has, for a quarter of a century, inculcated lessons of morality in thousands of human hearts, in view of which, the Recording Angel very probably has long since cancelled the poet's neglect of the parson's sermon, by a conclusive *per contra* of —*Fully Paid!*

Mr. CRAWFORD's muse—which represents only one side of a versatile mind—is energetic and melodious in its flow. He is hopeful of the future of the race, deprecates social rivalries, and emulates the approach of the time—

"When Wealth shall wear, like jewel'ry, the blessings of the poor."

He has, in addition, a superior lyrical faculty, and has had many of his beautiful songs wedded to appropriate music.

THE DRUNKARD'S RAGGIT WEAN.

A WEE bit raggit laddie gangs wan'rin through the street,
Wadin' 'mang the snaw wi' his wee hackit feet,
Shiverin' i' the cauld blast, greetin' wi' the pain;
Wha's the puir wee callan? he's a drunkard's raggit wean.

He stans at ilka door, an' he keeks wi' wistful' e'e,
To see the crowd aroun' the fire a' laughin' loud wi' glee,
But he daurna venture ben, though his heart be e'er sae fain,
For he maunna play wi' ither bairns, the drunkard's raggit wean.

Oh, see the wee bit bairnie, his heart is unco fou,
The sleet is blawin' cauld, and he's droukit through and through,
He's speerin' for his mither, an' he wun'ers whaur she's gane,
But oh! his mither she forgets her puir wee raggit wean.

He kens nae faither's love, an' he kens nae mither's care,
To soothe his wee bit sorrows, or kame his tautit hair,
To kiss him when he waukens, or smooth his bed at e'en,
An' oh! he fears his faither's face, the drunkard's raggit wean.

Oh pity the wee laddie, sae guileless an' sae young,
The oath that lea's the faither's lip 'll settle on his tongue;
An' sinfu' words his mither speaks his infant lips 'll stain,
For oh! there's nane to guide the bairn, the drunkard's raggit wean.

Then surely we micht try an' turn that sinfu' mither's heart,
An' try to get his faither to act a faither's part,
An' mak them lea' the drunkard's cup, an' never taste again,
An' cherish wi' a parent's care, their puir wee raggit wean.

——::——

BRIGHT WATER FOR ME!

O! COME, come with me to the stream in the glade—
The mossbank our rest, and the birch tree our shade;
With the echo we'll laugh—with the birds we will sing,
And dance 'mong the flow'rs round the murm'ring spring.
There's health at the fountain, and down to its brink
Come the birds of the forest to bathe and to drink,

And the song of the woodland it seemeth to be,
Bright water, cool water, pure water for me!
  Then come, come away to the stream in the glade;
  The mossbank our rest, and the birch tree our shade;
  And you'll dance in the wood 'mong the wild flow'rs with me,
    And our drink the cool water, pure water shall be.

In the dance of the gay, 'neath the bright gasalier,
Where circles the wine cup, I know there is cheer,
And I know that the wine and the brandy they sip
Give light to the eye, and a smile to the lip;
But the light of the eye, it must ne'er be forgot,
May turn to the dull, glassy glare of the sot;
And the wine-waken'd smile biddeth virtue to flee—
Oh, there's nothing like water, pure water for me!

There is joy in the wine, but I tremble to know,
More dreadful than war, 'tis humanity's foe;
Of the loved and the lovely it giveth to death
More victims by far than the pestilence breath.
Then throw down the goblet—then dash down the cup;
Though proffer'd by friendship, O! take it not up—
Turn away from the welcome that gives it to thee:
For there's nothing like water, pure water can be.
  Then come, come away to the stream in the glade,
  The mossbank our rest, and the birch tree our shade;
  And you'll dance in the wood 'mong the wild flowers with me,
    And our drink the cool water, pure water shall be.

——::——

I WEAR A JEWEL.

I WEAR a jewel near my heart, for gold I wadna sell ye,
A peerless gem—a lassie's love—it's worth I couldna tell ye.
Her beamin' e'e is heaven to me, her cherry mou', the pree o't—
In ae sweet kiss there's mair o' bliss than a' that gold could gie o't.

The envious stan' an' lift their han', an' glow'r that I should own it;
An' cantrip carls sairly blame an' swear that I hae stown it.
The gossips mak' an unco crack, but we can lo'e in spite o't,
An' if they lea' her love to me I'll tak' wi' that the wyte o't.

My heart it beats to hear her speak, wi' joy in every stoun o't,
An' oh! whene'er I hear her name, I love the very soun o't.
Tho' weel I ken her loving heart is a' that she can gie me.
Tho' freen may frown, an' fremet blame, I ken she'll never lea' me.

It maybe costs a tear or twa when nae ane's near to ken o't,
When thinkin' o' oor lang-tried love I canna see the en' o't;
An' maybe when I wankrife lie, when nicht an' mornin's meetin'—
That eerie hour o' mystic power—my heart is sairly greetin'.

Oh, that the warl' should ever ban twa hearts that lo'e ilk ither, [gither!
That love should burn, an' hearts should yearn, an' never come the-
But love that grew, we kenna hoo, will surely be forgiven;
For many a love is bann'd on earth that's no a sin in heaven.

THOMAS RUSSELL.

A MAN of good common sense, and a poet of very considerable ability, THOMAS RUSSELL, was born at Parkhead, near Glasgow, October 29th, 1822. The poet's grandfather was a farmer in Shettleston, but after three successive years of bad harvest, he gave up the business of farming, and removed with his family into the neighbouring clachan of Parkhead. George, the youngest son, and the poet's father, betook themselves to the carting of coals from the pit-heads at Parkhead to vessels at the Broomielaw. A toiler from his ninth year, our poet had to take lessons from his father after the long day's work was over. With the first shilling he could call his own, he set off to the Bazaar and purchased a second-hand copy of Burns, receiving two-pence in change. His blood got inoculated with the poetic craze, and he forthwith became a rhymer. "A' ye wha live by crambo-clink," he read; and the phrase "crambo-clink" was the inspiring shuttlecock which danced in music through his quickened brain. It was years, however, before he attained that mastery over the forms of verse, and thought, and poetic fancy which his later musings show. Analyzing his poetic genius as evinced in his poetry, he possesses sentiment, it may be briefly premised, but sentiment hardened into tough realism by rough contact with the toiling world; he has humour also, but his humour has an iron grit in it. His verses generally, however, are full of strong mature thought, are commendably free from weak poetic maunderings and rhapsodies, and discover nowhere a useless railing at fate. When his muse becomes declamatory it is in the hot condemnation of war, tyranny, slavery, and such like great sins of the world. In one of his quieter moods, he paints the moral of war in the following homely but quite delightful humorous etching.

——:: ——

WEE GEORDIE'S DAY-DREAMS.

WEE GEORDIE wi' his day-dreams, haith, he's unco soon began,
Altho' he's only nine year auld he thinks himsel' a man;
He's sittin' by the fire-side, workin' wi' great glee,
Building man-o'-war ships to sail upon the sea.
He's doing wonders for his age an's master o' his trade;
Wi' naething but an auld pen-knife wi' a broken blade
He howks them oot, an' rigs them up, an' fills them fu' o' men,
An' marks oot a' the officers that we their rank may ken.

He tak's his mither's washing-tub—it mak's an ocean fine,
An' launching ship in after ship he forms them a' in line;
On this side are the British ships, on that side are the foes',
Just waiting on the dread command to deal each other blows.
A British captain tak's the e'e wha flourishes his sword,
An' threatens death to ilka ane who dares to come aboard;
His men are standing at his back, just whaur they oeht to be;
For Geordie kens, like aulder folks, that Britons rule the sea.

He first manœuvres them awhile, and then gets in a rage,
Because he canna gar them fire nor han' to han' engage;
He grasps the warlike captain's ship, an' driving 't owre the tide,
He scatters a' the foemen's ships an' cowps them on their side.
Quo' I—"Ye act the tyrant's part, and that beyond dispute,
In trying to get them to fecht *wi' nocht to fecht aboot;*
I canna say I ken their thochts, but this to me seems plain,
There's wiser men wi' wooden heads than mony wha ha'e brain."

——::——

SONNET.

COULD I have known before I was created
A thinking soul, and into being thrust,
How Circumstance and I should stand related,
I had preferr'd to have remain'd in dust.
Therefore, I deem I have not broken trust
With my Creator,—as without consent,
Or knowledge of the things for which we lust,
I enter'd life without foregone intent:
I made no compact that I might repent:
My sorrow is that I have found me here.
Had the dark veil of time for me been rent,
And all my future set before me clear,
I should have said—"God, only for thy sake,
And at thy risk, will I such burden take."

COLIN RAE-BROWN.

DESCENDED from an old Argyleshire family, COLIN RAE-BROWN was born at Greenock, December 19th, 1821. The family having removed to Glasgow, where our poet's education was completed, he there entered upon an engagement with a Fine Art and general publishing firm. Afterwards, he became managing partner of a similar business in his native town. Early in 1847 he relinquished his Greenock partnership and proceeded to Glasgow to make business arrangements for the publication of the *North British Daily Mail*—the first daily newspaper published in Scotland. Subsequently the *Mail* changed proprietorship, and was floated through its early difficulties into financial prosperity and success. Under the present able and energetic editorship of Mr. James R. Manners, the *Mail* has been pushed to the front as a leading Scottish daily. Under the same control, the *Weekly Mail*, it may be stated, has attained a circulation of 225,000 copies—a success unapproached in Scotland. Mr. RAE-BROWN has thus the satisfaction of knowing, that the newspaper he assisted in founding, has become, in these recent days, an organ of primal influence and power. On the abolition of the stamp duty in 1855, he established the *Bulletin* newspaper—the first daily *Penny* paper published in Britain.

Patriotic at heart, as he is energetic in mind and purpose, Mr. RAE-BROWN originated, in 1856, the Glasgow movement which culminated in the erection of the National Wallace Monument on the Abbey Craig. He was also an instrumental factor in the origination and success of the great Burns' Centenary Celebrations in 1859; his active services in connection with the Glasgow Festival being afterwards acknowledged by the presentation of a massive silver tea service.

Regarding his poetical labours, his first volume of verse was issued in 1849 by Mr. David Chambers (of *Chambers' Journal*), then of Glasgow. Several volumes of verse from his graceful and engaging pen have since appeared, the best known of which are *The Dawn of Love*, and *Noble Love*, both of which volumes are well and favourably known.

For many years past, Mr. RAE-BROWN has been resident

in London, employing his well-earned leisure in literary pursuits. In 1874 he contributed his *Glimpses of Scottish Life* to the *St. James's Magazine*, which delightful sketches were afterwards reproduced in three-volume form by Messrs. Sampson, Low, & Co., London. So recently as 1881, he edited the collected poems of the late James Macfarlan, prefacing the book with an interesting memoir of that unfortunate but nobly-gifted poet.

—::—

THE CAGED LARK.

Poor prison'd Lark ! all thy regrets are vain,
  Thou canst not visit the green fields of May ;
Howe'er melodious may be thy strain,
  Here thou art doom'd in bondage close to stay.

What ! set thee free—to joy with thine own kind—
  To revel gladly in the summer air—
To join the throng harmoniously combined
  To banish from each listener gloomy care—?

Ah ! it were vain such freedom to bestow !
  They'd deem thee tainted by thy sojourn here,
Would rudely scorn thee—so increase thy woe—
  But here, though prison'd, scorn thou need'st not fear.

Dost note my word, and, noting, think them sage,
  That now thou pourest out thy heart in song ?
Art thou content to warble in thy cage—
  Means so that note so clear, so rich, so long—?

Let it be so ! I'll cherish thee, sweet bird !
  As fondly as a mother doth her child,
Will, daily, from the verdant, dewy sward,
  Cut thee a turf whereon the sun hath smiled—

Will bring thee stores of field-food, fresh and green,
  Will tempt thy palate with a wondrous choice,

Will strive to gladden thee from morn till e'en,
  And all but satiate thee with little joys :

When comes the sun to smile on youth and age,
  Reviving many a sick and drooping heart,
Outside my window, then, I'll hang thy cage—
  There thou shalt sing till his last smiles depart.

What !—louder !—still more joyous than before—
  Thou art content, sweet bird, to stay with me !—
Then, so am I, to tend thee more and more,
  And spend my leisure hours with books and thee.

——::——

SHAKESPEARE.

What glorious victories are here enshrined
In deathless trophies of immortal Mind !
What proud exemption from the common doom
Are lives that need no costly, storied tomb !
How rich the spoils from Death's cold clutches wrung—
How vast the fame that lives on ev'ry tongue !

Such fame is thine, thou first of human kind
By whom the soul's deep myst'ries were defined :
Thou held'st the mirror up to nature's view
And proved the false by setting forth the true :
Dissecting motives of the hidden will
With touch precise and anatomic skill,
Unlocking ev'ry chamber of the heart
That laughs—or weeps, at bidding of thy Art.

Sun of thy system ! whose effulgent rays
Dispel the filmy clouds of mental haze,
Clearing the lab'rinths of Life's devious way
Till darkness seems transparent as the day—
Still unapproach'd throughout the World of Mind,
All Coming Time shall fail thy like to find !

BONNIE INVERMAY.

I'VE roam'd afar where'er the star
Of Fortune guided me,
But till this day, sweet Invermay,
I've ne'er forgotten thee.
Time rolls along while sigh and song
In swift succession flow,
For smiles and tears, and hopes and fears,
Are all of life we know :
Yet dear to me shall ever be
The joy of life's young day,
And still shall I, till mem'ry die,
Love Bonnie Invermay !

I love the glens, the rocky glens,
Of our romantic land,
I love her hills, her heath'ry hills,
And mountains sternly grand !
O for the days, the happy days,
When Hope's bright cup ran o'er !
But all in vain I sigh again—
They'll gladden me no more :
Yet dear to me shall ever be
The joy of life's young day,
And still shall I, till mem'ry die,
Love Bonnie Invermay !

I love the streams, the bounding streams,
That Echo loves to greet,
That dance and play, and fall in spray,
Like diamonds at our feet ;
And should Fate's star lead me afar—
Or strew my path with care,
Till sorrows grow, and age's snow
Hath whiten'd every hair—
Still dear to me shall ever be
The joy of life's young day,
And still shall I, till mem'ry die,
Love Bonnie Invermay.

ROBERT GEMMELL.

ROBERT GEMMELL, the author of a volume of quiet, but beautiful verses, was born at Irvine, Ayrshire, on 11th January, 1821. He had a fair school education, and from his boyhood up has been a devoted lover of books. On leaving school he was apprenticed to the Shipbuilding trade, but before completing his trade apprenticeship, he enlisted in the 30th Regiment of Foot. After a brief military servitude, our poet was induced to purchase his discharge, and returning home, he obtained a clerkship in the office of a Railway Contractor. He subsequently entered the service of an Iron-founder in his native town of Irvine, and is at present employed at the Eglinton Street Station of the Glasgow and Paisley Joint Railway Company.

Mr. GEMMELL early discovered a talent for quiet, but impressive verse-writing. He has also a fluent prose style, and has written, in all, three volumes of poems and life sketches. He is now (1882) preparing material for a fourth volume. He writes with noticeable purity, sweetness, and taste.

THE BANKS OF AVONLEE.

THE trees are cloth'd in richest green,
  And flow'rs bedeck the meadows gay,
While to enhance the pleasant scene,
  The lark pipes forth a gladsome lay;
And gentle zephyrs lightly float,
  Which onward bear the humming bee,
While Love sails in a fairy boat
  Along the banks of Avonlee.

A maiden with a clear blue eye,
And shining hair of golden hue,
Is listening, with a look so shy,
Unto a tale that's ever new;
The youth who pleads is frank and brave,
And she is fair and sweet to see,
While glory gilds the rippling wave
Beside the banks of Avonlee.

The birds sing louder with delight,
The flow'rs a greater joy inspire,
The landscape more enchants the sight,
All nature wears a new attire;
And from the scene is heard to rise,
A sound, as if in sympathy
With those who love have learn'd to prize,
Beside the banks of Avonlee.

And still, while years shall swiftly glide,
New hearts, O Love, shall feel thy power,
And beauty hear with joy and pride,
The dear old tale in hall and bower;
And thus it was in days of yore,
And still throughout all time shall be,
In every land, on sea, and shore,
And by the banks of Avonlee!

——::——

GLOAMING.

O GLOAMING, thou art all supreme! None can thy power gainsay,
While those who court fair fancy's dream, would fain prolong thy [stay;
For lovely forms are in thy train, and many a spirit bright,
Which scar'd, when Night asserts her reign, soon vanish from the sight.

O gloaming, thou hast richly shed a gladness over me,
As thy pale mantle thou hast spread alike o'er land and sea;
And while I've wander'd forth alone in thy sweet tranquil hour,
I've soar'd in thought to worlds unknown, through thy enchanting power.

REVᴰ DR WALLACE
THOMAS KENNEDY
W D. LATTO
NEMO ME IMPUNE LACESSET
D CARMICHAEL
JAMES SHAW
WILLIAM C CAMERON

(200)

O gloaming, oft I've stood beside yon time-worn castle wall,
Where silvery waters softly glide, to watch thy shadows fall;
And there thy presence still would bring remembrance of the past,
And joy, to which the soul will cling, while life itself shall last.

O gloaming, thou hast brought delight 'neath many a hawthorn shade,
Where glowing Youth to Beauty bright, the vows of love hath made;
Those words that trembled on the tongue, while shone the light of
Came forth when lark no longer sung, beneath thy covering grey. [day,

O gloaming, many a sweet romance, its birth hath owed to thee;
Thy spell our dearest joys enhance, and makes each sorrow flee:
The stars give forth a chasten'd light, the moon a milder ray,
Whilst thou, sweet herald of the night, exerts thy magic sway.

O gloaming, thy pale shadows teach that life, like day, must close,
And may their mute appealing speech our thoughts aright dispose;
Lead us to prize that truth sublime, ere health and vigour cease,
Which at the end of our brief time, alone gives joy and peace.

DANIEL CARMICHAEL.

THE possession of the poetical faculty does not necessarily imply the absence, in the same mind, of a mathematical or mechanical aptitude. If genius is the rarest sense, there is no obvious reason why the poet should not show fairly well in the struggle of life. Robert Burns was a capital ploughman as well as an unrivalled poet, and was furthermore said to have had the handsomest cast of the hand in the sowing of seed of any husbandman adjacent to the poet's farm at Ellisland. As a gauger also, he kept a clear record and clean books. It would be easy to multiply similar evidence, but we shall pre-suppose the reader's intelligence on the point, and at once introduce our good old poetic friend, DANIEL CARMICHAEL, who is both mechanist and poet. He is, however, not a Burns — there is only one Burns, and the heart of Scotland is his perpetual prophet—but he is a thoroughly good and most interesting member of the numerous "bardie clan," of which Burns, by universal consent, is the undisputed head. DANIEL CARMICHAEL was born at Alloa, County of Clackmannan, in the year 1826. On account of the death of his father, he removed to Edinburgh, where he was apprenticed to the trade of engineering. Completing his apprenticeship, he afterwards went to Glasgow, where he got married, remaining in that city, and working in various engineer shops on the Clyde, for the following six or seven years. "I then went back to Auld Reekie," says Mr. CARMICHAEL, in a note now before us, "and afterwards returned to the service of the Messrs. Napier & Sons, and came round to Liverpool upon the completion of the Scotia, 1st March, 1862." Since then our poet has been employed in one of the larger engineering establishments on the Mersey.

Like the majority of poets, Mr. CARMICHAEL wrote verses early. A local phrenological lecturer had, on a public platform, read his head and attested his capacity for poetry, and growing out of his love for singing and dancing, he ultimately found his true vocation in verse-making when he had a leisure blink from toil. A rhymster by instinct from his earlier years, he now finds a solace in the muse, and obedience to its calls a pleasurable necessity.

In 1879, he determined on producing a volume, but seeing no possible way of achieving this desirable end unless by becoming his own type-setter, printer, and publisher, the admirable fellow secured the necessary types, and having with his own hands constructed a rude printing machine, he "set up" his own types, printed his own book, and shortly afterwards succeeded in selling it out *to the last copy*. It is simply an unique production in poetical literature. The little book is really well printed in view of the circumstances stated, and is astonishingly free from errors.

In 1880, Mr. CARMICHAEL published a second volume of dialect verse under the title of *Rhyming Lilts and Doric Lays.* Like the former volume, it was also set up and printed by the author's own hands, and that, too, in the leisure hours of the evening, after a hard day's handling of the hammer and chisel. The poetry has, all through, a hearty, cheery, manly ring, and is marked by much pleasant homeliness and artlessness of expression. The author follows no model, but writes immediately from his heart, and the sense and feeling of his verses is of a popular cast both in tone and expression. He sings with capital point the virtues of *Caller Water* and *A Glass o' Ale* in turn. To readers of unaffected tastes, Mr. CARMICHAEL'S pages—racy and graphic as they are in humour and dialect—appeal with welcome and uncloying freshness. His brain is quick and fertile, and he continuously notes by newspaper letter-writing or otherwise all new, social, educational, and industrial movements. He is full of poetical enthusiasm, and is a capital hand at a twa-handed Scotch crack. Although for long resident in England, he has not forgotten his "mither tongue," but speaks his thoughts in Doric as broad as a Kilmarnock bonnet, having presumably neither the wish nor the smart ability to conveniently forget it.

—::—

A GLASS O' ALE.

O THOU pure, sparklin' glass o' ale,
Nectar for gods an' fellows hale,
I carena by, tho' bigot's rail
        Misca's ye sair,
Ye was a freen' to me when frail,
        That I'll declare.

For when upon the bed o' pain,
Wi' fever ragin' on the brain,
'Twas ye alane that I could drain,
For only you,
Abune a' ithers it was plain,
Could pull me through.

Therefore I'll no stan' quaitly by,
While fules an' madmen ye decry;
But to the rescue I will hie,
An' thee defend;
Will praise thy virtues to the sky,
Solace an' friend.

A glorious thing is moderation,
I like it weel on each occasion,
In temperance speech as weel's libation—
Wid like to hear
A guid, soun', learn'd, grand oration
Aboot the beer.

But if thae fules had just the power,
They'd mak' a' moderates quickly lower,
Beneath their blichtnin' shadows cower—
That withoot fail;
By police law mak' us gi'e owre
The glass o' ale.

The strengthnin' ale, sae guid an' braw—
Prime Edinbro' or Alloa,
Famed Burton's pale, baith strong and sma';
The creamy brew
Wid soon be stopt if 'neath the paw
O' that mad crew.

Lang, lang the day ere that may be,
Ere tyrant law again we see,
Ere freedom's flag shall cease to flee
Prood in the gale,
Ere we're compelled nae mair to pree
A glass o' ale.

LUMBAGO.

If horror's cup is no yet full,
An' something left still in my skull,
Inspire me with an extra pull
Ye Muses nine,
That I the pangs sublime may cull
To grace my rhyme.

Auld grum'lin' toothache's had his day—
Has spun his discontented lay;
Why don't he stuff his stumps an' stay
His achin' jaw?
Or by a dentist's tak' his way?
'Twad flee awa.

Or if he finds that's no enough,
He needna therefore tak' the huff;
For I can put him up to snuff,
Withoot a doot:
Just tak' the deevil by the cuff
An' pu' him oot.

But try an' pu' Lumbago oot—
'Twill tak' us a' oor time I doot;
Or even let us try an' foot
Sax miles a day,
Or in oor beds e'en turn aboot,
Just if you may.

While on the back we lie an' groan,
He tickles up the marrow bone
Wi' torture's sublimated prong,
An' mak's us yell!
There's nane I ken can come't as strong
As he himsel'.

Rheumatics—hech! but ye're nae joke;
You're no the chap I'd like to mock,
Or e'en your anger to provoke
By jibe or jeer;
That ye're a gey revengefu' bloke,
The fact is clear.

Noo, in my time I've had my share
O' pangs an' sorrows, an' to spare,
An', by the gods! I here declare—
Jingo and Jago!
'Gainst a' the ills that flesh is heir,
I'll *back* Lumbago.

——::——

CALLER WATER.

Let ithers sing o' sparkling wine
Until their throats be sair,
The "nectar" o' the gods divine
Is but a devil's snare,
Inspirin' fules in their mad mirth
To spates o' senseless chatter;
Na, mine's a sang o' modest birth,
I sing guid Caller Water.

Guid Caller Water, pure an' bricht,
Sent richt frae Heaven's ain doors,
A coolin' draught that keeps us richt,
An' free frae drucken "scores."
Nae headaches after it we ha'e,
Enough oor wits to scatter;
We're clear an' bricht as dewy spray
After guid Caller Water.

Sae, join my sang wi' a' your micht,
Nor mind the senseless jibe,
On water ye will ne'er get "ticht,"
Though gallons ye imbibe;
Nor troubled be wi' doctors' bills,
But grow baith rich an' fatter,
If ye but drink the sparkling rills,
That flow frae Caller Water.

THOMAS KENNEDY.

A BORDER poet of considerable merit, THOMAS KENNEDY was born in the Cowgate of Galashiels—now known as Overhaugh Street—in 1823. The beneficent operation of the Factory Act was not yet legalised is his young days, and our poet, at the tender age of eight years, had to toil within a local factory for eleven hours of every working day—a species of training the reverse of favourable to the development of a budding poetical genius. Yet, the story of men's lives daily proves that, from such alien surroundings, the finest lights of art, invention, and poetry, have in all ages sprung.

Mr. KENNEDY, after having passed through the various progressive stages of drudgery incidental to a youth employed in a large woollen factory, was at length apprenticed to the weaving trade—an occupation very commonly associated, on the part of its representatives, with poetry and politics. At the present time he is employed in the pattern department of Messrs. Sanderson's Tweed Mill, Galashiels.

Mr. KENNEDY wrote early and well—the first characteristic of native genius. His verses are flowing, spirited, and oftentimes eloquent and forcible, and received on one occasion the unqualified praise of the Rev. George Gilfillan, who declared his centenary piece entited, *Scotland and Scott*—a poem certainly of much eloquence, force, and beauty—to be "about the best he had seen on the subject," with the approving comment that some of its lines were worthy of being "written in gold." The poem is much too long for quotation here, but will form a very fine leading poem to a book of his verses, when the author concludes on issuing such. The volume, we doubt not, would be very favourably received. The *Prayer of the Bruce* is a subject which has been often handled, but it loses nothing of its native poetic and inspiriting beauty in our poet's hands.

——::——

THE PRAYER OF THE BRUCE.

The clouds came down and hung upon the hills,
  And wrapp'd in drizzling mist wide moor and glen,
As if in pity for poor Scotland's ills
  They fain would screen, and hide her scatter'd men.
For o'er the land, in town and castled keep,
  The countless foe in insolence held sway;
Whilst in ravines and wild recesses deep,
  The Scottish brave were hunted as a prey.

In woods, in caves, 'neath rocks where cataracts pour'd,
  Lived Scotland's freemen, 'reft of all save life,
And that sweet prayer for vengeance, which the sword
  Yet amply answer'd in the deadly strife.
Deem not their prayer impious—'twas the appeal
  Of noble hearts to desperation driven;
Hearts which, against oppression hard as steel,
  Burn'd with that fire whose flame is lit in heaven,

Such were the times, and such this special day,
  When towards a lone hut, half hid in heather,
A warrior strode—one who, in fight or fray,
  Smote like the thunder when wild tempests gather.
Within the straw-couch'd tenement he lay,
  Mist-wet and weary, through the cheerless night,
His shield his pillow—for the dawn's first ray
  Might bring the foe, in fierce unequal fight.

Watching the first faint glimmerings of morn,
  Which through the broken roof began to steal,
He mark'd upon a rafter, scath'd and torn,
  A spider working with unflagging zeal;

Twelve times the anxious insect tried to swing
  And fix itself into a cosier bield;
Twelve times it fail'd, but still the tiny thing
  Toil'd with an energy that would not yield.

The warrior chief who, musing, watch'd below,
  Beheld the emblem of his own hard lot,
Twelve times in blood had the remorseless foe
  Reel'd from his onset, yet success came not;
Hope now was dying, and a heavy woe,
  Full of dark dreamings of the adverse past,
Was settling down upon his soul, when lo!
  He mark'd the spider win the goal at last.

With quickening pulse and kindling eye, he rose
  And bade despair and all its gloom depart,
His good sword-arm nerv'd for a thousand blows,
  And war's wild impulse leaping in his heart—
"Rise, thou brave sun, and chase the coward night,
  Whose doleful bodings would benumb the soul;
Shine out, for by the Holy Rood, thy light
  Shall gild great deeds where battle-echoes roll."

"Come, ye vile hordes, slaves to a base design,
  Come, till your dark-plum'd hosts cloud hill and heath,
Come—But, O, Heaven! if justice still be thine,
  England shall wail their ignomy and death;
On this good broadsword, dinted with long years
  Of brunt and battle for my country's right,
I swear yet to avenge her blood and tears,
  And, kneeling, ask thee to watch o'er the fight."

Humble and low he bent his head in prayer,
  Alone in that bleak tenantless abode,
No saint nor surpliced priest was needed there,
  The fervent spirit rose direct to God.
Few, but impassion'd were his words, that rose
  In throbbing accents through the morning air,
Up where entrancéd vision could disclose
  Ethereal forms, now hovering dimly there.

Shades from an hundred battlefields they came,
  Gory and grim, even as they fought and bled;
Many who gave their life, 'midst blood and flame,
  Still following where the kingly Bruce had led.
Like drifting fragments of some broken cloud
  Shaped into ghastly phantoms of the dead,
They drew together there, and in close crowd
  Spread out their arms, in blessing, o'er his head.

Oh! could those spirits, in their happier spheres,
  Forget the gall and grief which tyrants bring—
Forget their hero, kneeling there in tears—
  There own belovëd Scotland's warrior king!
They came, with love that would not die, to tell,
  And in their benedictions, to unveil,
Their country's future, glorious and well,
  And show that yet her valour would prevail.

Stooping, they o'er him hung in fond farewell,
  Then gazing up, as if they would return,
They vanish'd; whilst the breeze caught the soft swell
  Of dying echoes whispering, BANNOCKBURN.
The monarch rose, but on his visage now
  Gleam'd the bright glory of the times to be;
Scotland was saved, for on that kingly brow
  The fates had come and written—VICTORY.

——::——

ON SEEING A VERY EARLY PRIMROSE.

WHY come ye sae early, my bonnie wee flow'r?
  Sleety blasts drive and darken the sky;
        And patches o' snaw
        That are sweer, sweer awa',
On the moss-cushion'd cradle yet lie, sweet flow'r;
  O ye've wauken'd I fear but to die.

Gae back to thy slumbers, my bonnie wee flow'r;
  The pleasures thy beauty should gie
        Are banish'd wi' pain,
        For the snaw, sleet, and rain,

Blears thy tender and delicate e'e, sweet flow'r,
And ye look as ane weeping to me.

Loud and harsh roars the burn, my bonnie wee flow'r,
And its waters dash drumlie alang;
Gae back to repose
Till it cannier flows,
It will wauken ye then wi' a sang, sweet flow'r,
And the saft winds will then make thee strang.

O then ye'll be welcome, my bonnie wee flow'r,
When the dour drizzling winter's awa—
When the thorn and brier spread
Their young leaves o'er thy head,
And the sunbeams wi' blessings aye fa', sweet flow'r,
In the nooks where ye bonnilie blaw.

Then bairnies will seek thee, my bonnie wee flow'r,
In the woods, in the glens, and the dells.
They love when ye come
To carry thee home,
Blooming, spotless, and pure like themsel's, sweet flow'r,
As an emblem that summer foretells.

For dear are thy blossoms, my bonnie wee flow'r,
To auld age that can never mair be
In the woods and the fields,
The bow'rs and the bields,
Where thy kindred grow gladsome and free, sweet flow'r,
And the birds carol sweet in their glee.

Then gae back to thy slumbers, my bonnie wee flow'r,
Fierce winter yet whitens the hill,
But it winna be lang,
For he kens he maun gang,
Then let na his spite do thee ill, sweet flow'r,
Take another short nap and lie still.

JAMES SHAW.

JAMES SHAW, now a schoolmaster in the Parish of Tynron, Dumfriesshire, was originally a pattern-designer, and was afterwards a partner in a print-work, Barrhead. Withdrawing himself from the concerns of business while still a young man, he subsequently resolved on devoting his life to teaching. He had an early-formed literary bent, but latterly his mind has been more directly interested in scientific speculations. Several of his articles have been published in the *Transactions of the Dumfriesshire Scientific and Antiquarian Society*. Mr. SHAW also read two papers before the British Association in Glasgow, which were afterwards published in the *Anthropological Journal*. He has since contributed articles on scientific subjects to *Nature*, the *Graphic*, and *Science for All*, as well as lighter sketches to other magazines and periodicals.

Personally, Mr. SHAW is a man of excellent character, and the most genial instincts; and his abstruser studies have not in any way interfered with his native sense of the humorous side of human life and character, a subdued reflection of which is occasionally evidenced in his lighter poems.

—::—

PATE M'QUATTY ON HIS FIDDLE.

O, I WOULDNA swap my auld fiddle
For a' the pianos I ken,
Nor for the gilt-flute o' Tam Riddell,
Nor the chanter and pipes o' Tam Glen.

How it sets the fellows a-prancing,
  Like cowts when they're fed upon corn !
How it rouses the lassies a-dancing
  Till the wee short hours o' the morn !

My fiddle's a witch and a charmer,
  Its tongue is the tongue o' a lark,
Its whispers as soft and as warm are
  As the whispers o' love in the dark.

Its song 's like the song o' a maiden,
  Its croon 's like the croon o' a dove,
Its heart-strings are shaken and laden
  Wi' the innermost secrets o' love.

Its wrath is the wrath o' a brither,
  When fechting for sisters at hame ;
It wails like the wail o' a mither,
  Its sob 's like the sobbing o' shame.

Its glee is the glee o' a gossip,
  When the blithemeat's set down on the board ;
It exults like a slave that can toss off
  The fetters put on by his lord.

Of baith sun and moon independent,
  If I mind but to rosin the bow ;
If "brig" and if "strings" be new mended,
  I've daylight wherever I go.

——::——

SONNETS ON SAGES.

Pericles.

The stars of heaven look glorious in the night—
Wonders of space—but in the night of time
What star shines like the sage's brow sublime?
Few orbs so bright as Pericles. The sight
Of Athens glorious, active, great, and free,
Sailing down time as through an unknown sea,
And this brave pilot at the helm, whose voice
And eye bring triumph, gives me stern delight.

Men are not in his hands like gambler's dice ;
He knows the subtle laws that govern mind,
And battling for the greatness of his kind,
In few short years weaves Greece a statelier crown
Of living lustre and of far renown
Than ages wove for Persian slaves so blind.

—::—

MARCUS AURELIUS ANTONINUS.

FIRM, tender, just—sad in his very smile,
Tears in his wrath—a godlike noble King :
Let us join hands with Marcus, who did bring
For crown, a soul of truth, hating all guile,
Vain shows, luxurious living, every wile
Lying in ambush for a monarch's feet,
To trip him. Sun, rain, snow, and sleet
Saw thee, poor King, on that wild horse of thine,—
The Roman people—an uneasy seat ;
For the rough barb, ill train'd, though strong and fleet,
Kick'd, plung'd, and bit thee. But an aim divine
Upheld thee, stronger than applause or wine ;
Life is full short—work well while it is light :
No riot ! Harvest must be home ere night !

REV. ALEXANDER WALLACE, D.D.

THIS popular divine, who is a native of Paisley, is so well known and esteemed as a preacher of gospel truths that he is never thought of as a poet. Yet when a young man, and a student, first in Glasgow and afterwards in Edinburgh, he achieved distinctive honour as a writer of lofty narrative and descriptive verse, having obtained class prizes for such work in both of these time-honoured Universities. During the early years of his ministry these prize poems, with several minor efforts in verse, were issued in a volume, long since out of print, which attests the author's claim to poetic recognition. A number of his minor pieces first appeared in the *Harp of Renfrewshire.* The reverend doctor, however, has all along conscientiously subordinated the pursuit of poetry to the higher vocation of his ministerial calling. He pours all his poetry and pathos into his sermons, and is one of the most popular divines of the United Presbyterian Church. In April, 1857, he was inducted to East Campbell Street Church, which pastoral charge he still holds.

In May of the present year (1882), at a jubilee meeting of his congregation held in the Glasgow City Hall, Dr. Wallace was presented with a cheque for a sum approaching £500, which he was asked to accept as a token of the esteem in which he is held by the members of his congregation. Popular as a preacher, he is almost equally well known as a lecturer on literary and social subjects, in the treatment of which, his natural eloquence, feeling, and pathos are abundantly manifested.

——::——

A HOME IN STRATHSPEY.

HURRAH ! for the moors all aglow with the heather,
So bright with the dew at the break of the day,
Hurrah ! for the mountains, the glorious mountains,
The streams, and the glens, and the lochs of Strathspey.

Hurrah ! for the forests, the birch and pine forests,
Which shelter the deer from the sun's fiercest ray—
Vast temples of Nature, so peaceful and solemn,
That cover the hills and the dells of Strathspey.

'Twas a red-letter day when to Lainchoil I wander'd,
And mountain and moor wore their brightest array ;
But brighter the friendship that gave me warm welcome
To a home of leal hearts and kind hands in Strathspey.

O blest be that home on the braes of the Nethy
  In the glints of the morn, or when gloaming falls grey;
I'll waft it a blessing where'er I may wander,
  And cherish fond memories of it and Strathspey.

God bless the dear mother who sits by the fireside,
  Tho' her ninety-eighth summer has now pass'd away!
May her sunset of life gently melt into glory
  Like the calm after-glow on the hills of Strathspey.

And blest be the daughter who lives for her mother,
  With the warmest devotion that love can display;
A ministering angel to cheer the old pilgrim,
  Till the end of her journey be reach'd in Strathspey.

O Thou who temp'rest the wind to the shorn lamb,
  A guide to the blind, to the feeble a stay,
Let the stroke that will sunder fall lightly on lov'd ones,
  When the shadow shall rest on their home in Strathspey!

May the Saviour who wept where Lazarus was buried,
  Set His bow in the cloud, and their sorrow allay!
When the old arm-chair by the fireside is vacant,
  And the face long familiar has gone from Strathspey.

——::——

JESUS IN THE STORM.

What bitter thoughts and weary,
  Had prey'd upon my mind!—
A darkness deep and dreary
  Had made me sick and blind.
No star by night to brighten—
  No ray of hope by day;
No soothing word to lighten
  The load that on me lay.

I grop'd my way in sorrow;
  In vain I sought to find
Some promise that to-morrow
  Would leave all grief behind.

The morning broke in sadness,
  And fiercer grew the strife,
Till every form of gladness
  Pass'd from my wasted life.

But now, upon the ocean
  Of troubled thoughts, I see
My Saviour's graceful motion—
  He cometh unto me.
The winds and waves He stilleth,
  And all is calm again;
My soul with light He filleth,
  Like sunshine after rain.

The eye of faith is beaming
  With joy sent from above;
The rainbow cloud is streaming,
  The pledge of constant love.
My loosen'd tongue adoreth
  The greatness of His might;
His smile alone restoreth
  The darken'd soul to light.

WILLIAM C. CAMERON.

A POET of superior ability, WILLIAM C. CAMERON is the son of a Dingwall man, who was a schoolmaster in the 42nd Highlanders, and our poet was born in the army on the 7th of October, 1827. On receiving his discharge the elder Cameron returned to Dingwall, his native place, and dying shortly afterwards, his son—the future poet—was very early apprenticed to the trade of shoemaking. On becoming journeyman he left Dingwall and travelled south, working respectively in Kirkintilloch, Airdrie, and Coatbridge. He afterwards conducted, for a short time, business on his own account. At present, he is in the employment of a Glasgow and Edinburgh publishing firm.

An early adherent of the Muse, Mr. CAMERON has written copiously to the local press, and to other journals and periodicals. In 1875 a selection of his poems were issued in a neat volume by Maclehose, Glasgow, under the patronage of Lady Campbell, of Garscube, to whom the volume was "gratefully and respectfully inscribed." A brief commendatory note, from the pen of the Rev. Dr. W. C. Smith, prefaces the collection. Mr. CAMERON's muse is both prolific and varied. His book reveals no over-strainings of fancy, nor pretentious swell of diction. He sings heartily and inspiritingly of bright skies, happy birds, and bonnie bairns, and emulates the glory of toil, and the happiness of the workman's bench.

In the domestic vein, the reverend sponsor for the volume says Mr. CAMERON's special strength lies. His verse-pictures of child innocence and beauty are certainly the prettiest we have ever seen. There is a fairy brightness and sweetness of fancy appertaining to them which is in exquisite keeping with the delicately tender and beautiful theme. Mr. CAMERON's experience in life has been a very chequered one. He has shared something of the local fame and prosperity, but very much of the misfortune, which proverbially attaches to the ragged followers of the "Nine." We subjoin several specimens of his excellent and self-informed muse.

——::——

DREAM-LAND.

'TIS not knee-deep 'mong growing grass,
Nor is't inhaling breath of flow'rs,
That swift-wing'd Time with me doth pass;
Nor is it in the laughing bow'rs

Of indolence I sit and dream
  Away God's golden sunlit hours;
Nor do I loll where singing stream
  Lulls me into a calm repose;
  Nor does the fragrance of the rose,
Waft its sweet breath t' enamour me,
Beside the wide and flowing sea.
  I never see the red sun set,
Nor do I see the pale moon rise;
  I seldom see the violet,
Or soaring lark ascend the skies;
  Nor do I rest on couch of ease,
With all I want close at my hand,
  And everything to soothe and please—
Alladin-like—at my command.
  And yet, although these are not mine,
  I have a gift that's more divine!

I dwell within a giant town,
  Whose angry smoke pollutes the sky,
And heavy feet, like waves, come down
  In constant din, from passers-by;
And swarthy men, with Vulcan hand,
  And heavy tread, and deep bass throat,
Make where I dwell a Mammon land,
  Instead of an Arcadian grot!
  And yet, I dream! Yes, dream!—Why not?
The mind can make a heaven of hell,
  Yet live among the little lot
Of things with which we're forced to dwell!
  And yet I dream! Yes, mindless thing!
I dream—I see—I shape the form
  Of happy scenes that Time must bring
When pass'd away this Mammon storm
  That rages now:—When mind will be
  Man's rank—man's fame—man's majesty!

So here I sit and con my creed
  The live-long day, content to glean
From out Time's hidden womb, the seed
  That soon or late, in every scene

Which swells the tide of misery,
Must usher in the glorious day,
That rings the knell of giant Might,
As the day-giver scatters night,
Before his keen eyes' burning ray!
All this I dream!—All this I dream!—
Dame Fortune's step-son oft pass'd by;
With scarce a friend to clear my name
From mis-report and calumny!
When midnight reigns stars seem more bright,
And their sweet mysteries stand unveil'd;
The darkness of the tomb gives light;
And all that death has kept conceal'd
Shall beam upon my wond'ring sight;
And every "Why" shall be reveal'd,
For God *doth* reign—*and God is Right!*
Ah, yes! I see one vast wide stage,
Where all men stand alike! The Sword
Of Justice ne'er by deed or word
Has failed to give our heritage!

—::—

LITTLE JESSIE.

Come, see my little baby-girl—a toddling, winsome thing,
With yellow hair in golden curl, and eyes as bright as Spring!
Two little arms, so white and neat, that fold around my neck,
And make me laugh at Wizard Fate for little Jessie's sake.

Her rosy lips—a scarlet thread—unclose, and lo! I see
Two pearly teeth shine through the red as white as white can be!
Her tiny—plump—wee—fairy feet, encased in slippers blue,
Make music to my ear more sweet than words can ever do.

Oh, rapture rare! her lisping words lift me above my woe;
Oh! music sweeter far than birds from her quaint prattlings flow.
Come, see her in her snowy frock, and curls of sunny light,
As she her baby-doll doth rock—my little angel bright!

A MOTHER'S WEALTH.

GI'E to the winds the gowd, it has nae charms for me ;
My gear's enough, for I ha'e bonnie bairnies three.

I wadna gie the look o' their blue laughing e'e,
For a' the gowd sae rife wi' those o' high degree.

Their wee bit voice sae rich, steals saftly on mine ear,
Like music heard from far upon the waters clear !

A very wealth o' joy, their wee sweet tiny sang,
And while I ha'e them a' there's naething can gae wrang.

Their love's a crown to me—my joy—and yet my care,
The centre o' my thoughts, the burden o' my prayer.

O ! may the Pow'rs on high guard weel their sunny youth,
An' bless my toddlin' lambs wi' health and love and truth !

My blessings on them a'—my bonnie bairnies three ;
Their love is a' my gear, their smile is bliss to me !

ROBERT TENNANT.

THE subject of this notice, who was a "man of letters" in a double sense, was one of the many Scottish poets of the humbler type who pursue the habit of verse-making from no vain-glorious motives, but because it is as natural for them at times so to relieve the swelling feelings of the heart as it is for the bird to chirp on the bough. The higher spirits of song retain their commanding situations on the Parnassian heights, exposed for ever in strong light to the public gaze, but underneath the lofty peaks, in sunny and unassuming nooks, the lesser wild flowers of Song sweetly blossom, tinted with colouring sunlight and liquid with the purest dews.

ROBERT TENNANT, who may be not inaptly styled the "Postman Poet," was born at Airdrie towards the close of 1829. His parents died while he was still a child, and within a few weeks of each other. Shortly afterwards he was taken from school, and while still a mere boy was put to the trade of handloom weaving, at which occupation he continued to work until he had reached the age of eighteen. Not relishing the confinement of the loom, however, he by and by secured an appointment as post messenger in his native district, travelling daily the length of Salsburgh, near Shotts. In course of time he was transferred to the Rothesay Post-Office service; he was also a short time in the Greenock postal service, and was finally shifted to the General Post Office, Glasgow, in 1853, continuing there until his death.

It was in his twentieth year, and while still engaged in the Salsburgh service, that TENNANT began to put his thoughts into verse. He cherished to the last a deep love for the sunshine, the wild-flowers, and the woodland singing birds, and his accessibility to the enjoyment of these simple delights while on the road as a country post-runner first actively awakened in his mind the latent desire to express himself in song.

Pursuing the habit of verse-making in leisure hours, the productions of his Muse so accumulated on his hands in the course of years as to warrant him taking into favourable consideration the advice of friends anent the publication of a little volume. In the spring of 1872, his little collection of *Wayside Musings* accordingly appeared, and was received with considerable favour by the local press. Only a very limited edition of the book was ventured upon, and being chiefly subscribed for, the volume was out of print almost immediately it was issued. The poems are mostly local in tone, and are simple and unassuming to a degree, equally in treatment as in subject.

Simple and unaffected at heart, TENNANT dealt largely in diminutives. In his delightful little volume, "wee" Davie Daylichts, "wee" wild roses, "wee" singing linties, "wee" yellow primroses, and "wee" blythesome bairnies abound. At our suggestion, the excellent nursery ditty, *Wee Davie Daylicht*, was sent on to Mr. Andrew Stewart, of the *People's Friend*, author of *Sangs for the Bairns*, and that gentleman, quickly recognising its suitability, set it to fitting music, and afterwards incorporated it amongst other kindred gems in his book. To readers of unaffected tastes, TENNANT's sweet and simple effusions prove very interesting reading. The note of song struck is certainly not high, but that it is essentially sweet and clear most readers will admit. He is a minor poet in the best sense of the term, his verses being commendably free from strain, or elaborate effort.

During the second week of January, 1879, a suddenly acquired illness, beginning with a severe cold, laid the poet aside from active duty for a few days. Venturing abroad too early, he had a relapse, the trouble taking the form of acute inflammation of the lungs, of which he died, after a brief illness, January 27th, 1879. His unexpected demise was much and deeply regretted by all who knew him, as his kindly and unaffected ways had endeared him to many friends.

—::—

WEE DAVIE DAYLICHT.

WEE Davie Daylicht keeks owre the sea,
Early in the morning, wi' a clear e'e;
Waukens a' the birdies that are sleepin' soun',
Wee Davie Daylicht is nae lazy loon.

Wee Davie Daylicht glow'rs owre the hill,
Glints through the greenwood, dances on the rill;
Smiles on the wee cot, shines on the ha';
Wee Davie Daylicht cheers the hearts o' a'.

Come, bonnie bairnie, come awa' to me;
Cuddle in my bosie, sleep upon my knee.
Wee Davie Daylicht noo has closed his e'e
In amang the rosy clouds, far ayont the sea.

——::——

TO THE ALLANDER.

O sweetly flows the Allander, a mossy, winding stream.
The dewdrops on its grassy banks shine bright in morning's beam;
The wee wild flow'rs in beauty there in rich profusion grow,
In sunny spots and shady nooks, when summer breezes blow.

How sweet to roam by Allander, to breathe the balmy air,
When cloudless are the summer skies, and woods and fields are fair;
To see the skylark soaring high, and chanting on the wing,
While in yon woods near Calder Kirk the wild birds sweetly sing.

A ramble by the Allander can give a joy to me,
Unfelt by those who travel far, famed foreign lands to see:
A few miles from the smoky town a son of toil may find,
By wood and stream those blissful joys that cheer the heart and mind.

Flow on, flow on, sweet Allander, to Kelvin's classic stream;
While toiling in the busy town, of thee I'll fondly dream,
And I would seek no greater bliss than liberty to stray,
Along the banks of Allander, for one bright summer day.

——::——

THE WEE WILD ROSE.

The wee wild rose, the sweet wild rose, the soft winds fondly kiss it;
The balmy dews on summer eves drop sweetly down to bless it.
By Calder stream it brightly blooms; the wee birds sing beside it;
In leafy shades the lofty trees from scorching sunbeams hide it.

The wee wild rose, the sweet wild rose; the peasant, strongly toiling,
With loving look may gaze on it, in summer beauty smiling.
The cultur'd flow'rs with gaudy robes in shelter'd gardens growing,
Can never match the wee wild rose, in peerless beauty blowing.

The wee wild rose, the sweet wild rose, the playful children love it;
It seems a little fairy flow'r when skies are bright above it;
It proudly spreads its crimson leaves when morning's beams are
shining;
And folds the dewdrop in his heart when sultry day's declining.

The wee wild rose, the sweet wild rose, the poet loves it dearly,
And in its tender leaves can read this lesson, written clearly:—
That man is like the fragile flower—he blooms awhile, then fadeth;
But there's a realm above the sky that death's dark wing ne'er shadeth.

——::——

FAIRLIE GLEN.

O, THERE'S a glen, a bonnie glen, the bairnies lo'e it dearly,
The wee wild flow'rs they gather there when sunny skies shine
clearly,
When summer birds come owre the sea sweet nature decks it rarely;
A fairer spot there couldna be than yon wee glen at Fairlie.

In flow'ry June when days were lang, and birds were singing sweetly,
When woods and fields in summer dress were a' array'd completely,
I left the city far behind, where folk are worried sairly,
Some blissfu' hours o' joy to spend in yon sweet glen at Fairlie.

I heard the mavis sweetly sing, the blackbird piping proudly,
And through the list'ning leafy woods the cuckoo calling loudly.
I saw the lark, that angel bird, that greets the morning early,
When wild flow'rs bloom beside the stream, in yon wee glen at Fairlie.

Fair Summer's gane, the bonnie queen, who wore her robes sae
trimly;
And Winter's come, the surly loon, who grips puir folk sae grimly—
The wee birds in the leafless woods will feast, I fear, but sparely;
But Spring will come, and then they'll sing in yon wee glen
Fairlie.

THE WEE YELLOW PRIMROSE.

THE wee yellow primrose, sweet child o' the spring,
Looks up to the sky when the lark's on the wing;
And keeks frae its grassy bow'r, cosy and green,
To nod to the daisy, its bonnie wee freen'.

It grows on the bank and it grows on the brae,
And blooms by the streamlet that sings by the way;
It shines on the graves whaur oor lov'd bairnies lie,
And mithers come there whiles to weep an' to sigh.

It shines like a star on the woodlands sae green,
And cheers lonely spots, blooming often unseen;
But saft breezes kiss it and over it play,
And wee linties sing till't the lang summer day.

I've seen the blythe bee gang careerin' alang,
Aye humming fu' cheerie its sweet summer sang,
First licht on the Primrose's sweet dewy lip,
Then creep to its bosom the honey to sip.

I've seen the bright butterfly, bonnie wee thing,
When a' the green woodlands wi' music did ring,
Flee fluttering by in its white simmer vest,
Awa' to a feast on the primrose's breast.

The fairy dews fa' on't on calm summer eves,
And dream a' the nicht on its pure silken leaves;
Such beauty its Maker the primrose has given—
O, surely an angel cam' doon wi't frae heaven.

Some strive through ambition for wealth and for pow'r;
I seek not for these, but give me a wild flow'r,
A sweet warbling-bird, or a bonnie bit bairn,
And lessons worth learning frae them I shall learn.

ALEXANDER SMITH.

ALEXANDER SMITH, on the publication of the celebrated *Life Drama* in 1853, received at the hands of the press and public a greater ovation of praise than any Scottish poet before or since, saving, perhaps, Burns. SMITH was born at Kilmarnock, on the last day of December, 1830, but was early removed to Glasgow, where he followed for some years the business of a pattern-designer, his first volume having been published while the poet was still working at his profession in that city.

The causes which conducted to his sudden leap into fame are easy of explanation. SMITH was introduced to the public notice as a new poet of a high order, by the Rev. George Gilfillan, who was then the highest flier of balloon adjectives going, and who had, in consequence of that loud beauty, the ear of a large section of the reading public. The rev. critic bestowed upon his poetic *protegé* the most lavish eulogies, and the praise accorded, it must be admitted, was very much supported by the poem quoted from, which was shortly afterwards published entire under the title of *A Life Drama and other Poems.* The poem throughout is wild a little, and decidedly youthy, making no claim to dramatic conception, or construction. Yet its rich melody, affluent imagery, and gorgeous word-painting, caught the public ear at once. It was written in the first flush of the author's manhood—in the soul's full spring-tide, and is consequently jewelled to excess with the richest coinage of a lavish poetic fancy. Glancing briefly through it, we have an abundance of such phraseological beauties as the following—

"Her hair a cataract of golden curls,"

alternating with such bold and striking comparisons as these—

> "Rich opulent souls,
> Dropt in men's pathway's like great cups of gold ;—
> Grand master-spirits, who went down like suns,
> And left upon the mountain tops of death
> A light that made them lovely."

Not infrequently we come across such striking and finely melodious lines as the following—

> "The eye of God aglare
> O'er evening's city with its boom of sin,"

> "The moon
> Lies stranded on the pallid coast of morn,"

> "The old sea moaning, like a monster pain'd,"

or this, wherein a picture is done in a single line—

> "Woodland waters, full of silver breaks."

The poem is also occasionally vivified with sensuous beauty of imagery of a warmly adolescent type and hue—

> "Dame Venus, panting on her bed of flow'rs,
> And Bacchus, purple-mouth'd astride his urn."

But in addition to garish word-picturing of this sort, SMITH's first book abounded in splendid passages, evidencing the possession of a most opulent poetical genius. It would be difficult to fault, or to outrival, the following fine passage—

> "The bridegroom sea
> Is toying with the shore—his wedded bride.
> And in the fulness of his marriage joy
> He decorates her tawny brow with shells,
> Retires a space to see how fair she looks,
> Then straight runs up to kiss her."

The subjoined passage displays a massive majesty of conception worthy of the greatest poets—

"The sunset dieth like a cloven king,
In his own blood, the while the distant moon,
Like a pale prophetess whom he hath wrong'd,
Leans eager forward, with most hungry eyes,
Watching him bleed to death, and as he faints,
She brightens and dilates: revenge complete,
She walks in lonely triumph through the night."

Unfortunately for SMITH's fame, however, the *Life Drama*, magnificent in some passages though it undoubtedly is, was strewn throughout with verbal extravagances, and forced conceits, and the loud shout of applause with which it had been received had hardly died away, when the re-action set in, and it became suddenly fashionable to write and talk the poem down. The eager young poet, anxious to conciliate the critics, thereupon went into fatal training for a course of subdued poetics, and from being a free, high-blooded young roadster, taking in the fresh hill-side airs, his muse became ever afterwards a mere animal of the paddock, browsing languidly within correct conventional enclosures. In the interim, however, influential patronage had been freely bestowed on him, and an appointment to the post of Secretary to the University of Edinburgh was the fortunate result of the publication of his first volume.

SMITH's subsequent volumes of verse were not over-successful. His *City Songs* only half pleased the hyper-critics who had been gratuitously dunning him with stale advice, and disappointed also those of his early readers who had believed in and gushed over the rich warm colouring of the *Life Drama*, and who saw only a subdued reflection of it in his later volume. A third volume entitled, *Edwin of Deira*, on which SMITH had spent the leisure hours of four years, was still less successful, the sale being so indifferent that the author ultimately only realised some £17 as his share of the profits.

Dead beat in the art of making money out of poetry, SMITH, with the versatility characteristic of true genius, turned his pen to prose-writing, and quickly gained recognition as one of the most charming of recent essayists. *Dreamthorp*, a volume of delightful sketches, appeared in 1863, and was followed in 1865 by the publication of *A Summer in Skye.* In 1866, he contributed to *Good Words* a novel entitled, *Alfred Haggart's Household*, which is replete with the most charming descriptions of natural scenery, blended with interesting delineations of domestic incident and Scottish character. On the fifth of January, 1867, he died of a fever contracted in the November of the preceding year. He lies in Warriston Cemetery, Edinburgh, where a chaste monument, in the form of an Ionian Cross, has been erected to his memory by a few attached friends. He had scarcely completed his 38th year. His untimely death was much and very widely regretted, as occurring when he was doing his best work.

Poetic fame had been the early and burning dream of his soul, and the prospective contemplation of its felicity never failed to rouse an emulative ambition within his breast. Erewhile, in the fervid longing for recognition, and before the shining laurel was yet his own, he had nobly written—

"Like the sweet scent within a budded rose,
A secret joy is in my heart, and when
I think of poets nurtur'd 'mong the throes,
And by the lowly hearths of common men;
Think of their works—some song, some swelling ode,
With gorgeous music growing to a close,
Deep-muffl'd as the dead-march of a God—
My heart is burning to be one of those."

In the year following SMITH's decease, a volume of his *Last Leaves* was published. It was edited by Patrick Procter Alexander, himself a man of fine poetic genius, and is prefaced by a favourable and most interesting memoir of the lamented poet.

Mere quotation can scarcely do justice to SMITH's affluent genius, but the subjoined portion of his poem on *Glasgow*—a poem of finished expression and sustained power—should prove very interesting reading generally.

——::——

GLASGOW.

CITY ! I am true son of thine ;
Ne'er dwelt I where great mornings shine
Around the bleating pens ;
Ne'er by the rivulets I stray'd,
And ne'er upon my childhood weigh'd
The silence of the glens.
Instead of shores where ocean beats,
I hear the ebb and flow of streets.

I dwelt within a gloomy court,
Wherein did sunbeam never sport ;
Yet there my heart was stirr'd—
My very blood did dance and thrill,
When on my narrow window sill
Spring lighted, like a bird.
Poor flow'rs, I watch'd them pine for weeks,
With leaves as pale as human cheeks.

Afar, one summer, I was borne ;
Through golden vapours of the morn,
I heard the bleat of sheep :
And trod with a wild ecstasy
The bright fringe of the living sea ;
But, with emotion deep,
In thee, O City, I discern
Another beauty, sad and stern.

Draw thy fierce streams of blinding ore !
Smite on thy thousand anvils ! roar

Down to the harbour-bars !
Smoulder in smoky sunsets ! flare
On rainy nights ! with street and square
Lie empty to the stars !
From terrace proud to alley base,
I know thee as my mother's face.

When sunset bathes thee in his gold,
In wreaths of bronze thy sides are roll'd,
Thy smoke is dusky fire ;
And, from the glory round thee pour'd,
A sunbeam, like an angel's sword,
Shimmers upon a spire.
Thus have I watch'd thee, terror ! dream !
Till the dark night crept up the stream.

The wild train plunges 'mid the hills
And shrieks across the midnight rills ;
Streams through the shifting glare,
The roar and flap of foundry fires,
That shake with light the sleeping shires ;
And on the moorlands bare
I see afar a crown of light
Hung o'er thee in the hollow night.

At midnight, when thy suburbs lie
All silent as a noon-day sky,
When larks with heat are mute,
I love to linger on thy bridge,
All lonely as a mountain ridge,
Disturb'd but by my foot ;
While the black lazy stream beneath
Steals from its far-off wilds of heath.

All raptures of this mortal breath,
Solemnities of life and death,
Dwell in thy noise alone ;
Of me thou hast become a part—
Some kindred with my human heart
Lives in thy streets of stone ;
For we have been familiar more
Than galley-slave and weary oar.

ALLAN PARK PATON.

THE editor of an elaborate and valuable *Hamnet Edition* of the works of Shakespeare, now in course of publication, Mr. ALLAN PARK PATON is also known as a poet of original and appreciable poetical genius. In 1845 his poems were first issued in volume form, and in 1848 a second small octavo volume was issued by Longman & Co., London, which was very favourably received by the press and the reading public. In 1858, the same publishing firm published his striking novel *The Web of Life*, which is less known than its high literary finish seems to merit. The story abounds with passages of great verbal beauty and fine imagery, and makes deeply interesting reading throughout. For the past fifteen years, Mr. PATON has been librarian to the Greenock Watt Monument, and at the present time (1882) is devoting all his spare time to the completion and perfection of his new edition of Shakespeare.

Mr. PATON's verses are characterised by much grace and beauty of diction; uniting the gift of poetic conception with the grace of melodious flow.

——::——

RAIN AFTER DROUGHT.

(Time: four o'clock morning.)

AM I awake, or is it a dream?
Beside the fresh run of a streamlet I seem;
And, strange! o'er my head it seems to be flowing,
I hear it as over the roof it is going,
    And the eaves, ah, how lulling its strain!

Now it grows more distinct—it is tinkling and clear,
Oh, can it be it which is blessing my ear?
Rain it must be!—Hurrah, for the rain!
The bright-dashing rain!
The fresh-splashing rain!
Welcome reviver!—Hurrah, for the rain!

Oh, I could lie ever and listen thy fall,
At a season like this when thou'rt welcome to all;
But when all my green friends are again lifting up
Their branches with joy, as they drink from your cup,
Shall I but a hearer remain?
No, no! I must up! I must see thy return—
I must see the fires quenching that lately did burn:—
There thou art! Oh, hurrah, for the rain!
The sweet-singing rain!
The clear-ringing rain!
Welcome reviver! Hurrah, for the rain!

Hurrah, for the rain! Methinks through the land
I see her brown sons at their farm thresholds stand,
Awaken'd, like me, by thy hope-bringing sound,
And gazing with joy on their hard-labour'd ground,
Till, before them, of deep golden grain,
Large seas seem to rise, and in fancy are seen
Their cattle and flocks amid pasturage green
Browsing happy:—Hurrah, for the rain!
In their mind's eye already is groaning the wain,
And the barn is busy:—Hurrah, for the rain!
The fear-stilling rain!
The barn-filling rain!
Welcome reviver! Hurrah, for the rain!

How drippingly-fresh the large trees o'er the road!
(No sounds save from them, and the rain now abroad,)
And how glad-like, reliev'd-like, look tree, bush, and flow'r,
In our own little garden wash'd by the bright show'r;
Such a sight to the soul is a gain!
It adds to our hope, and it adds to our faith;
It is like fresh existence succeeding to death;
Such a sight!—Oh, hurrah for the rain!

From all idle frettings it makes us refrain ;
God is late, but is coming !—Hurrah, for the rain !
The crystal-glob'd rain !
The fairy-rob'd rain !
Welcome reviver ! Hurrah, for the rain !

——::——

SONNETS.

It is the morn indeed ! The night hath gone,
While we together with our favourite Keats
Have, through a country over-rich in sweets,
Follow'd the Dian-lov'd Endymion.
Like him, too, have we wander'd on and on,
Lured by inviting music in the air,
Till, leaving far below the vale of care,
We now are here, where fancy reigns alone !
And so much have we read of joys divine
Which thrill'd the Latmian's touch, but mock'd his sight,
That, as I linger'd at this wondrous line
My spirit flooded up with strange delight,
For such a mystic hand seem'd held by mine !—
But, Love, 'twas thine, so rarely small and white !

———

How sweet thus in an idle boat to lie,
Borne gently by the ebbing tide away—
In the cool wave a gurgling hand to play,
Watching the shore we dreamily glide by ;
Or fix our gaze upon the evening sky,
Where sinking Day, couch'd on the mountain'd West,
His gold-fring'd cloud-robes draweth round his breast,
And, like a king, prepareth him to die !
Hush ! it is music !—How it thrills the sense
As it comes trembling o'er the trancèd sea,
A rich and mellow voice ! oh, say not whence
(Say not from some becalmèd company ;)
And—my soul fill'd with yonder radiance—
A wandering spirit it will seem to me !

WILLIAM D. LATTO.

As the author of *Tammas Bodkin; or the Humours of a Scottish Tailor*, Mr. LATTO's name is likely to obtain permanency in connection with Scottish humorous literature. After the unrivalled *Mansie Waugh*, the vagaries and humours of *Tammas Bodkin* form undoubtedly the freshest and most original contribution to humorous Scottish story-telling of recent times. A native of Ceres, a snug little Fifeshire village lying about two miles to the south of Cupar, he in early life adopted the profession of a teacher, and having completed a Normal School course in Edinburgh, acted for some time as Free Church Schoolmaster at Johnshaven.

He wrote verses early, contributing his juvenile effusions to the Poet's Corner of the *Fife Herald*. Passing on to higher work, he afterwards became a contributor to *Hogg's Instructor*, a popular literary magazine, conducted with great ability, and published in Edinburgh in weekly and monthly issues.

Attracting attention by the vigour and fertility of his pen, he was invited in 1860 to accept the editorship of the *People's Journal*, to whose columns he had been, for three years previous, contributing fresh and racy sketches and stories, and that responsible position he still retains with great credit to himself, and presumable profit to the proprietors. The publication of the *Bodkin* papers in the *Journal* met with instant public favour, and assured the growing success of that popular broad-sheet. The best of the earlier articles were afterwards revised and published in book form, and have since run through numerous editions. In their collected form they make highly enjoyable and entertaining reading, and give everywhere the amplest evidences of native genius and humour. As recently as two years ago, Mr. LATTO issued a small *brochure*, entitled *Song Sermons*, forming a series of interesting and racy homilies on certain well-known old Scotch songs. The series makes capital reading throughout.

In politics Mr. LATTO is a thorough Liberal. He is an effective platform speaker, and a man of strong character and genial parts. He is also a keen angler; and is personally admired and beloved by a very wide circle of friends.

Mr. LATTO's life for the past twenty years has been so pre-occupied with the exacting duties of journalism, that his early affection for the muse has been necessarily much subordinated and confined. The few fugitive pieces at hand, however, are of capital quality, and make highly flavoursome and truly delightful reading. He is a genuine Scotchman, of the Victor Hugo type of head and countenance, and his gratifying success as a journalist—which has been great—has not affected his native common-sense, which is more admirable still.

——::——

THE TWA BULLS.

[In the heat of the "Papal Aggression" controversy in 1851, occasioned by the publication by Pio Nono of a Brief establishing a hierarchy of bishops and archbishops in England, in place of the vicars-apostolic who had governed the Anglo-Romish Church from the period of the Reformation, Mr. LATTO espoused the popular side, and published a satirical poem on the subject, entitled "*The Twa Bulls; a Metrical Tale for the Times.*" The "Bulls," whose sayings and doings are described in the satire, were John Bull, who stands up for the Protestant Episcopal Church, and Monk, or the Pope's Bull, which bore to have been issued from the Flaminian Gate, and by virtue of which Dr. Wiseman was elevated to the Cardinalate and the Arch-episcopal See of Westminster. The two bovine champions having concluded a "dreigh" debate, wherein the wrongs which the two rival Churches of England and Rome had sustained at each other's hands had been duly descanted on, the poem winds up as follows]—

THE parlance ended, Monk confounded
Stood speechless, motionless astounded,
Cast down his een, an' hung his lugs,
An' screw'd his chafts as pert as pug's.
Meanwhile, John kept baith watch an' ward,
Resolv'd the pawkie boy to guard;
O' every movement to be heedfu',
An' to repel by force if needfu'.
Amid Monk's luggage, John espied
A something Monk was fain to hide—
A ponderous box, wi' bolt an' bar
Secured, as dusky dungeons are.
"Pandora's box!" cried John, "ods rot 'em!
Hopeless most likely at the bottom!"
Wi' that he leapt among the trunks,
An' dang the luckless box to spunks;
When, lo! there lay exposed to view
To Monk's designs the fatal clew,
That a' his sage manœuvres foil'd,
An' a' his future hopes beguil'd.
Broad hats an' hosen painted red
Were snugly pack'd beneath the lid;
An' then a dozen past'ral crooks
Lay cleekit in ilk ither's hooks;
But last of a', an' warst of a',
The treacherous things that Johnnie saw,
Cam' boots, an' gyves, and brimstane matches,
To frichten contumacious wratches;
An' deeds of excommunication
T' expurgate frae the British nation,
As by the crossing-sweeper's besom,
The dross o' Johnnie's Sectarism!
This black discovery crown'd the whole;
John bit his lips, but couldna thole:
He growled awee, an' paw'd the ground,
Then set his horns an' made a bound,
Raised Monk aloft, and pitch'd him over
To fields beyond the Straits o' Dover.

"Noo, bide thee there," cried John, "an' study
Henceforth designs less black an' bloody!
Paint winkin' Virgins by the hunder,
To mak' the vulgar cattle wonder;
But don't expect to find, auld cronie,
A second Bonaparte* in Johnnie.
Thou might'st have still been playin' the flunkey—
As now thou strut'st a meddling monkey—
Had there been nane but John's dragoons
To fecht for foreign despot's croons."
This said, John slowly turn'd him roon'
An' snoov'd awa' an' humm'd a tune;
Survey'd his fields frae sea to sea,
An' bless'd his stars they still were free.
So, fear'd abroad, revered at home,
John quietly snapt his thooms at Rome;
Enjoy'd his future years in peace,
An' saw his wealth an' power increase;
An' rear'd his sons, a gallant band,
An honour to their fatherland.

——::——

RUSTIC COURTSHIP.

ANCE on a time twa gallant swains gaed forth upo' the spree,
An' they wad to yon castle go, their ladye-loves to see.
The tane he was a tailor bred, as I hae heard it tauld;
The tither (to complete my rhyme), he was a ploughman bauld.

The tailor's name was Bodkin Tam, frae Buttonhole he came;
The ploughman, he at Snipemire lived, an' Andro was his name.
Their cleedin' was as linen white, their faces black as coal;
Twa sweeter nosegays never bloom'd within a buttonhole.

O when they reach'd the castle door, an' tirl'd at the pin,
Their layde-loves leuch lood for joy, an' raise an' let them in.

---

* Louis Napoleon, then President of the French Republic, by whose interference Pope Pius IX., the Monk of the poem, had been recently restored to the Vatican, after he had been compelled to fly disguised as a flunkey from the fury of his own subjects.

"An' hoo's my darling Tibbockie?" the tailor he did cry;
"An' hoo's my winsome tailor lad?" the maiden did reply.

"What cheer, what cheer, my Peggy dear?" the ploughman he did
"Ou, brawlie, thank ye Snipie man!" replied the maiden gay. [say;
O then oor gallant gentleman into the hall did go,
An' fiddled, while the lassies tript the light fantastic toe.

But oh! alas! an' lack-a-day! for sic a set o' stupids!
A Bowman cam' an' shot a shaft, was keener far than Cupid's.
The ploughman in a press did hide; sauf's! hoo his heart was quailin';
The tailor near-hand hang'd himsel', when crawlin' owre a railin'.

The Bowman tane them ben, an' doon he bang'd the whuskey bottle;
An' there they sat, an' there they drank, till both o' them were dottle.
As blin' as bats they tane the gait, but tint themsels ootricht;
An' landit at the Horse Shoe Inn, at nine o'clock at nicht.

Syne to Mess John's the twasome hied, where they did rant an' roar,
An' kiss'd the servant queans, an' spew'd upo' the kitchen floor;
Till Gowlanthump cam' doon, his face wi' wrath as white as snaw,
An' threaten'd, if they didna flit, to tak' them to the law.

Neist owre the kirkyard stile they lap, wi' mony a frichtsome yell,
An' whuppit doon the tow, an' rang auld Geordie Mortclaith's bell.
They fled at last amid a storm o' divots, sticks, an' stanes;
But where they gaed, an' hoo they fared, the Gudeness only kens!

——::——

THE BACHELOR'S LAMENT.

When cauld winter ruffles the leaves frae the tree,
I'm as weary a bodie as weary can be;
There's no ane to cheer me across the hearthstane,
A' the lee winter nicht I maun dozin' my lane.
Dozin' my lane, dozin' my lane,
A' the lee winter nicht I maun dozin' my lane.

The thrush lo'es to sing i' the white bloomin' thorn,
The hare lo'es to gambol amang the green corn,
But naething in nature can mak' my heart fain,
For I ne'er can be blythesome while livin' my lane.
Livin' my lane, livin' my lane,
O I ne'er can be blythesome while livin' my lane.

I've an auld dowie chaumer juist twal' feet by ten,
An oot-house, an in-house, a but-house, an' ben,
A weel-plenish'd mailin', an' gowd a' my ain,
But nocht can delight me when livin' my lane.
Livin' my lane, livin' my lane,
O nocht can delight me when livin' my lane.

Though some blame the lasses I care nae a flee,
I'll e'en tak' my fortune, whate'er it may be;
Guid folk are richt scarce, but I'll surely find ane,
To mak' me far blither than livin my lane;
Livin' my lane, livin' my lane,
To mak' me far blither than livin' my lane.

An' gin a sweet wifey should e'er be my hap,
I'll wake like a lav'rock an' sleep like a tap,
I'll sing like a lintie, an' never complain,
But forget a' the sorrows o' livin' my lane.
Livin' my lane, livin' my lane,
O wha can be happy when livin' alane!

JAMES H. STODDART.

THREE years ago, a volume of noticeably excellent verse, entitled *The Village Life,* was issued from the local press, and appearing anonymously, excited some natural enquiry, which briefly satisfied itself with the conclusion that the author was JAMES H. STODDART, editor of *The Glasgow Herald* newspaper. The elegant impeachment has never been violently denied. Mr. STODDART is a Dumfriesshire man, having been born at Sanquhar, in 1831. Early evincing a literary bent, he was a contributor to the newspaper press when a mere youth. In 1862 he joined the *Herald* staff as sub-editor, and on the retirement of Professor Jack from that post in 1875, Mr. STODDART became editor-in chief, which responsible appointment he still worthily holds. In January of the present year (1882) at a representative gathering of his personal and literary friends, Mr. STODDART was presented with his portrait, as a mark of esteem, the Lord Provost making the presentation.

The volume of verse named, was issued by the eminent city publisher, James Maclehose, and the poems consist of a series of firmly-drawn and exceeding able sketches of village life and character. The book, from its design, rather than otherwise, lacks perhaps poetic massivity, but the poems are full of thought, flow, and conceptive force, and alternately bright, playful, tender, and incisive, glow everywhere with the keen lustre of accomplished verse.

In a purely literary sense we take *The Miller o' Birlstane* to be the finest poem in the book. It is a complete conception, most effectively wrought out, and embodies an under-current of spiritual meaning, which the competent reader will not fail to note. The poem is too long for quotation, but we give the following extracts from the fine sketch, entitled *The Blacksmith's Daughter*, which is drawn with a defter pencil than Crabbe's, and seems perfectly Wordsworthian in the subjective beauty and purity of its inspiration,—

——::——

THE BLACKSMITH'S DAUGHTER.

AWAY, philosophy and creeds!
Here in the honey-suckle's bower—
Which at the garden's farthest edge
Looks on the streamlet while it speeds,
Sunlit and gleaming through a shower,
Away o'er pebbles and through sedge—
Sits, with her needle, Isabel,
The Smith's young daughter, fair and tall,

As sweet a maiden for a song
As e'er did poet's heart enthral.

Her eyes are steadfast as a well
Of living water in its pit,
When to its depths immeasurable
A zenith star has lighted it.
Her face is ruddy with the health
Pure blood through all her body whirls;
And worth all gems of greatest wealth
Is the luxuriance of her curls.
She shakes them gaily in the sun,
Nor knows how witchingly they fall
About the marble of her throat.
Though dearly loved and prais'd by all,
She hardly knows she has begun
To blossom into perfect flower—
The perfect flower of womanhood.

. . . .

Much given to meditation's sway,
Nought loves she better than to see
The red light softly die away
Beyond the woods, beyond the moor.
Then steals she past the smithy door,
Rejoicing in her friend, the Night—
Her heart, her eyes, all brimming o'er
With youthful feelings of delight.
She seeks new life beneath the moon,
And happy thoughts that crave the boon
Of speech from her sweet lips, while high
Above, the stars are burning bright
In the blue lift, that to *her* eye
Seems veiling heaven from mortal sight.

The little stream is bubbling near,
And many a flickering gleam of light,
Through the dark trees and purple leaves,
Fall on its wavelets, soft and white.

. . . .

What thinks she, as her fair feet move
Along the margin of the stream?

Does she philosophise? or dream?
Her father's hard divinity
Is all she knows; and only knows
In her dear soul its better part—
Its softness and serenity,
Its loving, breathing, ardent heart.

. . . .

The Word by her,
In its pure life and loveliness,
Is freshly lov'd. Does it not stir
Within her heart on such a night
Holy emotions, like the bliss
Of perfect praise and saintly prayers?
Its beauty mingles with her faith.
The Lord of all, whose love she shares,
His Son divine, and human too,
Seem moving from the sphere of blue,
And, coming down upon the trees,
Are present in the mellow light
Of moon—are breathing through the night;
For beauty, love, and holy peace
Are theirs; and the fair earth reveals
Th' Eternal Presence that it feels.
Ah, gaze away, with shining eyes,
O'er all the mellow'd moonlight view,
Fair maiden, meditative, wise,
Deep thoughts will come, and feelings new;
For, just as shyly steals yon beam
Aslant the arch that spans the stream,
Till, in a corner, long in shade,
A dark-eyed pool its light receives;
So, on the calmness of thy soul,
A quickening beam of love will light,
Giving new hopes and strange delight,
Absorbing thoughts and passions—all!
And in the sacred inner shrine
Create an image half-divine,
A form of manliness and grace
To love, to cling to, and embrace:
Thy dawn of love, fair musing maid!

W. T. M^c AUSLANE
MATTHIAS BARR
THOMAS MILLER
IMPUNE
JAMES THOMSON
J BROWN
ROBERT ADAMSON

THOMAS MILLER

Is a native of Dunse, Berwickshire, born in the April of 1831. His mother, whom he warmly remembers as a most gentle and lovable being, was lady's maid to the wife of General Maitland previous to her marriage. His father also held employment in the Maitland family. In our poet's fourth year his parents removed to Dumbartonshire, and shortly afterwards to Glasgow, in which city he received the elements of a very ordinary school education. In his tenth year, he was put out to "herd kye" in a suburban park, and a year later he became a "tear-boy" in a local printfield.

An odd volume of Shakespeare's Plays which came into his hands awakened in his boyish mind a love of poetry and the drama, and the twin tastes thus early formed have survived the accidents of a chequered life, nobly and hopefully sustained. A final removal of his parents to Edinburgh, where they both soon died within six months of each other, left our poet to fight unaided the serious battle of life. In Edinburgh he has since remained, where his genial parts, joined to an excellent character and a ready ability, have procured him many attached friends.

Estimating Mr. MILLER poetically, he is more of the popular lyrist than the reflective poet, although he can indite excellent and impressive reflective verse when occasion requires. He has a faculty for popular song-writing, and has had the rare fortune of having his songs set to music and sung in the leading theatres and music halls in Scotland. Many of his lyrics are in popular request, and several of them are copyright property, an extract from one of which we append :—

MY HEART AYE WARMS TO THE TARTAN.

SCOTLAND, country of my birth,
My heart clings close to thee ;—
As clings the tendril to the vine,
And ivy to the tree ;—
The glorious East—the boundless West—
The sunny South's rich charms,
Are poor to him who Scotland loves—
Whose heart the tartan warms ;—
My heart aye warms to the tartan,
And wheresoe'er I roam,
I'll love the tartan kilt and plaid
As dearly as my home !

Dear Scotland, how thy mem'ries crowd
Within my fervent soul !
Thy fame shall make thy sons feel proud
While years and ages roll ;
Unconquer'd in the grand old days
By proud imperial Rome !
And still we've tartan'd warriors left
To guard our mountain home !—
My heart aye warms, &c.

Lang may the Rose of England twine
With Erin's Shamrock green !
And lang may Scotland's Thistle wave,
And Lion'd flag be seen !
God grant our land the joys of peace,
But should the war-blast roar,
The tartan'd kilt will to the front,
And conquer as of yore !
My heart aye warms to the tartan,
And wheresoe'er I roam,
The tartan kilt and plaid I'll love
As dearly as my home !

A LITTLE CHILD.

A FAIRY child! with eyes of lustrous blue,
  Soft in their glances, yet so deep and thrilling,
His very soul seem'd rising into view;
  And while you gazed, you felt its power instilling
Soft, soothing influence in your own like dew,
  And with the gentleness of Heaven filling
Your weary spirit with that peaceful rest
Which loves to linger in sweet childhood's breast.

Oh! blessed childhood! what a wondrous power
  Thy very helplessness of being wields,
E'en giant strength will at thy cradle cower;
  And wisdom wonder at the love it yields!
Weak as thou art, and tender as a flower,
  Thy very tenderness thy young life shields.
Sweet child, thou art a very Heaven to me,
For Heaven we know is made of such as thee.

And what a mystery is a little child!
  What powers, and possibilities, and parts
May all be slumbering 'neath these glances mild,
  Which yet may waken to enrich the arts;
And through thy ken may yet be reconciled
  Some cruel doubts, whose present influence thwarts
Our spirit's peace, and makes us sometimes own
  We're steering blindly o'er a sea unknown.

Rich are the realms that all around thee lie
  When once thy mind their mysteries can explore,
Rare are the treasures that will charm thine eye,
  And lead thee spellbound to their wondrous store.
Grand are the thoughts that reach the deep and high,
  Spreading for thee their intellectual lore—
Empires of wealth, by Heavenly power design'd,
  To meet the longings of the lofty mind.

We are, at best, but children all through life,
  For ever learning to be truly wise—
How weak at times 'gainst passion's deadly strife!
  How trifles fret us, and how sins surprise!

How hard the struggle when the powers are rife!
  What subtle discord 'neath the surface lies!
Wayward our will, and helpless in life's gale,
When clouds o'erwhelm, and doubts and storms assail.

Perchance thy spirit may be strong and wild—
  Restless and weary on life's dusty road;
Sick of the empty joys that once beguiled,
  And seem'd to ease the poor heart's weary load.
May all the tenderness that graced the child
  Return, and charm thee to the loved abode—
The dear old place—thy childhood's peaceful home,
Where blessings wait thee 'neath its hallow'd dome.

Wean'd from the world and all its passing show,
  Filled with the tender joy that thrills the breast,
When the chafed spirit, purged and bending low,
  Woos back the peace that conquers all unrest—
That gracious love that makes the heart o'erflow,
  And soothes the sorrows of the worst and best!
Oh! blessed influence, gentle and benign,
May all its wealth of healing power be thine!

And, when the shadows of Life's evening fall,
  And gathering mists frail Nature's powers obscure,
May Hope's bright star illume the dreary pall,
  And Faith stand firmer on its rock secure.
And when the signal's given to recall
  The spirit home to Him who washed it pure,
May life's last sigh be peaceful and serene,
And angels waft thee to the world unseen!

JAMES MACFARLAN.

One of the most remarkable poets the West of Scotland has yet produced, James Macfarlan was born in Kirk Street, Calton, Glasgow, April 9th, 1832. His youth was full of high poetic promise, but his habits were erratic, and the extraordinary promise of his earlier years was never effectively fulfilled. He inherited, in a large measure, that dangerous unbalance of mind which is too often the accompaniment of poetic genius, and his brief life, for the most part, was passed in purposeless dreamings amid the chill shades of penury and want. In justice to MACFARLAN, however, it is but fair to state that his moral up-bringing was wretched in the extreme. The son of a wandering Irish pedlar, poor MACFARLAN was early familiarised with vice and profligacy of every form and hue. It is noteworthy, however, that his poetry throughout presents a remarkable and sustained elevation and purity of thought and feeling. Poesy was the one bright, beautiful, and inspiring goddess which he lovingly worshipped. The husk of the body thrown aside, he breathes in his verse a rarified atmosphere, and delightedly bathes his wings in the empyrean ether of song. He was deficient in personal address. In the matter of dress and appearance he was indeed careless to a grievous fault, and his presence was the reverse of prepossessing. The most hopeful admirer of his genius could find but little trace of it in his features or in his conversation. The fact is, MACFARLAN was a Bohemian by birth, and by distinct preference; not choosing to be aught better. Utterly uneducated, without help or external promptings of any kind, but guided solely by his self-informing instincts, he emerged for a brief time from the thick obscurity of his surroundings with the sunlight of a splendid poetical promise on his brow. Proportionate, however, to the help and encouragement extended to him, he slackened his industry, and allowed his erratic habits to fatally impede his progress. Latterly he fell into confirmed ill-health, and for the last two years of his brief life retired into the obscurity of silence, deserted by all—friends, fame, hope—all except his proud genius, and the consumptive, hacking cough which stuck to him closer than a brother. Occasionally, to the very last, his fine strong genius would shoot out a lambent flame, but the lark of song was dead within his heart. It was but the *gutterings* of an expiring lamp-light within the socket. He died November 6, 1862, in the thirty-first year of his age, and was interred in Cheapside Cemetery, Glasgow, at the expense of a few admirers of his writings. Pegasus has too often proved a horse which carries poets to the poorhouse; but never, surely, was poor erring Hartley Coleridge's denunciation of the thriftless trade of rhyme-making more in point than in the case of JAMES MACFARLAN. Experience speaks—

"There never was a blessing or a curse,
So sweet, so cruel as a knack of verse:
When the smug stripling finds the way to rhyme,
Glad as the wild bee 'mid a bed of thyme,
Sure of the praise which partial friends bestow,
He breathes a bliss, if bliss may be below.
Pass some few years, and see how all will end:
The hireling scribe estranged from every friend;
Or if one friend remain, it's one so brave,
He will not quit the wreck he cannot save;
The good man's pity, and the proud man's scorn,
The muse's vagabond, he roams forlorn.
Oh, may all Christian souls, while yet 'tis time,
Renounce the world, the flesh, the devil, and vile rhyme!"

MACFARLAN was a great master of verbal melody, and his poems are replete with high thought and rich fancy, are ornate in diction, and impressive in their flow.

—::—

BOOKWORLD.

WHEN the dim presence of the awful night
Clasps in its jewell'd arms the slumbering earth,
Alone I sit beside the lowly light,
That like a dream-fire flickers on my hearth,

With some joy-teeming volume in my hand—
A peopled planet, opulent and grand.

It may be Shakspeare, with his endless train
  Of sceptred thoughts—a glorious progeny !—
Borne on the whirlwind of his mighty strain,
  Through vision-lands, for ever fair and free,
His great mind beaming thro' those phantom crowds,
Like evening sun from out a wealth of clouds.

It may be Milton, on his seraph wing,
  Soaring to heights of grandeur yet untrod ;
Now deep where horrid shapes of darkness cling,
  Now lost in splendour at the feet of God ;
Girt with the terror of avenging skies,
Or wrapt in dreams of infant paradise.

It may be Spenser, with his misty shades,
  Where forms of beauty wondrous tales rehearse ;
With breezy vistas, and with cool arcades
  Opening for ever in his antique verse.
It may be Chaucer, with his drink divine,
His Tabard old, and pilgrims twenty-nine.

Perchance I linger with the mighty three
  Of glorious Greece, that morning land of song,
Who bared the fearful front of tragedy,
  And soar'd to fame on pinions broad and strong ;
Or watch beneath the Trojan ramparts proud
The dim hosts gathering like a thunder-cloud.

No rust of time can sully Quixote's mail,
  In wonted rest his lance securely lies ;
Still is the faithful Sancho stout and hale,
  For ever wide his wonder-stricken eyes ;
And Rosinante, bare and spectral steed,
Still throws gaunt shadows o'er their every deed.

Still can I robe me in the old delights
  Of caliph splendid, and of genii grim,
The star-wealth of Arabia's Thousand Nights,
  Shining till every other light grows dim ;
Wander away in broad voluptuous lands,
By streams of silver, and through golden sands ;

Still hear the storms of Camoens burst and swell,
  His seas of vengeance raging wild and wide;
Or wander by the glimmering fires of hell,
  With dreaming Dante and his spirit-guide;
Loiter in Petrarch's green melodious grove;
Or hang with Tasso o'er his hopeless love.

What then to me is all your sparkling dance,
  Wine-purpled banquet, or vain fashion's blaze,
Thus roaming through the realms of rich romance,
  Old Bookworld, and its wealth of royal days,
For ever with those brave and brilliant ones
That fill time's channel like a stream of suns!

——::——

THE LORDS OF LABOUR.

They come, they come, in a glorious march,
  You can hear their steam-steeds neigh,
As they dash through Skill's triumphal arch,
  Or plunge 'mid the dancing spray.
Their bale-fires blaze in the mighty forge,
  Their life-pulse throbs in the mill,
Their lightnings shiver the gaping gorge,
  And their thunders shake the hill.
    Ho! these are the Titans of toil and trade,
      The heroes who wield no sabre;
    But mightier conquests reapeth the blade
      That is borne by the lords of labour.

Brave hearts like jewels light the sod,
  Through the mists of commerce shine,
And souls flash out, like stars of God,
  From the midnight of the mine.
No palace is theirs, no castle great,
  No princely pillar'd hall,
But they well may laugh at the roofs of state,
  'Neath the heaven which is over all.
    Ho! these are the Titans of toil and trade,
      The heroes who wield no sabre;
    But mightier conquests reapeth the blade
      Which is borne by the lords of labour.

Each bares his arm for the ringing strife
  That marshals the sons of the soil,
And the sweet-drops shed in their battle of life
  Are gems in the crown of Toil.
And better their well-won wreath, I trow,
  Than laurels with life-blood wet;
And nobler the arch of a bare bold brow,
  Than the clasp of a coronet.
    Then hurrah for each hero, although his deed
      Be unblown by trump or tabor,
    For holier, happier far is the meed
      That crowneth the lords of labour.

——::——

THE POET.

Alone, upon a path of fairy flow'rs
  That drank a wild sweet light from dying day,
Like a calm thought, across those sumptuous hours,
  A poet held his way.

He had been one whose earnest spirit dream'd
  By misty mountain summits, robed in rain:
Whose soul ran riot when the tempest stream'd
  Athwart the moaning main.

He had borne much of wrong, had tasted crime,
  'Mong holy martyrs trod with bleeding brows;
And with the minstrels of the olden time
  Held many a deep carouse.

He had stood oft 'mid ruins old, sublime,
  In classic climes whose airs enrich the globe;
Where old Decay, the sullen slave of Time,
  Sits in his ivy robe.

His soul had wander'd through the paths of change,
  On to the silent doorways of the dead;
In many a flight of vision, mystic, strange,
  Through the spher'd night had fled.

He had found beauty on the snow-robed plain,
 And mountain stream struck dumb by chilling frost,
And in the white skirts of the hurricane
 That swept the rugged coast.

Love had he felt in one wild rush of dawn,
 That, bright'ning, deepen'd into lustrous day,
Then slowly pass'd, o'er life's stern hills withdrawn
 In sunset rich away.

With calm, stern Nature in the wilds he trod—
 Felt the commanding joy that awes and thrills
When some wild sun-burst, like the glance of God,
 Smote all the wond'ring hills.

Before him lay the sea; on either hand
 The gloomy mountain ranges cloud-wrapt hung;
While over many a dreary league of land
 The solemn see-breeze sung.

Gilding with silver light the zone of stars,
 All wilder'd rose the white moon, lustrous, large,
O'er the wild tumult of the rock-ribb'd bars,
 And oozy, salt sea-marge.

There knelt the poet, girt with holy fears,
 His voice in soul-wrapt worship warbling loud,
Within the temple roof'd with burning spheres,
 And canopied with cloud!

W. T. M'AUSLANE.

WILLIAM THOMSON M'AUSLANE is well known as the author of a little volume of *Gospel Songs* published two years ago, and which was generally recognised as comprising some of the finest recent contributions to sacred poetry. He is a native of Tradeston, Glasgow, having been born there on the 18th of April, 1832, and is the sixth son of a numerous family, several members of which have adopted the ministerial profession. His youth was mostly spent in the Vale of Leven, to which district his parents originally belonged. A poet from his boyhood up, he issued in the spring of 1849 a small volume of poetical offerings entitled *Early Efforts*, inscribed to James Ewing, Esq. of Strathleven, LL.D. This was reproduced in an augmented form early in 1854. These youthful publications were received with much favour, as showing, amid defects incidental to early efforts, the possession of true poetic feeling, with a fine appreciation both of natural scenery and moral excellence, allied to considerable natural powers of thought and description. A few pieces in the Scottish dialect evince respectively real pathos and genuine humour. These volumes are long since out of print.

In 1850, Mr. M'Auslane entered the office of the *Daily Mail* newspaper, holding positions—first as a clerk, afterwards as book-keeper, and subsequently as reporter and sub-editor. In 1861 he transferred his services to the *Scottish Guardian*, was afterwards on the *Morning Journal*, and sub-edited for a short time the *Inverness Courier*, then conducted by the well-known and lately-deceased journalist, Dr. Carruthers. Securing a re-engagement on the staff of the *Daily Mail*, he returned to Glasgow, and held with much acceptancy the position of chief-reporter until his appointment, in 1875, to his present office of Secretary to the Association for the Relief of Incurables for Glasgow and the West of Scotland. It will thus be seen that our poet has had a busy journalistic career; and although his life has been crushed full of exacting work, the still small voice of poetry has never been completely silent in his heart. For many years back his name has appeared with welcome frequency in the *Sunday Magazine* and other first-class religious periodicals, attached to deep-toned but quiet and unobtrusively beautiful gems of sacred song. The favour with which those chaste and unassuming poetical offerings at the shrine of a pure faith were generally received induced the author to re-issue them in a collected form under the distinctive title of *Gospel Songs*. The hymns and sacred pieces comprising the little volume are indeed Gospel songs in the truest sense of the term. The collection was lately praised by Mr. Spurgeon, a tribute to his genius and Christian faith of which our poet may justly feel proud. The exquisite feeling, the simplicity, and yet oftentimes eloquent verbal flow of Mr. M'AUSLANE's verses, which secured for him the reputation of a poet years ago, are amply represented in his present volume of Gospel songs, several of which have been set to music by Mr. William Moodie, teacher of music, Glasgow, and are now in use in different academies. His genius is thoroughly sanctified, and his chief delight seems to be in Gospel themes. He is also the author of two prose publications—*Prayer, Pardon, and Peace*, a very useful guide to anxious inquirers, now in its third edition; and *Light in the Valley*, a touching and deeply-interesting religious biography.

——::——

MORNING AT BRODICK.

FAIR Brodick Castle by the sea
'Mong green embowering woods appears;
Behind, in bold sublimity,
Goatfell its graceful form uprears.
An altar to the Great Supreme
It looks, whence vapours slowly rise—
Chased by the morning's glowing beam—
Like clouds of incense to the skies;
While mutely hills around combine
To own their Maker's power Divine.

How sweet, this early summer's day,
  While Nature vocal is with joy,
To Shirag's steep to take my way,
  Or Rosa's vale, or quiet Glen Cloy!
By murmuring rivulet to stray,
  Less happy scarce than when a boy
I sported on the gowany brae,
  No cares to trouble nor annoy;
Or scented first the wild bluebell
In some remote, romantic dell!

How sweet to hear the brooklet sing,
  To mark the primrose by its brim!
The butterfly is on the wing,
  The glad birds chant their matin hymn;
The hawthorn fragrant makes the air,
  And, gazing on the peaceful scene,
From earth so bright to sky so fair,
  With not a cloud to intervene,
All things beneath, around, above,
Proclaim my God a God of love.

But storms will come, and thunders loud
  The echoes of the glens awake;
And guilty fears can seize the proud,
  And make the boldest rebel quake.
'Tis vain to speak of mercy then;
  For justice stern the soul pursues
And satisfaction seeks. But when
  Believingly the sinner views
Mercy and truth in Jesus meet,
Pardon is found and rest is sweet.

——::——

HOME AND WIFE.

Where in this world, where strife and guile abound,
Shall one calm spot, one faithful friend be found,
A refuge sweet from earthly toil and care,
A heart that will thy griefs and burdens share,

Whose love keeps true through all the scenes of life?—
Thy Home that refuge, and that Friend thy Wife.
Bound be thy heart to home by strongest ties—
'Tis Heaven in miniature beneath the skies;
'Mid other claims, neglect not duty here,
This be of usefulness thy choicest sphere;
In the dear partner of thy life confide,
Let mutual trust with mutual love abide;
Prefer the solid joys around thy hearth
To all the pleasures elsewhere found on earth;
Then shall in peace and honour pass thy days,
And God, approving, smile on all thy ways.

—::—

MUSINGS AT TARBERT, LOCHFYNE.

The sun shines brightly on Lochfyne,
  On Tarbert's castle, old and grey,
As near its ruins I recline,
  And all the landscape wide survey;
While thoughts of past years intervene,
And mingle with the present scene.

The land-locked harbour at my feet,
  Round which the white-washed village runs,
Is throng'd with skiffs—the fishing fleet;
  Sea-ward the battery points its guns;
And islets small lie here and there,
Like the wild hills encircling, bare.

In garb of blue, with hardy mien,
  The fishermen, the shores along,
Mending their nets and boats are seen;
  Some sit the scatter'd rocks among;
While servant girls, their washing done,
Spread out their labours to the sun.

East, north, and west, from side to side,
  The eye may wander or may rest,
From where fair Bute o'erlooks the Clyde
  To far Ben Cruachan's snow-white crest;

Or lovingly may seek repose
On heights the West Loch that enclose.

How sweet, beneath yon mountain's brow,
  Where streamlets run and lambkins play,
Where yellow whin and heather grow,
  To spend the early summer's day;
Inhale fresh breezes from the hill,
And let the fancy roam at will!

How sweet, remote from haunts of men,
  While nature's works around rejoice,
To walk through Rallock's lovely glen,
  And list the cuckoo's distant voice;
By Stonefield stroll, whose charms are shared
So freely by a generous laird.

But sounds of bustle from below,
  From thoughts like these recall my mind,
Pierward there comes a constant flow—
  Men, horses, carriages, combined;
The famed Columba I descry,
And the day's great event is nigh.

Onward the sovereign steamer rides,
  Of firth and lake acknowledg'd queen;
Nearer the floating palace glides—
  Glasgow in miniature is seen;
Arrived, some passengers she leaves,
And others in return receives.

Northward her course she then renews,
  While westward, on the Tarbert road,
The tide of life its way pursues:
  Some near the village find abode;
Others for Islay's steamer fast,
Or Campbeltown go driving past.

How changed the time since Bruce the Bold
  Dwelt in these halls in kingly pride;
Since, in more recent days of old,
  Here clansmen fought and bled and died;
Now the broad claymore and the targe
Have given place to net and barge.

JAMES THOMSON.

James Thomson, author of a volume entitled *Northumbria and other Poems*, recently issued as a third edition, was born October 21st, 1825, at the village of Rothes, situated on the river Spey. Receiving an ordinary village-school education, he was put to "herd cattle" at the age of thirteen; but showing a taste and inclination for the profession of a gardener, he was afterwards apprenticed to that calling on the estate of William Grant, Esq., Elchies, Speyside. He was afterwards in the service of Lord Cockburn at "Bonny Bonnally;" and latterly proceeded to England, where he has resided for the past thirty years.

Mr. Thomson wrote verses early. His latest volume, issued in 1881 from the "Ballantyne Press," Edinburgh and London, is most tastefully got up, and in point of typography makes about the neatest and clearest page of verses we have ever seen. The literary merits of the book are also of a superior order, and, in view of the author's position and opportunities, show the possession of real poetical talent. He writes with true poetic flow, close observation, and correct taste.

—::—

TO MY AULD PIKE STAFF.

My auld pike staff, my trusty frien',
Like hand and glove we aye hae been;
Mony a change we baith hae seen,
        Since first we met;
Atween us yet nae words hae been,
        I'm prood to say't.

Weel do I mind the April morn
I took you frae your parent thorn.
Although at times you've been the scorn
O' modern pride,
I ne'er could bide to hae ye shorn
O' bark or hide.

A varnish'd coat ye ne'er could shaw,
Like sticks that come frae far awa';
Nor were yê ever busket braw
Wi' dangling tassel;
But aye a sturdy shank could shaw,
To bide a brassel.

When I to kirk or market gaed,
You aye did help me in my need;
I didna want a hicc'ry reed
Like strutting spark;
They look nae better than a weed,
And dae sma' wark.

Owre hills and glens I've wander'd wide
With you aye faithful by my side;
Down craigs and rocks you've been my guide,
And kept me richt;
With you I ne'er felt dash'd nor fley'd
In darkest nicht.

On many a wild-goose chase we've been,
When I was thoughtless, young, and green,
Full forty miles we've often gane
On summer's day,
When some famed spot was to be seen,
Where heroes lay.

Tho' thoughtless folks may sneer and laugh
At you and me, my auld pike staff,
We'll little heed their idle chaff,
But toddle on;
You'll be my friend, my auld pike staff,
Till I am gone.

HEART MEMORIES.

There are mem'ries treasur'd in the heart which tongue hath never
told,
Nor would their rich possessors sell for worlds of glittering gold.
Our sacred treasure's guarded fast, with more than miser care;
We would not our bright gems display to the rude world's stare.

The heart that has no mem'ries dear is like an empty spring,
Which to the weary trav'ller's heart no healing waters bring.
But he whose soul is stored with these has more than jewels rare;
He carries daily in his heart a cure for biting care.

When tired of life's steep rugged road, he cheers his weary way
With mem'ries sweet of days long past, that seem but yesterday,
Perchance the forms of dear old friends up in review he brings;
They pass through memory's golden gate on soft and downy wings.

But there's a form, when all is fled, that ne'er doth pass away,
To mem'ry's eye 'tis never lost the livelong night and day;
Oft has that form brought peace and hope back to the troubled heart
And made the tears of bliss and joy unconsciously to start.

The soft sweet tear of memory, like blessed summer rain,
Quickens the dried-up weary heart, and bids it smile again.
Who has not felt the soothing power of mem'ry's soft'ning tear,
When into that rich treasure-house we enter without fear?

MATTHIAS BARR.

A poet of true genius, Matthias Barr was born at Edinburgh, December 6th, 1831. His father was a native of Germany, who married an Edinburgh lady, and carried on the business of a watchmaker in that city. Having received a liberal education at the High School and Academy of

Edinburgh, our poet paid a brief visit to Germany, and afterwards removed to London, where he held a respectable appointment for a number of years, devoting his leisure hours to the cultivation of his literary tastes. At the present time Mr. BARR successfully conducts, on his own account, a music-selling and publishing establishment in London.

In 1865 his first-published volume of poems appeared, and he has since then issued several interesting little volumes of beautiful, touching, and in numerous instances, exquisite verse. Like Burns and Wordsworth, he finds the inspiration of song in the commonest objects. The simplest scenes, the homeliest incidents, the commonest wild-flowers, are all in turn handled by Mr. BARR with rare delicacy and the truest poetic feeling. His poems and lyrics of child-life have earned for him the highest praise. Dr. Rogers, an eminent authority, has judged them as "unquestionably the best in the language," and we should certainly say, that for beauty and purity of fancy and perception, with exquisite melody of tone, it would be difficult to rival them. For an exhaustive review of Mr. BARR's career and high merit as a poet, we refer the reader to an article in *Hand and Heart* for September 23rd, 1881, from the pen of William Andrews, Esq., of the "Hull Literary Club."

——::——

TO A BIRD IN THE CITY.

AH, bird! I bless thee in my heart; God knows I love to see
Thy tiny form, for none can tell the thoughts you bring to me—
The happy thoughts of far-off times, times long'd for now in vain,
Of thoughtless nights and careless days I'll never know again.

O breezy hills, O balmy groves, O pleasant seas and streams,
O sunlit fields, and green, green lanes, I only see in dreams—
These, these, all these, and more, are thine : what joy, O bird ! for you,
While here I pine with burning brow the golden summer through !

Dear bird ! thy name is link'd with all earth's sweetest things afar :
Thou hast no place, thou simple one, where toiling thousands are :
The hedgerows, white with blossoms all ; the morning wet with dew ;
The tranquil eve—boon here unknown—these, these belong to you.

Then leave us, bird ! yet take with thee my blessing as you go,
And what of best and holiest thoughts my nature can bestow.
Thy gift will prove a richer dower than that I give to thee ;
A hoard of mem'ries shall be mine when thou art lost to me.

O life ! this is a bitter world—a world full stern and cold :
We need such signs to keep our hearts and thoughts from growing old ;
We need such signs to guide us here and help us on our way ;
Such things speak plainer far to me than all that man can say.

——::——

ONLY A BABY SMALL.

Only a baby small, dropt from the skies ;
Only a laughing face, two sunny eyes ;
Only two cherry lips, one chubby nose ;
Only two little hands, ten little toes.

Only a golden head, curly and soft ;
Only a tongue that wags loudly and oft ;
Only a little brain, empty of thought ;
Only a little heart troubl'd with nought.

Only a tender flower, sent us to rear ;
Only a life to love while we are here ;
Only a baby small, never at rest ;
Small, but how dear to us, God knoweth best.

MY BRIDE.

My Bride is a simple maiden,
  And Love is her all—her all;
But better is love in a garret
  Than hate in a gilded hall.
And brighter than all the jewels
  That flash on a monarch's brow,—
Ay! bright as the stars of heaven
  Are the eyes of this bride, I trow.

When sorrows invest my bosom,
  I look in her smiling face;
When friends like the snow have vanished,
  I weep in her wild embrace:
The thrill of her glance is rapture,
  The glow of her touch divine;—
And Poesy, darling Poesy,
  Is the name of this bride of mine.

——::——

MY WEE WIFE.

Oh, wha is like my wee wife,
  My wee wife, my wee wife;
Oh, wha is like my wee wife,
  Sae leal an' true to me.

The wee bit singin' birdie
  Is happy in its nest,
The laughin' dautit bairnie
  Upon its mither's breast;
The lammie on the brae side,
  The hare upon the lea,
An' my wee wife, my wee wife,
  Brings happiness to me.
    Oh, wha is like, etc.

When vex'd wi' pride an' folly
  I sit me doun an' sigh,
Or mourn that care an' sorrow
  Should ever come us nigh.
The clouds that hing aboon me
  Awa' awa' they flee,
For ae blink o' my wee wife
  Is sunshine aye to me.
    Oh, wha is like, etc.

When life is in the gloamin',
  An' eerie fa's the nicht,
An' gropin' in the darkness,
  We weary for the licht,
Oh, then, oh, then, thegither
  We'll lay us doun an' dee.
For heaven without my wee wife,
  It werena heaven to me.
    Oh, wha is like, etc.

JOHN BROWN.

JOHN BROWN is a native of Dumbartonshire. He was born at Alexandria, his paternal grandfather having migrated to the shores of Lochlomond from Ayrshire about the middle of the last century. Our poet's early boyhood was spent at the adjacent village of Dumbuck, where he first observed and loved the beauties of nature. The family afterwards removed to Glasgow, where John was put to the trade of pattern-designing in Todd & Higginbotham's works, under the supervision of his uncle, who was a leading hand in the department. Mr. BROWN still follows his first profession, and from natural taste and long practical experience, is considered to be a very successful designer, and has been long and acceptably employed by leading city firms.

To his artistic tastes, Mr. BROWN superadds a native talent for poetry, which he occasionally puts to modest, but effective and pleasing use. He is a man of excellent character, superior mental endowments, and unassuming habits. We quote several of his pieces with pleasure.

—::—

THE BATTLE OF LANGSIDE.

BIRDS sit on leafy bowers in Langside wood,
Singing love songs o'er the flowers in Langside wood;
Then come, my love, away,
Through the Queen's park let us stray,
Up by the old mill brae, to Langside wood.

There's a spell at gloaming grey in Langside wood,
When the silver moon holds sway in Langside wood;
Then in accents sweet and bold,
Fond lovers may unfold
Tales with more charms than gold, in Langside wood.

In fifteen sixty-eight, near Langside wood,
Queen Mary met her fate near Langside wood,
On the thirteenth day of May,
In the early morning grey,
Brave Regent Murray lay near Langside wood.

'Twas just a mile away from Langside wood,
She beheld the bloody fray, near Langside wood;
Dressed in her regal sheen,
Queenly beauty in her mien,
On Cathcart's castle green, near Langside wood.

Grange safely lay concealed near Langside wood,
But he soon his power revealed near Langside wood;
When Argyle came into view,
Like hail his arrows flew,
Then the armies closer drew to Langside wood.

The clash of steel to steel near Langside wood,
Made them stagger, faint, and reel, near Langside wood,

Till her army took to flight,
To the left and to the right,
Down the hill with all their might, by Langside wood.

In the panic of defeat, near Langside wood,
Pursued in hot retreat, near Langside wood,
Three hundred men were slain
Before they reached the plain,
And thus ended Mary's reign, near Langside wood.

Now, no more war's trumpet horn, near Langside wood,
Is heard at early morn, near Langside wood,
But the thrush and cooing dove,
And young Cupid's charms of love,
Are felt on hill and grove near Langside wood.

——::——

THE GLEN.

NEVER tread on the heels o' anither,
But stan' in your ain leather shoon,
An' if earth canna gie ye eneuch,
Then resort to the stars and the mune.

There's the rain, an' the snaw, an' the thunder,
An' the clouds that flee drearily by ;
There's the wind that whisks by like a spirit,
An' then there's the bonnie blue sky.

In the meantime I'll tak a bit peep
O' the glen near my auld mither's dwellin',
O'er the lea wi' the sheep and the kye—
By the wud whare the timmer's a-fellin'.

I will join in the sang o' the birds,
An' pu' the wild flowers for my dearie—
The hawthorn an' bonnie blue bells—
For 'tis Summer, an' Nature is cheery.

I will twine roun' the stem o' the rose
A frill wi' the red-tipped gowan,
An' the heather entwine wi' a string
O' the fruit frae the tree o' the rowan.

Enchanted I'll stan' on the rock
  An' watch the wild freaks o' the fountain,
An' list to the cry o' the deer
  As it bounds o'er the heath o' the mountain.

I will gaze on the dark pool below
  When the sun in the west is declining,
An' the trout frae his bed upward springs,
  While the moon's through the trees dimly shining.

But it's whispered that fairies an' witches
  In the glen after gloamin' appear;
Sae I'll aff to my ain wifie's ingle,
  For when there I hae naething to fear.

Then I'll muse on the fair book o' Nature—
  Recreation that never brings sorrow,
An' will ne'er let the joys o' the nicht
  Be the cause o' a pang on the morrow.

———::———

MY MAGGIE'S NO MORE.

Twittering, twittering over the meadow,
  Twittering, twittering over the stream,
Downy clouds playing at sunshine and shadow;
  Can it be real, or is it a dream?
Was it the swallow that I heard twittering?
  Is winter time past; is it summer again?
Was that the cuckoo that I heard fluttering?
  Has Flora returned with the flowers in her train?

Ah! yes, it is summer so blythsome and cheery,
  The storm of the winter's no more on the shore,
But summer or winter to me's alike dreary,
  When I think on the past, and my Maggie's no more.
Oh! sad was the summons, that left our home motherless;
  Woe's me for the babe that but lately she bore!
Oh God! give me strength that they be not left fatherless;
  For despair rends my heart, since my Maggie's no more.

ALEXANDER LOGAN.

AMONGST those who, to appreciable purpose, have earnestly striven to maintain the prestige of the beautiful Doric of auld Scotland in all its wholesome sweetness, simplicity, and purity, ALEXANDER LOGAN, the subject of this sketch, holds no inferior place. He is a native of Edinburgh, having been born there July 6th, 1833. His parents, who were in humble circumstances, but of highly respectable character, he lost while yet a mere child. Our poet was thus early sent forth to fight, on his own behalf, the trying battle of life; and getting apprenticed to the trade of a tin-plate worker in his native city, his subsequent career, both as an operative and a Scottish poet, clearly establishes his title as a man of character and poetic parts. He is at present in the employment of one of the leading firms in Edinburgh, and it is a significant fact that he has been in the service of that particular firm for a full quarter of a century.

Like the majority of true poets, Mr. LOGAN wrote verses early, but it was not until about 1862 that he ventured on sending his literary productions to the Scottish newspapers and journals. Many of his beautiful, though homely, little poems found their way across the Atlantic, re-appearing in the columns of the Scottish-American press; and the favour with which they were generally received induced him to issue them in a collected form in 1864, under the title of *Poems and Lyrics.* The little volume, replete as it is with much poetic beauty, pathos, and patriotism, was very favourably received by the critics, and is now out of print. Mr. Logan is never tired of singing, in true and sweet tones, of domestic love, parental felicities, and ingleside cheer.

ALEXR LOGAN
JOHN NICOL
GEORGE DONALD
NEMO ME IMPUNE ACESSE
JOHN FULLERTON
EBENEZER SMITH
QUINTIN BONE

He has, in addition, a true and natural note of pathos, which he uses with frequency and effect, as in *Life's Gloaming*, and in his equally touching poem—*Kiss my native Soil for Me!* He is also national to a degree, and his lyre, which, figuratively, is wreathed with heather, thistles, and tartan ribbons, rings out heart-stirring lyrics of fervent purpose and inspiriting flow. Several of his songs have been set to music and published in sheet form. It is in the homelier humorous and domestic effusions of his muse, however, that his genius is perhaps most evident. His Doric is pure, simple, and flowing, and he sings a true and hearty note of song, without artifice or obtrusive self-consciousness.

——::——

MACALLISTER'S BONNET.

In mony strange places on earth ha'e I been,
An' mony queer things in my travels ha'e seen;
But this I'll maintain till the last breath I draw,
Macallister's bonnet is queerest o' a'.
It serves for a scrubber to wash doon the stair,
A cushion to place on his auld easy chair;
It carries the tatties, the barley an' breid,
An' as for a besom he ne'er felt the need.
  Noo what could compare wi' Macallister's bonnet?
  Ay! weel ye may stare at Macallister's bonnet!
  An' wonder wha wrocht it! likewise where he bocht it!
  For ilka thing rare does Macallister's bonnet!

It carries the turnips when feedin' the kye,
An' answers his mare as a mooth-pock forbye;
A cosie bed mak's for the dog or the cat,
In short, it wad do for!—I kenna a' what.
It serves for a bucket to carry the coals;
If windows are broken it fills up the holes;
When shavin', he wipes wi' 't his jaws, mooth an' chin,
He'd use't for his brose, but it winna haud in!

When gaun to the market it's ever the same,
It serves for a basket the beef to bring hame ;
Wi' sheep heids an' trotters it's aye stappit fu' !
Forbye lots o' scran for the hens and the soo !
Nae marvel need be though it's envied by some,
It's sand-box or meal-pock, an' soops doon the lum !
The auld fail-me-never maist does ilka turn !
He'd mak' it a kail-pat, but losh ! it wad burn !
Noo what could compare wi' Macallister's bonnet ?
Ay ! weel ye may stare at Macallister's bonnet !
An' wonder wha wrocht it ! likewise where he bocht it !
For ilka thing rare does Macallister's bonnet !

——::——

YE NEEDNA FEAR FOR SCOTLAND.*

Ye needna fear for Scotland—firm as her native rock,
Her sons in danger's darkest hour withstand the battle-shock ;
As pours their purple heather-bloom its fragrance on the gale,
They fling their gallant slogan forth, and haughty despots quail.
Ye needna fear for Scotland—these mountaineers are mine !
To licht the path o' liberty their claymores ever shine !

Ye needna fear for Scotland—unsullied is her name,
In ilka clime beneath the sun kent is her matchless fame ;
The river owre its rocky bed may cease to seaward flow,
But never shall my trusty braves their backs turn to a foe.
Ye needna fear for Scotland—these mountaineers are mine !
To licht the path o' liberty their claymores ever shine !

Ye needna fear for Scotland—aggression's tide to stay,
In pride will rise the Thistle green, an' manhood lead the way ;
Her tartan plaid has never wrapt the bosom o' a slave,
Her banner soon amid the shouts o' victory will wave !
Ye needna fear for Scotland—these mountaineers are mine !
To licht the path o' liberty their claymores ever shine !

* "These men are mine—ye needna fear for Scotland !"—*Sir Colin Campbell.*

Ye needna fear for Scotland—her war-pipe's stirring strain
Anither brilliant link will add to glory's growing chain ;
High valour's quenchless fire within her noble clansmen burn !
My kilted heroes o' the north nae foe on earth may turn !
Ye needna fear for Scotland—these mountaineers are mine !
To licht the path o' liberty their claymores ever shine !

—::—

LIFE'S GLOAMING.

Noo I'm drawing near my gloaming, swiftly passes time awa' ;
Darker, and mair dark, the shadows deepen as they roond me fa'.
Frae the freends I soon maun sever I ha'e lov'd since Life's young day,
An' will honour while I travel doon the brae, doon the brae !

Feeble on a staff I'm leaning, lanely, sair, toil-worn an' auld ;
For the Shepherd kind I'm waiting, He'll convey me to the fauld.
There reliev'd o' ilka burden, I'll foregather and be gay
Wi' the freends that pass'd before me doon the brae, doon the brae !

They wha to my heart were dearest, lang, lang noo ha'e been awa' ;
Still, the sweet thocht mak's me happy, that I soon will see them a'
In a fair land, never darken'd by the dowie clouds o' wae ;
Smile, ye Powers aboon, an' cheer me doon the brae, doon the brae!

Gild my path wi gowden lustre, aid thae weary feet o' mine ;
Guide me on my hameward journey to the freends o' auld langsyne.
Let my lang lost bosom-treasures meet me on the seraph-way ;
Life is ebbing fast, I'm nearly doon the brae, doon the brae !

—::—

KISS MY NATIVE SOIL FOR ME ! *

Comrade, fareweel for evermair, soon rent will be the mystic chain ;
To part wi' thee my heart is sair, on earth we'll never meet again.
If spared to reach oor heather-land, that lies beyond the deep blue sea,
Bend thou thy knee upon its strand an' kiss my native soil for me !

* "Fareweel" said a brave young Scottish soldier, lying on his deathbed in India, to his comrade who was about to leave for home, also weary and worn. "Fareweel, dear comrade, an if spared to reach auld Scotland, kiss my native soil for me."

I'll speel nae mair oor bonnie braes, nor wander through the flow'ry glens;
I'll hear nae mair the linty's lays, the sweetest notes my bosom kens.
Far frae the land that I adore, alas! my narrow bed maun be;
Then kneel upon its rocky shore an' kiss my native soil for me!

Still to this sorrow-stricken heart the thocht o' auld langsyne and hame
Can sunny memories impart, an' fan affection's purest flame.
The hallow'd spot, wi' fond regard, in fancy I distinctly see;
Bend low upon its daisied sward an' kiss my native soil for me!

A kindly mither thou hast there, thy coming waits wi' open arms;
An' gentle sister, sweetly fair, to welcome thee frae War's alarms.
But nane ha'e I, an' death will seal, far, far frae hame, my hollow e'e;
Fareweel! my comrade dear, fareweel! an' kiss my native soil for me!

ROBERT ADAMSON.

A POET of homely, but true talent, ROBERT ADAMSON, was born in the near vicinity of the "auld grey toun" of Dunfermline, in the April of 1832. He was put to field-work very early, receiving only a very scant school education. He was afterwards put to learn the damask trade; but, after working for a considerable time amongst uncongenial "heddles and treddles," he struck out one fine morning on an opposition track, and rambling about for some time in search of new employment, he settled at last at Muirkirk, amid the smoke and din of engine-keeping. At Muirkirk, as an engine-keeper, he still remains.

Mr. ADAMSON, it may be mentioned, early evinced a decided love of books, and had his muse kindled into active emulation, like many more recent Scottish bards, on reading the works of Burns. Encouraged by the favour with which his poems had been received by the local press, he issued, in

1879, his *Lays of Leisure Hours*, which met with a very kind and encouraging reception. An introductory note from the genial pen of the Rev. Alex. Wallace, D.D., Glasgow, adds interest to the little volume.

Mr. ADAMSON's muse is a very interesting one. He sings with hearty voice the triumphs of Labour, and is proud of the healthy, mental, and moral manhood, born of honest toil. His quaint verses *Man an' Moose* will be read with genuine pleasure by all; saving, perhaps, the "douce" housewife, whose plundered aumry may interfere with the operation of her native humanity of feeling. The subjoined comparatively fine poem—*On the Moor*—represents him at his poetic best. Mr. ADAMSON is one of those self-informed peasant poets of whom Scotland has had a richer dower than, perhaps, any other nation, and of whom her rural population may justly feel proud.

——::——

ON THE MOOR.

OUT on the lonely moor, so quiet and still,
  Where undisturb'd the meditative mind
May nurse the thought that's uppermost at will,
  What pleasure it doth find!

Here, far away from all the bustling throng
  In headlong haste ambition's goal to reach,
There is no jarring of discordant song,
  No venal, vulgar speech.

Only the voice of Nature greets the ear,
  In lark's and linnet's song, and curlew's call,
The bleating lamb, the purling streamlet clear,
  And rushing waterfall.

Sweet simple singers, whose true, artless strains
  Of Nature's happiness and homage pure,
Make glad the heart, the burden of life's pains
  The better to endure.

While, 'mid soft breezes, whispering voices tell
Of life and immortality to be;
As of its parent ocean breathes the shell,
Time of eternity.

Here fair flow'rs nestle in the shady nooks,
As if afraid to be by mortals seen;
With all the graces in their loving looks
And modesty of mien.

Graces that warm the heart with gratitude,
As they unfold their Author's love divine;
Giving a foretaste of celestial food—
The angel's bread and wine.

Oh, lone retreat of peaceful, calm repose,
Who would not taste thy cup of pleasures pure,
And prize, in such a world of wants and woes,
A closet on the moor?

——::——

MAN AN' MOOSE.

WEE moosie, I ha'e catch't ye noo,
An' what I should dae wi' ye
Is mair than I can richtly tell;
But as ye are sae like mysel',
I think I will forgie ye.

For tho' ye ha'e at my expense
Ta'en mony a hearty dinner,
Since I hae fairly judg'd the case,
Truth tells me to my very face,
I'm faur the biggest sinner.

An' as enough an' mair is cast
Into the human happer,
To serve the wants o' man an' moose,
I think he shouldna craw sae croose,
Wha is the biggest pauper.

Ye've jist as guid a richt to live
  As him, tho' but a beastie,
An' ill aff wad he be for wark
Wha wad deprive ye o' the spark
  That's burnin' in yer breastie.

Sae, my wee freen', I'll let ye gang,
  Nae mair I houp to trap ye,
But mind ye, baudrons is aboot,
Watchin' a chance yer lugs to cloot,
  An' ten to ane she'll snap ye.

Sae rin for life, yet dinna mak',
  Like mony fules, a jest o't,
Tho' it's a battle at the best,
As wisest sages ha'e confess't,
  It's best to mak' the best o't.

JOHN NICOL.

A POET of real, though unassuming merit, JOHN NICOL was born at Parkhouse, near Ardrossan, 31st May, 1829. His school education completed, he entered the service of Messrs. Merry & Cunninghame, Coal and Ironmasters, in his eighteenth year, and still remains in their service. The "tender passion" first awakened his youthful muse, and he has since rhymed consistently and well whenever opportunity, or impulse, inspired him.

In 1880, he collected and published a well-chosen selection of his fugitive pieces, under the title of *Poems and Songs*, which the local press most favourably received. There are many quotable poems in the book, but the two following effusions very favourably represent Mr. NICOL's interesting and talented muse.

TO A WOUNDED SEA BIRD.

I SAW it in its beauty—in its freedom as it flew,
Like a snowflake from the heavens, o'er the waters, deep and blue;
And it left the clouds behind it, for the tempest was its way,
As it darted like an arrow through the pyramids of spray.

It rose above the mountain—it vanish'd in the deep,
And circled round the beacon, like a sickle set to reap.
It piped above the village, then hasten'd through the foam,
To meet the wave-toss'd mariner, and bid him welcome home.

I heard a musket rattle, and I saw a wreath of smoke,
And saw a treach'rous human form uprise behind a rock;
And with a clutch victorious, he grasp'd the helpless thing—
That flutter'd on the shingle, with bleeding, broken wing.

This "lord of the creation" I curse not, nor despise—
But pity much his cruel heart, and envy not his prize,
Go, fly, ye pretty sea birds! go, fly upon the sea!
And build your nests upon the crags—you're ever safe for me.

——::——

HOME AND COUNTRY.

VEXED with the toils and troubles of the day
  I gladly hasten to my humble home,
Where peace and pleasure soon drives care away,
  Where vice or sorrow seldom ever come.
How sweet it is, when one has been annoy'd,
To find one's self with homely tasks employ'd.

No joys so pure as those we find at home,
  No friends so true as those with whom we dwell
All hearts beat back, however far they roam,
  To some dear mountain, valley, plain, or dell.
One cannot find, no, not in all the earth,
A place so sweet as is one's place of birth.

Land of the brave, land of the free and fair,
  Thy every spot is classic, holy ground,

Where love and truth attune thy lyric air,
  And peace and plenty scatter blessings round ;
Though dark thy glens, though bleak thy rugged hills,
Thy very name thy child with transport fills.

Nor will I wander from my native vale,
  To seek a fortune in a land of slaves ;
But I will breathe bold Britain's genial gale,
  And leave my bones beside my grandsires' graves ;
And, looking up for greater bliss above,
Will shut my eyes among the friends I love.

GEORGE DONALD.

George Donald is a native of Thornliebank, Renfrewshire. In his twelfth year he was put to work in the printfields of the Messrs. Crum in that village. The unfortunate career of his father—the author of *Lays of the Covenanters*, and one of the principal authors of the Nursery pieces contributed to *Whistle Binkie*—had shortly before devolved on his mother the care and up-bringing of the family. At sixteen years of age our poet was apprenticed to the pattern-designing, which occupation he followed for twelve years. A stagnation of trade caused him to seek other employment, and he was successful in obtaining a situation on the reporting staff of the *North British Daily Mail.* This position he held for eleven years. He at present holds a situation in the office of the Govan Parochial Board.

Relative to the literary side of our poet's life, Mr. Donald, it may be mentioned, discovered an ability to rhyme as early as his sixteenth year. His educational advantages had been scant, but assiduously applying himself to a praiseworthy course of self-tuition in his spare hours, he succeeded in acquiring a fair English education, with a knowledge of the French language, and a wide acquaintance with general literature.

In 1865, Mr. DONALD issued his poetical effusions in a volume, under the title of *Poems—Reflective, Descriptive, and Miscellaneous.* His poetry is marked by much beauty and purity of thought and feeling, and the mechanism of his verse is perfect. He but seldom attempts the Doric, using, by a sort of selective instinct, the English language as that best suited to the fine tone of his thought and fancy. He has contributed to *Chambers's Journal*, and to other magazines and periodicals.

—::—

THE DAYS THAT ARE NO MORE.

"O, Death in Life, the days that are no more!"—TENNYSON.

THROUGH the dim past in fancy oft I stray,
Seeking amid its shadows for the lost;
For vanish'd joys too early snatch'd away—
All my heart cherish'd most;

For friends departed—those whose presence cheer'd,
Whose love lit up life's dark and weary round—
All the sweet sympathies that life endear'd,
And made earth hallow'd ground.

Oh, loved and lost! why was your stay so brief?
Why did you leave me through long years to mourn?
Is there no power can mitigate my grief,
Or bid the dead return?

Give, give me back the friends of other years,
Life's halcyon hours and pure delights restore—
Sepulchral voices mock my blinding tears,
And answer "Nevermore!"

Oh, nevermore life's vanish'd joys shall wake
  From the dead past to dissipate my gloom,
Nor voice of love and friendship ever break
  The silence of the tomb!

Ah, spake he well, that minstrel of old time—
  "Of all we suffer here, the deepest woe
Is the remembrance of past joys sublime
  We nevermore shall know."

Yet not for ever: while we trembling grope
  Amid life's passing shadows, cold and grim,
There beams afar, to cheer with faith and hope,
  A star not faint or dim.

O joy, to know not ever thus our doom,
  That we shall find, when ends this fleeting breath,
Our joys and friendships in perennial bloom
  Beyond the realms of Death!

——::——

THE LION OF FLORENCE.

(From the French of Millevoye.)

In the fair city of Florence, on a time,
Were gather'd once, brought from a distant clime,
Nature's wild denizens. It chanced one day,
Escaped, a lion roam'd the public way.
Amid the terror and disorder spread,
A frantic mother with her infant fled.
Oh, how can words that mother's anguish tell,
When from her arms the precious burden fell!
At the same instant, horrified, she saw
Her child beneath the monster's hungry jaw!
Aghast and motionless, as marble fixed,
She stood. 'Twas but a moment thus, the next
By fear o'ercome, by fear restor'd to sense,—
O charm of love! frenzy sublime, intense!—
Upon her knees she sank—"My child, my child—
Give me my boy!" she cried in accents wild.

Was it a miracle? the piteous cries
Moved the fierce beast: it turn'd on her its eyes,
Seem'd to divine a mother's heart implor'd
That her dear babe might be to her restor'd;
Rais'd tenderly the infant from the street
And laid the darling treasure at her feet;
Look'd on the child, now smiling and content,
Then slowly on its way it quietly went.

DANIEL M'MILLAN.

A WRITER of beautiful and interesting verses, DANIEL M'MILLAN, better known by his *nom de plume* of "Dalintober," is a native of Dalintober, Campbeltown, Argyllshire. He had a good ordinary school education, his boyish years being pretty equally divided between school attendance in winter, and the wild freedom of a "herd's" life in summer. Attaining his fifteenth year he was apprenticed to an ironmonger's business in the town of Campbeltown, completing which term of servitude he afterwards pushed his fortune in Glasgow, and is now sole partner in a manufacturing business there.

Mr. M'MILLAN has contributed for years, and with much acceptance, to the local press and to other quarters. He writes with quiet melodious flow, and with much beauty and purity of thought, diction, and feeling. He is a man of excellent character and parts, and is esteemed and beloved by many appreciative friends.

THE MORAL HERO.

HE may be rich, he may be great,
He may be poor and low;
Of high renown in church and state,
Or all unhonour'd go;

Yet what his station, where his place,
He is an honour to his race.

No partial part in church or state
He for himself doth claim;
A deed unjust to perpetrate
He deems an open shame;
For what he claims, his will bequeaths
To every human thing that breathes.

The love of truth, a fountain deep,
Disposes heart and will,
Alike when stormy tempests sweep,
As when the winds are still;
Though interest prompt, temptation try,
He will not make, nor act a lie.

Within his heart a lamp of love,
Such as a god might claim,
Burns like a sun-ray from above—
A pure and holy flame;
And folds beneath its ample wings
The God, and all created things.

Hail, mercy, hail! benignant shade,
Sweet friend of the oppress'd,
Thou like a holy dove hast made,
Thy home within his breast;
And where thou claim'st a covert meet,
To bear and to forbear is sweet.

Where pinching Want with leaden eye,
Hath singled out her prey,
He of his bounty doth supply,
And drives the wolf away;
And sees a deed the gods might share,
Provoke the smile of dull despair.

Where sickness, prelude of decay,
Hath fixed the barbéd dart;
Where death had reft the loved away,
From friendship's wounded heart,
He soothes the soul by sorrows riven,
And points the eye of faith to Heaven.

He sows the seed while sluggards sleep,
  O'er earth's unkindly sward;
Secure in Heaven at last to reap
  His guerdon and reward;
From youth to age his path hath been
The footprints of the Nazarene.

Rejoice, oh man, that such there be
  Thy right of kindred claim:
Rejoice and labour such as he,
  With high and holy aim:
Then wreathe the laurel round thy brow,
The man, the moral hero, thou!

——::——

THE SONG OF LIFE.

"The world is young, the world is fair,
With mirth and music everywhere;"
  Thus sang the careless child,
As wide he wander'd o'er the lea
As blithesome as the mountain bee,
  And as the lambkin wild.

"The world is young, the world is bright,
One changing scene of new delight;"
  The youthful lover sung,
As by the trysting tree he stood,
While thought prospective stirr'd his blood
  And trembled on his tongue.

"The world is moil, the world is toil,
To move the mart and till the soil;"
  Thus sang the man of might,
The fever fret of yesterday
Has unrewarded pass'd away,
  The watchword still is—fight!

"The world is old, the world is cold,
With cares and sorrows manifold;"

This sang the hoary sage.
The child, the youth, the man of might,
The play, the passion, and the fight,
Fade in the mists of age.

"Weep not, thy hopes all lowly laid,"
The soothing voice of Nature said;
"Howe'er thy hap be starr'd,
Who in the varied scenes of life
Display true virtue in the strife,
Shall reap a rich reward."

JOHN FULLERTON

WAS born in the village of Woodside, near Aberdeen, September 11th, 1836; and is both an interesting poet and a fertile prose-writer. In his tenth year he voluntarily forsook the school, and found employment as a "twister" in an extensive local cotton mill, and since then his career has been a varied one, showing a distinct upward rise, and an admirable application of talent and character all through. He is employed at the present time as a writer in a solicitor's office, Peterhead.

A versifier from his earliest years, Mr. FULLERTON issued, in 1870, a little brochure entitled *The Ghaist o' Dennilair*, which was highly praised by the local press, and rapidly ran into a second edition. The poem is likely to take a permanent place in local literature.

To numerous leading London journals and magazines Mr. FULLERTON has contributed with acceptance. In the *People's Friend* he has appeared at intervals for years back under the cognomen of "Robin Goodfellow," and of "Wild Rose," and the local press is frequently enriched by his ceaseless literary industry.

Personally, Mr. FULLERTON is a man of a kindly, sympathetic, and generous disposition; of retiring habits, but ever ready to help and encourage all. His poems and sketches —generous, eloquent, and superior in thought and diction— are the outcome of a gifted mind and a kindly sympathetic heart.

—::—

THE OLD CASTLE.

SHELTER'D 'mong the dark fir trees,
  Stands a castle old and grey;
Through its roofless rooms the breeze
  Wanders night and day.
Ivy climbs across its walls,
  Shells of what they once had been;
And in all the mighty halls
  Grass is growing green.

With a throbbing heart I tread
  Silent chambers where years gone
Sire and matron, youth and maid,
  Pass'd the night with song—
Song of love or fairy tale,
  Told or sung with bosoms light,
As the evening shadows fell,
  Deepen'd into night.

Here the warriors, brave and bold,
  Hung their swords and shields to rest;
Here the friars, young or old,
  Quaff'd of wines the best;
Here the merry and the gay
  Danced till morning streak'd the east;
Here was spread by night and day
  Aye the lordly feast.

All are gone—the grey-hair'd sire,
  Matron, youth, and maiden fair,
Wandering minstrel-bard whose lyre
  Thrill'd the brave hearts there;

All are gone—their graves are near—
  Grass o'ergrown on every side—
And nor sound nor voice I hear,
  Save the fretting tide.

——::——

AT THY GRAVE.

At thy grass-grown grave I kneel,
As the night's shades round me steal,
    Dost thou know me, darling, near?
Canst thou see my tearless grief,
O'er our year of bliss so brief,
    Comes my sorrow to thine ear?

Blossoms watch'd with tend'rest care
In Life's Garden, deem'd so fair,
    Wither'd lie beneath my feet;
And from leafy bower and shade
All the summer birds are fled—
    Hush'd their love-lays pure and sweet.

Love of mine, for thee no more
Shines the sun on sea or shore,
    Sings the lark his merry lay;
Where thou art, nor voice, nor song,
Breaks the silence deep and long
    O'er thee, sweet, by night and day.

From that far off home of thine
Wilt thou, love, revisit mine,
    Shadow'd now, and lone, and drear?
Come amid day's toil and flight,
Come in dreamings of the night,
    With thy smile and voice to cheer.

Mine is now a lonesome way,
Sunless all the summer day,
    And at night, within my cot,
Books and music scatter'd round,
Yet nor footstep, voice, or sound
    Greet me, meet me, cheer my lot.

At thy grave I linger still,
Night winds moaning on the hill,
    Sear'd leaves falling at my feet;
Home was Heaven a year ago,
Thy love, Mary, made it so.
    Where and when now will we meet?

EBENEZER SMITH.

A POET of vigour and fertility, EBENEZER SMITH was born in the High Street of Ayr, 4th January, 1835. His mother was surnamed Tannahill, and his maternal grandfather was a Robert Tannahill, poetically, a very interesting name. His father and grandfather were both shoemakers, and leaving school at the age of thirteen, young EBENEZER was put to the shoemaking trade. Completing a brief apprenticeship, he succeeded to their business while still a youth.

Conducting business on his own account, Mr. Smith was very successful for a long period, but with the fatality which too often clings to poetic genius, he now finds himself in the ranks of the working operatives once more.

Regarding the literary side of our poet's history, he began the practice of rhyming, it may be mentioned, as early as his twelfth year, and with occasional longer or shorter intervals, he has practised verse-writing ever since. Our poet was a bright and promising scholar when a boy, and excited hopes of a "career" in the mind of his schoolmaster. He has issued three volumes of verse, which the Scottish press have in turn very favourably received. His style is popular, rather than lofty or ideal. He has both promptitude and poetic flow, uniting to these indispensable requisites of success a very trenchant power of satire, the free exercise of which, in the celebrated poem of *The Pharisee*, dragged our poet into strong public notice in connection with an action for libel heard in the Court of Session in 1873, and known as the "Pharisee Case."

In the exercise of his fancy as a poet, Mr. SMITH has had moments of rapture such as the bulk of men never dream of, but beyond that, poetry has brought him no immediate reward. There are two versions of *The Pharisee*, one of which we append.

—::—

THE PHARISEE.

THE incarnation of all evil!
The first-born darling of the devil!
A creature formed to pray and prowl,
Without a heart, with little soul—
What wretch more odious can be
Than yonder smooth-tongued Pharisee?

Beneath that face of pious paint,
Whose pray'rful lips proclaim the "saint,"
Lie rows of teeth more cruel far
Than any Bengal tiger's are;
That mouth which o'er the sinner moans,
Can rend his flesh and crush his bones.

Intent on saving sinners weak,
He glides through life—slow, silent, sleek;
But ready always, night and day,
To turn and gorge himself with prey;
No more voracious shark than he
In all the earth-encircling sea!

Woe to the victim in his path
Who rouses his remorseless wrath!
No bear, urged on by Nature's law,
Uplifts a more unpitying paw;
No cobra's venom'd fangs can dart
With less compassion in its heart.

Yet, innocent as slumb'ring child,
With down-dropp'd eyes—how meek, how mild!
As serpent vile its victim charms,
He draws his prey into his arms,
Insulting God, without a qualm,
With placid prayer, and sounding psalm.

Ev'n in his moods of wrath or guile
He breaks upon you with a smile,
And hurrying on the hour of doom,
Shines gloriously amidst the gloom,
Like lightning gleam, which darts from Heaven
Before the oak beneath is riven.

He gives—but always in such way
That those who get must more repay;
He helps—but not till he has made
A slave of him who takes his aid;
He works for good, or ill's prevention,
But always with a bad intention.

To raise himself an inch he'd pray
The length of Summer's longest day;
To gain some paltry private end
He'd sacrifice his bosom friend;
And break, to gratify his hate,
His father's venerable pate.

The orphan robb'd, he says—"'Tis well!
Let's pray—God keep his soul from hell;
As for myself, my sins forgiven,
I'm going shoulder-high to Heaven;
Where I upon a throne shall sit,
And fresh enormities commit."

Thus mingling robbery and rant,
Deceit and holiness, the "saunt"
Goes, step by step, the downward road
That leads to Satan's dread abode,
And wakes astonish'd—with a stare—
To find a man so pious THERE.

QUINTIN BONE.

A POET of fine taste, and much artistic beauty of fancy and expression, QUINTIN BONE was born 4th April, 1836, at Dalrymple, a village finely situated on the classic Doon, and about six miles distant from the town of Ayr. He was educated at Dalrymple Parish School, under Mr. William Porteous, then well-known throughout Ayrshire for his professional enthusiasm and scholarly acquirements. In his sixteenth year, he accepted a situation in the office of Messrs. Foulds & Bone, merchants and shipowners, Greenock, serving a three years' apprenticeship with that firm as clerk and bookkeeper. Afterwards, he was appointed to the responsible office of cashier to the extensive ship-building co-partnery of Messrs. Robert Steele & Co., of the same town, which situation he retained till the Education Act (Scotland) came into operation in 1873, when the first School Board of Greenock Burgh unanimously appointed him their treasurer. About this time he began business on his own account as a public accountant. Subsequently, he was appointed auditor to the Greenock Parochial Board, and Treasurer to the Gourock Burgh and Local Authority, with various other offices of a public character.

Mr. BONE wrote verses successfully while yet a mere lad, and became, in due time, a constant and valued contributor of verses, sketches, and literary notices, to the local newspaper press. Early in 1860, he issued a selection of his poems, prefaced by a long leading piece, entitled *Valley Farm*. The principal poem—which reminds one of Alex. Smith's richly diffusive, and verbally sensuous style—is an effort of real poetical genius, and, despite its recurrent tendency to *spasm*, is wonderfully rich in fancy, melody, and distinct verbal beauty. Revelling in its felicitous picturings, the critic is disarmed of censure, and yields to the sense of beauty and melody which is everywhere rained around him.

In the maturity of his taste Mr. BONE now views the publication of *Valley Farm* as having been premature. In the intervals of an exacting business he has since then written many fine pieces, which have been contributed anonymously, for the most part, to various journals and literary magazines, and which he is likely to ultimately re-issue, along with other unpublished verses, in a complete and revised form.

Personally, Mr. BONE is a man of quiet but genial mind, uniting in himself the excellence of assured character, with business abilities of more than average mark. The exquisite lyric, *O, Go not yet!* very favourably represents Mr. BONE's fine poetical genius.

——::——

THE MUSIC OF THE SEA.

I LOVE the bold choir of the wild sea waves,
When the wind's fingers sweep along the strings
Of Neptune's harp, and wake its melody
Sublime and loud. Old Winter, hoary-lock'd,
Ere yet he flings him from the western steep,
As the gay step of rosy Spring is heard
Along the crisping earth, sweeps the loud chords,
And lo, as the high anthem swells aloft,
The listening continents and isles around,
And eager heaven with all its stars, are dumb,
Hanging on the deep thunder of its voice!
How sweet, when Summer-earth laughs out in leaves,
Is the low murmur of the sunlit waves.
Lo! in arcadian bower the Queen of May,
Wreathèd in robe of flowers, high honeymoon
Passes, with her sweet boy, the love-sick Year,—
And the fleet, perfume-wing'd, and tell-tale Wind

Whispers their mighty passion to the sea!
The eager-listening waves, through all their tents,
Murmur their sweet surprise, and big with joy
Exultant wake the echoes of their caves,
Then leap again to light, and laughing run
To fling the story on a thousand coasts.

——::——

O, GO NOT YET!

O, go not yet—not yet!
  Night veils her myriad stars,
  As now wide-shimmering bars
Of level moonlight flit
  Far o'er the glistering sea,
  And light, dear heart, on thee,—
O, go not yet—not yet!

O, go not yet—not yet!
  The moonlit air falls cold,
  But we, under this old
Grey oak and tall elm, sit
  Warm with love's passion-heat
  Hearing our hearts beat, beat;—
O, go not yet—not yet!

O, go not yet—not yet!
  I would this were each night,—
  That round thy neck snow-white,
These arms should ne'er unknit;
  Come quickly, happy day,
  When I shall not need say,—
O, go not yet—not yet!

——::——

THE IDLE SINGER: REACTION.

"Silence! brave words enough; now for your deeds."—*MS. Play.*

Have you a word for your brother
That will help him in his need?
O, by love, our great sweet mother,

Why this fluting through a reed,
And this singing in fine rhythm?
Poet, do not trifle with him—
Seems your song-flower but a weed,
Self its root—the devil's other—
Fame its hotbed; lo, a tare
That hath sprung instead of wheat;
Fruitless, can it well be fair
Or its garish bloom smell sweet?
With the world's wail swelling higher
Round life's sacrificial fire,
As the victims pale advance—
Sin, Pain, Want, and Ignorance—
All your verses in my heed
Are but idle fancy's ware,
Lifeless, loveless for most part,
And they weigh as light as air
In the balance with one deed,
With a word warm from the heart.
For athwart our spirits' ken
In awed hearing now and then,
Breaks the tumult of the sadness,
Of the badness and the madness,
In the great world-heart that rages,
Beating march-time in the battle,
Ever clashing life with death
Up the red slope of the ages;
And thy song seems idle prattle,
And thyself in simple childhood
Tranc'd by fairy story's spell,
Blowing bubbles with light breath,
Pleased with bauble coach and rattle,
Playing at heaven on the brink of hell.
With a passion of self-disdain,
With a sudden pang of pain,
From thy dream-life sickly sweet
Be thou shaken to thy feet.
Being is better than seeming;
Doing is grander than dreaming;
Worthy life than perfect poem—

Be it epic, drama, lyric,
With their faultless, fair ideal,
And their yearning, rapt, hysteric ;
And the human-hearted real,
With its homely heroism,
And its love-enrooted duty,
Having flow'r of Christ-like beauty,
Showeth dearer in God's sight
Than the muse's farthest flight
Through heaven's height or hell's abysm.

Idle dreamer by life's road,
Wooing beauty all day long—
Self is world's sorrow and wrong,
Leaden weight of its weary load—
Cease awhile ; life's noblest, highest,
Is not singing a great song ;
It is doing the will of God.
Life is real, and thou liest,
Lulling us with cozenings
And the rhythmic wave of wings—
And we dream within a dream
Till God wake us, all astart,
Thee and us, with awful beam
Of His daylight white and real—
Shaming tawdry fine ideal
Paling showman's tinsel art
Blear'd and sickly, pale and wan.
Live in doing, strive to be all
You have sung of in your sanity,
You have felt of our humanity,
O, awake thee, BE A MAN !

——::——

JAMES CHAPMAN.

THE subject of the following sketch—JAMES CHAPMAN—was born in the immediate vicinity of the village of Upper Banchory, on the river Dee, Kincardineshire, October 22nd, 1835. His father was a shrewd, homely, country blacksmith, eminently practical in his ideas, and with nothing of the romantic-poetical fancy characteristic of his talented son. In his sixth year JAMES was sent to school, and had a fair elementary education. The family having removed a few miles farther up the Dee, his father leased a farm called Craiglash, where our poet, after leaving school, wrought as a tiller of the soil until reaching manhood's estate.

In his twenty-fourth year, being anxious to see the world, Mr. CHAPMAN left home, and set off for Glasgow with not a great deal in his pockets, but with abundance of health in his body, and a fair share of hope in his breast. He shortly afterwards settled in Partick, and for a number of years back has served with acceptancy the burgh in various capacities. He was for several years a detective-officer, and at the present time holds a responsible appointment in the sanitary department under the Local Authority.

Referring to the literary side of Mr. CHAPMAN'S history, it was while still resident at Craiglash, with its bleak heaths, its dark pinewoods, grey rocks, and gloomy tarns—over which his memory yet lovingly lingers—that he first devoted himself to the study of poetry. Isolated very much from congenial companionship, our poet, in his leisure hours, sought and found fitting society in the pages of Scott, Byron, Ossian, Longfellow, and Poe. He had early discovered a facility in verse-making, and he became in time a frequent contributor to the local press, and to other quarters, writing largely under the *nom de plume* of "Gnome." In 1878 he ventured on the publication of a volume, under the title of *A Legend of the Isles and other Poems,* which was well received by the press, and was otherwise successful beyond his anticipations. He is presently (1882) preparing and arranging materials for a second volume, which will shortly be issued, and which will assuredly advance his reputation as a poet. Mr. CHAPMAN's poetry is highly ideal in tone. Mild of humour, and with no appreciable infusement of lyrical passion, his verses are, nevertheless, remarkable for their high idealism, their wealth of romantic fancy, and their purity and melody of tone. His muse lives in a world of her own fancy, meddling not much with everyday life, and still less with politics. Yet his mind is hopeful of the race, and his verses draw frequent inspiration from Christian faith :—

What of the future?—Doubt and Fear
Point down a vista dark and drear;
But o'er the mist-cloud dark and chill,
Hope, like an angel, hovers still,
White-wing'd and beautiful.

In addition to his poetical faculty, Mr. CHAPMAN inherits a very fine talent for sketching in colours. He also cuts monograms and engravings in wood very successfully. He is a man of quiet habits and fine gifts, and finds a beautiful solace for the fretting worry of life in his Christian hope, in the society of his wife and family, and, next to these, in the cultivation of the sister gifts of art and poesy which Nature has entrusted to his use, and which are rapidly ripening to fine issues in his hands. We quote several of his more popular and less ideal poems.

BUSIRIS THE PROUD.

In a silence like that of Sahara lies Goshen ;
  The stillness is weird—it o'erawes, it appals :
In the field there's no stir, in the city no motion,
  The wild dog prowls lonely 'mong desolate walls.

To the eastward away, 'neath the dust cloud that gathers,
  Dense masses stretch far, they are nearing the sea ;
'Tis the Hebrews, they hie to the home of their fathers,
  The God of their fathers leads on—they are free !

Can ye blame their elation, or tame its expression,
  As forth from Rameses they surge and defile,
Though the anguish'd Egyptians' wild lamentation
  Ascends with, and blends with, the moan of the Nile ?

Ye may weep if ye will, where bereavement yet raises
  Its plaint through the realms of Busiris the Proud ;
As for me, I will join in their journeys and praises
  Who follow I Am in His pillar of cloud.

But the sun seeks the desert, and Israel is rueing ;
  Night lowers on the wilderness—where shall she flee ?
In her rear rings the tramp of the war-horse pursuing,
  Her flank feels the cliff, in her front foams the sea !

Hath the Levite been false ?—will Jehovah forsake her ?
  Through dust and through gloom she looks timidly back,
And she feels like the fawn when her terrors o'ertake her,
  And tell her the jackal is hot on her track.

She is faint, she is faithless, yet God hears her 'plaining,
  His east wind hath cloven the billowy bar,
'Tween the waters she wendeth, her sandals scarce staining,
  While close on her rear rolls the Memphian car.

Down the vista of death rings the wild, mocking laughter—
  Insulting to man, and defiant of God—
But the swarthy cheek pales as, across the cleft water,
  Is stretch'd the avenging, the terrible rod !

At the 'hest of Jehovah the waves yawn asunder—
  Omnipotence wills it, down, bursting they come,
And the neigh of the war-steed is lost in their thunder—
  The shriek of the rider is stifled in foam !

Ah, the tyrant was proud, and his pride spread his pillow !
  He mingles his locks with the slime of the sea ;
O'er his cohorts careereth the merciless billow—
  The wilderness welcomes the feet of the free !

—— :: ——

THE ROUGH TYKES O' TARLAND.

Wi' the last o' the James's
  We saw our hopes perish,
Yet that name, o' a' names, is
  The ane we maist cherish ;
Though oor monarchs in thae days
  Heard Gaelic but rarely,
It was welcome in wae days
  To bonnie Prince Charlie.
When oor lads, led to death, wi'
  The Prince sought a far-land,
Then the war-pipes ga'e breath wi'
  "The Rough Tykes o' Tarland."
      The rough tykes o' Tarland—
      The dare-deils o' Tarland—
      'Twas his cause clad the heath wi'
      The rough tykes o' Tarland.

While on high ilka brow flung
  The bonnet and feather,
And as dawn's ruddy glow flung
  Its fire o'er the heather,
Round the auld parish kirk they
  March'd thrice ere they parted,
And they swore on the dirk they
  War' true and leal-hearted :
Then away o'er the hill, to

Their graves in a far-land,
While the echoes rang shrill to
"The Rough Tykes o' Tarland."
The rough tykes o' Tarland—
The dour loons o' Tarland—
But the cailachs spaed ill to
The rough tykes o' Tarland.

"'Tis but little we'll care for
Foreboding or omen,
When the claymore is bare for
The Sassanach foemen;
Let the Seer tell his dreams o'
The white rose down-trodden,
And the Baenshee's wild screams o'
'Culloden, Culloden!'
Bid him rave to the linn wi'
His havers frae star-land—
Bid the piper strike in wi'
'The Rough Tykes o' Tarland'!"
The rough tykes o' Tarland—
The blythe blades o' Tarland—
To be sad seems a sin wi'
The rough tykes o' Tarland.

Though the lassies war' wae, yet
The laddies war' lauchin',
They war' keen for the brae, yet
They paused at the clachan,
And the rough lip was wet wi'
The strong deoch-an-dhoras,
While the wailin's war' met wi'
The song's stormy chorus.
"To yer hames, maids and dames, and
Prepare wreath and garland;
For oor names shall be fame's, and
'The Rough Tykes o' Tarland'!"
The rough tykes o' Tarland—
The lost lads o' Tarland—
'Twas the last o' King James and
The rough tykes o' Tarland.

WILLIAM ALLAN

JAMES CHAPMAN

WILLIAM FREELAND

ALEXANDER BROWN

J. E. WATT

GEORGE MURRAY

"SCOTTIE!"

THE auld Scotch law is, "Brak his jaw
  Wha dares to ca' ye 'Scottie.'"
Sic' points ha'e a' some twist or thraw,
  But this yane's naewise knotty.
Just gi'e him a forget-me-not,
  He'll look baith blae an' blate for't ;
My proodest boast is, I'm a Scot—
  A norlan' Scot—thank Fate for't !

It's Scottie this, an' Scottie that,
  Whan ye gang o'er the border ;
But heeze the bannet o'er the hat,
  We'll haud the loons in order.
Steek ye yer neive as I wad mine,
  (The dirk is oot o' date for't)
An' gi'e them yane for auld langsyne.
  They'll aiblins no thank Fate for't !

Whare will ye get sic buirdly men
  As them wha tread the heather?
As for oor lasses, weel we ken
  They're peerless a' thegether !
This aye was true, it's naething new,
  There's neither day nor date for't,
An' I'm ane o' the favoured few,
  For I'm a Scot, thank Fate for't !

The Scottish breast is Freedom's shield—
  Grand are the thoughts that heave it—
Though no aye first to tak' the field,
  We're ne'er the first to leave it !
Though mony a name that's kent to Fame
  Gets cauld neglect an' hate for't,
They'll no mak' game o' Scots at hame,
  For I'm a Scot, thank Fate for't !

Some brag o' this, some brag o' that,
  The Cockney craws fu' saucy—
At bouncin' few can rival Pat—
  The Yankee croons the causey !

But I've a boast that beats them a',
I'm gratefu' ear' an' late for't,
Gae bide yer heids baith great an' sma',
For *I'm a Scot*, thank Fate for't!

ALEXANDER BROWN.

A WRITER of graceful and interesting verses, ALEXANDER BROWN, was born in 1837 at Lochhead, in the parish of Auchtertool, Fifeshire.

His ancestors, for generations back, had been engaged in agricultural and pastoral pursuits in the surrounding districts. Our poet was the eldest born of the family, and his father was manager of his own brother's farm. The moorland cot in which they lived was a humble dwelling, but if they lacked city comforts and luxuries, they had, by way of compensation, abundance of fresh air, while an ample potato and cabbage garden, with a stock of live poultry in addition, put absolute want at a comfortable distance. In his seventh year he was put to school at Lochgelly, but, on account of the long rough road, could only attend it during the fine summer weather. Latterly, when he had grown a bit, the arrangement was reversed. To suit family circumstances, he attended school in the winter months, and herded cattle during the summer season, or was put to outwork in the fields. Field-work in the summer-time he found to be rather a pleasant occupation; but if work in the fields was agreeable to his taste, the herding of cattle was not. And even the weary monotony of the latter occupation had (in our poet's view of it, at least) a still lower depth in the tending of sheep and lambs in Spring,—to him the very bondage of Egypt.

Having acquired the elements of an ordinary school education, he was, at the age of fourteen, apprenticed to the trade of cabinet-making at Milnathort. Completing his apprenticeship there, he afterwards removed to Edinburgh, where he still remains, following the same occupation, occupying the position of a foreman for the past fifteen years. Like, alas! too many of us, Mr. BROWN has not found life all sunshine and joy. The shadow which sooner or later comes to all men's homes has sat by his hearth, and unloosed the fount of tears in his heart. Yet he judges life to be, when wisely used, a good and enjoyable gift. He maintains good health, has always had plenty of work, and knows nothing of tyrannical masters. And if he sometimes realises the truth of Burns's lines satirising mankind as "an unco squad," he considers the ungenerous impression, often as it recurs, as due to his own over-sensitive nature, rather than otherwise. Regarding the literary side of his life, it may be stated that from the day he could fluently read he was a keen lover of books, although for years his opportunities of becoming acquainted with them were scant enough.

While still working out his apprenticeship at Milnathort, he attempted literary composition in a quiet way—more as a mental exercise than aught else—and he was greatly stimulated in his studies by attending the literary lectures of the two Dissenting clergymen of the village—at that time the Rev. Dr. Young, now of Glasgow, and the gifted Dr. W. C. Smith, now of Edinburgh, a poet of acknowledged genius. Our poet's growing tastes were further stimulated and confirmed through his connection with a small literary association in which the composition of original essays in prose and verse, alternated with the reading of choice passages from standard authors. His connection with this society, Mr. BROWN thinks, has very much, and very beneficially, influenced his life. Supplementary to what has been already detailed, he has been for the past twelve years, it may be mentioned, a regular, though unostentatious, poetical contributor to the local press, and to other quarters. His verses are uniformly good. He writes more gracefully, more evenly, and more sweetly than uneducated poets usually do. A vein of true and pure thought runs through all his musings. He never attempts to whip the winged Pegasus with a thong of fire, but keeps her well in hand, curvetting with a graceful and restrained action. He has not yet published in a collected form, but when that event is accomplished, his friends will be in possession of a volume of surpassing beauty and purity of verse.

——::——

A WOODLAND RHYME.

When Spring's sweet life is young and fair,
  While fields are green and woods are gay;
When apple blossom scents the air,
  And sheds its beauty o'er the way;
When snow-white clouds are sailing slow
  Across the sapphire depths of space,
And make alternate gloom and glow
  On earth's fair face:

What potent charm doth permeate
  All things around me, great and small:
The forest monarchs, high in state—
  The mosses on the mouldering wall;
The flowery carpet of the green,
  Inwrought in Nature's wondrous loom,
With fretted lights of sunny sheen,
  And tender gloom?

What stirs the life-blood of the oak,
  When Winter's freezing days are flown,

To from its naked boughs evoke
  The curly leaves of ruddy brown?
The sycamores that proudly tower
  Burst into leaf beneath its sway,
Nor can the ash befool its power
  By long delay.

O, sweet the light of forest glades
  In the first flush of Summer's green;
The fanning breeze, the waving shades,
  The glints of sunny light between;
That gladdens all the vista'd scope,
  And breathes a peace that seems divine—
A spirit full of life and hope
  That touches mine.

——::——

INTO CAPTIVITY.

Fair maiden, with the meek blue eyes,
In which the calm of summer skies
  The depth of waveless seas have met;
Upon the beauty of thy face,
Of heart-content and artless grace,
  An unseen hand the seal hath set.

When wandering eyes thy windows pass,
And see thee through the polish'd glass,
  Fair visions o'er the fancy come,
As of a cheerful, beaming light,
Whose glow makes all around it bright
  Within that dear paternal home;

Or, thro' imagination's dream,
Glides on a pleasant summer stream,
  With quiet music in its flow—
Where greener leaves are on the bow'rs,
And brighter tints are on the flow'rs
  That blossom where it murmurs low:

That ripples onwards till it meets
Another stream that seaward fleets,
  To merge in one for evermore—
Whose broader current, gliding on,
Is singing, in a softer tone,
  A deeper music than before.

Even so to thee—as bright and gay
As is a joyous summer day,
  With heart that hath no thought of guile—
Some gallant Knight, who, gadding by,
With dreams of conquest in his eye,
  Lured by the magic of thy smile,

Shall whisper words that witching prove,
And bind thee fast with cords of love,
  No more in fancy free to roam—
Shall hold thee captive in his power,
And shut thee in the highest tower
  And strongest Keep of Castle-Home.

And all thy life's sweet forces will
Become his servitors, until
  Thy brow is deep with lines of care,
And thou hast lost the bloom of youth,
And little fingers, void of ruth,
  Be tangled in thy braided hair :

Till, more than freedom was to thee
Shall be this sweet captivity,
  That every year will more assure ;—
The walls close up in every chink,
The chain grow stronger, link by link,
  The longer that it doth endure.

——::——

THE VILLAGE WELL.

Where summer basks on gowany braes,
  And whins in bloom are gay ;
Where labour rests at golden eve,
  And rosy children play ;

How sweet to hear, when evening's glow
  Is fading in the dell,
The lisping murmur of the spring,
  That fills the village well.

Sweet spring, the village dames by thee
  Recount each homely care;
The comely maiden looks in thee,
  And sees that she is fair.
There bashful lad and modest lass
  The tender tale will tell,
When gloaming gathers o'er the braes
  Around the village well.

But gossips say, the blooming maids
  Who bear the milking pail
Have found in thee a faithful friend,
  Whose bounty does not fail:
That by thy help, when times are hard,
  Their little gains they swell;
It is no unrequited love
  They give the village well.

The parchèd lip of honest toil
  Finds solace in thy stream,
And those who wander love to rest
  Beside thy rippling gleam.
Long many kindly thoughts of thee
  In simple hearts will dwell,
For only gentle memories cling
  Around the village well.

Long be the braes with gowans bright,
  The whins with blossom gay;
Long, village sons thy memory keep,
  Though far from thee they stray:
And long by thee may peaceful age
  With kindling glances tell
Of boyhood's days and boyhood's ways
  Around the village well.

NO!

Among the quaint maxims come down from our fathers,
  The fruit of experience rather than art,
Round which as you ponder, thought after thought gathers,
  Sinks into the memory, and will not depart;
I single out one that may comfort or chide us—
  May steady the careless, and quicken the slow,
Is pregnant with meaning to guard and to guide us;
  "He'll soon be a beggar that canna say No."

For round you will cluster the idle and thriftless,
  Who seek not for good, or but faintly pursue it,
Who love to do nothing, the lazy and shiftless,
  And beg your assistance to help them to do it.
As vultures swoop down on a camel that's dying,
  While its heart's latest pulses beat faintly and low,
So knaves hover round the too-weakly complying,
  Who fail in decision, and fear to say No.

The rascal whose story you failed in rejecting—
  Of hunger and hardship, and sparseness of wealth,
The while on your goodness you're sweetly reflecting,
  Within the next taproom is drinking your health.
Those fasts that would match Dr. Tanner to show them,
  And those better days that he knew long ago,
Dismiss with the hope that again he may know them,
  And think of the beggar that canna say No.

The wife whose sick husband robs life of enjoyment,
  And drives her abroad a subsistence to win;
The poor working-man who is out of employment,
  Because his last thought is the wish to get in;
The blessing of those who are ready to perish
  Upon you with gladness should gratefully flow;
But fear not when needful the spirit to cherish,
  That prompts you to answer, a good honest No.

Beware of the vicious, the scheming, the greedy;
  The life of the loafer's the star of their hope;
A dole unto one may be help to the needy—
  The need of another the end of a rope.

That the true man may prosper, the rogue may be branded,
So live—though the flippant may note it as slow;
And think of the thousands of lives that are stranded
For lack of the courage to boldly say No.

Be wary of friendship that gently incites you,
And pause and consider as over a brink;
When merely as formal it kindly invites you,
To write your cognomen in graphic black ink.
And if in your care a young life is expanding
To youth in its brightness of fervour and glow,
With intelligence teach, without blindly commanding,
The duty of Yes and the merit of No.

'Tis said in Italian, a good reputation,
Is like to the cypress that grows on the plain;
Cut down it is gone past rehabiliation,
And never can grow into green leaf again.
So when you are tried, let this motto suffice you,
It comes from the fountain where wisdom doth flow:
My children, consent not, when sinners entice you,
He'll soon be a beggar that canna say No.

WILLIAM ALLAN.

A WELL-KNOWN and very prolific versifier, WILLIAM ALLAN was born in Dundee, November 22nd, 1837. After completing his apprenticeship to the engineering trade, he wrought for a short time as a journeyman in several engine shops in Glasgow, and elsewhere. The force of his mind and character, however, joined to the advantage of a good technical education, soon marked him out for conspicuous service, and, after an adventurous career abroad as a "blockade-runner" during the American Civil War, he returned to Scotland, and in 1868 entered the service of the North

Eastern Marine Engineering Company, Sunderland. Two years later he was entrusted with the entire management of the works, and his energy, skill, and application have been such as to very materially develop, and most completely assure the success of the co-partnery of which he is now the managing head.

Mr. ALLAN has written very profusely. He is the author of not less than six goodly volumes of verse. He is a man of warm impulse, drawing his inspiration immediately from his own glowing and generous heart. He only sings of what he knows of, and be the theme stirring, humorous, or descriptive, his lyre is handled with an energy and spontaneity of flow far removed from studied imitation, or vapid commonplace. He has a free-flowing lyrical faculty, and several of his songs have been set to music and published in sheet form. In the delightfully amusing poem—*The Mutches*—which incident occurred in the experience of a fellow-craftsman in Hydepark Engine Works, near Glasgow—Mr. ALLAN writes with real Scottish humour and appreciable point.

——::——

THE MUTCHES.

I'M just like ither decent men, nae better nor nae waur, O,
An' a' I hae, an' a' I ken, is no eneuch by far, O;
But what o' that, I'm just a man, a mortal fu' o' fail, O,
Sae bear wi' me noo gin ye can an' I'se tell ye a tale, O.

Weel ken ye freens I like a dram o' Hielan' mountain dew, O,
I mak' nae mou's, I winna sham, it aften mak's me fu', O;
Daft things I do an' say, I'm tauld, whan it begins to rule, O,
I haver like a fishwife auld, an' blether like a fule, O.

I dauner'd oot the ither nicht against my wifie's will, O,
Wha vowed that she'd pit oot the licht upon the chap o' twel', O.
She sulk'd and gloom'd, but nocht I saw, save fancied crony-joy, O,
"Guidwife! I'll no be lang awa', it's just a freenly ploy, O."

A social hour aye swiftly gangs whan whisky weets its wings, O—
A crack, a dram, weel mixed wi' sangs, the pairtin' moment brings, O;
The lang hour rang gey strange that nicht, the whisky was aboon, O,
My feet wad ne'er stap oot aricht, my heid aye wanted doon, O.

Hoo aft I coup'd, hoo aft I fell, or duntit ilka wa', O,
Is mair than ony tongue can tell, yet I gat hame for a', O.
I aff my shoon whan at the door, my wifie was asleep, O,
Sae cannily I owre the floor upon my fours did creep, O.

The licht was oot, an' a' was dark, the fire was deein' wan, O,
I steer'd it up an' by its spark I saw a wee bit pan, O;
"What's this! what's this, she's cook'd for me? I left her dour an' angry, O—
For love she can my fauts forgie, she kent I wad be hungry, O!"

My gizzen'd lips I aft did wipe, I blest my happy fate, O,
By a' that's gude! 'twas tender tripe, an' sune the haill I ate, O;
Wi' thankfu' heart I gaed to bed, my thochtfu' wife I blest, O,
She wadna speak nor turn her heid, sae ae saft han' I kiss'd, O.

I wauken'd late, I wauken'd pain'd, I wauken'd like to dee, O,
My wife was up, an' as I maen'd she lauch'd wi' muckle glee, O;
"Guidwife! fareweel! I'm dune! I'm dune! I'm noo in Satan's clutches, O!"
"Ha! ha!" quoth she, "*It serves ye richt!—ye've ate my linen mutches, O.*"

—::—

THE VOICE IN THE GLOAMING.

I HEARD a voice in the gloaming-time
Singing out in the lonely street;
The notes rose up in a wailing chime,
Then fell with a sadness sweet.
I listen'd awhile and my heart was stirr'd,
'Twas a song of sorrow and pain,
I gently stole out in the darkness and heard
The last of the touching strain—
"Father above! Hear me to-night,
My mother I would save,
Cold is our home, no fire, no light,
Give me of bread, I crave."

I heard a voice in a dingy room,
  Crying out in a dying tone,
"My child, my child, how deep is the gloom,
  Come back to your mother, lone."
A footstep was heard on the creaking stair,
  And a shout—"O mother! I come;"
But a weeping child breath'd in silence a prayer,
  As a mother-soul went home—
    "Father above! Hear me to-night,
      O with Thy child abide;
    I'm but a sinner in Thy sight,
      Be Thou my only guide."

I saw a child by a grave-side stand,
  And the tears from her bright eyes fell,
As the sexton old, with a kindly hand,
  Hid all that she loved so well;
Then wandering away from a scene so dark,
  To a world all bright and fair,
Like the weary dove coming back to the ark,
  God had a friend waiting there—
    "I thank Thee, Father, God of Love,
      For all Thy tender care;
    I know that Thou in heaven above
      Hast heard the orphan's prayer."

——::——

BE A MAN!

In the battle rush o' life,
    Be a man!
In the never-ceasing strife,
    Be a man!
If at hammer, plough, or pen,
Show to a' your fellow-men,
Duty's creed ye only ken,
    Like a man!
Though your lot is unco hard,
    Be a man!
Though ye reap but sma' reward,
    Be a man!

Life is best when guid an' true,
Honest deeds ne'er sink frae view,
Richt repays, if ye pursue
Like a man!

When amid your lowly friends,
Be a man!
When success your path attends,
Be a man!
Bear a jealous neebor's hate,
Bear the cauldness o' the great,
Bear the troubles o' your fate,
Like a man!

If o'erwhelm'd wi' pain or grief,
Be a man!
Though your joys gi'e nae relief,
Be a man!
Stand erect before a foe,
Ne'er a coward's effort show,
Smile on Death's exultin' blow
Like a man!

JOHN HYSLOP.

JOHN HYSLOP is a Dumfriesshire poet, having been born in the rural hamlet of Kirkland, parish of Glencairn, 9th February, 1837. His father was then, and for nine years afterwards, in the employment of Sir Robert Laurie, whose fair ancestress—Annie Laurie—will fill an immortal niche in Scottish song. Failing health caused his father to remove with his young family to Thornhill, and the house income being but small, our poet's chances of education were of the most meagre description. His school attendance was all compressed within one year, and was mostly spent at an "auld wife's village schule."

Mr. Hyslop was early put to work, his first employment being that of a walking "craw-bogle," herding the birds off the seed in a nursery during the Spring months, rattling a huge pair of clappers, and "halloing" at them as often as he saw them alight. A removal of the family brought our poet into Kilmarnock, in which town he has lived for the past thirty years. Completing a five years' apprenticeship at the engineering, he forsook that handicraft, his health having suffered, and hearing of a vacancy in the local Post Office, was nominated to the situation of rural messenger in March, 1860. For the past twelve years he has acted as one of the town letter-carriers of Kilmarnock.

In the Spring of the present year (1882) he issued his poems and songs in a complete form under the title of *The Dream of a Masque and other Poems.* The volume was very well received, and favourably represents the author's poetic gifts. He writes with great fluency, and the happiest point; and is one of the many lowly and unassuming poets who have made, in their day and generation, the muse of Scotland a distinct and imperishable possession of the heart.

——::——

THE WEE STRANGER.

Noo, whatna totum's this we've got
  That mak's sae muckle din?
What angel ope'd the gates o' life
  An' let this fairy in?

It was on a Sabbath morning,
  In autumn o' the year,
When this waunert sprite sair greeting
  To our fireside drew near.

We clasp'd it up within oor airms,
  Happ'd it warm an' cosie ;
This queer wee fairy wife we've got
  Cuddling in oor bosie.

She winna let us sleep o' nichts,
  Her wee bit yaum'ring cry
Creeps to us in the land o' dreams,
  Whaur safe an' soun' we lie.

An' ye'll no want my bonnie pet,
  Though we should toil an' slave
Oor fingers to the bane, ye'll get
  Yer pick amang the lave.

There's sic a steer aboot the hoose
  Since Baby Janet cam',
She's made her hame in a' oor hearts,
  The wee bit guileless lam'.

Wee Nan's as prood as if she were
  The leddy o' the lan',
An' Jim, since put in the stirks-sta',
  Has grown a perfect man.

Big steering Jack, an' a' the lave,
  Maun ken whaur it cam' frae ;
They mak' us lee in spite o' fate
  Full twenty times a day.

God bless the bairns ! the future times'
  Braw women an' brave men—
A bairnless hoose maun surely hae
  A cheerless ingle-en'.

I pity sair thae soulless cuifs,
  Wi' hearts as cauld as airn,
Wha dinna loe the prattlings sweet
  And kisses o' a bairn.

They bring us glints o' Paradise,
  They'll big oor fun'ral cairns,
They cheer us baith in life an' death—
  God bless the bonnie bairns !

THE GLEN DOON THERE.

Wi' blythe an' merry tinkle, the bit bonnie wimplin' burn
Jinks through its banks o' cowslips, wi' mony a jouk an' turn;
Wi' mony a jouk an' turn, like a young thing free o' care,
Whaur I'll meet my Jess the nicht, in the glen doon there.
In the glen doon there, in the glen doon there,
I'll meet my bonnie Jessie in the glen doon there!

There's trig an' dainty lassies baith at hame an' far awa',
But for nane I care a preen, for my Jess owre-caps them a'—
For my Jess owre-caps them a'; she's juist ane beyond compare;
An' I'll meet her at the gloamin', in the glen doon there.

For she's stown my heart awa' wi' her saft bewitchin' een:
Sae I've trysted wi' Mess John, an' I bocht the ring yestreen—
I hae bocht the ring yestreen, an' my heart's as licht as air,
For I'll wed my Jess the morn, in the glen doon there.

Though we canna brag o' gear, nor hae binks o' gowden ore,
We've nae herds o' kye or sheep, but we've wealth o' love in store—
We hae wealth o' love in store; sae a fig for Daddy Care,
When link'd for life thegither, in the glen doon there.
In the glen doon there, in the glen doon there,
To bonnie winsome Jessie, in the glen doon there!

J. E. WATT.

The author of a lately-published volume of excellent Doric verse, J. E. Watt, was born at Montrose, February, 1839. His father's occupation, that of a salmon-fisher, necessitated the removal of the family soon afterwards to Dunninald, a secluded romantic little spot on the sea-coast, three miles south of Montrose. Another family removal in our poet's eighth year was made to the Glen o' Craigo, a bleak and barren-looking pine-forest district in the parish of Logie. The following year the future poet was put to work in the

Craigo Bleachfield, toiling for eleven hours each day for 2s. 6d. per week. In his thirteenth year, his parents having again removed to the town of Montrose, our poet was finally put to learn the trade of a brass-finisher. His education had been much neglected previous to this. But the native spark of genius resident in his breast inspired him to search after fountains of thought, and his leisure hours were now sedulously devoted to the reading of instructive books, and to the acquirement of the indispensable art of penmanship. He had very early discovered a knack of rhyming, but being unable to write down the verses he had hitherto let the talent lie in abeyance. Completing his apprenticeship at the brass-finishing business, he finally abandoned it—his health having suffered—and took to the weaving of floorcloth. He is presently employed in a large flax-spinning mill in Montrose, and it is to his credit that he has been with his present employers for over sixteen years.

Acquiring a facility in verse-making, and showing evident talent for the portrayal of character, Mr. WATT continued the practice of rhyming until the local repute he had gained induced him to issue his fugitive pieces in a volume, which resolution he consummated in 1880, his collected poems appearing under the suitable title of *Poetical Sketches of Scottish Life and Character*. The book was largely subscribed for, and was well received by the Scottish press. The volume is a welcome addition to the Doric minstrelsy of Scotland. Mr. WATT has a keen eye for odd, out-of-the-way characters and incidents in daily life, and sketches off the humour of such with a graphic pen. His poetry is not of an imaginative order. He writes a good, relishable, hodden-grey type of verse, and there is much in his book that is likely to obtain permanency in Scottish local poetry.

In addition to a distinct power of graphic portraiture,

Mr. Watt possesses a very fine note of pathos, and makes also capital use of the superstitious beliefs in charms and witchcrafts once common to country-side districts, and which still exercise a weird power over certain types of mind. Altogether, his poetical sketches of Scottish life and character, and his quiet but effective pictures of lowly and unassuming life, are certain to be relished by all readers of healthy natural taste, although in these times of great social and political excitement their modest claim to attention is apt to escape the notice they so well merit.

—::—

JOCK WABSTER'S AULD COAT.

An auld gaberlunzie, Jock Wabster by name,
Was the life o' oor clachan when he was at hame;
For he daunert aboot wi' his wallets an' bags—
A lump o' guid-humour encircl'd wi' rags;
His breekums were short by amaist a han' breed,
An' the croon o' his hat was sew'd in wi' white thread;
But the ae thing that made him a bodie o' note
Was a hap that he wore ca'd Jock Wabster's Auld Coat.

There were mony disputes 'mang oor billies at e'en
As to what the original hue o't had been—
Gif the ground o't had stood by ae colour? or twa?
Or had e'en been a queer combination o' a'?
It was weel kent that noo its great motely o' dyes
Embodied ilk hue o' the earth an' the skies;
Oh, there wisna anither in Scotland, I wot,
Had a thing in his aucht like Jock Wabster's Auld Coat.

Oor gentry, wha carena to wear their claes dune,
Their fashions may change maist as aft as the mune;
But Jock wi' his coat was mair fickle than they,
For the shape an' the hue o't he'd change ilka day,

While the sleeves wad be blue, the breists red, green, an' black,
A hail rainbow o' hues wad adorn the back;
While a daud o' tann'd claith frae the sail o' a boat
Made sonsy pouch-flaps to Jock Wabster's Auld Coat.

At the cottar's fire-side hoo blythely he'd crack,
As he o' some dainty bit alms wad partak';
An', oh, hoo the auld bodie's genius shone oot
When a trinket he'd get, or a piece gaudy cloot;
He pick'd up a' scraps frae the fields an' the wuds—
The verra craw-bogles he robb'd o' their duds;
E'en rags frae the ause-bings, despite mony a spot,
Were deem'd worthy a place on Jock Wabster's Auld Coat.

Ilk chiel rides the hobby that suits his ain whim,
But Jock's was a hobby that rode upon him,
Till his sides micht as weel hae been girth'd wi' a gird,
An' the wecht o't maist crush'd the auld stock to the yird.
Yet he was contented, an' deem'd his coat braw,
An' kept aye addin' til't, but took naething awa';
Sma' dread had oor sodgers o' shell or o' shot
Were they a' clad in duds like Jock Wabster's Auld Coat.

When the weather was dour, the wind gusty an' snell,
Jock keek'd like a tortoise frae 'neath his huge shell;
An' when he gat hame he aye fell til't amain,
An' clootit, an' clootit, an' clootit again;
Till belyve, as he drew to the end o' his course,
He'd a load on his back micht hae foonder'd a horse;
An' a chiel wad hae needed the strength o' a stot
To hae swelter'd a day in Jock Wabster's Auld Coat.

But, alack! 'neath this load Jock was destined to fa',
An' the Angel o' Death took his spirit awa',
To dwell, let us hope, in a world o' bliss,
In reward for the meekness display'd while in this.
An' the coat beneath whilk the auld bodie had reel'd
Is noo in a museum 'mang relics o' eild;
An' bodies wha kenn'd him whyles pairt wi' a groat,
Jist to get a fresh look o' Jock Wabster's Auld Coat.

A LEAF FROM GRANNIE'S SCRAP BOOK.

Sud I chance i' the gloamin' to meet an auld wife,
  Wi' a beard on her chin an' a staff in her hand,
I'd rin frae her gate as I'd rin for my life,
  Gif the deil were ahint me wi' a' his black band.

Sud I happen thereafter to see a black cat
  Loup through a wee winnock, or hole in the wa',
I'd look if a twig o' St. John's-wort I'd gat,
  Lest it sud be the same wither'd carlin I saw.

I like nae the corbie, his song is but harsh,
  As he sits on some blast-blighted stump o' a tree;
An' the muckle black taed that loups i' the marsh,
  O, I wish he were mony a lang mile frae me.

The wee yellow-yorlin I winna misca't,
  Lest it sud be mine to dree dool for my pains;
Richt fair are its feathers, but mind it has gat
  Twa-draps o' the Deevil's black bluid in its veins.

Guid keep me aye far frae the "mune-bowing tyke,"
  An' the pyot that chatters high up on the tree;
Frae the whittret that squeaks frae its hole in the dyke,
  For the sicht o't alane is richt gruesome to me.

In this wonderfu' age, whan the folk are gaun daft,
  An' hae new-fangled notions o' maist things atweel,
Hoo can we expect they'll believe in witchcraft,
  Whan they scarce can believe in a God or a Deil?

But though sceptical bodies sud e'en be sae rash
  As to laugh at an auld wife for wearin' a charm;
I will still prize a sprig o' the green mountain ash—
  Sud it dae me sma' guid, it can do me nae harm.

——::——

GEORGE MURRAY.

ALTHOUGH a native of the north of Ireland, GEORGE MURRAY is of Scotch extraction, and has, for the most part of his life, been residentin the western metropolis of Scotland. Coming to Glasgow when a boy, he became a clerk in a sewed muslin warehouse, and with the exception of a brief period spent in Londonderry as sub-editor of the *Londonderry Journal*—which appointment a failure in health caused him to resign—he has continued to live in Glasgow, where he now holds a responsible situation as corresponding clerk in one of the largest business warehouses in the city.

Showing an early taste and aptitude for poetry, Mr. MURRAY was in early life a successful and acceptable contributor, both in prose and verse, to many local newspapers and periodicals. He writes with correct taste, and with true poetic flow and fervour. He has not yet ventured on independent publication in a volume. His poems, however, are well worthy of being reproduced in a collected form, and would be well received publicly, besides being treasured by many appreciative friends. His capital song, *Work, Boys, Work!* is full of popular tone.

—::—

O, WORK, BOYS, WORK!

O, WORK, boys, work,
  And merrily let us toil,
As on we march to happiness
  Amid the world's turmoil:
While others sit repining,
  And "cruel fate" deplore,
Let us be up and working, boys,
  There's many a joy in store.
    O, work, boys, work, etc.

21

For honest independence
  We'll still keep striving on—
Far sweeter tastes the bread, my boys,
  The dearer it is won.
To clamber up the mountain
  We'll *work* as well as *pray;*
And for a just and manly name
  We'll bravely toil away.
      O, work, boys, work, etc.

While looking to the future
  For sunny days to come,
We'll labour in the *present*, boys,
  To form a happy home:
Then work without repining,
  The goal may soon be won—
Tho' cold and wintry be the day,
  The nearer is the sun.
      O, work, boys, work, etc.

And what tho' fortune darken,
  And troubles round us crowd,
There's still a bright and shining sky
  Behind the darkest cloud;
Then why should we feel envy,
  Altho' our store be small,
For, while we're strong and willing, boys,
  There's plenty for us all.
      Then work, boys, work,
        And merrily let us toil,
      Still marching on to happiness
        Amid the world's turmoil.

——::——

HUNTING CHORUS.

HARK! thro' the woods rings the Hunter's Horn,
From slumber rousing the drowsy morn!
The echoes rebound from the distant hills
And blend with the songs of a thousand rills;

The birds are up on the tireless wing,
And the woods with unnumber'd pæans ring.
Our pulses beat quick at the hounds' loud bay,
And the Horn is ringing! Away, away!
Ho! ho! how the plodders of earth we scorn
As we bound to the sound of the joyous Horn!
The Horn! The Horn!
The wild thrilling notes of the Hunter's Horn!

Rings out the Horn yet again, Hurrah!
We've willing steeds and a noble prey.
We dash along over hill and glen,
And heed not the shouts of excited men:
We wait not for riders who lag behind,
For on speeds the prey like the sweeping wind;
But, tho' he be fleet as the rushing blast,
We'll run him in triumph to earth at last.
Then hark! what exultant sounds are borne
To the joyous bands by the pealing Horn!
The Horn! The Horn!
The jubilant ring of the Hunter's Horn!

—::—

HAPPY DREAMS BE THINE!

LADYE, from thy slumbers wake,
One fond look bestow on me;
Ere the coming day shall break,
On the battle-field I'll be!
Yet, can I disturb thy rest—
Thou, who never may'st be mine?—
Sleep, then, darling, and may blest
And happy dreams be thine—
Sweet and holy thoughts, my love.
Calmer far than mine;
Peaceful visions from above,
And happy dreams be thine!

Should I, on the field of strife
Fall amid my country's foes,

When the ebbing pulse of life
From my quivering bosom flows—
Then, my latest prayer shall be,
Ere my soul this earth resign,
May each day bring peace to thee,
And happy dreams be thine—
Sweet and holy thoughts, my love,
Calmer far than mine;
Peaceful visions from above,
And happy dreams be thine!

But, should I return once more
Crowned with glory's noble wreath,
When the trumpet's blast is o'er,
And their swords the victors sheathe—
Ladye, at thy feet I'll lay
All the laurels may be mine,
Daily guard thee, ever pray
That happy dreams be thine—
Sweet and holy thoughts, my love,
Calmer far than mine;
Peaceful visions from above,
And happy dreams be thine!

WILLIAM FREELAND.

The author of a recently issued volume of superior verse, William Freeland is a native of Kirkintilloch, but early removed to Glasgow, where he now holds a responsible position on the city newspaper press. A journalist by profession, Mr. Freeland in his book—*A Birth Song, and other Poems:* Glasgow, Maclehose & Sons, 1882—shows a fresh proof, if proof were needed, that the native voice of song will not be silent in the human heart, but will assert itself under environments the most exacting and repressive. The volume is a charming addition to local poetical literature, and will bear favourable comparison with the most notable of the poetical works yet issued from the Messrs. Maclehose's select press. Liberal in tone throughout, the book is imbued with the noblest sympathies, and repeatedly reaches with affluent swell the high-water marks of modern thought and progress. In a more directly poetical sense, its pages abound with poems and lyrics of admirable feeling, fancy, and literary finish. Nothing could be finer in their way than many of Mr. FREELAND's exquisite little lyrics, the greater number of which will be somewhat familiar to the general reader as having appeared in different leading magazines during recent years.

——::——

DAWN.

IN the cool star-glimmer, night's dream of dawn,
When dew-bells blink'd on leaf and lawn,
I rose ere yet the lark's keen eye
Twitch'd to the first sun-pulse in the sky.
Downward I went by a forest way,
Companionless, to an ocean bay;
And all around the stillness hung
Like silence on a prophet's tongue,
Which may not speak the thing it knows,
Till heaven's fire on the altar glows;
And I alone of human birth
Seem'd all that walk'd the soundless earth.

In the blanket of her wing the wren
Slept far within the forest's ken;
The sinless mouse in her hollow sod,
Lay safe as in the breast of God;
In her honey-golden cell the bee
Humm'd in a dream of melodie;

And other tiny pensioners lay
Under the veiling mists till day.
Nor innocent things alone, but those
That make all living else their foes,
Were caught by the opiate clouds that fall
With the shadowy eve on the eyes of all.—
  The subtle snake lay coil'd at ease
By the cedar's many-cycled knees,
Acting perchance, in his curtain'd brain
The drama of paradise again;
Cheating once more, with golden lie,
The mother of all humanity.
  The tiger slept in his bosky land
Dark, like an inly-smouldering brand,
Which, touch'd by the faintest breath that came,
Would leap to life like a living flame.
  The eagle with talons and beak of blood,
Brooded above the plunging flood—
Fixed as from all eternity—
God of the moaning mystery.
  Under the billows in caverns dark
Hung suspended the long keen shark,
Till ocean should open his blood-red eye—
To dart on the white ship sailing by.

The forest was pass'd; I reach'd the bay
Haunted by silence all the way:
The far-borne murmur of the deep
Wak'd not the sleeping land from sleep;
The music of that tremulent noise
Seem'd audible without a voice,
According sweetly with the chime
That haunts the solemn calms of time.

Low-eastward, where dim ocean flows,
Swift points of glimmering spears uprose,
And through the shadowy lanes of light
Vanish'd the fawn-like stars in fright;
But stilly the forest began to stir
With stealthy wings in oak and fir

And round about each wrinkl'd root
Whisk'd horny claw and woolly foot :—
  Out of her blanket peep'd the wren
With eyes like the eyes of fairy men ;
The innocent mouse on nature's quest
Crept from her maker's genial breast ;
Forth from his citadel strumm'd the bee
Blowing the trump of industrie ;
The tiger, at the bird's sweet note,
Woke with a blood-hound at his throat,
And shot apace with a burning mouth,
And dropp'd like a star in the sedgy south ;
Out of his coils, as from an abyss,
Flash'd the old snake with a startled hiss,
And, chased by the ghost of his vision, fled
As if some heel had bruis'd his head ;
A motion I saw on the motionless sea,
Rushing between the Dawn and me,
Silent and black as an upturn'd keel,
Swift as death on an edge of steel—
'Twas the shark who follow'd in hungry joy
A ship with a death-doom'd sailor boy ;
The eagle, melancholy shape
Fate-like, calm, on the shadowy cape,
Oped an unfathomable eye
Full on the Dawn's grey-vizor'd sky,
Then rose on wide heroic wing,
Making the cool air quiver and sing,
And upward wheel'd through many a spire
To bathe in the solar surge of fire !

——::——

"THE EARTH IS THE LORD'S."

LORD of the lambkin and the lion,
Lord of Benlomond and Mount Zion,
  Of Israel and Italy,
  Watching in sweet tranquility,
      I worship Thee !

Lord of the glow-worm and the planet,
Lord of dim Patmos and green Thanet,
  Of Jordan's flood and Highland Dee,
  Touch'd by their waves of harmony,
    I worship Thee!

Lord of the sunrise and the sundown,
Lord of Jerusalem and London,
  Of ruin'd Babylon, Rome the free,
  Awed by sad tales of tragedy,
    I worship Thee!

Lord of the well-spring and the geyser,
Lord of Jew Paul and Roman Cæsar,
  Of England and great Germany,
  Dreaming of wondrous times to be,
    I worship Thee!

Lord of the lark—heaven's happy roamer
Lord of King David and blind Homer,
  Of Scotland and green Galilee,
  Illumed by fires of memory,
    I worship Thee!

Lord of pale Dante, Pluto olden;
Lord of grand Milton, Shakespere golden;
  Of Knox—of fearless Luther, he
  Who gave the world new eyes to see,
    I worship Thee!

Lord of the dew-drop and the ocean,
Lord of each heart's divine emotion,
  Of heaven-born science piercing free
  To the sweet soul of mystery,
    I worship Thee!

Teach me, dear God, and make me lowly,
Purge me with light, and make me holy;
  Let me be crucified, and be
  Christ-like, with Christ's humility—
    Adoring Thee!

INVOCATIONS.

Arise, O sun and bring
Upon thy genial wing,
The vigour of the morning-tide, the wholesomeness of day.
Arise, and wake the lark,
That, all the dewy dark,
Amid the green concealing grass, wrapt in a dream song lay.

Awake, O drowsy bee;
Flow'r-bosoms pant for thee
And ope, and bloom with beauty, and drip with hydromel;
Awake and join thy hum
To the enchanting sum
Of mirthfulness and melody that now begins to swell.

Open thy beauty, rose;
For now the south wind blows;
And, from the east, thy bold bridegroom is rising from the sea.
The birds thy praises sing,
And flash their merriest wing,
For there is not, in all the world, a flow'r to equal thee.

O lover, ope thine eyes,
And feed no more on sighs,
Or those delicious maladies that make thee lean and weak.
Cast out, not sense, but fear,
And whistle, cool and clear,
And soon the maid, who wavers now, will not be long to seek.

O maiden why so coy?
Seize, seize the proffer'd joy!
And join the music of thy heart unto the pulse of man;
And ye two, being one,
Shall march beneath the sun,
A legion, to repel despair by heaven's diviner plan.

——::——

JOHN TAYLOR,

Artist and poet, was born near Huntingtower, Perth, in 1837. His grandfather occupied the farm of Huntingtower for many years as Grieve to —— Turnbull, Esq. His father, James Taylor, the writer of some poetical pieces of merit, and a prize-taker in several rhyming competitions, having shown distinct artistic taste in his youth, was apprenticed to the pattern-drawing at Ruthven print-works. In 1840, the family removed to Glasgow, where they have lived at the same address ever since. His mother belonged to an old Perthshire stock, said by the family tradition to be connected with the Dalhousies. One relative was Provost of Perth about the beginning of the century, and another was a royal chaplain and minister of St. Enoch's, Glasgow, for about forty years.

The subject of this notice became a pupil teacher and Queen's scholar in the Free Normal Seminary, and on leaving it in 1857, was engaged for a few years as a tutor in England. Previous to this, however, his inclination towards both pen and pencil had become decided, and he had attempted portraits both in chalk and oil, as well as had a few short articles published. He paid two lengthy visits to France, in 1860 and 1865, during the first of which he painted several pictures in Paris. His first exhibited picture was a series of outline illustrations to Longfellow's "Excelsior" in the Glasgow Fine Art Institute, 1862. He continued to accept engagements as a visiting master, teaching drawing, etc., in several higher class schools till 1867, when he finally gave up teaching.

Though occasionally sending pictures to some of the principal exhibitions, Mr. Taylor has not had any in the Glasgow Institute since 1870. He has contributed to various periodicals, including the *Art Journal*, *Chambers's Journal*, *Hedderwick's Miscellany*, *etc.*, but he is perhaps best known by his poems and songs in the *People's Friend*, and in his rhymes contributed to the *Ayrshire Argus*, 1866-80. He has also contributed poems and pencil sketches to *Quiz*, a Glasgow comic paper.

Mr. TAYLOR is a man of retired habits, and fine tastes. His poetry—which is excellent in itself—represents only one side of a highly-gifted mind.

——::——

TO BIRTHLAND.

IN sunny boyhood's golden time—but yesterday it seems—
My life was radiant with the light of bright and happy dreams;
And then, O bonnie Scotia! my own dear land of birth,
I held thee as the fairest and the freest land on earth.
Thy mountains and thy valleys all, so fair and dear to me,
Were fairer still and dearer in the light of liberty;
And joy went thrilling through me as, with buoyant, bounding tread,
I wandered o'er thy bonnie braes among the heather red.

O, happy, happy, happy time! so nearly linked to heaven,
That not to man through all his years on earth below is given
Another time of joy so pure—so like the joys above—
However bless'd his life may be in wealth, or fame, or love.
Through every varied season then there shines a glow sublime,
A sweet soul-filling peacefulness, not of the earth and time;
And, light of heart and full of glee, with buoyant, bounding tread,
Youth wanders o'er the bonnie braes among the heather red.

O, happy, happy, happy time! but yesterday it seems—
And yet how dim and distant now its bright and joyous dreams.
'Tis almost as if one awoke on some strange, eerie shore—
Awoke and wondered where had fled the "tender grace" of yore;
As if the forms once known and loved he found, with sad surprise,
Become like masks whence alien souls looked out with callous eyes;
And all the mystic glory gone that once so sweetly spread
Its wondrous beauty o'er the dear old hills and heather red.

O, sunny boyhood's golden time! O, native land so dear!
O, lov'd companions who made both so bright and fair appear!
There is a grief, a desolate and dull entrancèd woe,
That they have had a blessèd boon who ne'er had cause to know,—
A strange, sad loneliness that owns no spot of earth as best;
The heart seems to have lost the trick of north, south, east, or west.
All aimless, then, the steps that once, with buoyant, bounding tread,
Went wand'ring o'er the bonnie braes among the heather red.

O, native land! the pride that glowed at thy dear name is cold;
No more with love and light art thou enhaloed as of old;
From boyhood's patriotic dream the gleam of glamour fades,
And seeming true men stand revealed as simulacral shades.
Ay, many once deemed fair and free are leagued in craft and guile,
And cunningly veil Cain-like hearts with hypocritic smile,
While o'er their gentler fellow-men with cruel feet they tread;—
No wonder on thy bonnie braes the heather grows so red.

And yet, O Scotia! thou hast had some noble sons and true,
Who went not with the many when the right was with the few;
Who thought but of the freedom that for others they might win,
And, single-handed, held the breach when foes came thronging in.
What though they fell, and, falling, filled—when flesh could do no more—
The gap through which the enemy his mighty force did pour;
The one last gift they had to give they gave that we might tread
As freemen o'er thy bonnie braes among the heather red.

Thy peasants, too, and preachers, have been men who dared be free—
Who dared to live, and think, and speak, as conscience gave decree;
Who every worldly hope resigned in Freedom's holy cause,
To stand, though but a feeble band, against tyrannic laws;
And oft expecting nought from earth beyond a mossy shroud
In some lone spot among the hills, "far from the madding crowd."
With these thy truest, noblest sons, thou knowest how it sped;—
No wonder on thy bonnie braes the heather grows so red.

A freeman standeth by the right, though one against the world,
With honest word, or pen, or sword, and banner fair unfurled;
Forth like the knights of long ago adventuring his way
Against the social reptiles who make human kind their prey.

True freedom owneth all on earth as one wide family,
And lives already in the time "when all shall brothers be."
"Of old sat Freedom on the heights,"—O! that it might be said
She dwelleth still in thee, dear land of hills and heather red.

But of the eternal soul of truth thou art not yet bereft,
And of the faithful none may say that he alone is left;
Ten thousand, thousand there may be who have not bowed to Baal,
And there is One who will not let His own true people fail.
While gentle, kindly mothers are in hall or humble cot,
And sons are born within whose breast there is one manly spot,
There still will be a hope for thee, still some sweet radiance shed
From the far sun of glory on thy hills and heather red.

A' LANE, LANEY!

I'VE had my share o' sorrows; they've been neither few nor sma'
But noo I feel sae canty that I clean look owre them a';
For I've a kindly wifie, and a hoosie a' my ain,
And a bonnie wee bit bairnie that will soon can rin his lane;—
It's a' lane, laney, and it's a' lane, lane,
Frae his faither to his mither his wee lea lane!

The king I dinna envy, though he wears a gowden croun,
For crouns are heavy bonnets, and micht weigh a body doun;
And thrones hae nae sic comfort as my cosie muckle chair,
When I watch the wee bit tottum toddlin' back and forrit there:—
It's a' lane, laney, and it's a' lane, lane,
He's worth the wealth o' kingdoms his wee lea lane!

If e'er I'm dull or weary when the lang day's wark is through,
On my heart the bairnie's lauchin fa's refreshin' as the dew;
I'm sure he makes me nobler—could I e'er for very shame
Dae wrang and think to tak' him on my knee when I gaed hame?—
It's a' lane, laney, and it's a' lane, lane,
He's just a very blessin' his wee lea lane!

Bright visions o' the future in my fancy whiles I see;
If spared to grow man muckle, wha kens what he yet may be?

Yet neither fame nor fortune may be in the Maker's plan,
But oh! I fain would see him a guid-hearted honest man;—
It's a' lane, laney, and it's a' lane, lane,
A joy to a' that ken him, his wee lea lane!

What wealth could gie sic pleasure to his mither, or to me,
As the kindly earnest glancin' o' his wonder-lichted e'e?
Oh, earth to some folk's fancy may be desert cauld an' stern,
To me it's just like Eden wi' the wife and that bit bairn;—
It's a' lane, laney, and it's a' lane, lane,
The sunshine o' oor summer his wee lea lane!

But summer wears to winter—the leaf fa's frae the rose,
And sorrow comes unbidden, and the day draws to a close;
And I often think how eerie—if the wife and me were gane—
Would be the wee bit bairnie in the world left alane;—
It's a' lane, laney, it's a' lane, lane,
Baith faitherless and mitherless, his wee lea lane!

I ken there's kindly neebors that wad tak him to their fauld,
But the stranger's bread is bitter, and his bed is hard an' cauld;
Yet there's Ane aye watchin' owre us wi' a love abune compare,
That mak's the wee bit lammies a' His ain peculiar care;
I ken that I can trust Him, and I needna mourn or maen,
He winna leave the bairnie his wee lea lane!

JANET HAMILTON.

A POETESS of wide repute, and of remarkable genius, JANET HAMILTON was born in the parish of Shotts, Lanarkshire, October, 1795. The story of her life has, of late, been so often and so ably told, that we will not do more than briefly advert to it here.

The daughter of a shoemaker in lowly life, she never had the advantage of an attendance at the village school; but her mother taught her to read; and she invented a kind of rude writing for her own use, when over fifty years of age.

Mrs MORTON

Mrs HARTLEY

JANET HAMILTON

E C NICHOLSON

MARY CROSS

In her thirteenth year she was married to James Hamilton, her father's young journeyman, and reared a family of ten children. After a happy, but laborious life, she died in the October of 1873, having just completed her seventy-eighth year.

Her poems appearing in collected form when she was considerably over three-score years, attracted much attention, and gained for the aged poetess immediate and permanent fame. Numerous editions of her poems and essays have since appeared, and have been well taken up. The *Memorial Edition*, recently issued, is entirely worthy of her fame.

JANET HAMILTON was undoubtedly one of the most remarkable female singers that has ever appeared in lowly Scottish life. Her auld world pictures are most delicious additions to the Doric minstrelsy of Scotland, and to persons whose native tastes are not emasculated by the cant of culture, their perusal offers perennial sources of enjoyment and delight. Several years previous to her demise, we were favoured with her correspondence, and privileged to sit beside her at her own fireside, and her "crack" we found to be as graphic, and almost as interesting as her excellent poetry. In the midsummer of 1880 a memorial Fountain, of simple but chaste design, was erected to her memory in Langloan, the district so long and so interestingly associated with her name.

——::——

A BALLAD OF MEMORIE.

NAE mair, alas! nae mair I'll see young mornin's gowden hair
Spread owre the lift—the dawnin' sheen o' simmer mornin' fair!
Nae mair the heathery knowe I'll speel, an' see the sunbeams glancin',
Like fire-flauchts owre the loch's lane breast, owre whilk the breeze
is dancin'.

Nae mair I'll wander owre the braes, or thro' the birken shaw,
An' pu' the wild-wud flowers amang thy lanely glens, Roseha'!
How white the haw, how red the rose, how blue the hy'cinth bell,
Whaur fairy thim'les woo the bees in Tenach's brecken dell!

Nae mair when hinnysuckle hings her garlands on the trees,
And hinny breath o' heather bells comes glaffin' on the breeze;
Nor whan the burstin' birken buds, and sweetly scented brier,
Gie oot their sweets, nae pow'r hae they my dowie heart to cheer.

Nae mair I'll hear the cushie-doo, wi' voice o' tender wailin',
Pour out her plaint; nor laverock's sang, up mang the white clouds
  sailin';
The lappin' waves that kiss the shore, the music o' the streams,
The roarin' o' the linn nae mair I'll hear but in my dreams.

When a' the house are gane to sleep I sit my leefu' lane,
An' muse till fancy streaks her wing, an' I am young again.
Again I wander thro' the wuds, again I seem to sing
Some waefu' auld warld ballant strain till a' the echoes ring.

Again the snaw-white howlit's wing out owre my heid is flaffin',
When frae the nest 'mang Calder Craigs I fley't her wi' my daffin';
An' keekin' in the mavis' nest o' naked skuddies fu',
I feed wi' moolins out my pouch ilk gapin' hungry mou'.

Again I wander owre the lea, "an' pu' the gowans fine;"
Again I "paidle in the burn," but, oh! it's lang-sin-syne!
Again your faces blythe I see, your gladsome voices hear—
Frien's o' my youth—a' gane! a' gane! an' I sit blin'lins here.

The stars o' memory lichts the past; but there's a licht abune
To cheer the darkness o' a life that maun be endit sune.
An' aft I think the gowden morn, an' purple gloamin' fa',
Will shine as bricht, an' fa' as saft, when I hae gaen awa'.

TO OCTOBER.

Not changeful April, with her suns and showers,
Pregnant with buds, whose birth the genial hours
Of teeming May will give to life and light:
Rich in young beauty, odorous and bright.

Not rose-crown'd June, in trailing robes of bloom,
Her flowery censers breathing rich perfume,
Her glorious sunshine, and her bluest skies,
Her wealth of dancing leaves where zephyr sighs !

Nor fervid July, in her full-blown charms,
Shedding the odorous hay with sun-brown'd arms ;
Nor glowing August, with her robe unbound,
With ripening grain and juicy fruitage crown'd !

Nor thee, September, though thine orchards glow
With fruits, ripe, rich, and ruddy—laying low
The yellow grain with gleaming sickles keen,
With jest and laugh the harvest song between.

I sing October, month of all the year,
To poet's soul and calm deep feeling dear ;
Her chasten'd sunshine, and her dreamy skies
With tender magic charm my heart and eyes.

JESSIE D. M. MORTON.

A POETESS of true genius, Mrs. MORTON, was born at Dalkeith about the year 1825. She early evinced a remarkably fine talent for verse-writing, and contributed frequently to the local press while little more than a girl in years.

In 1866 her poems were handsomely issued by an Edinburgh publisher, and met with a most gratifying reception. In the following year a second augmented edition was issued.

Judged as a Scottish poetess, Mrs. MORTON must be accorded a high place. She has a touching vein of pathos, and writes with great beauty and purity of sentiment. In the line of humour she has also made a distinct mark. Her *Broken Bowl*—which has been often imitated but never equalled—is one of the best and most characteristic Scottish readings of the century. At present, Mrs. MORTON occupies a stationery and new-agent's shop in Dunfermline.

——::——

THE BROKEN BOWL.

WHAUR Neidpath's wa's wi' pride look doon
Upon a gude auld burgh toon,
A crankie cratur leev'd langsyne,
Amang the gude auld freen's o' mine:
But weel I wat ye sune sall see
She wasna ae drap's bluid tae me.
  Ane o' the awfu' cleanin' kind,
That clean folk clean out o' their mind;
An' aften as we've seen betide,
Clean gude men frae their ain fireside.
A fykie, fashious, yammerin' yaud,
That could the gear fu' steevely haud;
An ill-set, sour, ill-willy wilk—
She had a face 'twad yearnèd milk,
Forbye a loud, ill-scrapit tongue
As e'er in human heid was hung.
To girn an' growl, to work an' flyte,
Was aye the ill-spun wisp's delight;
O heaven, I'm sure that Tibbie's meanin'
Was ae great everlastin' cleanin'.
Frae morn to nicht she ne'er was still—
Her life was like a teugh threadmill.
She was jist like an evil speerit,
She ne'er could settle for a minute;
But when a dud she made or clootit,
Then a' the toon wad hear aboot it.
  Whene'er folk couldna keep her clues,
She heckled them about their *views;*

But when the wrath began to boil,
She grew real "fear't about their sowl."
'Twas queer! (but nocht's sae queer as folk)
Then to the workin' she wad yoke
Thro' perfect spite an' fair ill-natur';
An' the deil's-buckie o' a cratur'
Was o' the "pipe" a mortal hater.
  John, honest man, had aye to hap,
For peace-sake, o'er the weeshen stap;
But e'er the lintel he wad pass,
'Twas, "Man, for gudesake, min' the bass;
Tak' care o' this, tak' care o' that,
Haud aff the hearth noo when it's wat,
When ance it's dry, syne tak' a heat;
Tak' care, man, whaur ye set your feet!
Fa' tae yer parritch, an' beware
Ye let nae jaups fa' on the flare;
Weel, o'er the bicker haud your snoot,
Nor fyle my weel-wash'd table-clout.
To toil, noo, 'deed I'm no sae able,
(Keep yer black dottle aff the table!)
Ye never think hoo sair I'm wrocht
Waes me! but ye ha'e little thocht—
To ha'e things richt when hame ye come—
(Confound ye! smoke it up the lum!)
  Some men wad ha'e the mense to say,
Ye're sair for-foughen-like the day—
Puir body! 'od I'm sure ye're wearit?—
The like o' that wad gi'e ane speerit.
But you! whane'er ye've claw'd ye're coggie,
Ye mak' this hoose a fair killogie.
Inowre the door there's no a steek
But's pushion'd wi' yer 'bacca reek;
An' tho' I clocher till I'm chokin',
I winna pit ye past yer smokin'.
What needs I toil? what needs I care?
Yev'e blawn mair siller i' the air
Than wad ha'e built a house and mair.
Yer neist guidwife'll mend the matter—
She'll no be sic a tholin' cratur';

She'll gi'e yer weel-hain'd gear the air,
My certie ! lad, she'll kaim yer hair ;
An' wi' the saut blab in yer e'e,
Ye'll min' the patience I've ta'en wi'e.
 D'ye want to scomfish me ootricht ?—
Ye've ne'er laid doon the pipe the nicht ;
For a' I've said ye're never heedin'—
Begin, ye scoondrel, to the readin' !"
 Owre weel John ken'd his hoose was clean,
An' keepit like a new-made preen ;
That a' frae end to end was bricht,
For Tibbie toil'd frae morn to nicht.
So he, to hain the weary wark,
Ance hired a lassie stoot an' stark—
A snod bit lassie, fell an' clever ;
But Tibbie was as thrang as ever,
Nae suner was the cleanin' through
Than cleanin' just began anew.
 Noo, on a bink, in stately pride,
Her favour'd bowls stood side by side ;
Braw painted bowls, baith big an' bonny—
Bowls that were never touch'd by ony ;
For they were honour'd vessels a',
An' servile wark they never saw,
Save when a dainteth she was makin',
She whiles took ane her meal to draik in.
 Ae day, the lassie a' thing richtin',
W' canny care the bowls is dichtin',
An' puir thing ! tho' her care increases,
She breaks ane in a thousand pieces.
"What's that ?" screech'd Tibbie, "Losh preserve us !"
Is this the way the fremyt serve us ?
De'il speed the fummlin' fingers o' ye—
Owre Cuddy Brig I'll tak' an' throw ye ;
Ye glaikit gude-for-naething jaud,
Ye'll break us out o' hoose an' hand,
My fingers yeuk to ha'e ye whackit—
Tell me, ye cutty, hoo ye brak it ?
Ye donnert slut ! ye thochtless idiot !
Tell me, this moment, hoo ye did it ?

"In Embro toon thae bowls were coft,
An' sax-an'-twenty miles were brocht,
Weel packet up an' kindly carrit,
An' gien tae me when I was marrit.
In name o' a' that e'er was wrackit
In a' the warl', hoo did ye brak it?"
The lassie sabbit lang and sair,
But Tibbie's tongue could never spare;
Loud was its clear an' wrathfu' tenor,
When in John stàppit to his denner—
An' as he drew inowre his seat,
Her tongue brak owre him like a spate;
He heard o' a' the sad disaster,
An' aye the tongue gaed fast an' faster;
An' aye there cam' the ither growl—
"Lassie! *hoo did ye brak the bowl?*"
"Wheesht! wheesht!" quoth John, "nae mair aboot it.
Od sake! ye've plenty mair withoot it."
But ere anither word was spoken—
Wi' face thrawn like a weel-wrung stockin'—
She squeel'd—"D'ye want to break my heart?
Ye monster; will ye tak' her pairt?
Is this my thanks for a' my toil?
Hoo could the gipsy brak my bowl?"
Patient John heard the endless clack
Till his twa lugs were like to crack;
An' risin', stappit to the shelf
Whaur whummilt stood the gaucie delf,
An' lookin' owre the precious raw,
He raised the biggest o' them a',
An', withoot steerin' aff the bit,
Clash loot the bowl fa' at his fit;
An' as the frichtit flinders flew,
Quoth he, "Ye ken the way o't noo,
For, sure as I'm a leevin' sowl,
That's hoo the lassie brak the bowl!"

——::——

THE TWA GOWANS.

Twa wee gowans bloom'd on a gowanie lea,
Whaur a'things were bonnie as bonnie could be;
The ane had a tinge o' the red heather-bell,
An' the ither was white as the snawdrap itsel'.

The white ane was genty—was winsom' an' wee,
The red ane was braw as a gowan could be;
An' couthie they grew frae they sprang to the licht,
When their hearties were young an' their headies were licht.

An' aye when the wind wad blaw gurlie an' dour,
The red ane aye bent owre the genty bit flow'r;
When drappies o' rain on its breastie wad fa',
It tenderly lootit an' kiss'd them awa'.

When aft-pitten breezes a daffin' wud fa',
An' a' the braw floories wad touzle an' blaw,
The wee gowans joukit an' jinkit ajee,
They boo'd an' they beck'd, an' waflled wi' glee.

But, ah! whan the red ane was ta'en frae the lea,
The wee ane lay doon on its divot to dee;
It lay in its beauty sae heedless o' a',
Like a wee drap o' gowd on a wee flake o' snaw.

For a' roun' the roots o' the floorie sae kind,
The white ane's wee threedies had lang been entwin'd;
Their hearties were ane, an' they wadna be twa,
An' the bonnie wee floorie sune wither'd awa.

—::—

MY FIRST-BORN.

She came to my soul like a sunbeam of bliss—
 Like a ray of God's gladd'ning light;
My fond spirit folded her under its wings,
 And I wept with a holy delight.

I gazed on her beauty, I heard her soft breath,
 With feelings I never had known—
I trembled with joy as I lovingly dreamt
 That the beautiful gem was my own.

A rapturous dream was that dream of my soul,
  Too bright and too blessèd to stay;
Forgive me, O God! the wild moment of doubt,
  When the child of my love pass'd away.

Some griefs have a gloom, while they sadden the soul,
  A solace would seem to impart;
'Tis the veil the angels hang over the soul,
  While they bind up the wounds of the heart.

But O, there are wounds that they never bind up!
  In silence they let them bleed on;
They know that till death they can only be wash'd
  By the tears that are shed when alone.

Believe not, though smiles light the mother's pale cheek,
  One drop of her sorrow is gone;
Ah, no! every smile has its tribute to pay,
  In the tears that she sheds when alone.

They are sacred to truth—they are sacred to Heaven,
  And hopes that for ever have flown;
They spring from the fathomless deeps of the soul,
  The tears that are shed when alone.

ELIZABETH HARTLEY.

A VERY interesting poetess, of good local repute, Mrs. HARTLEY was born at Dumbarton, in the year 1844. Her father held a respectable situation for many years as gardener to the late Sheriff Steele of that town. She was a delicate and extremely sensitive child, and the confinement of the school-room disagreeing with her, she was withdrawn in her eighth year, completing in a fair way her school education at home. She had an extraordinary memory when a child, and as early as her tenth year could repeat from memory nearly the whole of the *Lady of the Lake.* She contributed verses to the local press while still a girl, and issued a volume in her eighteenth year, which was re-issued, in an augmented form, in 1870, under the title of *The Prairie Flower and other Poems.*

Mrs. Hartley has a fertile fancy, correct and flowing diction, and writes with much beauty, power, and purity of feeling. Her little volumes have had encouraging receptions accorded them, and are locally prized.

—::—

MY NATIVE LAND!

How grand are Scotland's rugged hills, where mountain torrent foam!
How still and lovely are her glens, where Highland maidens roam!
What land can boast more gallant hearts than Scotia's honour'd clime?
What land so rich in love and fame, so grand and so sublime?

Ours is the land where freemen trod—the land where tyrants fell;
Amidst whose lofty mountain peaks oppression dare not dwell.
The land where martyrs' tombs arise beside the patriot's grave;
The land where Scotland's Thistle wild shall ever proudly wave.

And from her heath-clad Highland hills what dauntless heroes came—
No false detractor's coward hand can mar their wreath of fame.
Waken'd from peace by Honour's call, the sword of death to wield,
The plaided warriors of the north were foremost on the field.

When, conquering all the world beside, the Roman legions came,
The dauntless spirits of the north they vainly strove to tame.
While Scotland's mountains lift their heads, her title still shall be
Engraved in lines of living fire, the birthplace of the free.

And dost thou ask her of her sons a token to produce?
She points upon the scroll of fame—a Wallace and a Bruce.
O! well may Scotland's bosom glow at Wallace—glorious name—
He won her many a laurel wreath on fields of deathless fame.

But who so base as he who seeks to slight his native land,
Who open'd first his infant eyes on Scotia's honour'd strand,

Yet seeks to cast aspersion false upon her patriots brave—
See, Scotland, with indignant frown, disclaims the recreant slave.

Who fain would slight the noble blood shed for her battles won,
She spurns the traitor from her side, nor owns him as her son.
No—let him fly to burning climes, where slavish terrors reign;
He likes not our cold mountain land—it yields him but disdain.

Let him be fann'd by crouching slaves in some more kindred land;
Let no pure Scottish maiden give to him her heart or hand;
But let him learn that Scottish hearts still dwell upon her strand;
That Scotia's Thistle leaves a wound when clutch'd by foeman's hand.

ELLEN C. NICHOLSON.

A GIFTED poetess of real genius, ELLEN C. NICHOLSON is the daughter of the well-known Scottish poet James Nicholson. She was early trained for the profession of teaching in the Glasgow Free Normal School, and as a candidate for the Queen's Certificate passed the highest on the list for Scotland. Several years ago she obtained a situation as head-teacher of a girls' school at South Shields. It is to her credit to state that two of her pupils have lately passed highest on the list for all England, so that professionally she may feel justly proud of her success.

In conjunction with her father, she lately issued a selection of her fugitive poems, and the press generally accorded the collection a generous note of praise.

Miss NICHOLSON's genius, with cultivation, would give her a leading place as a living Scottish poetess. Her verses suggest on the part of the fair authoress the possession of many of the attributes of impressive and successful verse-writing. Her fine poem, *The Ae Wee Room*, will be very generally admired.

THE AE WEE ROOM.

It's years sin' last we left it—oh, sae weel's I mind the day!
My hair was broon an' bonnie then, that's noo sae thin an' grey.
Waes me! for a' the years hae had o' gladness an' o' gloom,
They've gi'en me naething dearer than my ae wee room.

Sae weel's I mind the wee bit hoose—the burn—the bonnie yaird—
The lauchin' o' the bairns ootbye upon the sunny swaird—
The summer scents o' thymey knowes an' clover leas in bloom,
The breezes brocht at e'enin's to my ae wee room.

It had but little plenishin'; the wa's were unco bare;
But John was young, an' I was young, an' love was wi' us there!
An' but-an'-ben my Johnnie wrocht an' liltit at his loom,
While I wad croon the owercome in oor ae wee room.

An' oh, the happy simmer e'ens for John, an' bairns, an' me!
Sic daffin' doon beside the burn—sic racin' owre the lea—
Sic pu'in' o' the gowans an' the bonnie yellow broom,
To deck the shinin' dresser o' oor ae wee room!

The simmers noo are unco blae, the winters cruel cauld;
It's maybe that thae twa-three years I've grown sae frail an' auld.
But, oh! langsyne, though snaws were deep an' gurly skies micht
gloom,
We aye had simmer sunlicht in oor ae wee room.

Noo John has land and hooses braw, an' mickle warl's gear;
An' we hae left the ae wee room for sax-an'-thretty year;
But through them a' I've miss'd the sangs he sang me at his loom;
For Love seem'd left ahint us in oor ae wee room.

I've miss'd my bonnie bairnies, for the youngest dee'd ere lang;
The eldest sail'd across the seas; the bonniest gaed wrang.
Oh! purses may be fu', I trow, and hearts be unco toom,
We'd better kept oor bairnies in oor ae wee room.

There's heaven afore us a', they say; but heaven's ahint for me—
The wee cot-hoose, the bonnie yaird, the burnie, an' the lea!
The dreary muir o' cauldrife age has still a spot o' bloom—
The thocht o' puirtith's happy days in ae wee room.

SONNETS.

MARSDEN BAY, NEAR SOUTH SHIELDS.

WERE I an artist, I should paint the scene
  In many views and aspects. One by night—
  The moon upon the waters, weirdly bright ;—
One lonely barque, with sails of silver sheen,
Filling the foreground. Outlined dark, yet keen,
  The rugged line of limestone cliffs should lie
  Athwart the fitful radiance of the sky.
Nearer—the great, lone rock that guards the bay—
The shadowy stretch of sand—the shimmering spray.
  That were the fairest scene. There should be more :
Views in the twilight, subtly soft and grey—
Views sunlit—views of storms and flying cloud—
  Of cliff fantastic—sea-gull haunted shore,
And weed-grown rock, and cavern heavy-brow'd.

TO A DEAD FRIEND.

Do you rest sweetly in your wintry grave,
  Beyond whose trampled turf I cannot see ?
Do never dreams or memories, wave on wave,
  Sweep through the silence sund'ring you from me ?
  Has death but fetter'd you ; not set you free ?
Else why so silent ? Many days ago,
  You lay all rigid on a snowy bed—
Oh woe is me, who ever see you so !—
  And would not answer when I asked you, weeping,
  What lies beyond the grave in Death's dark keeping ?
What is this secret that you will not tell ?
  Can no wild prayer of mine disturb your sleeping ?
Oh hapless Living ! Oh most happy Dead !
  Those dear, dumb lips can keep their secret well.

——::——

MARY CROSS

Is another young lady poetess of high and certain promise. She at the present time resides in Glasgow; and although young in years has already contributed meritorious poems, sketches and stories to numerous newspapers, periodicals, and magazines. She is very widely read in English literature, and, possessed of fine taste and a highly receptive mind, has enriched her native gifts, and formed her finished and effective prose-style, by an appreciative study of the masterworks of modern English literature. In the Spring of the present year (1882) she contributed to the *People's Friend* a novel entitled *What's his History?* Engaging in style, the story is otherwise full of interest and genius. She has also contributed novelettes and sketches to *Household Words*, and to other London magazines.

A facility in both rhyming and prose-writing Miss Cross discovered very early. Her verses are full of fine feeling, and glow with chaste and beautiful fancies. She has not yet published her poems in a collected form, but her name is familiar to newspaper readers all over Scotland. She has all the fertility and ardour of true poetical genius, and writes with inspirational warmth and flow.

——::——

ON THE SHORE.

A glow of crimson glory floods the west,
  And clouds assume the purple robe of kings;
I hear above me, rushing to the nest,
  The sweep of "sunset wings;"
Hear, too, the rhythmic chiming of the waves
  Scattering a shower of light upon the sand;

As twilight with her train of misty haze
  Walks slowly o'er the land.
From some far church the bell of vesper rings—
  A voice to tell the hour of prayer and praise ;
I deem it, as in solitude I stand
  The requiem of days.

O thou to-morrow, as yet dimly seen !
  O dawn of morn unknown, and yet to be !
What, as you glimmer o'er the changing scene,
  What bear you unto me ?
In vain I try to pierce the misty veil,
  I vain I bend towards you a listening ear ?
I neither mark a swift advancing sail,
  Nor seas by winds swept clear ;
No holy anthem echoes o'er the sea,
  Your skies and clouds are tremulous and pale ;
What passage in the chapter of the year,
  Trace you in my Life's tale ?

Monotony ? The sleepy swell of waves
  That neither rise to storm nor sink to rest ;
Or—sand and sea-weed rent from hidden graves ?
  I wonder which were best !
To dream at ease where winds are soft and low,
  And sky and sea meet cloudless far away ;
Or where the storm clouds hurry to and fro
  O'er a wild world of spray.
Make answer, oh ! thou soul within my breast,
  To sleep, and dreams, and pleasure, answer No !
I turn from these to living, acting day,
  Where deeds like stars may glow.

——::——

TO A SCEPTIC.

In the silence and calm of the night-time,
  When the stars shine serenely above,
And softly to earth, in the moonlight,
  The wind breathes its whispers of love,

I gaze from my window, e'er watching
  The white moonbeams float on the sea;
Is it strange that thus lonely and pensive,
  My spirit is yearning for thee?

I think of thy voice, and its music
  Still lingers, though faint, in mine ear;
I think of thy face and its beauty,
  And fancy that yet thou art near.
Not lost! thou art mine and forever
  In the joys I even may share;
There's a chain that yet binds us together;
  Its links are of gold—for 'tis prayer.

Then the Sceptic's hand blots out the picture;
  He tells me I dream and I rave;
Oblivion alone can await us;
  No Heaven but only a grave!
His soul can know naught of the comfort,
  Hope breathes in her heart-stirring words,
The harp of his mind is left silent,
  No angel-hand sweepeth its chords.

Alas! his is not the sweet doctrine
  Taught by the Saviour who came;
Strange that His teaching existeth—
  That wisdom still bows at His name—
When a mind such as yours is, O Sceptic,
  Sees only a fable, a myth,
And preaches its own wondrous doctrine,
  That everything closes with death.

Well, you may some time awaken,
  And cease in the darkness to roam;
Your heart may say in repentance,
  "O, Father! thy child has come home!"
There is hope e'en for you, O Sceptic,
  As you lean for support on a reed;
I look to that figure on Calv'ry,
  And know not in vain did He bleed.

DANTE.

SUBLIME the music—poet of the dead—
  Thy heart pour'd forth in wild impassion'd strain;
Through mystic chords of wonder and of dread,
  There throbs a note of living woe or pain.
I see thee, glory-robed, on Fame's high throne,
  And crown'd with laurel and pale asphodel;
But, oh! the yearning pathos of those eyes,
  The shades of sadness that within them dwell!—
Like clouds that dim the great sun-lighted skies!
I deem thy sad lips breathe one word alone,
The name of her who might have been thine own;
  But thou hast now the bliss on earth denied,
  And it may be thy spirit's spirit-bride
First bade thee welcome to God's paradise.

——::——

A SPRING DAY.

'NEATH the shady forest clusters
  Where winds were soft and sweet,
Where the sunshine's golden lustres
  Seem'd lances long and fleet,
Where the blackbird and the starling
  Sang anthems to the May,
We wander'd, oh, my darling,
  That bygone happy day.

We cared not for the morrow,
  The present was our own,
And not a shade of sorrow
  Across our path was thrown;
We saw wild-roses blushing
  Beneath each stately tree,
We heard the river rushing
  To join the distant sea.

The sea as blue and boundless
  As was the arching sky,

And stately, calm, and soundless
  We saw tall ships go by.
We cared not to remember
  That evening follows noon,
That snow-flakes of December
  Make bleak the ways of June.

Oh, day of perfect gladness,
  Oh, day of golden hours,
I gather without sadness
  The dead leaves of your flow'rs,
For though it all is over
  It brought me joy divine;
I dream in grey October
  Of Mays that once were mine!

ROBERT BUCHANAN.

A POET of distinguished genius, ROBERT BUCHANAN was born of Scotch parentage at Caverswell, Staffordshire, 18th August, 1841. The family removed to Glasgow while the future poet was still a child, who received his education at the High School of that city. He afterwards attended classes at the Glasgow University. He early showed remarkable ability, and issued a small volume of verse in his seventeenth year. In 1860 appeared his *Undertones*, a volume of remarkable promise, which his career as a poet and man of letters has amply fulfilled. It is not necessary that we should here detail the successive volumes of poetry, criticism, and fiction, which have from year to year flowed from his fertile and brilliant pen. It is sufficient to say, that he is, beyond comparison, the foremost living Scottish poet, and has permanently enriched English literature with

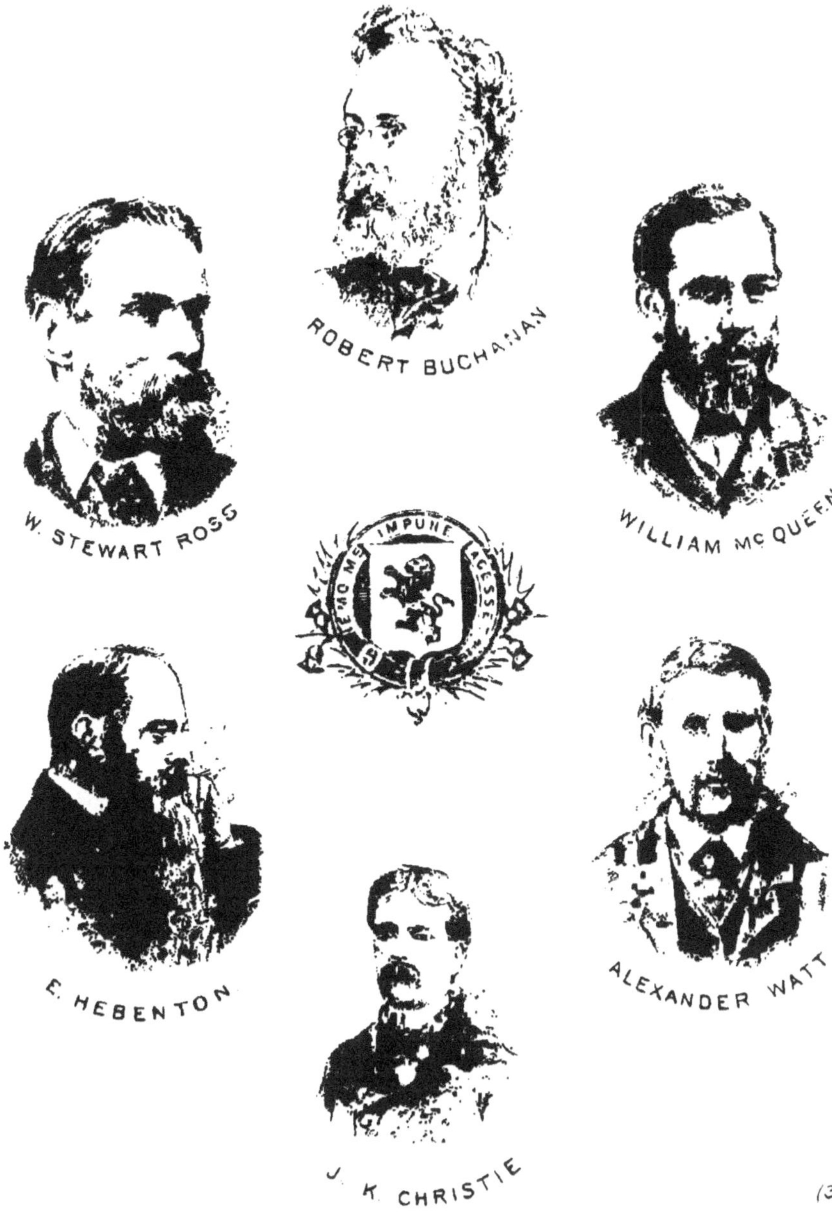

ROBERT BUCHANAN

W. STEWART ROSS

WILLIAM McQUEEN

E. HEBENTON

ALEXANDER WATT

J. K. CHRISTIE

1352

some of the noblest poems of the present century. He possesses in affluence, dramatic insight, imagination, humour, and pathos, and is, perhaps, the most variously-gifted, as he is certainly the most illustrious of living literary Scotsmen.

Recently he broke ground as a dramatist, and at the present time he is taking a leading place as a writer of prose fiction. His *Child of Nature* is a story full of charm, and his higher and more imaginative work—*God and the Man*—has been pronounced one of the most remarkable and notable of modern novels.

His selected poetical works are at present in course of republication by Chatto & Windus, the well-known London publishing firm. Mr. Buchanan enjoys a pension on the Civil List, which Mr. Gladstone granted him in 1870, in consideration of his literary merits.

——::——

THE BATTLE OF DRUMLIEMOOR.

(Covenant Period.)

Bar the door! put out the light, for it gleams across the night,
  And guides the bloody motion of their feet;
Hush the bairn upon thy breast, lest it guide them in their quest,
  And with water quench the blazing of the peat.
Now, wife, sit still and hark!—hold my hand amid the dark;
  Oh Jeanie, we are scatter'd e'en as sleet!

It was down on Drumliemoor, where it slopes upon the shore,
  And looks upon the breaking of the bay,
In the kirkyard of the dead, where the heather is thrice red
  With the blood of those asleep beneath the clay;
And the Howiesons were there, and the people of Glen Ayr,
  And we gather'd in the gloom o' night—to pray.

How! Sit at home in fear, when God's voice was in mine ear,
  When the priests of Baal were slaughtering His sheep?

Nay! there I took my stand, with my reap-hook in my hand,
  For bloody was the sheaf that I might reap;
And the Lord was in His skies, with a thousand dreadful eyes,
  And His breathing made a trouble on the deep.

Each mortal of the band brought his weapon in his hand,
  Though the clapper on the spit was all he bare;
And not a man but knew the work he had to do,
  If the fiends should fall upon us unaware.
And our looks were ghastly white, but it was not with affright—
  The Lord our God was present to our prayer.

Oh, solemn, sad, and slow, rose the stern voice of Munroe,
  And he curst the curse of Babylon the Whore;
We could not see his face, but a gleam was in its place,
  Like the phosphor of the foam upon the shore;
And the eyes of all were dim, as they fixed themselves on him,
  And the sea fill'd up the pauses with its roar.

But when, with accents calm, Kilmahoe gave out the psalm,
  The sweetness of God's voice upon his tongue,
With one voice we praised the Lord of the fire and of the sword,
  And louder than the winter wind it rung;
And across the stars on high went the smoke of tempest by,
  And a vapour roll'd around us as we sung.

'Twas terrible to hear our cry rise deep and clear,
  Though we could not see the criers of the cry;
But we sang and gript our brands, and touch'd each other's hands,
  While a thin sleet smote our faces from the sky;
And sudden, strange and low, hiss'd the voice of Kilmahoe,—
  "Grip your weapons! wait in silence! they are nigh!"

And hark'ning, with clench'd teeth, we could hear across the heath,
  The trampling of the horses as they flew,
And no man breath'd a breath, but all were still as death,
  And close together shivering we drew;
And deeper round us fell all the eyeless gloom of hell,
  And the fiend was in among us ere we knew!

Then our battle shriek arose, and the cursing of our foes,
  Nor face of friend or foeman could we mark;

But I struck and kept my stand, trusting God to guide my hand,
  And struck, and struck, and heard the hell-hounds bark;
And I fell beneath a horse, but I struck with all my force,
  And ript him with my reap-hook—through the dark.

As we struggl'd, knowing not whose hand was at our throat,
  Whose blood was spouting warm into our eyes,
We felt the thick snow-drift swoop upon us from the lift,
  And murmur in the pauses of our cries;
But, lo! before we wist, rose the curtain of the mist,
  And the pale moon shed her sorrow from the skies.

Oh, God! it was a sight to make the hair turn white,
  And wither up the heart's blood into woe,
To see the faces loom in the dimly lighted gloom,
  And the butcher'd lying bloodily below;
While melting, with no sound, fell so peacefully around
  The whiteness and the wonder of the snow!

Ay, and thicker, thicker, pour'd the pale silence of the Lord,
  From the hollow of His hand we saw it shed,
And it gather'd round us there, till we groan'd and gasp'd for air,
  And beneath was ankle-deep and stainéd red;
And soon, whatever wight was smitten down in fight,
  We *buried* in the drift ere he was dead.

Then we beheld, at length, the troopers in their strength,
  For faster, faster, faster, up they stream'd,
And their pistols flashing bright, show'd their faces ashen white,
  And their blue steel caught the driving moon, and gleam'd;
But a dying voice cried—"Fly!" and behold, e'en at the cry,
  A panic fell upon us and we scream'd!

Then we fled!—the darkness grew!—'mid the driving cold we flew
  Each alone, yea, each for those whom he held dear;
And I heard upon the wind the thud of hoofs behind,
  And the scream of those who perish'd in their fear;
But I knew by heart each path through the darkness of the strath,
  And I hid myself all day, and—I am here!

PROTEUS.

INTO the living elements of things
  I, Proteus, mingle, seeking strange disguise;
I track the Sun-god on an eagle's wings,
  Or look at horror thro' a murderer's eyes,
In shape of hornéd beasts my shadow glides
Among broad-leavéd flow'rs that blow 'neath Afric tides.

A wind of ancient prophecy swept down,
  And wither'd up my glory—where I lay
On Paris' bosom, in the Trojan town;
  Troy vanish'd, and I wander'd far away,—
Till, lying on a virgin's breast I gazed
  Thro' infant eyes, and saw, as in a dream,
The great god Pan, whom I had raised and praised,
  Float, huge, unsinew'd, down a mighty stream,
With leaves and lilies heap'd about his head,
  And a weird music hemming him around,
While, dropping from his nerveless fingers dead,
  A brazen sceptre plung'd with hollow sound;
A trackless ocean, wrinkling far away,
  Open'd its darkness for the unking'd day.

Moreover, as he floateth on, at rest,
  With lips that flutter'd still and seem'd to speak,
An eagle, swooping down upon his breast,
  Pick'd his blank eyeballs out with golden beak.

  Thro' wondrous change on change—
Haunted for ever by a hollow tune
Made ere the birth of Sun, or Stars, or Moon—
  I, Proteus, range.

  Nay, evermore I grow
Darker, with deeper pow'r to see and know:—
For in the end, I, Proteus, shall cast
  All wondrous shapes aside but one alone,
And stand (while round about me in the Vast,
The Earth, Sun, Stars, and Moon, burn out at last)—
  A Skeleton, that kneels before a Throne!

WILLIAM M'QUEEN.

A POET, and well-known story-writer, WILLIAM M'QUEEN, was born at Pollokshaws, December, 1841. While still a child he was removed to Glasgow, in which city he continues to reside. At Kingston, and afterwards at St. Enoch's Parish Schools, he had a good ordinary education. He was in time bred to a manufacturing business, but had always a love for literature, and started an MS. Magazine in connection with a literary society, along with several young companions, when only sixteen years of age, which existed for several years. During the time of the American war he went to sea for a couple of years, and returning to Glasgow he afterwards held a responsible position as managing clerk in a power-loom factory. Failing health caused him to relinquish this situation, and he has, for the past ten years, been almost exclusively devoting his time and talents to literary avocations—embracing story-writing, and general journalistic work.

In 1875 he issued a small *brochure* of verses, under the title of *Songs and Rhymes*, which met with a gratifying reception. He has also had published in book-form, his interesting story, *Peter Sannox's Heir*. To various English magazines and journals Mr. M'QUEEN's ready and prolific pen has contributed. He writes with apparent flow, and with an irresistibly engaging smartness of style. The poetical side of his mind, if less developed, is equally attractive. His rhyme on *The Sturdy Beggar* is a capital picture of the auld Scotch gaberlunzie of wandering propensities, easy morality, and picturesque habits and attire;

and his catching little nursery ditty, *Johnny's got a Bawbee*, is equal, in its way, to anything in *Whistle-Binkie*. He has contributed to leading London magazines.

—::—

THE STURDY BEGGAR.

I'M a beggar auld, fu' o' cracks an' canty,
Facing Boreas bauld wi' my step sae jaunty.
Wallets strung oot-owre ilka raggit shouther:
Baith in shine an' show'r I'm aye blythe and throu'ther.

Roving here and there, paying ne'er a lawin';
Reaping everywhere withoot the fash o' sawin'.
Ne'er a care ha'e I, rowing aye in plenty;
Ilka ane lays bye for the beggar denty.

The rarer flow'rs o' life, let ithers sing their praises;
They're only got by strife, and I'm content wi' daisies.
I jink whaur ithers fecht, and troth I wadna niffer;
In bearing poortith's wecht it's this makes a' the differ.

A beggar's mode o' life is often viewed wi' scorning;
But ithers oot o' Fife can live and lauch by sorning.
And wherefore shouldna I be as proud o' my vocation
As ony noble high, wha fattens on the nation?

Singing o'er the lea, hirpling through the clachan;
It's a' the same to me—banning, begging, lauchin',
Free o' ony plan, and a' the cares attendant;
I'm the only man, truly independent.

—::—

THE INN AT LOCH RANZA.

THERE'S a neat little inn cuddled close by the hills,
Near the side of a loch where the tide ebbs and fills,
Where no stinted welcome the weary heart chills;
Need I name it?—the Inn at Loch Ranza.

There Mary the maid, who has cheeks like a rose
Freshly blown, with deft skill, when the ruddy fire glows,
Will toss you a pancake or brew Athole brose
To cheer the tired guest at Loch Ranza.

Perhaps no such brands as "Martell" or "Margaux"
Can be tapp'd, yet the liquor to win a guffaw
From the saddest of lips is the pure Usquebah
Drank "neat" in the Inn at Loch Ranza.

With a boat on the loch, when the twilight lies still
On the sea from the Newton to lonesome Pirn Mill,
The angler may cast in the shade of the hill
Who puts up in the Inn at Loch Ranza.

When Narrachan blinks in the beams of the moon,
Take a turn with your pipe through the fairy-like toon,
Where sweet Highland voices an evening lilt croon
Within sight of the Inn at Loch Ranza.

Here the plaids of the lassies, warm hearted and true,
Are woven so large, with a squeeze they'll hold two,
And an empty place might (who knows?) happen for you
Not far from the Inn at Loch Ranza.

——::——

PENNY-A-YARD.

THERE's an auld wizzen'd figure
That crawls alang the street,
Wi' a coul upon his head,
And wi' bauchles on his feet;
He keeps ayont the kerb,
And he croons until himsel',
But the words come soughing saft,
Like the echoes doon a well—
Penny-a-yard! penny-a-yard!
Only a penny! penny-a-yard!

Owre his shouthers and his duds
Hang the proceeds o' his craft,
Shining bricht against the rags,
Like a ray on cob-webb'd laft,

Fa'ing through a colour'd winnock ;
  And they clink a treble part,
To the low yet quaint refrain
  That seems welling from his heart ;—
      Penny-a-yard ! etc.

In half-text, upon his sleeve
  Preen'd, are words will mak' ye quail
Gin ye're squeamish ; for wi' stumpy
  He's a desperate haun to rail,
At everything and ocht,
  In big words he canna spell ;
And he sweers some awfu' sweers
  When he's fou and disna' sell.
      Penny-a-yard ! etc.

For he drinks, the body, whyles—
  'Deed, as often as he can,
Jist to prove he's no a beast,
  But a reasonable man.
A thing micht else be dooted,
  As ye watch him creep alang,
Dark and thrawn, unkempt and crooket,
  Tearing fiercely at his sang.
      Penny-a-yard ! etc.

He's a sair forfoughten body
  Even at the very best ;
He's a bit o' Auld St. Mungo
  If a bit o' an auld pest ;
And there's mony fouks wad miss him
  Should he cease to snooze alang
Wi' his chains and wi' his pliers,
  And the burden o' his sang.
      Penny-a-yard ! etc.

——::——

JOHNNY'S GOT A BAWBEE.

Johnny's got a bawbee—how will he ware't?
Will he buy a pownie, or a muckle cairt?
    Hey ! for the waring o' the big bawbee,
    We maun send for something owre the saut sea.

Buy a whup for horsey, or a roon drum;
Buy a French peerie that can dance and hum.
Hey! for the waring o' the big bawbee,
We maun send for something owre the saut sea.

Buy a tin whistle, or a cat and dug;
Something that can skirl in a body's lug.
Hey! for the waring o' the big bawbee,
We maun send for something owre the saut sea.

Buy a wee brither frae a kail stock,
Brocht by the doctor in a black pock.
Hey! for the waring o' the big bawbee,
We maun send for something owre the saut sea.

Ne'er mind what ye buy, only buy it sune,
Gin it be but something that'll mak' a din.
Hey! for the waring o' the big bawbee,
We maun send for something owre the saut sea.

GLOAMIN' TIME.

I SET me doon and think when the fire burns bricht,
For the rhymes they kind o' clink in the gloamin' licht,
When the darkness creeps aboon,
And the shadows gather roon,
As the day resigns the croon to the starry nicht.

Hoo ane minds o' things lang gane in the witching hour!
And strange mem'ries seize the brain wi' a giant pow'r,
Till the strongest drap a tear,
And the reckless quake wi' fear,
And far's nearer than the near in the heart's lone bow'r.

It's trying to the maist is the gloamin' licht;
For a' folks hae a ghaist that's no buried richt,
That will come withoot a ca',
And refuse to gang awa'
While the shadow's on the wa'—though the fire burns bricht.

Yet the gloamin's but a blink—it was meant to be sae,
And we mauna sit and think a' the livelang day.
We maun up and strive oor best,
Dae oor wark wi' cheerfu' zest,
And oor future will be blest whaure'er lies oor way.

THOMAS STEWART.

THOMAS STEWART, locally known as "Rustic Rhymer," is a Lanarkshire poet, having been born in the autumn of 1840, at the farm-steading of Harelees, parish of Dalserf (now in the *quoad sacra* parish of Larkhall), and about a mile distant from the village of Larkhall. The little thatched cottage—now roofless—was centred in the heart of a fine orchard, and our poet's happy recollections of the place are mixed up with white roses, red apple blossoms, bright berries, and rosy-cheeked apples. In the poet's bright memory of it, winter never seems to have visited that Eden home of his childhood, and all his recollections of boisterous mirth—the "dookin'" at Hallowe'en, the "curling," and the "snaw-ba' battles," go back to Harelees Hill, a locality a little farther west, whither his father—who was manager of a small colliery there—had removed with his family in 1846. His father, it may be incidentally stated, was a man of sterling moral worth, and dying early, left his surviving family the poor yet rich inheritance of a good name. As early as his eighth year, our poet was put to work in the pit, and being of a not over-robust constitution, he suffered from the continued confinement of the mines, and up till his twelfth year could only put in occasional appearances among his brother miners. Ill-health and early toil interfered also very materially with his chances of school education, which were never ample. At the age of fourteen he found himself a regularly qualified miner, struggling, with noble purpose, to achieve a full day's "darg" with stronger men, and so surprise his widowed mother with the amount of weekly wages earned. He very early felt his bosom fired with a desire to rhyme, and as he grew into manhood he grew also into poetry and local fame. For years he supplied the "Poets' Corner" of the local newspapers with doric verses of homely but excellent merit, obtaining such proficiency and encouragement in the art that in 1875 he was enabled to issue his fugitive pieces in a little volume, under the title of *Doric Rhymes.* Many of these rhymes are merely local, and of necessarily confined interest. A number are domestic in subject, and a goodly proportion reflective and general. He has flow, quiet, pawky humour, reflection, and good descriptive force. He never attempts the heroic, but wisely sings his homely note of song, without artifice, and with pleasing and varied intonation of feeling and voice. Mr. STEWART now holds a responsible situation as manager of the Local Gas Company of the district. He is a graphic prose-writer as well as a fluent poet, and has lately indited for the local press some very interesting sketches of "pit-life" in the Lanarkshire mining districts.

——::——

LOVE'S FIRST KISS.

I, MUSINGLY, in mem'ry, cast my eyes
  Back o'er the busy scenes of life I've past,
And wonder, 'mid its griefs, its cares, and joys,
  Which joy perfection's mantle o'er me cast,
That which was sweetest in the happy past,
And whose impressions, deep, will longest last.

In joys of childhood, simple, and sincere,
  Gain'd from a fading flower, or fragile toy,
E'en ere they fade, their beauties disappear,
  Though bright, and true, how short each childish joy ;—
One moment bright, with nothing to annoy,
Now 'whelm'd in grief, the little lisping boy.

My schoolboy days, when pride began to peep,
  Ambition, newly born, with envious eye,
And greedy grasp, on Learning's ladder steep,
  Each new step gain'd, how great my rising joy !
But schoolboy bliss ambition can destroy,
And so, e'en this, was an imperfect joy.

But ruder toils my op'ning manhood brought,
  A widow'd mother's comfort was my care,
To soothe her lonely soul was all I sought,
  And deem'd the task a joy beyond compare ;
But brightening youth sought brighter spheres than this,
To bask in beams of social love and bliss.

I loved a maid, for long my heart had yearn'd
  On some pure breast to breathe the balm of love ;
"I'm thine," she sigh'd, how warm my bosom burn'd
  With, joy of joys ! the joy of saints above ;
No purer bliss a mortal mind can move,
Than blest my breast that e'en in Avon grove.

From countless cups I've sipp'd the sweets o' joy,
  I've woo'd an' won the pleasures of applause,
The charms of music, pride of tinkling toy,
  I've found them fleeting, fading as their cause ;
But joy the purest, unalloy'd bliss,
The dearest, rarest, Marion's maiden kiss.

Her maiden kiss, that e'en in Avon grove,
  The stream of bliss that flows from mutual love,
'Tis dearer, far, than all the joys of earth,
  In lordly hall, or lowly humble hearth ;
A sacred stream, its fountain-head above,
  A glorious gleam of heavenly light is love ;
The flash of fame may fade with earthly years,
But love's pure flame shall light eternal spheres.

THE WEE COLLIER LADDIE.

SAD the widow'd one gazed on her wee collier laddie,
As, dowie an' drowsie, he crept frae his nest,
An' threw, wi' a grue (for 'twas dirty an' duddy),
The sweat-soakit sark o'er his fair, fragile breast.

An' she sigh'd as she saw hoo her hopes had deceiv'd her,
For, fair in the future, sae fair seem'd his fame,
Ere death o' her dearest on earth had bereav'd her,
An' blotted the bliss o' her humble wee hame.

"Ah, my bairn! maun the buds o' rare genius be wither'd
That lang heaz'd my hope, an' that still I can see?
Maun the fire that thy fond faither saw aye be smother'd
By soul-crushin' toil for my bairnies an' me?

"But I boo to the will o' my Heavenly Faither;
Ambition is often the offspring o' Pride;
He kens what is best for my bairn an' his mither—
The Lord is unerring, 'the Lord will provide.'"

Sae she wrapp'd his weel-clooted coatie around him,
To shield his bit bosom, for breezes were snell,
An' strove to speak cheerie, she wished nae to wound him
Wi' cares, cruel cares! that were crushin' hersel'.

An' there flow'd frae the fount o' his filial affection,
A stream, pure an' holy, untainted wi' guile;
An' his only ambition, his aim in each action,
Was to brichten the beam o', an' bask in her smile.

Sae he sang in the dawn, as he brav'd biting Boreas,
"Though cauld be thy breath, bonnie spring, wi' what glee
Will I hail smiling morn wi' the mavis in chorus,
When 'Primrosy Glen,' in her glory I see.

"Ambition may urge me to aim at the pleasures,
The glories that beam in the beauties o' Art,
When the gleam o' a gem, frae some rare bardie's treasures,
Thro' the mists o' the mine pours its rays on my heart."

But can pleasure, mair pure, bless the bard's glowing bosom?
Though fair be his fame, an' though boundless its flow,
Than the wee collier's bliss, than the joy that o'erflows him,
An' soars in a sang, hailing morn's golden glow.

ALEXANDER WATT

Is the son of William Watt, author of *Kate Dalrymple*, and was born at East Kilbride, February 4th, 1841. His desultory attendance at the village school ceased with his tenth year, and he was then sent to serve as an assistant in a weaving shop, and was afterwards put to the loom. He subsequently engaged himself to a local jobbing slater, at which work he wrought for some ten years. He afterwards wrought for several years with the Calderwood Roman Cement Co., contiguous to his native village, but a recent suspension of mining operations on the part of the firm caused him to accept, for the time being, a still humbler position as a day labourer, at which he at present remains.

Descended from a line of poetic ancestors more or less locally known as rhymsters, Mr. WATT wrote verses early, and his chief delight is still in poetry and music. He inherits a gift for music, and conducted for five years a local flute band, receiving from his brother bandsmen a substantial token of their appreciation of his talent and services. In 1880 he obtained a prize volume for a poem on Janet Hamilton, the Langloan poetess, offered by a local newspaper, and has contributed to the same quarter numerous interesting local sketches and poems. Mr. WATT is a man of excellent character and native genius, and is well fitted for, as he is certainly deserving of, a better position in life than he has hitherto been permitted to fill.

——::——

A LAY O' LANGSYNE.

WHEN whins had tint their gowden bloom, an' fields nae mair look'd cheerie,
An' 'mang the woods, in fitfu' thuds, rose winter's prelude drearie,
To drive the langsome nicht awa', across the muir we stappit,
To yon laich biggin' near the law, that snug wi' thack was happit.

Auld Johnnie in the muckle chair was aye fu' blythe to see us,
An' Bell, wi' kindly, couthie air, soon seats apiece did gie us.
The big snuff-mill was haudit roun', an' naethin' was sae pleasin'
To Johnnie than when Taddy's broun did set us callans sneezin'.

Syne wad he tell us langsyne cracks, that did ilk fancy tickle,
'Bout ploughin', thrashin', theekin' stacks, an' wieldin' o' the sickle;
Hoo he at fairs an' markets baith did cudgel menseless cowpers,
Or put to flicht sic ill-bred graith as turbulent lan'-loupers.

But whaur's the group o' younkers gay that aft round Johnnie's ingle,
'Neath sacred friendship's warmest ray, in bygane days did mingle?
Some to the muckle toon ha'e gane to dree life's weary battle,
Whaur commerce, leagued wi' lusty gain, maintains an endless brattle;

While ithers 'neath far distant skies, to keep life's wheels in motion,
Howk whaur the precious nugget lies, in lands beyond the ocean.
But let them be whaure'er they may, their thochts will aften wander
To the lov'd scenes o' youth's bright day, an' on their pleasures ponder.

THE CHRISTENING.

AN INCIDENT IN THE LIFE OF THE BAREFIT LAIRD.

'Twas Foorsday, an' the blinding drift
Cam' swurling frae the murky lift,
An' Hittock's course thro' Freeland Glen
Lay wreathed an' hid frae mortal ken.
But tho' in winter's fleecy gear
The kintry round lay sad an' drear,
In yon snug cot beside the burn
Nae face look'd sad, nae heart did mourn,
When 'twas declar'd a son was born
To the douce Barefit Laird that morn.
The laird—a man o' upright heart—
Was fain to act a faither's part;
To do as his guid sires had dune,
An' hae the bairnie christen'd sune
By ane wha taught wi' heart an' will,
Like Cameron, Renwick, and Cargill.

But in the westland congregation
There was twa Sabbaths o' vacation,
Whilk was owre lang for ane sae douce
To keep a heathen in his hoose.
Aft had he heard his gutcher tell
O' bairnies bound wi' elfin spell,
That werena o' kirk rites possess'd,
An' by a holy pastor bless'd;
Forbye, the guidwife erst had seen
A fairy form attired in green,
An' as it gade its mystic round
Had aften glintit at Rosemound.
Sae ere sax suns did rise an' set,
Their bairnie christen'd they maun get.

Soon as the Sabbath morning broke,
The wean was dress'd in 's christening frock,
His mou' was moisten'd weel wi' toddy
By Meg, the ancient clachan howdie,
And then consign'd to Nannie's care,
Wha maun wi't to the kirk repair.
She row'd it in a pirnie plaid,
An' wi' the guid laird by her side,
Weel 'fended by his hodden greys,
They soon were speelin' Cathkin Braes.
Belyve in auld Saint Mungo's toon,
Awhile they wander'd up an' doon,
Till that they found a grave Divine
(Ane o' the Covenanting line),
Wha scorn'd to feed the soul that yearns
For pastures green on blastit birns.
Before his congregation sune
The sacred rite was duly dune;
Syne Nannie an' the laird bedeen,
Wi' licht hearts hameward cross'd the Green;
Tho' dour the wind, an' deep the snaw,
They murmur'd na', but trudg'd awa';
An' after strooslein' hard an' sair,
Unskath'd they reach'd Rosemound ance mair.

The leal guidwife, wi' prudent care,
A mensfu' blythemeat did prepare,
In honour o' the sweet wee treasure
That garr'd her bosom glow wi' pleasure.
As weel beseem'd that loved retreat,
The day was closed wi' converse meet;
An' free o' ostentatious airs,
Arose to heaven their evening prayers.

A' ye wha o'er Fame's brawling flood
Loudly proclaim your deeds o' guid,
Yet canna see that truth an' beauty
Lie in the sober path of duty,
On Time's muck-midden fling your pride,
An' cast your canting zeal aside;
Be for ilk worthy act prepared
To imitate the Barefit Laird.

EDWARD HEBENTON.

A WRITER of thoughtful and interesting verses, EDWARD HEBENTON was born at East Memus, parish of Tannadice, Forfarshire, 8th May, 1842. He had a fairly good school education, and in his seventeenth year entered a solicitor's office. He was an early and consistent lover of books. The discovery of his talent for verse-writing was made under rather accecidental circumstances. The account we give in our poet's own words:—"A fellow-clerk and I," he says, "got into a trivial dispute one evening in the office, and a good deal of smart badinage passed between us. Our further argument was interrupted by the entrance of a client, but my opponent was too keen a disputant to let the matter drop, and accordingly he scribbled a verse or two, assailing my arguments, and passed them across the desk to me. I replied in verse. Next day the dispute diverged from the subject at issue to the quality of our respective verses. This new difference was referred to another desk-mate for settlement, who suggested that we should test our poetical powers by each choosing a theme, writing thereon, and submitting the poems to the editor of the *People's Journal.* The suggestion was adopted, with the result that while my opponent's piece went to the waste basket as containing 'nothing new,' my verses, according to the editor's verdict, 'would have passed muster had they not been already overstocked.' This was so very gratifying to me that I was induced to fresh attempts, and I have indulged in the *ars poetica* ever since."

Mr. HEBENTON is at the present time a clerk in the Register House, Edinburgh. He has not yet ventured on the publication of a volume, but has contributed poems and well-written sketches with welcome frequency to the local press, and to other quarters, for many years back. His verses are thoughtful, rather than sentimental. He has fine poetic flow, and writes with great clearness and point.

——::——

MUSINGS.

IN days bygone mayhap I dream'd the laurel might be mine,
While yet Parnassus hill I deem'd within my power to climb.
But *then* life's sky was brightly blue, and rosy-colour'd hope
Still beckon'd on, no height in view with which I could not cope.

Ah, me! 'twas but the strength of youth, as yet by cares untried—
The ignorance of the hard ruth that might in time betide.
Ah, me! I am not sighing now o'er these bright vanish'd dreams;
I reck them not, though life, I trow, a shade more sober seems.

I am but musing on the past, when youth, in fever-heat,
Sought not to know its joys would last, provided they were sweet.

I am but musing on the past—on what alone I'd sought,
Ere yet my mind had taken cast from life's maturer thought.

'Tis not, I ween, a crime to glance at days of long ago;
Such retrospect tends to enhance the present joys we know.
And, therefore, though my thoughts may turn back to the days of
'Tis not that I the present spurn, or what may be in store. [yore,

Ah, no! mine are not vain regrets; and for the future, why?
I'll leave its working with the Fates, nor in it seek to pry.
Enough for me it is to feel the clasp of kindly hand;
Or meet the glances that reveal those sympathies that stand

Unlessen'd 'midst the woes of life, untouch'd by all its cares,
And prove whate'er its moils and strife, heart to heart pity bears.
Enough! What more could one desire to fill his cup than this?
I know not, nor would I aspire to higher form of bliss.

——::——

LONE WERE THE WAY.

Lone were the way o'er Life's dark hills,
And hard, oh, hard the climbing,
If down the rugged slopes no rills
Flow'd, with the babbling joy that stills
Our wearied soul's repining.

Lone were the way and sad the lot,
And deep, oh, deep the sorrow,
If for each heart there were no spot,
Where draughts of rosy hope are got,
To cheer the darksome morrow.

Lone were the way, no stars to guide
Our weary feet when stumbling,
If there were never by our side
A heart to which we could confide
The why our hopes are crumbling.

Lone were the way, had Providence
Not made a wise division
Of love, of hope, of joy; and hence,
Amidst our woes we know still whence
To seek life's full fruition.

'TIS SWEET.

'Tis sweet to roam in early Spring through meadow, wood, and lea,
When flow'rs are op'ning to the sun, and birds sing cheerily.
'Tis sweet to rest in sultry June beneath the green trees' shade,
Or in the softly murmuring brook with naked feet to wade.

'Tis sweet to join the merry game that speeds the winter night;
'Tis sweet to list to tale of love—of gallant deeds in fight.
'Tis sweet to hear of friend's success—of wanderer return'd
From foreign climes to those fond ones who long his absence mourn'd.

'Tis sweet to know that one's good deed has eased a mind of pain;
'Tis sweet to know that kindness will return to us again.
'Tis sweet to know there are in life so many varied things,
From each of which, to comfort man, some jet of joy upsprings.

A SUMMER SONG.

Oh, come, my love, the woods are green,
The wild birds warble free,
The daisies deck the fairy scene,
The lambs skip o'er the lea;
Then come, my love, from city dust,
And smoke, and swelt'ring weather—
Come from the seat of Mammon's lust,
And rove among the heather.

Adown the glen the burnie rins
With murmur soft and low,
The yellow bloom is on the whins,
The birks their tassels show;
Then come, my love, let these beguile
To go with me a-roaming,
Where Nature basks in beauty's smile,
From summer morn till gloaming.

Come while the fields are fair, my love,
With sweetly-scented clover,

While in the woods the cushat-dove
Coos soft 'neath leafy cover;
For rural scenes are fair, my love,
When blythe the birds are singing,
And all the echoes of the grove
With their sweet notes are ringing.

J. K. CHRISTIE.

A NATIVE of Paisley, J. KNOX CHRISTIE, can lay claim to a fair portion of the poetic afflatus with which the inhabitants of that ancient town are commonly accredited. An early repugnance to the formal routine of school life made him hate books when a boy as sincerely as he now loves and values them. When in his ninth year, he left home for school one Monday morning as usual, but instead of going there he sought and found immediate occupation in a local lithographer's workshop. The step was taken outside the knowledge of his parents, but he was allowed to remain, and only left it for other employment after three years' service. When about eighteen years of age our poet entered the postal service at Dunoon, where he remained for a period of three years, employing his leisure hours in the cultivation of his literary tastes, and in the correction of an early neglected education. On leaving Dunoon he removed to Glasgow, where he has since been connected with the Glasgow postal staff. From his boyhood up, Mr. CHRISTIE has all along been an energetic contributor to the poetical columns of the local press, and to various magazines and periodicals. In 1877, he issued his fugitive pieces in a collective form, under the strikingly alliterative title of *Many Moods, in Many Measures*, which met with a gratifying reception. The volume, save in a few poems of obviously early date, shows throughout the deft hand of the accomplished versifier, and is instinct with true poetical feeling and fancy.

In consonance with the title of his book, Mr. CHRISTIE has written down his poetic thoughts in many moods and many measures, and his muse, which is still active and fertile, shows, as we have indicated, correct and forcible diction, fertile fancy, and poetic flow. His mind delights also in moral verses, leavened with a spirit of a pure and unobtrusive evangelicalism of faith, and to the religious periodicals of the day he has contributed many truly sweet and beautiful sacred pieces.

Personally, Mr. CHRISTIE is a man of quiet habits and fine tastes. He is a good prose-writer as well as a fluent poet, and as he has written much superior verse since the publication of his first volume, he is likely to ultimately re-issue it in an augmented form.

We quote a few pieces conceived in his lighter and more popular style.

——::——

A BEVY OF BEAUTIES.

WITH paper, pen, patience, and pleasure as well,
  Hand resting on chin, we are sitting here musing,
And doing our best to decide which is belle,
  But all must allow it is rather confusing.
'Mongst five lovely ladies to say which is best;
  'Tis this makes our task seem the hardest of duties,
For fixing on one may offend all the rest,
  And who would offend such a bevy of beauties?

Now each has a charm that her neighbours may lack,
  Of form or of feature that's piquant or pretty,
And then we are sternly aware of the fact
  That each may ere long be perusing this ditty.
You know the safe truism, old as the rocks,
  That money at all times of evil the root is,
Yet some say 'tis women—'tis one of their jokes—
  There can't be much ill in a bevy of beauties.

Be pleased to excuse us should we write amiss,
  Our previous stanza does seem rather hazy,
But then we intend to be lucid with this,
  And introduce, therefore, at once, our friend Daisy.
A sweet, gentle face, somewhat sombre at times,
  Is one of her charms ; and how neat, too, her foot is,
And tender her heart ! and—but some of our rhymes
  Must be kept for the rest of our bevy of beauties.

Fair Susan is winsomely friendly and free,
  With more in her face of bright June than October ;
An elegant figure, in truth, too, has she,
  And lovable ways, be they merry or sober.
But what of bright Lizzy ?—she's modest and shy,
  To get at her heart try her eyes, there the route is :
To travel that way some beau ere long will try,
  And now for the next of our bevy of beauties.

Brave Maggie appears with a frank winning smile,
  A lady-like form, and a heart truly human.
The reader might travel for many a mile
  And never behold a more genuine woman.
And last, though not least, at blythe Kate we arrive,
  Whose petite, piquant form quite as smart as her foot is,
Or shapely gloved hand, say now, which of the five
  Would you claim as your choice from this bevy of beauties ?

——::——

THE PERNICKETY WIFE.

My wife's a weary, waefu' wife,
  Tho' ane mair trig there couldna be;
She's been the plague o' a' my life,
  And yet she's unco gude to me.
She dusts and cleans the hale day lang,
An' aye fin's oot there's something wrang;
The chairs an' me aboot are dang
  Because she's sae pernickety.

A speck o' dust she canna thole,
  An' faith her een are gleg to see;
A wee bit mite o' dirt or coal
  Mak's her at ance, to clean it, flee.
The flair is nearly worn awa',
The chairs are maist withoot a flaw;
A cleaner hoose ye never saw,
  My wife is sae pernickety.

We hae a cosy but-an'-ben—
  For twa the hoose is nane owre wee,
An' a' her time the wife maun spen'
  In makin' things look spruce and spree.
She aye pursues her daily plans—
She polishes the frying-pans,
An' rubs an' scrubs the pots and cans,
  The body's sae pernickety.

When I come back frae work at nicht
  To tak' my hamely cup o' tea,
She glow'rs me owre to see a's richt
  Before a bite is gien to me.
Gude faith, if glaur is on my buits,
She ca's me a' the dirty bruits,
An' turns me oot to clean my cuits,
  The body's sae pernickety.

A' things maun aye be in their place
  At nicht; it's just the same wi' me;
She gies me an allotted space,
  From oot o' which I daurna jee.

I'm seated in a corner chair,
In case I fyle hearthstane or flair,
An' maunna move ance oot o' there,
The body's sae pernickety.

An' then she sets to scrub again,
For scarce a meenit has she free—
At stoup, or clock, or window-pane,
At fender, grate, or crockery.
Aye wash an' splash, and scrub an' rub
At mantlepiece or bowl or tub;
She's never oot o' the hub-bub,
The body's sae pernickety.

I'm sure she thinks me in the way,
An' will be till the day I dee;
The scrubbing-brush and dusters hae
Her hale concern an' company.
Could she just use me like the delf—
For ance I think she'd please herself—
First scrub, then put me on a shelf,
My wife is sae pernickety.

——::——

BRAVE DAYS OF OLD.

The brave days of old, were they better than now?
That often have power to move us
When memory chases the cloud from our brow,
And tenderly seems to reprove us.
A fast-fading vision, a dim, distant dream,
Those brave days of old to our memory seem,
As Life still goes on like a fast-flowing stream,
The same sun still shining above us.

Forgetting the trials and struggles we knew—
Forgetting the tears and the sighing,
We lovingly linger o'er days short and few,
When Joy all our cares was defying;

When friends group'd around us, young, merry, and strong,
With bright, happy faces, with laughter and song,
Each brief, careless hour, as it pass'd would prolong,
And blithely each brief hour went flying.

How fondly we think of the brave days of old,
As friends that have vanish'd for ever—
Of faces now lying beneath the grim mould,
And forms that have cross'd the wide river;
The earth still is bright, and the skies overhead,
Yet dearly we muse over days that are dead,
Of hopes, passing fair, and of visions long fled,
Brave days we can see again never.

PETER GARDINER.

A FLUENT and impressive prose-writer, as well as an interesting poet, PETER GARDINER, is a native of Edinburgh, having been born in one of those quaint old "closes" which still form a marked characteristic of the narrow, strangely-crooked, time-and-weather-worn streets of that part of the city known as the "Old Town." At an early age, he was put to Duncan Street School, Newington, to form a "friendship with the three 'R's,' and a hatred for the master's tawse." While still a school-boy, he evinced a native aptitude for literary work by securing a first prize for an essay, entitled, "Oor trip to Musselburgh." Being naturally of a studious and reflective turn, and having been thrown much, and very early, on his own resources, he took to miscellaneous reading with pleasure, and devoured books with avidity. With a poet's instinct, however, he preferred Blind Harry's *Wallace* to Lindley Murray's Grammar, and the ballad of *Sir James the Rose* to the School Arithmetic. His mother had a taste for the ballads and poetry of her native country, and from her lips he first learned to know and respect the names of Burns, Scott, Ramsay, Hogg, and Tannahill.

In his eleventh year, he was withdrawn from school, and apprenticed to the trade of a blacksmith. Having completed a five years' apprenticeship, he took passage for New York, and landed there in May, 1864, from whence he went to Philadelphia, and settled for twelve months among some relations resident in that town.

In 1865, incited by an adventurous spirit, our poet joined the United States Marine Corps, and was serving in the Barracks at Washington when President Lincoln was assassinated. He formed one of the guard of forty odd men detailed to watch over the misguided men arrested in connection with the assassination, and the equally dastardly attempt on the lives of the leading members of the Cabinet. He stood guard, also, two hours over the lifeless body of John Wilkes Booth, who murdered the good President with a pistol-shot in Ford's Theatre. Shortly afterwards, he was drafted, as one of a guard of forty-two men, on board the United States sloop-of-war, *Hartford*—a staunch vessel, carrying twenty-one guns, and flying a Commodore's pennant at the main. Aboard the war-ship, he had an extended cruise of three years, during which they sailed from New York to Rio de Janeiro, thence to Cape Town, thence to Java, and on to Hong Kong, *via* the Spice Islands. Cruising around, they afterwards made the passage through the Inland Sea of Japan, visited Yokohama and other places, returning again to the Chinese coast. This cruise had the effect of very materially expanding and maturing Mr. GARDINER's mental powers, as well as widening and broadening his sympathies. Especially, however, was his soul taken with the grandeur and sublimity of the mighty ocean—

seductively beautiful in its peaceful hours; in wrath, terrible as the Destroying Angel,—and the vast seclusion of the sea first awoke his muse to conscious effort. On account of a failure of health, he returned to Scotland about 1869, and is, at the present time, employed as an operative mechanic in Edinburgh on his own account.

As a poet, Mr. GARDINER must be conceded a distinct place, although we certainly think he attains his highest development as a thoughtful and impressive writer of prose. His mind is much and highly gifted, and he unites to an evident power of thought, a strength and beauty of expression which is rare amongst the unlettered sons of toil.

—::—

DEAR SCOTLAND!

DEAR Scotland! my country, mine own rugged land,
  When in childhood thy mountains I wander'd,
No blue-bell was torn from its couch by this hand,
  On the breezes abroad to be squander'd.
Thy heather, thy thistle, were sacred to me;
  And the mist-plaided mountains above me
Seem'd the haunt of the souls of the fearless and free—
  Dear Scotland! my country, I love thee.

A stripling, I stray'd on a far foreign strand,
  And dreamt of the days of my childhood;
And in fancy re-gazed on the cliff-guarded land,
  Where the fierce eagle nurtures her wild brood.
My heart gave a bound, and my pulses beat high,
  I frown'd on the clear blue above me;
I sigh'd for the mist, while a tear dimm'd mine eye—
  Dear Scotland! my country, I love thee.

In manhood I tread thee, mine own cloudy land,
  Love's fire in my soul brightly burning;
She touches my heart with her weird-wizard wand,
  Thy name in its chambers in-urning.

I bow to my mistress—I kneel to my God—
And I smile on the grey sky above me,
While the wild blood leaps high as I spring o'er thy sod,
Dear Scotland! my country, I love thee.

Dear Scotland! my country, though Time's shrivell'd hand
Be heavily laid on my forehead;
Though sapp'd be youth's fire, still love for thy strand
Will re-kindle the eyes in my hoar-head.
Though Death strikes me down, still live shall my strain,
While my soul from its haven above thee,
Defying his power, shall murmur again,
"Dear Scotland! my country, I love thee."

——::——

A MOTHER'S LAMENT FOR THE DEATH OF HER BOY-CHILD.

THE warm simmer sun in his glory is shinin',
An' tranquil an' blue is his path to the west;
In the east-lift a wee snaw-white cloud is reclinin',
Like a bairnie asleep on a fond mother's breast.
But my een, sair wi' greetin', my heart cauld an' stony,
Through thick mists o' sorrow nae beauty can see;
The snawy-white cloudie reminds me o' Johnnie,
As, wrapped in his gounie, he slept on my knee.

The saft westlin' win' soughs alang the gay meadow,
An' flutters the green plumes that nod on the trees;
Through the leafy-roof'd aisle, strip'd wi' sunshine an' shadow,
Flow'r-scents an' burd-warblin's are borne on the breeze.
Here my bairnie an' me aft hae wander'd thegither,
O! Death, thou hast robb'd me o' a' earthly joy;
The sparrow's wee fledgeling can chirp to its mither,
But mute is the voice o' my bonnie wee boy.

At nicht when the starnies are timidly keekin',
Wi' tearfu' wee een frae the face o' the sky,
Then my puir bruisèd heart goeth aimlessly seekin',
The spot where the spirit o' Johnnie may lie.

O! they tell me he's safe in the Shepherd's warm bosom,
  They say that it's sinfu' to grieve or repine,
But O! when I see a wee bairnie that's lo'esome,
  God help me! I canna help yearning for mine.

On the face o' the heaven—the bosom o' nature,
  Wherever, distracted, I turn my sad e'e,
There is something recalls to my mind ilka feature—
  The image o' Johnnie is *a'where* to me.
Kind Heaven! if we only could a' gang thegither,
  Then Death wadna seem sae remorseless an' stern;
But hoo can a bairnie dae wantin' its mither?
  Or hoo can a mither dae wantin' her bairn?

——::——

THE LOSS OF THE CONCORD, OF NEWHAVEN.

'Twas morning, and the ruddy sunbeams fell
  Upon the surf-chafed coast of bleak Dunbar;
The sea-gull sped from her spray-portall'd cell,
  And flash'd athwart the waters like a star;
The fishing-boats rode on the white-topp'd swell,
  Out on the deep a sail was seen afar.
The breezes bore the surf's hoarse voice along,
The circling sea-gull's scream, the fisher's snatch of song.

Out to the deep the Concord cleft her way;
  Staunch was the boat, and fearless were the crew—
Of many hearts the pride, the hope, and stay,
  The gallant Johnstones—hardy, bold, and true—
Whose polar-star was duty. Ah! the day
  Dawn'd not on braver ploughers of the blue;
Their goal the sail which, bird-like, gleam'd afar;
Their task to steer her safe across the harbour bar.

A frown swept o'er the sapphire dome of heaven,
  Swathing in gloom the sun-god's flaming crest;
In fitful gusts inconstant winds were driven
  Across the dim, dark ocean's heaving breast;

ALEXANDER ANDERSON
L J NICOLSON
PETER GARDINER
NEMO ME IMPUNE LACESSET
JAMES M NEILSON
ROBERT FORD
H C WILSON

(382)

Then like a sightless Cyclops, madness riven,
  The storm-king leapt upon the trembling yeast;
Then winds and waters grappled in the gloom,
And the staunch Concord's crew stood face to face with doom.

Alone upon the deep! Brave pilot band!
  "No eye to pity and no hand to save."
Firm-lipp'd they stood, as Scottish men can stand
  When death confronts them, and the yawning grave;
Undaunted and unvanquish'd, hand in hand,
  They sank beneath the tempest-wrestling wave.
Their children's faces flash'd before their eyes,
And with a cry to God, they entered Paradise.

No more the pilots' sail shall fleck the deep,
  Their keel no more plough furrows in the Firth;
And Sympathy shall mourn and Pity weep
  Over the death-glean'd sheaves of sterling worth;
And lamentation's voice shall heavenward leap,
  Wailing the dear ones snatch'd away from earth.
The cries of babes, the tears by women shed—
O, Heaven! these have no power to summon back the dead.

To Thee, O God, we turn in mute despair,
  In speechless agony of heart and mind.
Make thou the widows Thy peculiar care,
  Their broken hearts with Thine own hands upbind.
The mother, Lord, in thy great love let share,
  The fatherless in Thee a Father find.
"*The dead shall rise!*" then may the pilot band,
  With mothers, wives, and babes, be found on *Thy right hand.*

W. STEWART ROSS.

A TRUE poet, and a man of remarkable business energy and enterprise, WILLIAM STEWART ROSS is a Galloway man, having been born at Kirkbean, March 20th, 1844. Sent to school in his ninth year, he became an omnivorous reader of books, and by the age of twelve, was familiar with the writings of Burns, Byron, and Scott. Showing a remarkable aptitude for school acquirements, he became a schoolmaster, on his own account, as early as his seventeenth year. He was afterwards, for a period of two years, principal assistant to his former master at Hutton Hall Academy, passing from thence, in the winter of 1864, to an attendance at Glasgow University, in view of a completion of his varied and desultory studies. Subsequently, he supported himself for years by writing for newspapers and magazines. Possessed of a versatile fertility, springing from a root of genuine intellectual power, nothing in the way of literary work seems to have come amiss to him during this early and struggling portion of his career. Latterly, he formed a business connection with an Edinburgh publisher, which connection was ultimately severed through Mr. Ross establishing himself as a publisher in London; he being now head partner of the well-known educational publishing firm of W. Stewart & Co., the Holborn Viaduct Steps.

Mr. Ross's career presents a noble spectacle of genius, energy, and native strength of character, manfully asserting itself, and overcoming all obstacles to success. An enterprising London publisher, he lately signalized himself as being still a poet at heart, by carrying off the Prize Medal recently offered for the best poem in connection with the inauguration of the Dumfries Burns Statue. Brief in compass, but superb in conception, expression, and sustained elevation of tone, we take Mr. Ross's noble poem to be one of the very finest tributary odes ever laid on the shrine of Burns. In the present year (1881) he issued his *Lays of Romance*, a book of romantic-historic verse aglow on every page with the energy of a true and high poetical genius. In addition to the Burns poem, we quote the splendidly-bold and stirring ballad of *Richard Lion-heart*.

RICHARD LION-HEART.

"Ha! ha! my veins are raging hot, my hectic senses reel!
Pshaw, fever! Bring my harness, squire, my morion of steel.
I cannot live supine like this, and die like coward slave:
Ho, reeling front of battle be the death-bed of the brave!

"No, no, my Berengaria! take that bandage from my head,
And bring me, gentle wife of mine, the iron helm instead:
And put thy snow-white favour in my plume, so dark and high;
Steel harness be my winding-sheet, a soldier let me die!

"Know, in this sainted Palestine, the Saviour died for me;
And my good sword and strong right arm shall strike for Him and thee;
And ne'er shall heathen sandals tread, and heathen banners wave,
O'er the garden of his agony, the glory of his grave!

"No! o'er the Moslem turban, and the flashing scimitar,
We'll pour the hosts of England in the thunder-crash of war.
On, warriors of the high crusade, bended bow and swinging sword,—
And wave o'er Pagan Ascalon the banner of the Lord!

"Gird on my heavy armour, bring my war-horse from the stall;
Sound the trumpet, shout Jehovah! forward, onward to the wall!
Come, gentle Berengaria,—through the vizor bars, a kiss;
And I'll leave to weak old women a dying bed like this.

"Let Leopold of Austria die thus, when die he may;
Let craven Philip breathe his last far from the battle fray;
The couch of Richard Lion-heart must be the crimson sod,
Where, 'neath the banner'd cross, he fought for glory and for God.

"See, holy Carmel's dark with shame, red blushes Jordan's tide,
That Saladin should hold a day the land where Jesus died;
Ho! where the dead lie thickest upon earth's groaning breast,
At eve search for King Richard, and lay him to his rest!

"And not in dear old England lay you your leader dead,
But deep within this holy land lay you his helmèd head;
Not English oak, but Syrian palm, shall guard his soldier's grave
In the sainted land he lived to love—the land he died to save!

"O Salem, for thy Holy Tomb, O England, for thy throne,
King Death shall find King Richard with his armour girded on;
He'll greet thee, King of Terrors, o'er Jordan's mortal flood,
With a forehead wreath'd in laurel, and a hand imbrued in blood!

"Come, laggard knights, I charge you, haste, ere the sun go down,
And bear me on your shoulders to the ramparts of the town!—
Plunge him amid the battle shock, the grapple, yell, and groan,
That Death may find King Richard with his armour girded on!"

—::—

ROBERT BURNS.

All hail, O Nithsdale's furrow'd field, a Marathon art thou;
The fire of God in his great heart, of Genius on his brow,
Thy patriot bard strode o'er thy sward, his triumph car the plough!
The laverock in the early dawn, the merle at evening grey,
Sang pæans as the ploughman trod his more than laurell'd way;
And the red ridge of Scottish soil behind him grandly lay,
Prink'd with the daisy's "crimson tip," the "rough burr-thistle's" head,
And rough print of the ploughman's shoe—shoe of the deathless dead.

'Tis o'er, the rig is dark with night, the "lingering star's" on high,
And Song-land's gain'd another wreath of flow'rs that never die.

In Nithsdale, as a dreamy boy, in wild ecstatic turns,
I've grasp'd the plough to follow, rapt, thy shade, O Robert Burns!
As "spretty nowes have rairt and risk't" I've seen thee standing nigh,
'Mid visions of the Throne of Song too grand for mortal eye:
The hills around burn'd into verse, an anthem vast and dim,
The "fragrant birk" an idyll grew, the "stibble field" a hymn!

O Sword, rust o'er thy mighty dead, pent in their funeral urns,
Plough, by Elisha sanctified, and glorified by Burns,
Thine is no roll of tears and groans, the dying and the dead,
Thou writest on the wintry fields, the prophecy of Bread—
I'll drive my share o'er vanquish'd Want, my coulter's edge uprears
The banners of the yellow corn, the rye's unnumber'd spears.
God speed thy "horns"—no altar horns so sacred are to me,
The Prophet and the Muse of Fire their mantle bore to thee!

Yet, would a tyrant weld our chains? then, Victory or the Grave—
The trumpet blast of "Scots wha hae" will make the coward brave!
Then onward, Valour, "red-wat-shod,"—glory to him who dies!
Be his eternal infamy, the "traitor knave" who flies!

Dumfries, thy cold hands hold his urn, thou guard'st his iron sleep,
O shrine that draws the universe to worship and to weep!
What tribute grand of brass or stone can thy poor hands bestow?
What bronze or marble worthy him who lies so cold and low?
Of the brave man whose fight is fought, whose weapon's sheath'd, whose banner's furl'd,
Though still his fire and force of soul throbs in the veins of half the world:
Australia loves him, India too, as though he had but died yestreen;
Columbia knows the Banks o' Doon, and Afric sings of Bonnie Jean!

Hast seen athwart the midnight stars a cloud its shadow fling?
Hast seen the stain from the cage's bars upon the eagle's wing?
Impeach I will not; but, Dumfries, I cannot do him wrong,
Thy street-mire stain'd the singing-robe of the great King of Song:
Look sorrowing back on the grey hairs too early o'er his brow,
And, grateful, what he lack'd in bread, give him in garlands now.

. . . .

Joy in thy solemn heritage, breaking Oblivion's wave,
O grandest city of the world, for you have Burns's grave!

JAMES M. NEILSON.

JAMES M. NEILSON is one of several poets who, of late years, have put in a distinct claim to be remembered in the Doric minstrelsy of Scotland. He was born in the parish of Campsie, March 2nd, 1844. Whether or not he was born a poet, we have heard the bard himself facetiously remark he would not take upon himself to say, but he is morally certain he was not born a gentleman, as he had to stump out to work at a very early age. Bye-and-bye when he had entered upon his teens, he found employment in Lennox Mill, becoming an apprentice to the business of an engraver for calico-printing work. His first public appearances in verse were made as early as his eighteenth year, in the *Stirling Gazette*, then the property of, and edited by, Dr. C. Rodgers. About this time he began to write local notes for the *Stirling Observer*, and later on he became a district correspondent of the Glasgow *Daily Mail*, with general local acceptance. With the born persistency of the true poet, however, he stuck to rhyme under every shade and colour of circumstance, with the result that his poems had soon so thickly accumulated on his hands that the publication of a volume became in the end an inevitable sort of necessity. This undertaking he successfully accomplished in the Spring of 1877. The book was largely subscribed for, and very well received, the author's claim to the name of a poet being generously admitted.

Mr. NEILSON, it may be remarked, is essentially Scottish in the cast of his mind, and his book is largely imbued with the national tastes. The subjects poetically descanted on are mostly Scottish, and even local in tone, and they are treated by preference in the native lowland Doric. Few will regret this, as Mr. NEILSON is especially happy in the use of his native West of Scotland dialect, and he is never so effective as when using it. Ample evidence of his ability as a poet, and his competency to handle worthy and sensible subjects in homely dialect verse, is to be found in his fine poem, *Grandfaither's Knee*, in his kindly and beautiful verses, entitled *Grannie's Ingle-side*, and in other kindred poems.

Like the majority of Scottish poets, Mr. NEILSON blends pathos with humour, and the Scottish language has perhaps nothing tenderer, in its way, than his pensively-beautiful and touching little cradle song, *The Mither but no the Wife.* Furthermore, he has written a number of spirited songs, several of which have been set to music and published in popular sheet-form.

—::—

GRANDFAITHER'S KNEE.

By the ingle auld grandfaither's sittin',
His nichtcap drawn owre his bauld pow;
'Mang his scant locks Time's frost's gat a fittin'
That Death's breath alane noo can thow.
Like a licht 'mang the mist o' the mornin',
Subdued is the flash o' his e'e;
But his heart dings owre Age an' ilk warnin'
To get at the bairns roun' his knee.

When the bairns leave their play 'mang the heather,
Leave paidlin' the mossy broon burn,
Wi' the bloom on their cheek they there gether,
To grandfaither's knee they return;
An' like clusters o' ripe fruit they swing on't—
Richt glad is the auld vintner's soul,
An' he fin's nae the burden they bring on't,
For love mak's him stronger to thole.

While their faithers may rival sae keenly
For honours in Kirk or in State,
There's rivalry scarcely mair freen'ly
'Mang bairns for their favourite seat;
For grandfaither's haun's a croon kin'ly,
Like royalty's robe's his embrace:
Wi' his knee for a throne, 'maist divinely
True happiness brichtens ilk face.

On the ae day, wi' grandfaither's bawbee,
They're listed into the Dragoons,
An' they've mounted his knee an' awa', see,
To ride through the enemy's touns.

On the next day they join the blue jackets—
  The *Black Prince* gaes reddin' the sea,
But they're safe aye frae rifles an' rackets—
  A snug place is grandfaither's knee.

There they're schul't in the gaits they sud gang in,
  Whar thorns will be fewer to fash ;
An' for fear they dae oucht there is wrang in,
  They're ne'er to dae onything rash.
It's their altar—the Holy Beuk's spread on't,
  He reads aboot ilk Bible bairn ;
An' their wee heids sae flaxen are laid on't,
  Their earliest prayer to learn.

But, ochone, for the dool they've been hearin',
  Their wee hearts blude sair wi' the stang—
He has told them the nicht-fa' is nearin',
  His day wi' them canna be lang.
Owre ilk rosy cheek Sorrow's dew's dreepin',
  Gude's haun in't they canna yet see ;
An' they segh loud an' lang till they're sleepin'
  Their sairs hale on grandfaither's knee.

—::—

GRANNIE'S INGLE-SIDE.

The craw the highest fir may tap,
  The bee the sweetest blossom seek,
The thistle's hame be Scotland's lap,
  The swain may court the rosy cheek ;
But, ask the bairnies whaur they'd be—
  What's best owre a' the world beside ?—
They'll haud their flaxen heids fu' hie,
  An' shout—"It's Grannie's Ingle-side ! "

When buskit oot in braw new claes,
  Auld Grannie's hansel's never miss't ;
Wee feet wi' thorns, an' trampit taes,
  Are buckl't best when Grannie does't.

For orra ailments o' the bairns,
  Her ready skill can sune provide ;
For muckle, muckle Grannie learns
  Frae first she owns an Ingle-side !

When mither owre them craws sae croose,
  An' faither threats to use the tawse,
A kind word's aye in Grannie's hoose—
  Their fortress is their Grannie's wa's.
When bairns wi' bairns fa' oot at play,
  An' on some wee dispute divide,
Auld Grannie's sowers't wi' her say—
  They're sune made freens at her fireside.

When strings o' stories Grannie tells,
  'Bout giants, witches, ghaists an' a',
That skelpit owre the ferny fells,
  An' cantrips play'd in castles braw,
Their faces never brichter shone—
  Ilk day frae morn till nicht they'd bide ;
As loyal subjects to a throne,
  Are they to Grannie's Ingle-side.

She counsels them on wrang and richt,
  An' guid advice she'll aften gie ;
She warns them o' the ills that blicht,
  An' snares spread oot to please the e'e :
For she has kenn'd the warld fu' lang,
  An's e'en a tried an' trusty guide ;
Her counsel has sic wecht amang
  The bairns aroun' her Ingle-side.

But Grannie's gettin' auld an' frail,
  As bairns grow up to maids an' men ;
The day's at han' maun tell a tale
  On wrinkled three-score years an' ten.
But maids an' men she'll leave ahint
  Will count the gowden hours wi' pride
They've treasur'd up in Memory's mint—
  The days at Grannie's Ingle-side !

A MITHER, BUT NO A WIFE.

A CRADLE SONG.

WHIST, my bonnie bairnie, dinna greet sae sair,
Mither's heart is breakin', dinna rack it mair;
Whist, my darlin' tootie, cradlie-ba' an' sleep—
Nicht is unco eerie, life is unco steep.

An' the waefu' win's sough, wailin' in the lum,
'Minds me o' the kirkyard, whaur are sleepin' some
Wadna' see us wrang't sae; tho' there's ithers keep
Steekit doors against us—sleep, my bairnie, sleep.

Fausely did the man woo, wily did he win,
Then he left me—whist, doo—to the lash o' sin;
Left the burden a' mine—hoo it crushes doon!—
Sorrow drooks the hale warl', an' the heavens froon!

Frien's, wha wad be guid folk, banish me frae hame,
Thinkin' in this big toon they may hide the shame:
Aiblins they may fin' yet, in this warl wide,
Want o' kindly pity, worth o' hollow pride.

Hidden lies the future—O, it's dark to me!
But for *your* sake, tootie, I could thole to dee,
Sittin' in the shadows hope can ne'er dispel,
Dreedlin' aye the warst comes, e'er on sinner fell.

Gin ye winna sleep, bairn, come to mither's arms;
Ay, ye'll lauch an' craw noo, prood as ye had farms
Growin' owre wi' ripe corn: lauch an' craw awa',
Thy smiles the only sun-blinks ever on me fa'.

—::—

THE BAIRNS A' AT REST.

From Good Words.

THERE was din, as ye ne'er heard the like,
'Mang our bairns the nicht roun' the fire-en';
A' were busy as bees in a bike;
A' were blithe as the birds in the glen.

What wi' castles an' kirks built wi' stools,
  What wi' rhyming at spellings a' roun',
What wi' playing at ball an' at bools,—
  But there's peace noo, they're a' cuddled doun.

Now, the bairns are asleep, and a calm
  Has fa'n roun' like a saft gloaming shade,
And a kind hand unseen sheds a balm
  O'er their wee limbs in weariness laid.
On their fair chubby faces we see
  Sic an evenly sweetness o' rest,
That ye'd doubt but they borrow'd a wee
  Frae the far-awa' realms o' the blest.

Like wee birds in a nest do they cow'r
  By ilk other so cozy and kin';
O, their bed's like a rose-bed in flow'r,
  And our glances o' love on it shine!
Awa' wi' your glairy gowd crown,
  Frae the cunning cauld fingers o' Art!
But, hurrah for the bairns that hae grown
  Like a living love-wreath roun' the heart!

Ha, let's wheesht. As we warm in their praise,
  We micht waken some flaxen-hair'd loon;
See, already shot out frae the claes
  Just as lithe a wee limb's in the toon!
Hap it o'er, hap it o'er. Bonnie bairn,
  Whaur awa' may that wee footie pace?
The richt gait o' the world's ill to learn,
  And fair Fortune is fickle to chase.

There are hid 'neath these lashes so long,
  The full een that are stars o' the day;
There lies silent the nursery song,
  On these lips fresh as morning in May;
And there beats in these bosoms a life
  Mair o' promise than Spring-buds are giv'n,
That must meet the world's favour or strife,
  And shall make them or mar them for heav'n.

Will ye guard them, ye angels o' Peace,
In this haven, in the curtains o' night?
Will ye guide them when dangers increase,
Heaving out in their day-ocean fight?
For O, whaur, frae the bairnie so wee
To the bairnie the biggest of a',
Is the ane we'd first part wi' and see
To a bed in the grave taen awa'?

LAURANCE J. NICOLSON.

A POET of emotional purity, and much beauty of verse, LAURANCE J. NICOLSON, was born in the town of Lerwick, Shetland Isles, 26th April, 1844. On account of his nativity he has been not inappropriately styled the "Bard of Thule." His father, who was a general merchant and ship agent, died when the subject of this sketch was only eleven years old. His mother was the daughter of Walter Gray, who held, as the last of many generations, the estate of Cliff, in Unst—the most fertile isle of the Shetland group. Of seven children LAURANCE was the youngest, and on the death of the father the whole family removed to Dalkeith, where the eldest son held a clerkship. What education the poet had closed at this time, and it only amounted to what is termed "elementary." A strong desire to enter upon a sea-faring life, in imitation of an elder brother who had adopted that profession, was put aside in deference to the wish of his mother, and he was shortly afterwards apprenticed to the trade of cabinetmaking in Dalkeith, completing a five years' term of servitude to that handicraft.

He early inherited from his beloved mother—a woman of gentle mind and manners—a decided taste for poetry, but it was only at her death, happening, as it did, just as he had finished his apprenticeship, that he was taken with a strong desire to express himself in verse.

A serious illness succeeding the death of his mother left him bodily weak, inducing the poet to seek a less exacting occupation than the cabinetmaker's bench. In this he so far succeeded as to find temporary employment at a clerkship in the Burgh Engineer's Office, Edinburgh, and afterwards in a builder's office in Dalkeith.

Mr. NICOLSON has not yet ventured on the publication of a volume, although he is ultimately certain to do so. His verses merit such distinction, being characterised by high thought and emotional fervour, with much grace and beauty of diction. He has also a fine lyrical flow, and has written many truly beautiful songs. His subjects are for the most part drawn immediately from his own heart-suggestions, and their treatment is correspondingly subjective in tone. Occasionally, however, he adventures on impersonal topics, and under the inspiration of an earnest purpose, writes impressively, and invariably well. As a vehicle of thought he has but seldom attempted the Scottish Doric. His mind is, perhaps, too serious for effective success in that walk, presenting as it does no specially humorous side in his writings. He has been for a number of years back an energetic contributor to the Scottish newspaper press, and to the periodical literature of the day; but his verses are, all through, far above the level of the ordinary newspaper poem, both in thought and diction, and collected into a volume, would form a very acceptable little book.

——::——

THE LAST FIGHT.

He left his home with failing hope and breath,
To fight it out with death;
Death whisper'd, as he look'd within his eyes,
"A noble prize."

Where'er he went no land could give him life
For such unequal strife;
At last, his one hope left—Death pressing nigh—
Home! home to die!

From morn till noon and night, from night till dawn,
The good ship hasten'd on;
And hasten'd on the shadow o'er the tide,
Nor left his side.

The happy earth-light faded in his eyes,
And died, as daylight dies;
The silent valley open'd unto him
Its entrance dim.

Adown the valley, grasping now Death's hand,
He heard the cry of—"Land!"
And backward, upward to the light of day,
He dragg'd his way.

And they that loved him met him on the shore,
And kiss'd him o'er and o'er;
He whispered, smiling, as his spirit pass'd,
"Home! home at last!"

——::——

NELLIE.

What ails thee, little rosebud of my heart?
The birds are singing in the sunny sky,
And yet my little one from all apart,
Can only answer with a wailing cry.

The am'rous breeze but woos the gentle flow'rs
  To steal their souls, and wander heedless by;
We wait beside thee through the silent hours,
  Yet see we nought but sorrow in thine eye.

And like forget-me-nots bedrench'd with dew,
  Thine eyes look strangely up from beds of snow;
Thine eyes look up—thy spirit shineth through—
  "Forget-me-not?" No, little darling, no!

The summer sunshine bids the heart rejoice,
  And earth, and sea, and sky in rapture meet;
When shall we hear the music of thy voice
  Keep happy time to little patt'ring feet.

Thy brother pauses in his lonely play,
  And with a wearied sigh, yet patiently,
"To-morrow," little darling, he will say,
  "Will Nellie rise? and will she play with me?"

"To-morrow," with its sunshine, never came—
  My little boy is standing at my side,
And clasping still the mem'ry of a name,
  With wond'ring eyes he whispers—"Nellie died."

O, sweet forget-me-nots, bedrench'd with dew!
  Dear eyes that follow me where'er I go;
Entreating still from death-calm depths of blue.
  "Forget-me-not?" No, little darling, no!

——::——

CHRIST IN BONDS.

"He came, and yet His own receiv'd Him not!"
    We read in ancient lore;
For Truth and Freedom's sake He chose His lot,
    And suffering bore.

"The foxes have their holes, the birds of air
    Their nests, and yet," he said,
"The Son of Man he hath not even where
    To lay his head!"

Oh Truth! oh Freedom! is it gain, or loss,
Ye count the Christmas morns?
For love of you He bore the bloody cross,
And crown of thorns.

Behold! ten thousand temples rear'd on high,
To Christ of Nazareth;
And there the heirs of Freedom creed-bound lie,
In living death!

Oh Satire! greater never saw the light—
A people still in chains!
Who cry from out the darkness of the night,
"Christ Jesus reigns!"

——::——

SHALL WE BIND THE CHAIN.

"Help! oh help! shall Freedom die?"
"No!" the Cossack makes reply.
"What though all men else be dumb,
"Brother, ho! we come! we come!"

Over mountain, ice, and snow,
Deeply sworn to strike the blow;
Death! or Freedom! on they go,

On, resistless as thy tide,
Mighty Danube; far and wide,
Sweep they down the Tyrant's pride.

Shall we stem that tide,
Freedom's rushing river?
Wake again the strife?
Give oppression life?
Never! never! never!

Battle-drum is heard no more,
Clash of swords, nor cannon's roar;
But the wail above the dead
Pierces through the gloom o'erhead.

"Has the storm and darkness gone?
When—oh when, will break the dawn?"
Cry they, still with tearful moan.

Hearing that beseeching cry,
Shall the hope within them die?
Brothers—what shall we reply!

Shall we bind the chain
  Blood and tears now sever?
Wake again the strife!
Give oppression life?
  Never! never! never!

FRANK SUTHERLAND,

BETTER-KNOWN to North Country newspaper readers by his *nom-de-plume* of "Uncle Peter," is a Morayshire poet, and was born in 1844. He is a hairdresser to trade, and at present conducts a business in Elgin. He is an expert angler, a musician, and a crack shot with the rifle, as well as a writer of flowing and competent verse. In 1879 he was the successful competitor for a five guinea prize song on *Morayland*, offered by the London Morayshire Club. Regarding Mr. SUTHERLAND's musical abilities, it may be stated, that our poet is the eldest of a family of musicians—well-known over the North of Scotland—and who have performed at all the high-class festive gatherings in the seven surrounding counties for many years past.

A volume of his poems, we learn, are now in course of preparation, and which will be issued under the distinctive title of *Sunny Memories of Morayland.*

MORAYLAND.

Air—"The Bonnie Briar Bush."

Ance mair aroon' this festive board convenes our social band:
A lot o' leal an' loyal loons frae dear auld Morayland—
Yon sunny clime we lo'e sae weel, far north ayont the Tay,
The land whar gentle Lossie winds, deep Fin'ron, an' the Spey.

'Twas there, langsyne, whan gleesome loons we chased the gird an' ba'
Wi' early freens whase very names sweet memories reca'.
The land whar Punchie wander'd lang wi's trusty rod an' reel,
Whar Cutler Jamie sat and sang o'er's skirlin' timmer wheel.

Whan bravely climin' life's steep hill or creepin' canny doon,
We like to tak' a leisure hour to rest an' look aroon';
Though far remov'd we still can see yon shady Oak Wood dell,
The auld Bow Brig, green Lady Hill an' tricklin' Marywell.

Some loons, by Mossat's ripplin' rills, in fancy tak' a turn,
While ithers roam o'er Cluny Hills or stray by Wishart's Burn.
Ay! mony a time we wander aff, though only but in dreams,
To clim' far-distant sunny braes or muse by silv'ry streams.

A kind auld mither Moray is, her sons are leal an' fain,
An' though they aften rove aboot, she coonts them still her ain.
'Mang ither worthy sons frae hame she ever proodly croons
O' unco mindfu' bairns she ca's her London Moray loons.

Though weel they lo'e big London Toon an' a' its fowk sae kin',
Their fondest thochts aye wander back to scenes o' auld langsyne.
Then pledge wi' me, wi' three times three, an' a' the honours grand—
My Toast is "London's Moray Club, an' dear auld Morayland."

——::——

CHILDHOOD'S HAPPY HOME.

I've followed Fortune's footsteps far, o'er many a sunny strand,
But Fate allured me o'er the wave back to my native land;
Back from the wildwood's eerie shade, across the trackless foam—
Back to the sweetest spot I've seen, my childhood's happy home.

Once more I see the dear old cot, half-hid by woodbine leaves,
While up the tott'ring, roofless porch, the faithful ivy weaves.
A gloomy stillness hangs around, where all was once so gay;
My presence e'en disturbs the calm—grim ruin here holds sway!

ROBERT (WANLOCK) REID

WILLIAM AITKEN

J. TATLOW

F. SUTHERLAND

ALLAN S. LAING

ROBERT LEE CAMPBELL

(400)

The trickling stream is winding still near by the cottage door,
But gone the little rustic bridge I cross'd in days of yore;
The wild rose and the tassl'd broom hang o'er its crystal tide,
While underneath their friendly shade the troutlets coyly hide.

Night's silv'ry lamp hangs in the blue behind you far off hill,
While softly steals the gloaming grey o'er moorland, stream, and [rill.
Oh! guiding star of promises, oh! whispers soft and low,
Where are the hopes you gave to me in twilights long ago?

I ope the shatter'd garden gate, pass through with hurried feet,
And touch a little mound near by, once mother's favourite seat.
My fondest wish is thus fulfill'd; though tears steal down my face,
I turn away—I've seen enough—and leave the dear old place.

ALEXANDER ANDERSON.

A POET of wide celebrity, ALEXANDER ANDERSON, better known as *Surfaceman*, was born at Kirkconnel, April 30th, 1845. He got the rudiments of a plain elementary education at the village school, Crocketford, a small hamlet at the lower end of Galloway, whither the family had removed; but, like many celebrated in after life, he evinced no special cleverness, nor remarkable aptitude for learning. He showed an early taste for sketching, however, obtaining, while still a boy, a local fame for colouring. As his mind expanded, books took possession of his leisure hours, and he eventually turned his attention from colours to word-painting. Like other born bards, he lisped in numbers from his boyish years, writing in the course of his early youth a quantity of satires, epistles, and poems, which he afterwards despairingly destroyed. Returning from Crocketford to his native village of Kirkconnel, our poet afterwards, and while still a youth, wrought for a time in a neighbouring stone quarry.

It was while working as a quarryman that he first resolutely began that self-culture which afterwards shone out so completely in his books of verse. Such was his ardour in the pursuit of knowledge, that he subordinated for several years his inmate genius for the muse to that end. A desire to read the great masters of foreign literature in their own tongues caused him to diligently apply himself to the study of German and Italian lexicons, and he was finally able to say—"Now I can appreciate in my own way in their own tongues the mighty voices of Goethe, Schiller, and Dante." Leaving the quarry, he finally became a surfaceman on the G. & S. W. line of railway, adjacent to his native district. The desire to express his thoughts in verse returning upon him, he sent about this time (1870) a poem entitled *John Keats,* to the *People's Friend,* then newly started; and Mr. Andrew Stewart, the acting editor—who first perceived his fine talents, and whose friendship, next to the poet's own genius, has most efficiently factored Mr. ANDERSON's progress in poetical reputation—warmly encouraged him to further efforts, with the result that from that time forward he became a regular contributor to its poetical columns. The connection served an efficient purpose, as it ultimately enabled him to appear before the public with a volume of verse entitled, *A Song of Labour and Other Poems,* which was entirely bought up by subscription, and was otherwise very successful. Two years later he issued *The Two Angels and Other Poems*—a volume of remarkable verse, which the Scottish press generally accorded a generous welcome. Since then he has issued two more volumes, which have gained for the author, in a certain measure, the ear of the English reading public. Briefly analysing his genius as evidenced in his poetry, his humour, it may be remarked, is mostly a subordinate quality, and his pathos seems occasionally elaborated rather than real. In other veins, however, Mr. ANDERSON's books present remarkable features of study. His poetry, throughout, is imbued with a depth and beauty of feeling, a fire of conception and expression, an energy of movement, and a recondite culture, which is astonishing, in view of his position in life.

In his second publication—*The Two Angels*—occurs a remarkable series of Sonnets entitled, *In Rome*—describing the legends and ruins of the Imperial City, whither the poet by an act of poetic volition had in imagination transplanted himself. Mr. ANDERSON, thanks to the generosity of a patron, has since been privileged to visit in reality the scene of his longest, and, perhaps, finest poem. Declamatory in tone, these Sonnets are, throughout, rhetorical rather than poetical. Yet they are instinct with the noblest sympathies, displaying a firmness, a grasp, and an eloquence, worthy of the lofty theme.

In the department of nursery poetry, ANDERSON has achieved distinct success. His *Cuddle Doon* and *Jenny wi' the Airn Teeth* are perfection in their way, and have obtained a wide currency. In 1880 Mr. ANDERSON received an appointment as sub-librarian, Edinburgh University, which situation he still retains.

——::——

THE OLD SCHOOL-HOUSE.

AH ! often when coming from labour,
  When I hear the children play,
There rises within me a vision
  Of the school-house far away—

The old, dark, humble school-house,
  That stood by the little stream
That babbled and splash'd in the sunshine,
  Or slipp'd into pools to dream.

And, again, as I think of my childhood,
  And its circle of sunny land,
Comes the wish to stand by that streamlet,
  As of old I used to stand—

Just to listen again to its murmurs
  As I did in that early time,
When my life—before and behind me—
  Had the ring of a poet's rhyme:

Or to stand on the bridge with the children,
  And give one long, deep shout,
That might sweep from my bosom's chamber
  The dust of manhood out.

For I weary and fret at the knowledge
  This manhood has brought to me,
And forever look back with a longing
  To the glory that used to be.

But vain is that pent-up yearning,
  And wish for the summer gleam
That ran through my young existence,
  Like the plot through a fairy's dream.

It has sunk away as the sunshine
  May fade from the breast of a hill,
And the shadow that now is around me
  Is misty and drear and chill.

But still, when I come from my labour,
  If I hear the children play,
Then my heart goes back to the school-house
  And the village far away.

——::——

JENNY WI' THE AIRN TEETH.

What a plague is this o' mine, winna steek his e'e,
Though I hap him owre the head as cosie as can be.
Sleep! an' let me to my wark, a' thae claes to airn:
Jenny wi' the airn teeth, come an' tak' the bairn;

Tak' him to your ain den, where the bowgie bides,
But first put baith your big teeth in his wee plump sides;
Gie your auld grey pow a shake, rive him frae my grup—
Tak' him where nae kiss is gaun when he waukens up.

Whatna noise is that I hear comin' doon the street?
Weel I ken the dump-dump o' her beetle feet.
Mercy me, she's at the door, hear her lift the sneck;
Whisht! an' cuddle mammy noo closer roon' the neck.

Jennie wi' the airn teeth, the bairn has aff his claes,
Sleepin' safe and soun', I think—dinna touch his taes;
Sleepin' weans are no for you; ye may turn aboot
An' tak' awa' wee Tam next door—I hear him screichin' oot.

Dump, dump, awa' she gangs back the road she cam';
I hear her at the ither door, speirin' after Tam.
He's a crabbit, greetin' thing, the warst in a' the toon;
Little like my ain wee wean—Losh, he's sleeping soun'.

Mithers hae an awfu' wark wi' their bairns at nicht—
Chappin' on the chair wi' tangs to gi'e the rogues a fricht.
Aulder weans are fley'd wi' less, weel aneuch, we ken—
Bigger bowgies, bigger Jennies, frichten muckle men.

——::——

CUDDLE DOON.

The bairnies cuddle doon at nicht, wi' muckle faucht an' din;
O, try and sleep, ye waukrife rogues, your faither's comin' in.
They never heed a word I speak; I try to gie a froon,
But aye I hap them up, an' cry, "O, bairnies, cuddle doon."

Wee Jamie wi' the curly heid—he aye sleeps next the wa'—
Bangs up an' cries, "I want a piece"—the rascal starts them a'.
I rin an' fetch them pieces, drinks, they stop awee the soun',
Then draw the blankets up, an' cry, "Noo, weanies, cuddle doon."

But ere five minutes gang, wee Rab cries oot, frae 'neath the claes,
"Mither, mak' Tam gie owre at auce, he's kittlin' wi' his taes."
The mischief's in that Tam for tricks, he'd bother half the toon;
But aye I hap them up, an' cry, "O, bairnies, cuddle doon."

At length they hear their faither's fit, an' as he steeks the door,
They turn their faces to the wa', while Tam pretends to snore.
"Hae a' the weans been gude?" he asks, as he pits aff his shoon.
"The bairnies, John, are in their beds, and lang since cuddled doon."

An' just afore we bed oorsel's, we look at oor wee lambs;
Tam has his airm roun' wee Rab's neck, an' Rab his airm roun' Tam's.
I lift wee Jamie up the bed, an' as I straik each croon,
I whisper, till my heart fills up, "O, bairnies, cuddle doon."

The bairnies cuddle doon at nicht wi' mirth that's dear to me;
But sune the big warl's cark an' care will quaten doon their glee.
Yet, come what will to ilka ane, may He, who sits aboon,
Aye whisper, though their pows be bauld, "O, bairnies, cuddle doon.'

—::—

H. C. WILSON.

Hugh C. Wilson, author of two little volumes of humorous, descriptive, and lyrical verse, was born at Dumfries House —which occupies the centre of a beautifully-wooded district on the banks of the Lugar, Ayrshire—about 1845. In his twenty-first year he set off for London, and has since held, for extended periods, responsible situations as head gardener in various parts of England.

Discovering a rhyming faculty early, he contributed for years to the local press, and issued his fugitive pieces in a collected form in 1874, under the title of *The Rustic Harp*. His second venture, *Wild Sprays from the Garden*, he published as recently as 1879. His later volume marks a distinct advance on its predecessor, and shows real and effective lyrical fluency and power. Mr. Wilson has lately had several of his flowing lyrics set to stirring music by Mr. Ross, the Queen's piper. He is a man of genial mind and native poetic genius.

NE'ER JAUP ANITHER'S FACE WI' GLAUR.

Ye many who, in manhood's race, are lagging, left behind the few,
Your shrugs discard for lifted hats, give manly, honest worth its due:
A comely face is fair to see, a bonnie sang is noted far;
But sweetest, chastest things are aye the easiest jaupit owre wi' glaur.

Wha is't but kens some wee bit fau't upon his neighbour's shady side—
Or wha but kens that o' himsel' frae ither een he fain would hide?
Deal gently then wi' ither's fame, for meddling often ends in war,
And rather wipe away a stain, than jaup a bonnie face wi' glaur.

We grudge to see another rise, while we obscurely stand—or fa';
And spite soon finds some wee bit wrang, to put a neighbour to the wa'.
We a' ha'e sins, Gude kens, enough, then, lest we make the matter waur,
Let each one look at hame afore he jaups anither's face wi' glaur.

—::—

SPREAD THE SHEET TO THE WIND.

Spread the sheet to the wind, let's away, let's away!
See the moon in her pride shining soft in the bay;
Let us skirt where the shade of the rocks bathe in light,
Spread the sheet to the wind, let's be merry to-night.

How my heart rises up with each pulse of the tide!
And the light sparkles clear on the wave's foaming side.
Now the land fades away, my lads, steadily, ho!
With the blue sky above and the blue waves below.

Spread the sheet to the wind, to the oar, to the oar!
Let the murmur of song in a dream reach the shore.
With the breeze blowing fresh, the waves rolling in light,
Spread the sheet to the wind, let's be merry to-night.

COME DOON THE HOWM.

Come doon the howm and meet me by the gate o' rustic spars;
Above our heads the spreading tree, above the tree the stars.
We'll track the verdant woodland path among the hazels green,
Where hunters stalk at morning hour, and rabbits whid at e'en.
Then doon the howm, come doon the howm, where peep the early stars;
Then doon the howm, come doon the howm, and meet me by the spars.

Come doon the howm and meet me, love, when song-birds leave the spray,
And list the brisk and dauntless song among the rising hay.
The corncraik woos and wins his mate with rude untutor'd art,
And bids me tell with simple faith the feelings of my heart.
Then doon the howm, come doon the howm, when peep the early stars;
Then doon the howm, come doon the howm, and meet me by the spars.

ROBERT FORD.

An ingenious and happily-humorous poet, Robert Ford was born at Wolfhill village, parish of Cargill, Perthshire, 18th July, 1846, where he continued to reside till his seventeenth year. With the prevailing sense of humour which is characteristic of his mind, Mr. Ford tells us that he has no recollection of the fact of his birth—the interesting event happened so early in his life; "and if," he says, "the proverbial *silver spoon* was in my mouth, it must have found its way into the Howdie's pouch, and gone to feed the gab of another than the original owner." His parents belonged to the humbler class, but were rich in heart-love and moral worth. In his seventeenth year he left the cover of the parental roof, setting out to fight the battle of life with a bundle under his arm, and a twofold blessing on his head. Gravitating to Dundee, he wrought there till 1874, first as a cloth measurer, and afterwards as a clerk. Latterly he removed to Glasgow, where he still continues, having been fortunate in finding more lucrative, and much more agreeable employment as a clerk in one of the larger soft goods warehouses in the city.

To the local journals, and to other quarters, Mr. FORD has contributed poetry and sketches for a number of years back. The success of a series of humorous prose papers from his pen, appearing in the *People's Journal* under the title of *Matilda Towhead*, first encouraged him to persevering literary effort, and in 1878 he collected and published his fugitive poetical pieces—*Hamespun Lays and Lyrics*, which met with instant success, having been almost entirely bought up by subscription. In 1881 he issued a small volume of *Humorous Scotch Readings*, which had a similar success. As a poet, the out-standing characteristic of his verses is a hearty humour, expressed in the graphic Doric peculiar to the North of Scotland. He has a clear perception and evident enjoyment of a joke, and is, indeed, by natural instinct, the happiest of Doric humorists. He possesses, also, a very fine lyrical talent, and many of his songs—several of which have been set to music and sung—are of the happiest turn.

——::——

CUPID IN THE TEMPLE.

I CANNA, winna cloak the fact—
  Tho' sairly to my shame it's spoken—
On Sunday gane—immodest act—
  Wi' Cupid I'd a lively yokin'.

To kirk I gaed in high resolve
  To weld my fancy wi' the sermon;
Lat naething else my thochts involve,
  Nor hear, nor see, but Dr. Hermon.

But Dauvit's hymn was jimply read,
  When *bang* a dart gaed thro' my waistcoat—
A lass afore me turn'd her head,
  Her charmin' face I gat a glisk o't;
It set my being a' alowe,
  An' a' day lang that face seem'd bent on's;
Lat Doctor Hermon rant's he dow,
  I couldna catch a single sentence.

His ilka lang-drawn metaphor
  Seem'd but word-etchin's o' her features,
An' in the pulpit, smitsome fair,
  I saw *her* face instead the preacher's;
When praises well'd frae every heart,
  I heard but ae sweet voice afore me;
An' when we kneel'd, as when we sate,
  Her roguish een were beamin' o'er me.

By conscience thrice I felt rebuk'd,
  An' thrice I made renew'd endeavour;
Towards the preacher firmly look'd,
  Determin'd on improved behaviour;
But a' was faucht to nae avail,
  For lood as conscience lik'd to faut me,
I couldna help my sinfu' sel',
  Wi' twa sic een aye lookin' at me.

As hame I hied the birdies sang—
  "A bonnie lassie! bonnie lassie!"
I saw her cheeks the briers amang,
  I saw her in the very causey.
When mither speir'd me for the text,
  Quo' I, "'twas in the books o' Moses."
"The *words?*" quo' she. I answer'd next
  "Oh!—sky-blue een an' cheeks o' roses!"

Ah! roguie Love, yer fu' o' pranks,
  Nor wait for time an' place befittin';

Ye smit the sodger in the ranks,
  The merchant owre the ledger sittin'.
But hear me, lad—a victim flytes—
  As ye regaird yer reputation,
Employ the week as fancy dites,
  But cease your Sabbath desecration !

—::—

BARBER WILLIE'S BONNIE DAUCHTER.

THERE leeves a lass in oor toun-en'—
  We've few sae fair, an' feint a fatter—
She's cuist a glamour owre oor men,
  An' set the gossips' tongue a-clatter.
Gang East or Wast, or North or South,
  At ony keyhole list the lauchter,
In ilka hame the crack's the same—
  It's Barber Willie's bonnie dauchter.

A rosy lassie, five feet lang,
  Clean-fittit, toshly built, an' sturdy,
Can dance a fling, and lilt a sang,
  Shampoo a pow, or shave a beardie ;
An' sic a gift o' trapping hearts—
  A fortune to the dad that's aucht her ;
There's few I ken, but fidges fain
  To be possess'd o' sic a dauchter.

Wi' witchin' grace she saips the chin
  O' auld an' young, o' rich an' semple,
An' shaves sae glegly oot an' in—
  She ne'er was kent to jag a pimple ;
An' nane she shaves but looks his love,
  An' fain wad to his bosom claucht her ;
But envy lowers amang the wooers
  O' Barber Willie's bonnie dauchter.

Frae morn to nicht it's crop an' shave,
  Shampoo, dress, an' strap, an' lather ;
Some customers but ill-behave,
  Their brains wi' love are sae thro'-ither ;

Young blades wi' scarce a root to scrape,
  Three times a day beseek the favour
O' ha'ein' their gabs besmear'd wi' suds
  By Willie's witchin', wily shaver.

An' buirdly men wha late cud brag
  The bauldest beards oot owre their cravats,
Hae scarcely noo a tuft to wag,
  Save twa-three hairs about their baffits;
It's saip them here, an' scrape them there,
  The case is really yont a' lauchter—
Oor toun-en's scarce o' hearts an' beards,
  Thro' Barber Willie's bonnie dauchter.

Oh, that some chiel wad trap her heart,
  An' win her hand wi' slee palaver—
Wad rin her aff wi' coach or cairt,
  An' rid us o' the wily shaver.
Or could it reach the Fiscal's lug,
  He'd aiblins chairge her wi' manslauchter;
An' save oor men—heart, beard, and brain—
  Frae Barber Willie's bonnie dauchter!

TWA PU'D FLOWERS.

I PU'D a flower in yonder vale,
  Ae bonnie morn in June,
I set it gaily in my breist,
  And bore it to the toun;
I kiss'd its velvet lips at e'en,
  And laid it saftly by,
But when the day cam' round again,
  Nae bonnie flower had I—
A' licht o' life had left its e'e—
  Its sweet wee head hung dowiely.

A maiden gentle, sweet, and young,
  And glad as opening day,
Was woo'd and won amang yon braes
  That skirt oor native Tay.

Unto the toun, a rosy bride,
  She cam' in Winter's train,
And ere the Autumn tinged the wolds
  They tauld me she was gane;
"Ah! like my little flower," I sigh'd—
  "My violet, that droop'd, and died."

ROBERT (WANLOCK) REID.

Robert Reid, better known by his poetical *nom-de-plume* of Rob Wanlock, was born in the village of Wanlockhead, County of Dumfries, July 8th, 1850. He had a fair education, and at the age of fifteen removed to Glasgow for the purpose of entering the counting-house of Stewart & M'Donald, a well-known manufacturing firm. He remained there for the space of four years, removing thence to Belfast. In the autumn of the year succeeding his removal to Belfast (1870), the offer of a more suitable situation brought him back to Glasgow, where he entered the service of William Cross, shawl manufacturer, and author of *The Disruption*, a well-known Scotch story, and a number of really good Scotch songs which originally appeared in *Whistle Binkie*. In the winter of 1877 he again left Glasgow to fill a situation of trust in Montreal, Canada, where he still remains. Regarding the poetical side of his history, it may be briefly stated that Mr. Reid early discovered a talent for poetical composition, and indulging the fancy in leisure hours, made rapid and distinct progress in the art. He contributed regularly to local and other journals for several years, with the result that the publication of his fugitive pieces became in the end a sort of *non*-escapable necessity, if we may be allowed the expression. In 1874, and while the author was yet in his twenty-fourth year, his excellent volume of *Moorland Rhymes* was accordingly issued. The book, showing as it undeniably does uncommon beauty and purity of dialect verse, was generally very favourably received by the Scottish press. The volume otherwise evinces a remarkable variety of metre, with much vigour and versatility of thought. The English pieces are all thoroughly good, but the author is at his happiest and best only when handling essentially Scottish themes in his native pure and sweet southlan' dialect.

—::—

THE WHAUP.

Fu' sweet is the lilt o' the laverock frae the rim o' the clud at morn :
The merle pipes weel in his mid-day biel', in the heart o' the bendin' thorn ;
The blythe, bauld sang o' the mavis rings clear in the gloamin' shaw :
But the whaup's wild cry in the gurly sky o' the moorlan' dings them a'.

For what's in the lilt o' the laverock to touch ocht mair than the ear !
The merle's lown craik in the trangled brake can start nae memories dear ;
And even the sang o' the mavis but waukens a love-dream tame
To the whaup's wild cry on the breeze blawn by, like a wanderin' word frae hame.

What thochts o' the lang grey moorlan' start up when I hear that cry !
The times we lay on the heathery brae at the well, lang-syne gane dry ;
And aye as we spak' o' the ferlies that happen'd afore-time there,
The whaup's lane cry on the win' cam' by like a wild thing lost in the air.

And though I hae seen mair ferlies than grew in the fancy then,
And the gowden gleam o' the boyish dream has slipp'd frae my soberer brain,
Yet—even yet—if I wander alane by the moorlan' hill,
That queer wild cry frae the gurly sky can tirl my heart-strings still.

JOSEPH TATLOW,

PRINCIPAL Assistant to the General Manager of the Glasgow and South Western Railway Company, although not born on this side of the border, may, in a certain measure, be regarded as a Scottish poet, on account of his extended residence in Glasgow, coupled with the fact that his muse first awoke to conscious effort upon Scottish soil.

Mr. TATLOW was born at Sheffield in 1851, was educated at Derby, and at the age of fifteen entered there the offices of the Midland Railway, where also his father held a position of responsibility. Very prosaic, probably, he found office work, but he was one of those happy spirits who, mindful of duty and always industrious, manage to agreeably lighten their work; and possessing strong artistic taste and talents, he employed much of his leisure time in etching. Mr. TATLOW came to Glasgow about ten years ago, is married and settled, and seems destined to live the busy useful life of a douce Glasgow citizen. By dint of industry and devotion to duty he has worked himself up to a good position in the Railway service, and has had only odd hours to devote to the cultivation of his literary tastes. He is not the man to neglect the serious business of life for merely intellectual pleasure, yet for several years he has attentively and successfully cultivated his Scottish-born muse, his poems having from time to time appeared in the *People's Friend*, *Society*, *Life*, *Masonic Magazine*, and other publications. He has also written and published several stories, but with a deepening love for poetic composition has of late confined himself to verse-writing. Mr. TATLOW, it may be mentioned, is Secretary in Scotland for the Railway Benevolent Institution, and the Railway service in this part of the kingdom owes him a deep debt of gratitude for his efforts towards having a Scottish Branch, with almost entirely independent management, established in Glasgow. Of an ardent enthusiastic temperament, Mr. TATLOW's somewhat sedentary tastes and habits are corrected by a *penchant* for congenial society. His verses evince the possession of fine taste, united to a graceful and engaging fancy. Chaste in language, and full of a sweet and pure melody, Mr. TATLOW's musings awake in the reader's mind the interest and beauty of quiet, but not the less real, poetical genius.

—::—

THE MINSTREL.

A MINSTREL sang—his notes were glad,
Like laughter or the trill of birds;
They sooth'd me not, for I was sad—
They vexed me like discordant words.
O, minstrel, cease that jarring sound,
Which serves but to embitter pain;
Could some more fitting theme be found,
I'd gladly hear thee sing again!

He smote the strings, his voice uprose—
With gesture proud and kindling eye
He sang in martial strain of those
Who erst had dared to do or die;
Unmov'd, I still withheld my praise,
But said—"O, minstrel, sweet and true,
I care not for these ancient lays,
Nay—chafe not boy, but sing anew!"

He smiled, and then with gracious mien
Awoke once more his trembling lyre,
And sang of Love, that daintie queene,
Who fills the heart with sweet desire;
Said I—"*Now* singest thou aright,
Full well I know the tender theme
That charms us with supreme delight;
So, sing on, minstrel, whilst I dream!"

A HAPPY HOUR.

I ROSE one happy morn with beating heart,
  Ere bright Aurora with a radiant blush
Swung joyfully the Eastern gates apart,
  And bathed the purple hills in rosy flush.
Adown the mead a wayward impulse led
  My footsteps glad, until I came to where
A smooth full-bosom'd stream on flowery bed
  Voluptuous flowed, and unexpected there
I saw my love, who, like a Naïad bright,
  Stood on its marge, a vision of delight.

With quicken'd pulse I ran an eager race
  'Gainst warm Apollo for the first fresh kiss;
But Love outstripp'd e'en his enamour'd pace,
  And won the beamy god's intended bliss.
I press'd soft lips ere sleeping daisy heard;
  Her sweet voice thrill'd me ere the lark rose up
From grassy couch, or wanton zephyr stirr'd
  The dew-brimm'd chalice of the buttercup;
And my enraptur'd soul, in joy, confess'd,
  Of all Love's happy hours, that was the best!

—::—

MIST AND MOONLIGHT.

MY love, do you ever remember
  A night that is long gone by,
In the mellowy time of Autumn,
  When the golden grain stood high?

We had been to the quaint old chapel,
  Which stood where the river flow'd,
And we saunter'd towards the city
  By the old familiar road.

Oh, peaceful and soft was the twilight,
  Till a mist rose o'er the lea,
When the air grew heavy with sadness,
  Like the doubt which burden'd me.

And the pines that skirted the wayside
  A darkness around us threw;
It seemed to my heart a foreboding—
  What life would be without you.

At length we emerged from the shadow,
  And stood in the open night,
You still may remember, my darling,
  The scene that burst on our sight:

How the moon in her queenly splendour
  Beam'd full on our startled eyes;
How we paused in a sudden wonder,
  And gazed in a glad surprise.

Her beams, with a silvery brightness,
  Fell soft on your upturn'd face,
And a flood of effulgence hallow'd
  Your form with a mystic grace.

And oh! as I gazed on your features,
  My heart cast out all its fears,
For I read in your eyes a secret,
  Through a mist of unshed tears!

—::—

AGNES.

As stars are dimm'd when full-orb'd Dian fills
  With her resplendent light an Autumn sky:
As fragrant musk all fainter perfume kills,
  And roses shame the flow'rs that blossom nigh:
So Agnes, pale and pure, thy charms outvie
  The brightest stars in fancy's boundless space;
Soft as an od'rous zephyr is thy sigh,
  And fairer than a lily is thy face.
But brighter still, and purer, and more fair
  Than outward beauty, draped in cloth of gold,
Are those rich ornaments thy soul doth wear—
  Truth, Hope, a Tenderness of depth untold,
A helpful Instinct, sweet as it is rare,
  A Patience that abides, a Love that grows not cold!

'TIS HARD TO BEAR.

'Tis hard to bear unmerited reproof,—
 To live a life misjudged, misunderstood;
To see our once warm friends now stand aloof,
 More credulous of whisper'd ill than good;
'Tis hard when Fate environs us with wrong,
 And slander spreads untouch'd by sense of ruth,
'Tis hard when circumstance must tie our tongue,
 And those who blame us know but half the truth.
This we must bear, dissembling with the fear
 That holds the soul subdued in patient thrall;
And trusting Time to make the darkness clear,
 We'll dream of sunshine though the shadows fall.
The Light *must* shine at last! Be of good cheer,
 Our wrongs shall righted be, for God is over all!

WILLIAM AITKEN.

A GENIAL and successful follower of the Doric muse, WILLIAM AITKEN was born in the quiet little upland village of Sorn, Ayrshire, March 26th, 1851; or on what is better known in the graphic parlance of the district as the "Wee Race Day." The village of Sorn is one of the most picturesquely situated hamlets in the whole West of Scotland. It lies in the song-celebrated valley of the Ayr, whose crystal waters meander past it, enclosed between rich and wildly-wooded banks of more than ordinary opulence and beauty. While our poet was still a child, his father removed with the family to Brig-End, a neighbouring country village, containing about a score or so of house holders, and situated within a few miles distance of those worshipful shrines of Scottish poesy—Mauchline and Mossgiel. Here he was sent to school; but, at the early age of ten years, was put to learn the operative trade of shoemaking. After completing his apprenticeship, and while still a young man, he applied for, and obtained a situation in the service of the Glasgow and South-Western Railway Company. He is now a traffic inspector on the Greenock section of that company's extensive system. It was while he was still a "knight of the leather apron" that Mr. AITKEN first began to cultivate an acquaintance with the muse. His mind early presented a sharp, analytical side, and his first efforts in verse were in the form of charades and rhymed puzzles. In this department of recreative verse-making he has all along been a successful prize-taker, as numerous valuable books in his library attest. Acquiring thus a mastery over the different forms of verse, with a growing facility of composition, he ultimately passed on to higher work, with the result that in 1880 he issued a successful volume of verse under the title of *Rhymes and Readings*. Estimating Mr. AITKEN as a poet, the first characteristic that strikes the mind is his broad and hearty humour—which never fails him—his quick-working fancy, and his general facility, flow, and promptitude of execution. His book was well received by the Scottish press generally, and has had a rapid and gratifying sale. At the present time (May, 1881,) he is preparing for publication, a small volume of Railway poems, under the distinctive title of *Lays of the Line*, which will certainly advance and widen his poetic reputation. Want of space alone forbids ample quotation from the numerous beautiful and impressive poems which distinguish his new volume, the publication of which will assure his growing fame.

——::——

RODGERSON'S DOUG.

IN oor famed sugar city o' tierces and bags,
Wi' its rich folk in satins and puir folk in rags,
Where it's mud to the ankles frae July to June,
Where the rain only stops for the snaw to begin,

Where the sailors prepare for the weather in store
Wi' a dip in the sea as they're comin' ashore,
If ye've time for a meenit to len' me yer lug,
Ye will hear o' a dweller in't—Rodgerson's doug.

Since the new Ayrshire line to the West End was made,
He's been yin o' the great railway's little "unpaid;"
His hale heart and min' seem sae fix'd on the wark
That he scarce can get time for a freen'ly bit bark.
Nae maiter what pairt o' the yaird ye may be,
If yer gaun up the hill or awa roun' the quay,
Jist point to the break-bogie, up gangs each lug,
And he's in't in a twinklin'—Rodgerson's doug.

Though he's no up to muckle wi' pencil or pen,
Nor yet shown on the pay-sheet alang with the men,
No a haun' in the wark's half sae constant as he,
He's as shairp as a razor in baith ear and e'e.
He can staun' like a man, he can jump, he can sklim,
'Twad be tellin' us a' were we active like him;
No a shift o' the wagons, or shunt wi' the pug,
But what's seen and taen note o' by Rodgerson's doug.

He's oot like a lark at the break o' daylicht,
And he never leaves off till the latest at nicht;
He's no like a wheen o' yer sleepy-heid folk,
He's as shairp to the hour as the haun o' a clock.
It's a quite common thing wi' the best workin' men,
For a yairdsman or guard to sleep-in noo and then;
Till the breakfast bell rings they the blankets may hug,
But we ne'er kent him sleepin' in—Rodgerson's doug.

Nae maiter what happens, he hears and sees a',
Could he speak, he could tell us a story or twa;
He could tell when the "bothy" was burned, and the hoo,
Where the whisky cam' frae that fill'd Gaffer Gibb fou';
Hoo the casks o' molasses were knockit agee,
And hoo the goods wagons got into the sea.
Nae amount o' rough shuntin', nae quick stop or rug
E'er knock'd oot o' the break-bogie Rodgerson's doug.

O' the men's dinner pieces he'll eat a' ye bring,
But he wadna taste drink gin ye made him a king;
Na, faith! he kens better than pree siccan stuff;
Wi' the food God provides he's contented enough.
When I look at the dougie I think noo and then
That he's gifted wi' wisdom far mair than some men,
And the world wad hae less o' turmoil and humbug
Had some men the judgment o' Rodgerson's doug.

—::—

A PARTING SONG.

We met—'twas a meeting—our journeys must part;
God speed thee!—the greeting went heart into heart,
As one after another his tribute let fall,
But the voice of our brother was sadder than all.
'Twas the hour that must sever our lives' golden chain,
And oh! we might never behold him again.

Hearts that seldom knew sorrow for once felt the sting;
For we knew what the morrow was destin'd to bring—
Tears to our eyes starting 'mid silence profound,
As our tokens of parting were handed around.
'Twas the hour that must sever our lives' golden chain,
For oh! we might never behold him again.

Not the short-lived affection grown up in an hour,
Like the rainbow's reflection that shines with the show'r;
Not the butterfly kinship a summer day rears,
Ours was more—'twas a friendship, the outcome of years.
But the wild waves must sever our lives' golden chain,
And oh! we may never behold him again.

ROBERT WOOD

Is an Ayrshire man, having been born at Newmilns, May 12th, 1850. His parents belonged to the working classes, and Robert was early put to learn the staple occupation of the district—handloom weaving. Disliking the monotony and confinement of the "loom," he removed to Glasgow while still a youth, and at present is employed in the packing room of a city warehouse.

His mind is of a religious and deeply sympathetic cast, and he delights in moral and reflective verse. He has great fluency of *impromptu* composition, and writes with a certain liquid ease and beauty of tone. Unassuming in mind, Mr. WOOD has cultivated publicity less than his talents would seem to warrant.

—::—

THERE IS A PATHWAY.

THERE is a pathway glorious
To the angels' happy home,
Where the thousands gone before us,
Are now waiting till we come.

Emanuel's love hath made it,
From the cross to yonder sky;
In his sorrows deep he laid it,
And the Father bringeth nigh.

Safely through the dreaded river,
I can trust the piercèd hand,
(For his promise faileth never)
Till I reach the spotless Land.

All my griefs are clouds refreshing,
That dissolve in tearful showers;
And behind them comes the blessing
Of the sunlight and the flow'rs.

From the mountain top in glory,
I shall wonderingly survey,
All my life's unfinish'd story,
In the light of perfect day.

Every conflict won by daring
In the battlefields of years,
Will bring trophies worth the wearing,
When the jewell'd crown appears.

J. G. PHILLIPS.

JAMES GORDON PHILLIPS was born in the picturesque little village of Newmill, in the parish of Keith, Banffshire, 7th February, 1852. At the early age of nine years he was engaged as "herd" to a farmer—as is generally the case in the North with sons of humble parentage; and was afterwards apprenticed to a tailor in Keith.

From his very earliest years he has had a strong love of literature, every book that he could lay hold of being eagerly read. At an early age he began to indite a homely note of song in the local newspapers, and soon gained considerable local reputation as a verse writer. Archæology and Natural History also engaged his attention, and in both fields he showed such proficiency and success that when the Secretary and Curator of the Elgin and Morayshire Literary and Scientific Association died, he was elected to fill his place, which situation he now holds.

In 1881 he issued a collection of his fugitive poems and sketches, under the title of *Wanderings in the Highlands*, which was locally well received. The prose sketches make very interesting reading, and the poems, which conclude the volume, all evince appreciative and distinctly progressive merit.

—::—

LAND OF THE BRAVE!

SCOTLAND! I love thee, thou land of the mountain,
  Land of the heather bell, rock, and deep cave;
Land of the cataract, land of the fountain;
  I love thee my country, thou land of the brave!

Thy glens may be bleak when the wintry winds whistle,
  And dreary thy hills when the wild tempests rave;

But there's kind hearts and true in the land of the thistle,
  And arms to shield thee, thou land of the brave!

The voice of the tyrant ne'er ruled o'er thy valleys,
  Though Rome's conquering legions swept over the wave;
With bright shining eagles, and gold bedeck'd galleys,
  They fought, but they fell, in the land of the brave.

And England's fierce Edward with all his proud power,
  Rush'd over the border thy sons to enslave;
But thy valiant and strong made him rue the dark hour
  That e'er he set foot in the land of the brave.

When Gaul's gloating eagle, with pinions all gory,
  Soar'd over Hispania and no one to save;
Not the last in the cause of bright freedom and glory
  Were the sons of Auld Scotia, the land of the brave!

Then who would not love thee, when each hill and corrie
  Are cradles of freedom, to tyrants a grave;
When your bright deeds of fame writ in legend and story,
  Hath seal'd thy proud name as the land of the brave.

Then hey for the land of the mist and the blue bell!
  The land that ne'er crouch'd, nor for mercy would crave!
Land of the flashing stream, land of the flowery dell,
  Land of the strong and true, land of the brave!

JOHN DOUGALL REID.

A POET of considerable promise, JOHN DOUGALL REID, who commonly writes under the *nom de plume* of "Kaleidoscope," was born in Glasgow on 4th February, 1853. His father was a native of Old Kilpatrick, and an engineer in the service of the Cunard Company. He died when John was six years of age, leaving his mother in very straitened circumstances. He was for some time in the Old Normal School, where he proved but a dull scholar, as he says. The departure for India of an uncle, who took an interest in

John, compelled his mother to withdraw him from school. Running about wild in the fields, he declares he learned more from the open book of nature, than ever the school put in him. Adopted by an aunt, John went to reside at Helensburgh, where he attended the Parish School, and made considerable progress in learning. We next find him employed as an apprentice to a draper and clothier, to which he never took kindly. To stand, he says, "for hours, bowing and scraping, and serving out ribbons, laces, and small talk to the ladies, while the waters of the Firth of Clyde were dancing and sparkling under my very eye, went decidedly against the grain." On the completion of his apprenticeship, he went to London, but did not succeed in the Metropolis, and as a roving life seemed to have a strange fascination for him, he enlisted in the 78th Highlanders in November, 1876—and he is now with the regiment at Benares, East India, a private in the ranks.

Mr. Reid has, undoubtedly, the true poetic gift. His muse is naturally of the soaring order. Subdued within the bounds of law and order, his fancy is rich and fertile, and he produces poems of much invigorative beauty, and lyrical excellence. He is a versatile poet, and is equally at home in weird ballads, love lyrics, and humorous songs and readings. He writes also able prose sketches, and being yet but a young man, with a genius only partially developed, he may be reasonably expected to achieve distinct future success in his beloved poetical studies.

——::——

BLUE, BLUE E'EN.

Amang yon yellow broom yestreen
I watch'd the fairy gloamin' fa',
An' heard alang yon woodland green
The wastlin' breezes lownly blaw.

The hour sae calm, the scene sae fair,
  Bade peace ilk fleetin' moment crown!
An' happy Nature's joy to share,
  I wistna a' my ain was stown.
      Blue, blue e'en, an' a mou' sae sweet,
        Blue, blue e'en, an' a form sae fair;
      Wi' angel face and dew-wet feet,
        An' a rose in her gouden hair.

Doon by me cam' a barefit lass,
  Wi' young love laughin' in her e'e;
Wi' white feet 'mang the green, green grass—
  Oh, wae for the hour she cam' to me!
"Love," sang a bird the wood within,
  An' "Here" made answer this breast o' mine!
She cam' an' gaed wi' the sun an' win',
  An' my heart has been sair sin' syne.
      Blue, blue e'en, etc.

Then dowie hameward through the nicht
  I took ootowre the muir my gate,
An' aye I saw in dark or licht
  The laughin' e'en I lo'ed sae late.
In valley deep, owre mountain high,
  I seek this lass I mayna name;
For waefu' maun my days gang by,
  Till my rose an' my love come hame.
      Blue, blue e'en, etc.

ALLAN S. LAING.

A YOUNG poet of very considerable promise, ALLAN S. LAING was born in Dundee, June 24, 1857. He is come of humble, but respectable parents, and was sent out to work in his tenth year. In course of time he was regularly apprenticed to the trade of an upholsterer, and wrought at that handicraft for over eleven years. Not finding steady employment at his trade, he engaged himself in 1879 as collector to a local book agent, but has lately left that service and started business, in Dundee, on his own account.

Mr. LAING wrote verses early, and first appeared as a poet in the pages of the *People's Friend*, in whose columns so many poetic fledglings have been encouraged and helped to a successful use of their wings. He has not yet ventured on the publication of a volume, but is certain to do so ultimately. He writes with progressive merit and effective point, and will take a future place among the long bead-roll of Scottish minstrels.

—::—

YEARS AGO.

SITTING alone and silent, by the light of the dying fire,
Watching the embers deepen to caves of glowing red,
Sweet Memory gently touches the chords of her hidden lyre,
And murmurs a mystic music of voices long hush'd and dead;
And faces crowd around me, and spirit hands touch mine,
While the flush of an olden love stirs into a sudden glow
The smouldering fires of my spirit, as the heart is warm'd with wine,
And I see the sweet face of my darling who loved me years ago.

Ah! we were young and happy, and life was a paradise, [bloom,
With the tree of knowledge untouch'd, the fruits in their pristine
And we each loved each, and walk'd in the light of each other's eyes,
As if all the world were lovely, and death were an unknown doom;
And when, with the joining of hands, our lives merg'd into one,
The voices of sin and sorrow for us were hush'd and low, [sun,
And we stood on our new home's threshold, and, watching the setting
Saw new joys dawning for us in that bright time years ago.

Years came, and greeting us, pass'd with their burthen of joy and
Into the realm of silence, as the sun dips into the sea, [hope
And as he from his couch in the ocean climbs up the shining slope,
So brightly the new years dawn'd with promise of joy to be.

The music of childish prattle, and patter of baby feet,
  Mingle themselves with the murmur of voices that come and go,
And the golden hair of the children, their bright eyes, blue and sweet,
  Sun my old eyes and bless me, as they bless'd me years ago.

One dear face ever present, bright halo-crown'd with love—
  One dear voice like sweet music, filling my soul with peace—
Voices and visions only! but precious as heaven above
  To the heart of an old man, weary of sorrows that seldom cease.
Long on my head have fallen the white rose-leaves of time,
  And I wait but the voice of the angel of God to bid me go,
Where hand in hand we shall walk, as in our olden prime,
  And shall love—my darling and I—as we loved long years ago.

——::——

A TRIO.

In a nook apart from the busy street,
Aside from the rushing of restless feet,
Where the hurrying hum is but faintly heard,
And the waves of ambition are never stirr'd,

Three maidens dwelt; a sisterhood
Whose lives were pure as their deeds were good;
Whose beauty, once seen, on the heart would be
As the echo of exquisite melody.

The first of the three was tall and fair,
With a glistening glory of golden hair,
Her eyes were stars in their steady light,
Her lips twin rose-leaves of crimson bright.

She seldom smiled, but her glorious eyes
Flash'd courage where apathy 'gan to rise,
She set in the heart of the faint a flame;
And men said "Faith" was the maiden's name.

The second was sunny, and frank, and free,
Her breast o'er-brimming with buoyant glee,
Her laugh was like echoes of silver bells,
Or the ripple of waters in leafy dells.

Oft seem'd to deceive, yet was loved the more,
For she touch'd every heart in its inmost core;

She soften'd sorrow and sweeten'd care,
And "Hope" was the name of this maiden fair.

But how shall I limn, with my puny pen,
The maiden who rules in the hearts of men
With a sway so soft that its tyrannous powers
Are sweet to the soul as the sun to flowers.

Her gentle presence is ever felt,
And stony hearts at her impulse melt;
All souls in her influence upwards move,
For she reigns supreme, and her name is "Love."

These three had a dwelling but poor and small,
Yet the light of their presence shone over it all,
And burn'd into brightness its every part,
Though it was but a humble human heart.

ROBERT LEE CAMPBELL.

ONE of the youngest and most promising of our rising poets, ROBERT LEE CAMPBELL was born at Edinburgh, November 12th, 1863. Losing his parents early, our young poet has had to shift for himself, and face the world earlier than falls to the lot of most men. Character and genius will assert themselves, however, and at the present time (1882), he finds himself an *alumnus* of the University of Edinburgh, and a journalist by profession. In his seventeenth year he earned his first guinea for a leader in a daily newspaper, and since then has had to continue journalistic and other literary work as a means of immediate income. With the versatility of real genius he can also strike at will a neat and most engaging note of song. Although yet under twenty years of age, he has contributed poems and articles to *Chambers's Journal*, the *People's Friend*, and to numerous other journals and periodicals. Mr. CAMPBELL inherits high mental gifts, and will take, in good time, a leading place in the profession of journalism, to the pursuit of which he consistently adheres, and which will eventually bring him distinction and reward.

——::——

AT A GRAVE.

DREAMINGS are ever in my heart,
  Dreamings of sadness and love,
That sigh to my yearning spirit,
  Like music from above.
They come with the perfume of song,
  Through the avenue of years,
And the echoes of happier hours
  Are kissing away my tears.

Dreamings that thrill with the sunshine
  Of summers and golden days,
Lit up by a fairy presence
  That has left earth's weary ways;
In the arms of Death's sweet angel,
  With his smile upon her face,
And we're left alone with the mem'ry
  Of her shy and tender grace.

'Twas the sad time when roses die,
  In their sweet and rare perfume,
Our darling pass'd, like a rose's breath,
  In the blush of her maiden bloom,
Away from regrets and the mortal pain
  Of this sad world's shadowy night.
To rest in the crimson heaven,
  In fragrant love and light.

And still with our spirits yearning,
  With our sorrow and heart's fond strife,
A sweet thought ever commingles
  The union of after life;
When souls that have long been sever'd,
  Throb back again to rest,
In the tender bonds of a heavenly love,
  On a Saviour's tranquil breast.

SUMMER.

Under the beams of the mid-day sun
  The lake is rolling its waves of gold,
The spirit of Summer has kiss'd the banks,
  And the sweet flow'rs smile as of old.
From the skies, so soft, like dewy rain,
  Comes the song of the skylark, lost to sight,
As it rises and fades in the crystal blue,
  Like a far-fled dream of delight.

Now to the blossoms that faint in the air
  With odorous breathings of love,
The burden'd bees are winging their flight,
  Kissing each flow'r as they rove.
The birds are trilling their joyous notes
  From amid the leafy nest,
And the zephyr sighs to his love, the rose,
  While he plunders the sweets of her breast.

And the murmuring air is fill'd with song,
  As Nature joys at Summer's return,
While fragrant thoughts twine round the heart,
  And rob it of griefs that burn.
In golden books we read of a time
  When the earth with Summer was ever fair;
Oh, for that season's return to our hearts,
  And to live in that purer air!

PRINTED BY H. NISBET AND CO., STOCKWELL STREET, GLASGOW.

NEW BOOKS AND NEW EDITIONS.

ANGLING REMINISCENCES OF THE RIVERS AND LOCHS OF SCOTLAND. By THOMAS TOD STODDART. Post 8vo. Price 3s. 6d.

If not the most useful, this is at least the most interesting of all Stoddart's angling works, of which there are three in number. The above is not to be confounded with "The Scottish Angler" on the one hand, or "The Angler's Companion" on the other, though from the same pen. The present work is colloquial throughout, and teeming with the richest humour from beginning to end.

THE WHOLE FAMILIAR COLLOQUIES OF ERASMUS. Translated by NATHAN BAILEY. Demy 8vo. Price 4s. 6d.

A complete and inexpensive edition of the great book of amusement of the sixteenth century. Probably no other work so truly and intensely depicts the life and notions of our forefathers 350 years ago, as does this inimical production of the great Erasmus.

There are 62 dialogues in all, and an immense variety of subjects are dealt with, such as "Benefice-Hunting," "The Soldier and the Carthusian," "The Franciscans," "The Apparition," "The Beggar's Dialogue," "The Religious Pilgrimage," "The Sermon," "The Parliament of Women," etc., etc. The whole work is richly characteristic, and is full of the richest humour and satire.

THE COURT OF SESSION GARLAND. Edited by JAMES MAIDMENT, Advocate. *New edition, including all the Supplements.* Demy 8vo. Price 7s. 6d.

A collection of most interesting anecdotes and facetiae connected with the Court of Session. Even to those not initiated in the mysteries of legal procedure, much of the volume will be found highly attractive, for no genuine votary of Momus can be insensible to the fun of the Justiciary Opera, as illustrated by the drollery of the "Diamond Beetle Case," and many others of an amusing nature, such as "The Poor Client's Complaint," "The Parody on Hellvellyn," "The King's Speech," "Lord Bannatyne's Lion," "The Beauties of Overgroggy," etc., etc.

ST. KILDA AND THE ST. KILDIANS. By Robert Connell. Crown 8vo. Price 2s. 6d.

"A capital book. It contains everything worth knowing about the famous islet and its people."—The Bailie.

"Interesting and amusing. It includes a lively description of the daily life of the inhabitants, the native industries of fishing, bird catching, and the rearing of sickly sheep and cattle, and gives a vivid picture of the Sabbatarian despotism of the Free Church minister who rules the small population."—Saturday Review.

THE PRAISE OF FOLLY. By Erasmus. *With Numerous Illustrations by Holbein.* Post 8vo. Price 4s. 6d.

An English translation of the "Encomium Moriae" which has always held a foremost place among the more popular of the writings of the great scholar. This work is probably the most satirical production of any age. It is intensely humorous throughout, and is entirely unique in character. This edition also contains Holbein's illustrations, attaching to which there is very considerable interest.

HUMOROUS AND AMUSING SCOTCH READINGS. *For the Platform, the Social Circle, and the Fireside.* By Alexander G. Murdoch. Second Edition. Post 8vo. Price 1s. Paper Covers.

Humorous and amusing Scotch readings, fifteen in number, and illustrative of the social life and character of the Scottish people, than which the author believes no more interesting subject can be found. Among other readings may be mentioned, "Mrs. Macfarlane's Rabbit Dinner," "The Washin'-Hoose Key," "Jock Broon's Patent Umbrella," "Willie Weedrap's Domestic Astronomy," etc., etc.

ANECDOTES OF FISH AND FISHING. By Thomas Boosey. Post 8vo. Price 3s. 6d.

An interesting collection of anecdotes and incidents connected with fish and fishing, arranged and classified into sections. It deals with all varieties of British fish, their habits, different modes of catching them, interesting incidents in connection with their capture, and an infinite amount of angling gossip relating to each. Considerable space is also devoted to the subject of fishing as practised in different parts of the world.

THE DANCE OF DEATH: Illustrated in Forty-Eight Plates. By JOHN HOLBEIN. Demy 8vo. Price 5s.

A handsome and inexpensive edition of the great Holbein's most popular production. It contains the whole forty-eight plates, with letterpress description of each plate, the plate and the description in each case being on separate pages, facing each other. The first edition was issued in 1530, and since then innumerable impressions have been issued, but mostly in an expensive form, and unattainable by the general public.

THE LITERARY HISTORY OF GLASGOW. By W. J. DUNCAN. Quarto. Price 12s. 6d. net. *Printed for Subscribers and Private Circulation.*

This volume forms one of the volumes issued by the Maitland Club, and was originally published in 1831. This edition is a verbatim et literatim reprint, and is limited to 350 copies, with an appendix additional containing extra matter of considerable importance, not in the original work.

The book is chiefly devoted to giving an account of the greatest of Scottish printers, namely, the Foulises, and furnishes a list of the books they printed, as likewise of the sculptures and paintings which they so largely produced.

GOLFIANA MISCELLANEA. Being a Collection of Interesting Monographs on the Royal and Ancient Game of Golf. Edited by JAMES LINDSAY STEWART. Post 8vo. Price 4s. 6d.

A collection of interesting productions, prose and verse, on or relating to, the game of golf, by various authors both old and recent. Nothing has been allowed into the collection except works of merit and real interest. Many of the works are now extremely scarce and, in a separate form, command very high prices. It contains twenty-three separate productions of a great variety of character—historical, descriptive, practical, poetical, humorous, biographical, etc.

THE BARDS OF THE BIBLE. By GEORGE GILFILLAN. Seventh Edition. Post 8vo. Price 5s.

The most popular of the writings of the late Rev. Dr. Gilfillan. The author, in his preface, states that the object of the book was chiefly a prose poem or hymn in honour of the poetry and the poets of the Bible. It deals with the poetical side of the inspired word, and takes up the separate portions in chronological order.

ONE HUNDRED ROMANCES OF REAL LIFE. By LEIGH HUNT. Post 8vo. Price 3s. 6d.

A handsome edition of Leigh Hunt's famous collection of romances of real life, now scarce in a complete form. The present issue is complete, containing as it does the entire hundred as issued by the author. All being incidents from real life, the interest attaching to the volume is not of an ordinary character. The romances relate to all grades of society, and are entirely various in circumstance, each one being separate and distinct in itself.

UNIQUE TRADITIONS CHIEFLY OF THE WEST AND SOUTH OF SCOTLAND. By JOHN GORDON BARBOUR. Post 8vo. Price 4s. 6d.

A collection of interesting local and popular traditions gathered orally by the author in his wanderings over the West and South of Scotland. The author narrates in this volume, thirty-five separate incidental traditions in narrative form, connected with places or individuals, all of a nature to interest the general Scottish reader, such as "The Red Comyn's Castle," "The Coves of Barholm," "The Rafters of Kirk Alloway," "Cumstone Castle," "The Origin of Loch Catrine," etc., etc.

MODERN ANECDOTES: A Treasury of Wise and Witty Sayings of the last Hundred Years. Edited, with Notes, by W. DAVENPORT ADAMS. Crown 8vo. Price 3s. 6d.

The Anecdotes are all authenticated and are classed into Sections—I. Men of Society. II. Lawyers and the Law. III. Men of Letters. IV. Plays and Players. V. Statesmen and Politicians. VI. The Church and Clergy. VII. People in General.

In compiling a work like this, Mr. Adams has steadily kept in view the necessity of ministering to the requirements of those who will not read anecdotes unless they have reason to know that they are really good. On this principle the entire editorial work has been executed. The book is also a particularly handsome one as regards printing, paper, and binding.

THE LITURGY OF JOHN KNOX: As received by the Church of Scotland in 1564. Crown 8vo. Price 5s.

A beautifully printed edition of the Book of Common Order, more popularly known as the Liturgy of John Knox. This is the only modern edition in which the original quaint spelling is retained. In this and other respects the old style is strictly reproduced, so that the work remains exactly as used by our forefathers three hundred years ago.

THE GABERLUNZIE'S WALLET. By JAMES BALLANTINE. Third edition. Cr. 8vo. Price 2s. 6d.

A most interesting historical tale of the period of the Pretenders, and containing a very large number of favourite songs and ballads, illustrative of the tastes and life of the people at that time. Also containing numerous facetious illustrations by Alexander A. Ritchie.

THE WOLFE OF BADENOCH. A Historical Romance of the Fourteenth Century. By SIR THOMAS DICK LAUDER. Complete unabridged edition. Thick Crown 8vo. Price 6s.

This most interesting romance has been frequently described as equal in interest to any of Sir Walter Scott's historical tales. This is a complete unabridged edition, and is uniform with "Highland Legends" and "Tales of the Highlands," by the same author. As several abridged editions of the work have been published, especial attention is drawn to the fact that the above edition is complete.

THE LIVES OF THE PLAYERS. By JOHN GALT, Esq. Post 8vo. Price 5s.

Interesting accounts of the lives of distinguished actors, such as Betterton, Cibber, Farquhar, Garrick, Foote, Macklin, Murphy, Kemble, Siddons, &c., &c. After the style of Johnson's "Lives of the Poets."

KAY'S EDINBURGH PORTRAITS. A Series of Anecdotal Biographies, chiefly of Scotchmen. Mostly written by JAMES PATERSON. And edited by JAMES MAIDMENT, Esq. Popular Edition. 2 Vols., Post 8vo. Price 12s.

A popular edition of this famous work, which, from its exceedingly high price, has hitherto been out of the reach of the general public. This edition contains all the reading matter that is of general interest; it also contains eighty illustrations.

THE RELIGIOUS ANECDOTES OF SCOTLAND. Edited by WILLIAM ADAMSON, D.D. Thick Post 8vo. Price 5s.

A voluminous collection of purely religious anecdotes relating to Scotland and Scotchmen, and illustrative of the more serious side of the life of the people. The anecdotes are chiefly in connection with distinguished Scottish clergymen and laymen, such as Rutherford, Macleod, Guthrie, Shirra, Leighton, the Erskines, Knox, Beattie, M'Crie, Eadie, Brown, Irving, Chalmers, Lawson, Milne, M'Cheyne, &c., &c. The anecdotes are serious and religious purely, and not at all of the ordinary witty description.

DAYS OF DEER STALKING in the Scottish Highlands, including an account of the Nature and Habits of the Red Deer, a description of the Scottish Forests, and Historical Notes on the earlier Field Sports of Scotland. With Highland Legends, Superstitions, Folk-Lore, and Tales of Poachers and Freebooters. By WILLIAM SCROPE. Illustrated by Sir Edwin and Charles Landseer. Demy 8vo. Price 12s. 6d.

"*The best book of sporting adventures with which we are acquainted.*"—ATHENÆUM.

"*Of this noble diversion we owe the first satisfactory description to the pen of an English gentleman of high birth and extensive fortune, whose many amiable and elegant personal qualities have been commemorated in the diary of Sir Walter Scott.*"—LONDON QUARTERLY REVIEW.

DAYS AND NIGHTS OF SALMON FISHING in the River Tweed. By WILLIAM SCROPE. Illustrated by Sir David Wilkie, Sir Edwin Landseer, Charles Landseer, William Simson, and Edward Cooke. Demy 8vo. Price 12s. 6d.

"*Mr. Scrope's book has done for salmon fishing what its predecessor performed for deer stalking.*"—LONDON QUARTERLY REVIEW.

"*Mr. Scrope conveys to us in an agreeable and lively manner the results of his more than twenty years' experience in our great Border river. . . . The work is enlivened by the narration of numerous angling adventures, which bring out with force and spirit the essential character of the sport in question. . . . Mr. Scrope is a skilful author as well as an experienced angler. It does not fall to the lot of all men to handle with equal dexterity, the brush, the pen, and the rod, to say nothing of the rifle, still less of the leister under cloud of night.*"—BLACKWOOD'S MAGAZINE.

THE FIELD SPORTS OF THE NORTH OF EUROPE. A Narrative of Angling, Hunting, and Shooting in Sweden and Norway. By CAPTAIN L. LLOYD. New edition. Enlarged and revised. Demy 8vo. Price 9s.

"*The chase seems for years to have been his ruling passion, and to have made him a perfect model of perpetual motion. We admire Mr. Lloyd. He is a sportsman far above the common run.*"—BLACKWOOD'S MAGAZINE.

"*This is a very entertaining work and written, moreover, in an agreeable and modest spirit. We strongly recommend it as containing much instruction and more amusement.*—ATHENÆUM.

PUBLIC AND PRIVATE LIBRARIES OF GLASGOW. A Bibliographical Study. By THOMAS MASON. Demy 8vo. Price 12s. 6d. net.

A strictly Bibliographical work dealing with the subject of rare and interesting works, and in that respect describing three of the public and thirteen of the private libraries of Glasgow. All of especial interest.

THE LIFE OF SIR WILLIAM WALLACE. BY JOHN D. CARRICK. Fourth and cheaper edition. Royal 8vo. Price 2s. 6d.

The best life of the great Scottish hero. Contains much valuable and interesting matter regarding the history of that historically important period.

THE HISTORY OF THE PROVINCE OF MORAY. By LACHLAN SHAW. New and Enlarged Edition, 3 Vols., Demy 8vo. Price 30s.

The Standard History of the old geographical division termed the Province of Moray, comprising the Counties of Elgin and Nairn, the greater part of the County of Inverness, and a portion of the County of Banff. Cosmo Innes pronounced this to be the best local history of any part of Scotland.

HIGHLAND LEGENDS. By SIR THOMAS DICK LAUDER. Crown 8vo. Price 6s.

Historical Legends descriptive of Clan and Highland Life and Incident in former times.

TALES OF THE HIGHLANDS. By SIR THOMAS DICK LAUDER. Crown 8vo. Price 6s.

Uniform with and similar in character to the preceding, though entirely different tales. The two are companion volumes.

AN ACCOUNT OF THE GREAT MORAY FLOODS IN 1829. By SIR THOMAS DICK LAUDER. Demy 8vo., with 64 Plates and Portrait. Fourth Edition. Price 8s. 6d.

A most interesting work, containing numerous etchings by the Author. In addition to the main feature of the book, it contains much historical and legendary matter relating to the districts through which the River Spey runs.

OLD SCOTTISH CUSTOMS: Local and General. By E. J. GUTHRIE. Crown 8vo. Price 3s. 6d.

Gives an interesting account of old local and general Scottish customs, now rapidly being lost sight of.

A HISTORICAL ACCOUNT OF THE BELIEF IN WITCHCRAFT IN SCOTLAND. By CHARLES KIRKPATRICK SHARPE. Crown 8vo. Price 4s. 6d.

Gives a chronological account of Witchcraft incidents in Scotland from the earliest period, in a racy, attractive style. And likewise contains an interesting Bibliography of Scottish books on Witchcraft.

"*Sharpe was well qualified to gossip about these topics.*"—SATURDAY REVIEW.

"*Mr. Sharpe has arranged all the striking and important phenomena associated with the belief in Apparitions and Witchcraft. An extensive appendix, with a list of books on Witchcraft in Scotland, and a useful index, render this edition of Mr. Sharpe's work all the more valuable.*"—GLASGOW HERALD.

TALES OF THE SCOTTISH PEASANTRY. By ALEXANDER and JOHN BETHUNE. With Biography of the Authors by JOHN INGRAM, F.S.A.Scot. Post 8vo. Price 3s. 6d.

"*It is the perfect propriety of taste, no less than the thorough intimacy with the subjects he treats of, that gives Mr. Bethune's book a great charm in our eyes.*"—ATHENÆUM.

"*The pictures of rural life and character appear to us remarkably true, as well as pleasing.*"—CHAMBERS'S JOURNAL.

The Tales are quite out of the ordinary routine of such literature, and are universally held in peculiarly high esteem. The following may be given as a specimen of the Contents:—"The Deformed," "The Fate of the Fairest," "The Stranger," "The Drunkard," "The Illegitimate," "The Cousins," &c., &c.

A JOURNEY TO THE WESTERN ISLANDS OF SCOTLAND IN 1773. By SAMUEL JOHNSON, LL.D. Crown 8vo. Price 3s.

Written by Johnson himself, and not to be confounded with Boswell's account of the same tour. Johnson said that some of his best writing is in this work.

THE HISTORY OF BURKE AND HARE AND OF THE RESURRECTIONIST TIMES. A Fragment from the Criminal Annals of Scotland. By GEORGE MAC GREGOR, F.S.A.Scot. With Seven Illustrations, Demy 8vo. Price 7s. 6d.

"*Mr. MacGregor has produced a book which is eminently readable.*"—JOURNAL OF JURISPRUDENCE.

"*The book contains a great deal of curious information.*"—SCOTSMAN.

"*He who takes up this book of an evening must be prepared to sup full of horrors, yet the banquet is served with much of literary grace, and garnished with a deftness and taste which render it palatable to a degree.*"—GLASGOW HERALD.

THE HISTORY OF GLASGOW: From the Earliest Period to the Present Time. By GEORGE MAC GREGOR, F.S.A.Scot. Containing 36 Illustrations. Demy 8vo. Price 12s. 6d.

An entirely new as well as the fullest and most complete history of this prosperous city. In addition it is the first written in chronological order. Comprising a large handsome volume in Sixty Chapters, and extensive Appendix and Index, and illustrated throughout with many interesting engravings and drawings.

THE COLLECTED WRITINGS OF DOUGAL GRAHAM, "Skellat," Bellman of Glasgow. Edited with Notes, together with a Biographical and Bibliographical Introduction, and a Sketch of the Chap Literature of Scotland, by GEORGE MAC GREGOR, F.S.A.Scot. Impression limited to 250 copies. 2 Vols., Demy 8vo. Price 21s.

With very trifling exceptions Graham was the only writer of purely Scottish chap-books of a secular description, almost all the others circulated being reprints of English productions. His writings are exceedingly facetious and highly illustrative of the social life of the period.

SCOTTISH PROVERBS. By ANDREW HENDERSON. Crown 8vo. Cheaper edition. Price 2s. 6d.

A cheap edition of a book that has long held a high place in Scottish Literature.

THE BOOK OF SCOTTISH ANECDOTE: Humorous, Social, Legendary, and Historical. Edited by ALEXANDER HISLOP. Crown 8vo., pp. 768. Cheaper edition. Price 5s.

The most comprehensive collection of Scottish Anecdotes, containing about 3,000 in number.

THE BOOK OF SCOTTISH STORY: Historical, Traditional, Legendary, Imaginative, and Humorous. Crown 8vo., pp. 768. Cheaper edition. Price 5s.

A most interesting and varied collection by Leading Scottish Authors.

THE BOOK OF SCOTTISH POEMS: Ancient and Modern. Edited by J. Ross. Crown 8vo., pp. 768. Cheaper edition. Price 5s.

Comprising a History of Scottish Poetry and Poets from the earliest times. With lives of the Poets and Selections from their Writings.

*** These three works are uniform.

A DESCRIPTION OF THE WESTERN ISLES OF SCOTLAND, CALLED HYBRIDES. With the Genealogies of the Chief Clans of the Isles. By SIR DONALD MONRO, High Dean of the Isles, who travelled through most of them in the year 1549. Impression limited to 250 copies. Demy 8vo. Price 5s.

This is the earliest written description of the Western Islands, and is exceedingly quaint and interesting. In this edition all the old curious spellings are strictly retained.

A DESCRIPTION OF THE WESTERN ISLANDS OF SCOTLAND CIRCA 1695. By MARTIN MARTIN. Impression limited to 250 copies. Demy 8vo. Price 12s. 6d.

With the exception of Dean Monro's smaller work 150 years previous, it is the earliest description of the Western Islands we have, and is the only lengthy work on the subject before the era of modern innovations. Martin very interestingly describes the people and their ways as he found them about 200 years ago.

THE SCOTTISH POETS, RECENT AND LIVING. By ALEXANDER G. MURDOCH. With Portraits, Post 8vo. Price 6s.

A most interesting resumé of Scottish Poetry in recent times. Contains a biographical sketch, choice pieces, and portraits of the recent and living Scottish Poets.

THE HUMOROUS CHAP-BOOKS OF SCOTLAND. By JOHN FRASER. 2 Vols., Thin Crown 8vo (all published). Price 5s.

An interesting and racy description of the chap-book literature of Scotland, and biographical sketches of the writers.

THE HISTORY OF STIRLINGSHIRE. By WILLIAM NIMMO. 2 Vols., Demy 8vo. 3rd Edition. Price 25s.

A new edition of this standard county history, handsomely printed, and with detailed map giving the parish boundaries and other matters of interest.

This county has been termed the battlefield of Scotland, and in addition to the many and important military engagements that have taken place in this district, of all which a full account is given,—this part of Scotland is of especial moment in many other notable respects,—among which particular reference may be made to the Roman Wall, the greater part of this most interesting object being situated within the boundaries of the county.

A POPULAR SKETCH OF THE HISTORY OF GLASGOW: From the Earliest Period to the Present Time. By ANDREW WALLACE. Crown 8vo. Price 3s. 6d.

The only attempt to write a History of Glasgow suitable for popular use.

THE HISTORY OF THE WESTERN HIGHLANDS AND ISLES OF SCOTLAND, from A.D. 1493 to A.D. 1625. With a brief introductory sketch from A.D. 80 to A.D. 1493. By DONALD GREGORY. Demy 8vo. Price 12s. 6d.

Incomparably the best history of the Scottish Highlands, and written purely from original investigation. Also contains particularly full and lengthened Contents and Index, respectively at beginning and end of the volume.

THE HISTORY OF AYRSHIRE. By JAMES PATERSON. 5 Vols., Crown 8vo. Price 28s. net.

The most recent and the fullest history of this exceedingly interesting county. The work is particularly rich in the department of Family History.

MARTYRLAND: a Historical Tale of the Covenanters By the Rev. ROBERT SIMPSON, D.D. Crown 8vo. Cheaper Edition. Price 2s. 6d.

A tale illustrative of the history of the Covenanters in the South of Scotland.

TALES OF THE COVENANTERS. By E. J. GUTHRIE. Crown 8vo. Cheaper Edition. Price 2s. 6d.

A number of tales illustrative of leading incidents and characters connected with the Covenanters.

PERSONAL AND FAMILY NAMES. A Popular Monograph on the Origin and History of the Nomenclature of the Present and Former Times. By HARRY ALFRED LONG. Demy 8vo. Price 5s.

Interesting investigations as to the origin, history, and meaning of about 9,000 personal and family names.

THE SCOTTISH GALLOVIDIAN ENCYCLOPÆDIA of the Original, Antiquated, and Natural Curiosities of the South of Scotland. By JOHN MACTAGGART. Demy 8vo. Price raised to 25s. Impression limited to 250 copies.

Contains a large amount of extremely interesting and curious matter relating to the South of Scotland.

THE COMPLETE TALES OF THE ETTRICK SHEPHERD (JAMES HOGG). 2 vols., Demy 8vo.

An entirely new and complete edition of the tales of this popular Scottish writer.

GLASGOW: THOMAS D. MORISON.
LONDON: HAMILTON, ADAMS & CO.

www.ingramcontent.com/pod-product-compliance
Lightning Source LLC
Chambersburg PA
CBHW022017110726
47901CB00006B/1562
* 9 7 8 3 3 3 7 2 3 4 0 4 1 *